THE
= QUESTION =

Matt's hands gradually crept up her satin skin leaving a cascade of warmth from the hot springs. "Caroline," he said in a low tone. He groped for the words, hoping he could find them this time. "Caroline . . . I . . ." He tried again but did not know how to continue.

"What are you trying to say?" she gently chided him.

"I'm trying to say . . ." As if of their own accord, his hands guided her closer, but he willed himself to go no further until he spoke the words. "I want to say that I love you."

Caroline's hazel eyes searched solemnly into his, finding their focus even through the darkness. "Well," she spoke, hushed, barely above the burble of the water, "do you?"

BIG SKY BURNING

DAPHNE HARTWIG

HarperPaperbacks
A Division of HarperCollins*Publishers*

HarperPaperbacks   *A Division of* HarperCollins*Publishers*
10 East 53rd Street, New York, N.Y. 10022

Copyright © 1992 by Daphne Hartwig
All rights reserved. No part of this book may be used or reproduced in any manner whatsoever without written permission of the publisher, except in the case of brief quotations embodied in critical articles and reviews. For information address HarperCollins*Publishers*,
10 East 53rd Street, New York, N.Y. 10022.

Cover illustration by Diane Sivavec

First printing: February 1992

Printed in the United States of America

HarperPaperbacks and colophon are trademarks of HarperCollins*Publishers*

10 9 8 7 6 5 4 3 2 1

For Glenn

CHAPTER

1

CAROLINE WALKED INTO
her farmhouse kitchen. The wooden screen door
slammed loudly behind her. "Still got to get to that
door," she said as her eyes, blinking and squinting,
were greeted by sudden, blinding shade. Stopped in her
tracks and still trying to focus, she smudged her sweaty
forehead with the back of a dirt-dusted hand and
smiled broadly at the kitchen's pleasant coolness
within the midsummer heat. She waited a moment longer, absentmindedly unbuttoning her blouse until her
eyes adjusted enough for her to see across the 1890s
homestead kitchen to the microwave oven in the corner. Caroline pushed off dirt-caked sneakers without
untying them and slipped off socks that spattered out
the grit from her vegetable garden. She wiggled her toes
and renewed her smile as she let her hot, bare soles
absorb the chill from the linoleum.

As Caroline walked through the high-ceilinged dining room and living room, her open blouse flapped and cooled her ribs, but after climbing the steep wooden stairs to her bedroom, she ran into a wall of hot, stuffy air. It was only nine-thirty, and already the day promised to be another scorcher. Caroline headed for her open bedroom window on the side wall, automatically reaching for the white wooden shutters. She stopped abruptly.

"This is silly," she told herself, as she had so many times before. "There isn't a soul around who can see." She left the shutters untouched and was caught by the sight that lay beyond her open, oversize window.

She lingered almost involuntarily as she looked out upon the unspoiled Montana landscape. Even after viewing this vast panorama every morning and night for the past three months, what she saw still held the power to make her pause and marvel anew.

Caroline looked over a low and grassy plain. Once, in years with more rainfall, this flat plain was home to a wide and shallow river, but now the river had dwindled to a series of running creeks that serpentined their way into the clear distance. The plain unfolded for three or four miles and at last evolved into sloping timberland. Caroline smiled with satisfaction, knowing that a sizable amount of that very timberland belonged to her. The timber forests rose higher, covering the huge mountains that spanned the horizon. Some were far enough away to seem like charcoal-shadowed hulks with chalky, rock-capped peaks. Others were green-gray ridges close enough for Caroline to still be able to identify the outlines of the sparser groups of pines.

These mountains were grand to her, but even they

were humbled by what unbounded from their peaks. The term "Big Sky" didn't even scratch the surface in describing what never failed to impress her the most: an infinite dome of clear, deep-hued sapphire that both dwarfed her in its massiveness and at the very same time drew her eyes deeper skyward, making her want somehow to rise into the endless blue expanse.

Looking out her window like this, she was once again awed by all that uninterrupted sky. This reaction always surprised her because she'd certainly seen plenty of sky as a child growing up in the flat prairies of Illinois, where the horizon consisted of equal halves of land and sky. Even in her recent life in Chicago, the view from her Lake Shore Drive condo was always half lake and half sky, however gray and indistinct each were. But this Montana sky with its unlimited presentation of the heavens—this was all so different.

Caroline's gaze traveled back to the grassy hills around her house. It was late July and the grasses were already parched, blending anywhere from dull green in the lower areas to wheat-colored atop some slopes. Even the land around her vegetable garden, where she'd just watered, was drying up fast. She looked past the mile of low hills that bordered her neighbor's land, only to observe more drying grassland.

Now she squinted with curiosity, as she had times before, toward the faraway house perched atop a craggy hill. This was her only neighbor for many miles within this uninhabited region but since she'd arrived last April, she could discern no signs of anyone living there. From her window she could just see, but without much detail, the large, dark amber log house in the distance. It looked tall and multifaceted, with lots of roofs sloping off in several directions. Caroline suspected the place to be modern and probably sizable, considering how much she could see even from this distance. So far she'd never noticed anyone moving around there or any lights on at night.

One bright morning just a few weeks ago, Caroline had acted on her curiosity and driven up the dirt road that led from her place to where she thought her mystery neighbor's house might be. From the road she'd seen a spot where a driveway might start, but no sign at all of the log house that was so well hidden and distanced behind the hills. Whoever her neighbor was, she'd concluded as she'd driven back to her own roadside farmhouse, they had a strong sense of privacy.

Finally, Caroline turned from her window to finish undressing. As she did, she surveyed with satisfaction the bedroom that she had recently renovated. For nearly three weeks she had thrown her energies wholly and completely into this room, as much for the renovation's sake, she had to admit, as for the way the single-minded busyness of the task offset the emptiness she felt in her newly solitary life.

The bedroom spanned the whole back length of the house and was so long and open that Caroline sometimes wished she had roller skates. It included two nooks for gabled windows and a fieldstone fireplace in the end wall. The oak frame windows, built in the 1890's, had given her the most trouble, and the fireplace had fallen into disrepair, but Caroline had thoroughly enjoyed devoting all her energies to these tasks. It was good to move and be busy again. It made her feel more at home in her new surroundings—made her feel that slowly, room by room, this place could really be her home.

The result of her efforts was a huge, high-ceilinged bedroom painted in a feminine blush of salmon pink—the color of the ballerina skirts she and her kid sister, Celeste, once had as children. She had decorated the top borders of the room with a series of spring green nosegays stenciled over a ribbon of darker pink. The floor, the old-fashioned wide baseboards, and other trims were all white, giving the whole room a delicate, reflected glow in the morning sunshine.

Caroline had furnished as sparsely as possible so as not to spoil the airiness of the huge room. "Keep things simple," Dr. McAllister had warned her, and she intended to heed his advice, outwardly as well as inwardly. Her bed was at one end of the room: a white four-poster with pale pink dust ruffles and a profusion of pink-toned pillows, all atop a sea-green-and-pink cotton coverlet. There was also a silver-gray rattan dresser decorated with tiny, sea-green, wood-carved flower garlands that had been in her and Celeste's room since they were kids. Atop the dresser stood a silver, hinged tri-frame for photographs. In the center oval was a picture of Caroline's mother and sister, their features not much alike except for wide, identical grins. The right oval framed two plump cats. The left frame held blank, gray cardboard.

Tossing her clothes aside, Caroline walked naked out of her bedroom and headed for the towel closet at the end of the upstairs hall. As she approached the full-length mirror that was attached to the closet door, she regarded herself, noting how much she'd changed since she had left St. Louis. Her hazel eyes had regained their warmth, but her figure was still a little too gaunt, she thought. Her pelvic bones stuck out from her lower abdomen, and the rosy-red scar, shiny and raised, stretched across one side, a reminder as to why she was here.

Caroline got some towels from the closet and went into the bathroom. She stepped into a bathtub that was elevated by eagles' claw legs and turned on the shower. Once again she noticed that lately the dry weather was lowering the water pressure.

Standing directly under the shower, she tilted her head up and for a long, relaxing interval let the water run down her copper-brown hair. Caroline liked the long-forgotten sensation of her hair on her shoulders. For practical reasons it had been very short in Chicago and in St. Louis, but now that she had come to Montana she had decided to let it grow long.

The rich smell of coconut shampoo surrounded her as she sudsed her hair and thought to herself that she needed to drive to Hawkeye today to see if Ray had finished the cutting on the upper tract. This was as good an excuse as any for making the trip to town and thereby having something to occupy her afternoon. Now that she had finished all her dawn-to-dusk tasks of renovating, settling in, and getting Ray Banes as foreman of her logging business, she was at a loss as to just what she ought to do with herself, how to handle all the idle time. Idle time, Caroline discovered, dramatically lowered her defenses against loneliness, missing her mother and Celeste, and even something that she didn't expect to miss, being part of a family unit back in Aunt Libby's house in St. Louis. She didn't miss Aunt Libby—that would be like missing a head-to-toe case of poison ivy in August—but she did miss the security of a familiar house with familiar people around her.

As Caroline reached for more shampoo, the stream of water from the shower head slowed to a thin spray and then to a dribbling trickle. She opened the faucet knobs all the way, but with no results. Grumbling, she got out of the shower and tried the knobs on the sink. Nothing but a dribble there, too. Now she could add finding a plumber to her list of things to do in town— that is, if a town the size of Hawkeye even had a plumber.

CHAPTER
✦
2

CAROLINE   DESCENDED
the stairs dressed in a blue chambray skirt and a pink
sleeveless blouse that gave her complexion a girlish,
rosy glow. She raked her hands through her poker-
straight hair to finish drying it as she walked through
the living room.

Caroline had made this room as different as she
could from her old one in Chicago. She'd gotten rid of
all the stark, modern furniture she used to have and had
taken with her only the comfortable stuff plus some old
family pieces her mom had been storing in Aunt
Libby's basement. "Simple is better," she had told herself, and she planned to continue to follow that philoso-
phy. Practicality also weighed heavily into this line of
thinking now that she had invested most of her money
and was budgeting the rest of it. Caroline was sure of
her financial security, but she could no longer afford to

be as flagrantly spendthrift as she'd once been back in Chicago. There, she used to buy shamefully expensive jewelry to reward herself at the end of an especially frustrating day. New sets of designer sheets replaced dirty ones every time she was lax in doing her laundry. On her lunch hours alone she had amassed more department store lipsticks and eye shadows than she cared to admit. Now, however, Caroline's motto had changed from "Because I'm worth it" to "Less is better." The difficulties of the recent past had graced her with a clear perspective of what was really necessary in life and what was just greed. Right now, having her health and security was more than enough.

Caroline strode past the dining room through the long kitchen, where she grabbed her purse from a wooden bread box, and stepped outside the door to the back porch. Even as she turned the key to the door's lock, she reprimanded herself, "There's another dumb habit I've still got to break." But she locked it anyway and headed for the red Camaro parked in front of the barn. Small, dried-mud paw prints dotted the car's wide hood. Opening the driver's door, she was greeted by a wave of heat. Grimacing, she threw her purse onto the passenger seat, rolled down the windows, and waited outside for the car to air out.

From the shade beneath the car emerged a gray, mackerel-striped cat, its tail held straight up in greeting. It made a burbling noise at her.

"Well, there you are, Humphrey," she said, bending down and scratching its head. "I'll see you later." The cat, however, sat itself directly in her path, staring up with round yellow eyes that held the essence of patience. Humphrey had kept this steady countenance the whole time Caroline's mother had taken care of him and her other cat, Tinky, in St. Louis. Caroline remembered how this little animal had loyally waited for her during that lost time—that horrible, anguished past year. Humphrey burbled hopefully. Caroline bent down again, smiling, and scratched the cat right under both jaws until he purred. "Now, scoot," she said gently before she climbed into the car and started it. The cat ran for the barn as she crunched down the gravel driveway toward the road.

Hawkeye was twenty-five miles away—about a thirty-minute drive over a series of wide, rolling plains. Today, as was usually the case, Caroline's was the solitary car on the rough-textured, two-lane blacktop. The tires hummed pleasantly as she drove. At the crest of one of the higher hills, she could see, stretching ahead, a black strip of road, "straighter than a preacher," she recalled from a country-western song she'd heard over the areas's one and only radio station. But straight as the road was, the hills that it crossed made it undulate like a softly unfurling ribbon. Caroline enjoyed the drive. It was just like riding a long, gentle roller coaster.

It occurred to her, however, that the drive in winter, when these hills turned to ice and snowdrifts, might be another story. Even as she gazed over the grassy landscape, she told herself that in autumn she would have to trade in her lovely red car for a more practical, jeep-type vehicle with four-wheel drive.

Who would have ever thought, Caroline marveled to herself, that I'd end up driving some kind of truck here in the middle of nowhere. She thought, and not for the first time, either, how this life she had begun in

Montana contrasted so startlingly with where and who she was before.

Back in Chicago she had been a successful career woman about to be made a vice president in the high-powered advertising and public relations agency of Cahill, Flynn and Zinder. This was the first time a woman, much less a young woman, had been promoted to the ranks of VPs.

Caroline had worked long and hard to attain the position. In fact, she had attacked her account executive job with three times the velocity of any of the male vice presidents in the agency. And she did it cheerfully, acquiescing to the other execs when she should, always volunteering to hostess the luncheons and dinner meetings where a woman's social graciousness made potential clients feel at ease with the agency. She liked the people in her agency and always made time to listen to their jokes and anecdotes, but she knew, also, how to keep her distance.

Mostly, she worked hard. She knew that was the real key to success—that hard work was the only way she, a woman, would ever be taken seriously enough to succeed in a no-nonsense agency like C. F. and Z. She had set her sights, and after only nine years out of college and with the agency, she got what she wanted. Of course, the price tag on what she wanted was steep, but she never once entertained the idea that she couldn't handle it. She had simply devoted her life to the pursuit of success, and she'd gotten it.

Caroline suddenly remembered the conversation she'd had with Mort Zinder the day he had first considered her for a vice presidency. Mort was a man who possessed a driven kind of energy that belied his fifty-two years and all gray hair. That day, dressed in an impeccably tailored navy blue suit, he strode into Caroline's office and in his usual forthright manner prefaced his proposal with his assessment of Caroline. Some of Caroline's colleagues accused Mort of being insensitive, even tactless, in his direct style, but Caroline suspected that they simply didn't like to admit that Mort was always carefully factual about anything he said. Mort's approach to delivering both criticisms and compliments was uncomfortably straightforward to some, but it was always honest and logical. The day he discussed the vice president's position with Caroline was no exception.

Pulling a chair to Caroline's desk, Mort sat down, folded his hands on the desk top, and got to the point.

"I know you've had your eye on the vice president's position, Caroline, and I'm nearly convinced you've got the spirit and spine for it. You've been extremely competent in your business dealings, and you show a good sense of control, yet you've never lost your humor or your femininity to it." Mort's face, showing an expression of full approval, altered to something more serious.

"Sometimes you drive yourself way too hard and won't relent until you're done with the job. And at those times, Caroline, no one in the office wants to say 'boo' to you. But, on the other hand, it's that very trait of never backing down or crumbling under stress that sets you apart."

Mort shifted on his chair, kept his eyes locked with Caroline's, and continued. "So. It's pretty simple. The Garner-Rolke folks are hard to please, slow moving, and very big. I'd like to have them with the agency." Mort smiled at Caroline. "You land the Garner-Rolke account within a year's time, and the position is yours."

Caroline responded with a broad grin and a "Thanks, Mort."

"Don't thank me yet," he warned. "The Garner-Rolke people are tough. But I think you've got a bright mind. If anyone can do this, you can."

Caroline grinned at Mort's compliment. She greatly admired the man, and his words of approval meant a lot.

Caroline supposed that Mort, having delivered his message, would leave. Instead he settled farther back on his chair.

"Tell me, Caroline, what are your long-term goals?"

"I want the vice president job, Mort. Once I get good at it, then I want to go on to whatever's next in line."

"Like what?"

"Well . . ." Caroline's grin surfaced again, along with a twinkle of humor in her eyes. "Someday I'd like to see my name on the building. Nothing flashy, mind you, just something permanent."

Mort was the only person in the office with whom Caroline could be completely open, and as she expected, he smiled at the joke, or half joke, before he continued. "Any other goals in your life? I mean, besides agency goals."

For a moment Caroline faltered. She shot Mort a brief, quizzical expression, then she caught on. "Sure. Lots. I want to see the Grand Canyon, visit San Francisco before it disappears . . ." She thought a moment longer. "I also want to learn how to play the clarinet and"—she looked sheepish—"I'd like to ride the tea-cups at Disneyland."

Mort smiled at her response but still didn't look satisfied with what she'd said. His smile faded. "Is that all?"

Caroline knew that whenever Mort had trouble eliciting the response he wanted from a person, he would approach from a different direction. Without waiting for her to reply, he continued.

"Landing this account will mean an increased workload. Keeping it after that will mean an even greater level of commitment to the job than what's ever been expected of you before."

Caroline nodded to imply that she understood. She was thinking that Mort sounded just like her father when he had first handed her the keys to the family car.

"Once you get this account and the VP spot, I'd like some kind of assurance from you, Caroline, that you would neither take clients away with the intent of beginning your own agency nor leave us in the near future."

"You know I wouldn't do that, Mort. I want this job, with this agency."

Mort's face registered an expression that Caroline didn't recognize. All she could read from it was that he was either puzzled or perturbed or both. She wondered if she'd said something wrong. "What's the problem?" she asked.

Mort, who always carried an aura of businesslike confidence, looked at this moment clearly uncomfort-able over what he was about to say. This was so out of the ordinary for Mort that it made Caroline uncomfortable, too. He hesitated a moment, then asked, "Is that all you want?"

"For right now, yes," she replied steadily.

Mort fingered the pages of the desk calendar and continued. "You've been seeing a young man for some time now, haven't you?"

"Yes, we've been together for nearly a year. His name is Jim Simmons."

"Right." Mort nodded in vague recollection. "Do you ever think about marrying and having children?"

Caroline was just about to answer with the reproachful words "Oh, Mort, I can't believe you're asking me the old are-you-going-to-run-off-and-leave-us-to-have-babies question," but upon seeing his face, she stopped short. A swiftly passing image of a similar expression flashed through her mind, and, briefly, she recognized the same look of concern her own father used to have for her.

"Yes, Jim and I are very close. Someday I think we'll marry."

"Is this the dark-haired young man who comes for you after work?"

"Yeah, you've met him. But as far as babies are concerned, maybe I'm abnormal or something, but I'm just not so sure that I want to give up what I've worked to accomplish here for years of changing diapers." Caroline waited for him to respond. When he didn't she continued. "A big part of why Jim and I have such a good relationship is that we're both workaholics and we understand each other's needs about our careers."

Mort silently thumbed the pages of the desk calendar, avoiding eye contact.

"What is it?" blurted Caroline impatiently.

"Okay. What if your Jim eventually—say, a few years down the line—really wants, insists upon having, a family? How would you go?"

"Well, I don't know." She thought for a while about decisions she had assumed were already set in place. Yes, she wanted this vice president's position. Yes, she wanted someday to marry Jim. But as far as a family was concerned, she could never envision Jim and herself in parental roles long enough to think it through. She looked wide-eyed at Mort and shrugged her shoulders.

"I don't know, Mort."

"That's some answer, Caroline." He smiled good-humoredly at her and went on to explain the steps he expected her to take to land the client and the promotion.

When Mort left her office, Caroline began wrestling with unanswered questions. Why was Mort sending her two contradictory messages? And why was he being so uncharacteristically nondirect about it? "Succeed with the agency. Commit yourself to it." That made sense to her. "Is that all you want?" That bothered her. Just what had he been trying to say?

Driving down the road to Hawkeye and remembering her agency days, Caroline could see so clearly now what Mort had been hinting at, what she had been so blind to back then: that she had tunnel vision when it came to the pursuit of success, driven to the pursuit simply for the sake of pursuit. The reward she sought so repeatedly back in those times was a feeling of her own self-worth. But that kind of self-worth had a way of fading so that it always needed renewal. Its pursuit overshadowed the other rewards of the job so that they meant little—an' elegant Chicago condo where she spent little time and a growing bank account that she had no leisure to enjoy.

It was that same bank account that had put her on this preacher-straight blacktop to Hawkeye. Her considerable savings from Cahill, Flynn and Zinder had bought her the homestead farmhouse completely free and clear. Except for a working bank account that would comfortably cover her living expenses for the next two or three years, she had invested the rest of her savings in a large tract of timberland rich in both hardwoods and pines. The maples, oaks, and cherries would be marketed to a commercial wholesaler for furniture, and the white and ponderosa pines would be sold to any of the local lumber mills between here and Butte.

Caroline had carefully studied the idea of owning timberland as a small business, and it appealed to her on several levels. Although she knew immediately that she both shouldn't and couldn't run a logging business by herself, it pleased her to know that the very money she had so frantically earned by producing slick advertising amid the clatter of Chicago's Loop had been transformed into everlasting forests passively reaping profits that would keep her safe in this peaceful place.

And it was a peaceful place all right. Extremely peaceful. Three months of peaceful, to be exact, she thought. Now that her preoccupation with settling in was completed and only one more month was left of summer, Caroline realized with an uneasiness that it could become, perhaps, too peaceful.

CHAPTER

3

*I*T WAS JUST PAST TEN-thirty, and the hot August sun made the distant road quiver with heat waves. Caroline peered ahead as she drove down the blacktop. The mountain range loomed behind her, looking patently scenic in the rearview mirror. Just ahead, the plains area she now traversed ascended into another set of minor mountains. Here, she would follow the blacktop through the pass that skirted the side of one of these mountains.

The route to Hawkeye was a series of treacherous inclines and hair-raising descents. With the practice of repetition, Caroline had not only learned the route by heart but had mastered the skill to maneuver it. Once the force of gravity had careened her car down the last of the mountain passes, she swallowed to relieve her ears of thirty minutes' worth of popping. She drove past the regional high school on the outskirts of town and headed for Hawkeye proper. Two gas stations, one on

either side of Main Street, marked the beginning of
town. On the right was Hawkeye's largest unattached
building, the IGA supermarket, a painted cinder-block
structure surrounded on all sides by its parking lot.
Caroline pulled in here and parked her car. She would
do her food shopping later, but first there were errands
to attend to.

Down the cracked, Depression-era sidewalk,
Hawkeye's stores stood in a row: Sears Catalog Outlet,
the True Value hardware store, Barney's Dinette City.
One the next block, straggly philodendrons hung from
macramé ropes in the high windows of the Bitterroot
Cafe; after that came the brilliantly lit Rexall drugstore,
with Hawkeye's only pay telephone outside its doors,
and a small Woolworth's whose sparsely stocked
shelves held, it always seemed to Caroline, the dustiest,
most forlorn merchandise she'd ever seen. A storefront
Baptist church followed, then an empty lot and a few
old houses, and Hawkeye ended there.

Crossing to the other side of the street, Caroline
faced the rosy bricks of the Municipal Building. Enter-
ing, she stepped into the open door of the post office to
a wall of post office boxes: there was no mail delivery
beyond Hawkeye's boundaries. Caroline opened her
letter-combination box and emptied its contents. She'd
gotten more than usual this week: a letter from her
mother, *Time* magazine, some mail-order catalogs, and
a mint green slip of paper telling her to pick up a
package from the postmaster's counter.

Caroline walked into the next, smaller room of the
post office, where a raised nameplate on the wide, gray-
green countertop read Irwin Corwell, Postmaster. Caroline touched the little please-ring-for-service bell, and

the postmaster appeared from behind the sorting table. He was a short, wiry, white-haired gentleman whose face and manner always reminded Caroline of the Pepperidge Farm man on television.

"How do?" he said, automatically surveying Caroline up and down. "How can I help you, young lady?"

"Well"—Caroline smiled, offering the slip—"I'm supposed to pick something up."

Mr. Corwell took the slip, squinted at it for a moment, and left without a word toward the mailroom. Caroline waited, reading signs explaining the four Priority Mail zones. Finally Mr. Corwell returned with a padded mailing envelope.

"Mizzz Caroline Atkinson?" Mr. Corwell asked, giving haughty emphasis to the "Ms." on the address label.

"Yes, that's me," Caroline answered pleasantly, noting the tone but wondering equally what the package was.

The postmaster arched a snowy eyebrow at the package. "It's come quite a distance." He paused to look exaggeratedly impressed. "Boston."

Without really wanting to, Caroline found herself explaining. "Then that would be from my sister."

Mr. Corwell squinted critically at the return address corner as he handed the parcel over to Caroline. "I thought you were from St. Louis or Chicago or some such?"

"I am. My sister's in Boston, though," was all Caroline wished to add, although she did so smilingly.

"That so?" said Mr. Corwell. "Hot weather we've been getting, don't you think?" Without letting Caroline reply, he continued. "Tell me, young lady, your neighbor back yet from wherever it is? I've got a stack of mail piled up and not much more room tah hold it all."

"No," Caroline answered, trying to follow the line of conversation while her mind assessed the shape and possible contents of her package. "I mean, I don't really know. I don't think there's anyone home over there. Or, at least, I've never seen anyone." She shrugged. "I don't even know who they are."

"Van Zandt's your neighbor's name, miss. Lived here for five, maybe six years, but not all of the time. Off and gone for long stretches. Lots of mail backup."

"Oh."

"Supposed tah be retired, but I'm not so sure. Wealthy, you know?"

"Uh-huh."

"Friends with most everyone around Hawkeye," continued the postmaster, "but real private, too." He nodded in affirmation and added, "Lived somewhere in the South before coming tah Hawkeye, but no one knows where."

"I see." Caroline had wondered who her neighbors were, but now Mr. Corwell's account of the older, retired Van Zandts didn't rouse her curiosity all that much.

"Well, good talking tah you, Miz Atkinson. If I can be of any further service, you be sure tah let me know."

Caroline's mind snapped back to business. Yes, she did have a question for the postmaster. "Mr. Corwell, you wouldn't happen to have seen Ray Banes come in for his mail yet today, or know if he's got business in town today, would you? You see, I'd like a word with him." She smiled, then added, "If he's around."

"Ray Banes," Mr. Corwell repeated. "He's seeing tah your trees, isn't he?"

"Yes," Caroline replied, wondering where Mr. Corwell got this correct but unannounced information about her logging business. Ray Banes, who uttered probably no more than ten essential sentences over the course of a year, wouldn't have been the source.

"Well," said the postmaster, "it just so happens that Mr. Banes was in here not more'n an hour past. When I asked him what he was up tah in these parts, he said he was headed for lunch at the Bitterroot and something about Fairbanks beyond that."

"That's great." "I'll catch him there. Thanks, Mr. Corwell."

Caroline backtracked down Main Street. A wide-bed pickup rumbled down the street parallel to her. It was only one of the ever-present four-wheel-drive, jumbo-wheeled vehicles-of-choice in the area. The back cab window always sported a double gun rack, while the front cab window revealed a bearded man wearing a baseball cap imprinted with the name of a feed or construction company. When Caroline had first come to Montana she'd been surprised to see so many men with beards. Now she hardly noticed except if the beard neared Z. Z. Top proportions. She was beginning to notice, lately, that if a man's face was clean-shaven, he almost invariably wore a cowboy hat and cowboy boots. The bearded men usually wore lumberjack boots.

When Caroline reached Fairbanks Hardware and Army/Navy, she crossed Main Street and headed for the social center, the communications hub—in fact, the very heart of Hawkeye: the Bitterroot Cafe.

CHAPTER

4

*T*HE WOOD-SHINGLED WALLS of the Bitterroot Cafe rose a "titch" above eye level, just enough to make sidewalk passersby have to tiptoe if they wanted to look in the windows to see who was inside. Even if you were somehow able to maintain a casual stroll on the balls of your feet or if you were tall, all those hanging philodendrons in their macramé cords and tassels blocked the view anyway. You looked a lot less silly if you simply went inside to satisfy your curiosity. Realizing this, Caroline reached for the pink-and-brown door of the Bitterroot.

A wave of cold air snapped at her when she entered. The sound of the air conditioner rumbling at full tilt above the door mixed with the din of clattering dishes and the hum of a dozen conversations. She stood near the cash register at the end of a long Formica lunch counter.

Suddenly Caroline felt unsure about intruding on Ray Banes's lunch. After all, it wasn't as if the taciturn, sixty-year-old Banes was her hireling or even an employee. He was a logger in his own right with his own land and not to be regarded as someone over whom she wielded authority. The deal they had arranged was that when Banes wasn't harvesting the timber on his own property, he and his men and equipment would work on Caroline's land. There would be plenty of time to fill both their annual quotas, and he had set her a deadline schedule for both softwoods and hardwoods.

It was the schedule Caroline wanted to ask him about. The first run of hardwoods should have been cut and readied for transport nearly two weeks ago, yet she hadn't heard a word from Banes. Caroline wondered if maybe he wasn't the right person to depend on. True, he had a lifetime's expertise in the field, plus long experience as a foreman. On the other hand, she was paying him and his men a very fair price, and she expected results or at least an explanation as to why there were no results. Still, Caroline told herself, she was fortunate to have found him to "see to her trees," as the postmaster had phrased it. Thinking on this, she wondered if, perhaps, in questioning him, she would be overstepping boundaries.

Nah, she told herself. The truth was that she felt intimidated by the crusty Ray Banes. Not that he ever bullied her in any way: he was a gentleman, both courteous and well respected by all. It was just that he disliked talking, so he didn't.

Not having a conversational wedge immediately in mind and still unsure as to the propriety of barging into his private lunchtime, Caroline decided on a quick postponement. She turned her attention to the community bulletin board on the wall next to the cash register. The Novi Historical Society was sponsoring a lecture, "Sheep Husbandry: Then and Now"; the Medallion County La Leche League was meeting at Jeanette Thibodeau's home; bales of barbed wire were for sale by various individuals. Time to talk to Banes.

Caroline turned past the cash register and stood at the outskirts of the dining area. She gazed over the tables and booths that seated the early lunch crowd. She didn't want to stare at people but was careful to glance quickly at everyone. By the time her gaze reached Ray Banes, he was solemnly beckoning her with one hand.

He sat alone at a center table, a stockily built man in a cotton plaid shirt. His well-tanned face was set in its usual expression of mild concentration.

"Sit down."

"Thanks, Mr. Banes."

"Ray."

Caroline smiled and pulled out a wooden, pink-seated chair that squealed on the linoleum. Sitting, she saw that Ray was in the middle of an extensive lunch that involved an array of side-order dishes.

"Mr. Banes—I mean, Ray, please don't let me stop you from eating."

As if to illustrate that she hadn't, Banes had cut and downed a piece of his strip steak just as Caroline finished her sentence. He drank a gulp of coffee from a thick, tan-colored mug and motioned to the black, faux-leather menu wedged between the sugar and the napkin holder.

"What are you having?"

"Oh. Um . . . well, Ray, I didn't really come here to eat. I was kind of won . . ." Caroline trailed off when she realized that she was talking to Ray's back. Ray, in the meantime, had silently caught the eye of the middle-aged waitress, who now approached with a place setting for Caroline. Caroline made a quick study of the menu as the waitress noisily poured ice water into a plastic tumbler that was so scratched from dishwashing that it seemed frosted white. The waitress, who wore a pink pocketed smock, and a black skirt, spoke as she poured.

"How's the food, Ray?"

"Real good, Sally."

"Glad to hear it. Now, tell me, how's Winona these days?"

"She's fine."

"Well, good. You tell her I said hi, won't you?"

Ray nodded.

Sally turned to Caroline and chirped, "You ready to order, honey?"

"Yes, I'll have a chicken-salad sandwich on white toast and a cherry Coke."

"Oh-kay. . . ." Sally scribbled as she spoke. "How 'bout you, Ray? Anything else?"

"Nope."

Sally pivoted and was gone. Ray concentrated on eating for some time, then spoke. "They send you the check yet?"

"What check?"

"Nope. Didn't get mine, either." He cut off more meat.

"What check?"

"For your first run of hardwood. Sent it up to

Butte. Duke took it." Ray was nearly done with the steak.

"You mean you got the first run cut, loaded, and transported?"

"Yup." Ray switched his empty oval dinner plate with the side dish heaped with hash browns and reached for the salt.

"When?"

Sally came by, clunked down Caroline's lunch, and refilled Ray's coffee mug.

"Thanks," said Caroline, then to Ray she repeated, "When?"

"Two weeks ago. The North Star Mill. Give them another week or two to get the check to you."

"That's really great. Thank you, Ray." She bit into the two-inch-thick sandwich that she'd been holding in midair. It was delicious, flavored lightly with lemon and dill and not too much celery. Well, thought Caroline, so much for my questions about the schedule.

The two of them ate in silence for a while. Ray switched the empty hash brown plate for the one filled with buttery brussels sprouts. He motioned his empty fork at Caroline and said, "Two things."

"What are they?" Caroline had to thumb an errant glob of chicken into the corner of her mouth.

"One, I'm going up to see the rodeo at Great Falls next week, so I won't be around."

"That's nice—I mean, that you're going to the rodeo."

"Yup. State fair. The big one."

Caroline smiled and sipped her cherry Coke.

"Used to be a rodeo man up there myself." Brussels sprouts got traded for cinnamon-sprinkled applesauce. "Two, you've got some defoliation in your hard-wood maples. Doesn't look real serious, but it's worth a check with the cooperative extension. I'll give them some samples before I go to Great Falls."

Caroline nodded seriously. "What do you think it is?"

"Some kind of insect pest. You'll probably end up having to spray next spring: kill the eggs before they can take hold next season." Ray sipped the last of his coffee and continued. "Not to worry, the spray isn't too expensive. Still, I'm surprised to see this kind of thing so early on in the summer. Usually it's autumn." He patted his lumpy shirt pocket and removed a pack of Camels and a Zippo lighter. "Probably on account of the dry spell." He eased out a cigarette, gave the tip a cursory tap on the table, and lit it with a click-snap of the Zippo. "Mind if I smoke?"

Caroline started the other half of her sandwich as Ray puffed smoke and concentrated on the lunch counter, which was beginning to fill up with more customers. Caroline attempted conversation.

"Was the work difficult for the first run of wood?"

"Same as usual."

"Was the dry weather a problem?"

"Nope."

"Are you looking forward to Great Falls?"

"Yup."

Clearly, Caroline surmised, Ray was done talking. They sat there in silence. Ray smoked contemplatively, and Caroline sipped, ate, and caught snatches of the conversations in progress at their neighboring tables.

Two women sitting directly behind Caroline were talking about how someone really ought to be put in charge of coordinating the potluck dinners at the Church of the Nazarene. At the booth to Caroline's right, three teenage girls dressed in semipunk attire—which was as much as they could get away with in a place like Hawkeye—shared a plate of French fries and giggled a lot. Caroline noisily slurped the last of her cherry Coke through its ice. Ray squashed out his cigarette stub and looked around. It was high noon, and people were pouring into the Bitterroot at a brisk pace.

Over at the cash register, a tall, well-built man dressed like a ranch hand grinned widely at Caroline and Ray. He hesitated an instant, then took off his cowboy hat and loped toward them. His hair, Caroline noticed, was as golden as sunlight.

"Howdy."

"Hello, Jody," said Ray. "You know Miss Atkinson, don't you?"

"I sure do." Jody Landis was somewhere in his early thirties, but his grin was that of a boy's. "Mind if I join you?"

"Please do," said Caroline, craning her neck to see Jody sweep back a lock of golden hair that had fallen over his eye.

"Here," said Ray as he squealed his chair away from the table and stood up. "Have a seat, son. I was leaving anyway."

Caroline saw that Ray was actually smiling. Jody's presence seemed to do that to people. Ray left a tip for Sally, scooped up both his and Caroline's tab slips, and nodded good-bye.

"Thank you, Ray." said Caroline, both surprised and flattered by the gesture. "You have yourself a great time in Great Falls."

"You going to the rodeo, Ray?" Jody asked.

"Yup." He smiled again.

"Well, you've got to tell me everything about it when you get back. Okay?"

Caroline tried to imagine Ray's describing anything in much detail, but as he left Ray nodded that he would.

Jody slipped quietly onto Ray's chair. Caroline could tell by the sheepish look on his face that he felt both uncertain as well as pleased to be there with her. That was just about how Caroline felt about him, too.

"You sure look good today," Jody said. His eyes sparkled at her, and she was held involuntarily by his strong, steady gaze. Caroline didn't say it out loud, but her mind said, You do, too.

To Jody, she smiled and said, "Thanks." Jody's eyes, clear and ocean blue, focused so directly onto Caroline's that it made her uncomfortable.

CHAPTER

5

*"H*I THERE, JODY!" blared Sally as she began to gather the dishes from Ray's lunch. "Excuse me just a moment." She swiftly clattered the dishes into a pile while smirking mischievously at Jody, aware that she had jolted him out of his unabashed regard of Caroline. "Be right back." She winked over the dishes at Caroline and departed.

"Does she know everyone who comes in here?" asked Caroline, again snared by Jody's eyes. He had longer eyelashes than any man had a right to.

"Suppose she does," Jody answered as he relaxed onto his chair. Caroline's gaze followed as Jody reached for the salt shaker and held it slightly tilted. His hand was large, square, and callused in places. The long fingers wore no ring; the sturdy wrist, no watch. The well-tanned hand suggested a toughness earned from hard daily labor, yet it held the small salt shaker with a gentle grace. Jody studied the rice grains that were mixed into the salt. After a moment he returned the shaker and quietly fixed his gaze on Caroline. She did her best, this time to return it.

"So, my young friends . . ." Sally was back, smiling at the two of them as she arranged Jody's place setting. "Have you thought at all about what you might want for lunch yet?" Without waiting for a reply, Sally addressed Caroline directly. "Sorry for interrupting, sweetheart. If I had our local Robert Redford all moon-eyed at me the way he is at you, the last thing I'd want to be hearing about is a lunch order. But . . ." Sally smirked at Jody and then said to Caroline, "Hand him a menu, honey, and get him to decide on something. I'll be back in a bit."

Caroline watched as Jody, sheepish from Sally's teasing, took a black leatherette menu and studied it. What a strange blend of strength and innocence he is, Caroline mused, her eyes fixed on the broad shoulders and the new blush of sunburn over the already tanned, square-jawed face. I wonder if he realizes how incredibly attractive he is.

Jody, absorbed in reading the menu, absentmindedly raked his hand through his hair with a slow, peculiarly masculine kind of unconscious grace. Sensing Caroline's direct regard of him, he grinned up at her from the menu, then returned to it.

No, Caroline concluded, he's got absolutely no idea. He was so open, so simple and unpretentious. Perplexed, Caroline wondered why a man so handsome and good-natured and who owned a successful small ranch hadn't gotten married before this. Surely the local ladies must have been lining up at his door. She paused to ponder as she gazed at Jody's hands holding the menu.

Maybe he was like me, she thought. Maybe, for him, the trade-off was his ranch. Caroline felt a sudden, unexpected pang of sadness for Jody's work-roughened hands. Pushing this feeling away, she thought instead of how she knew about Jody's trade-off.

She'd met him last April in Fairbanks Hardware. In fact, it was on her very first visit to Hawkeye, and Jody was the very first person she'd met. Maybe that was a good omen. It seemed, certainly, that ever since then, whenever she'd needed someone more capable than herself, Jody was always reliably there. In the first instance at Fairbanks, Caroline had just finished buying all the lumber for her sewing room shelves. She was outside in front of the loading dock, trying to stuff all the planks into the windows of her car. After she'd set four planks diagonally across the seats, it became obvious that they weren't all going to fit in a car the size of her Camaro. She was going to have to go back and ask them to hold the custom-cut boards until she could return. It would take a good two or three more trips up and down that damn mountain to get them all home.

Annoyed at her own lack of planning, Caroline grumbled as she hit open the loading door back into Fairbanks. There was Jody. He'd been watching her folly with the lumber and was smiling with amusement at her aggravation. For some reason, his infectious grin dissolved Caroline's bad mood. In his typical sweet-shy manner, he introduced himself and offered to load all the lumber on his pickup and bring it out to her place. Funny, she thought later, she had no qualms of distrust in letting this stranger follow her home. But then Jody was like that. Anyone could read his face like a book.

He came to see Caroline a lot after that, always on the pretense of casually dropping by to see if she needed his help with things like jammed windows and broken floorboards. The fact that his own ranch was ten miles on the opposite side of Hawkeye didn't seem to affect his habitual introduction that he was "just by way of your neighborhood," so he thought he'd "stop by to see how the renovation was coming along." Caroline never questioned him on it, mainly because he always seemed to show up when strength surpassing her own was needed.

Sometimes he did the heavier chores that Caroline might never have accomplished on her own. Other times he finished tasks for her that, really, she would have rather done by herself even if it did take her twice the time. Still, Caroline enjoyed having a visitor and enjoyed, too, their quiet talks over tall glasses of lemonade. There were even times when Jody forgot a portion of his shyness and spoke—in patches, at least—about his past.

The fact that Jody had survived a hard life said much about him. The fact that his good-natured temperament was still intact said even more. He grew up with his mother and an older brother in an old section of Helena. He never once mentioned a father, and Caroline never asked. As soon as Jody finished high school he went to work as a full-time ranch hand along with his brother. After many years of scrimping their earnings together, they finally had enough to go partners on the small ranch west of Hawkeye.

When his brother died in a horrible highway accident five years back, Jody was devastated. The loss of the one person who mattered in his life left him utterly bewildered. And he wasn't at all sure he could handle the ranch or its mortgage on his own. But somehow, as was always the case with him, Jody saw his way through those tough years and came out modestly ahead. Caroline suspected, also, that besides making a go of the ranch, Jody was the sole support of his mother in Helena.

Caroline could also see that Jody's uphill climb through life's obstacles didn't leave him fifteen minutes for a social life of any kind, much less for finding a girlfriend. Caroline saw clearly, now, that the ranch was indeed Jody's trade-off. He could have so easily sold it and become a salaried ranch hand again. She admired him for refusing to retreat and was glad that it had turned out so well for him. He had a hired hand, fresh livestock every year, store-bought feed, and books showing only black ink. Jody was ready to join the world now, if only he could get the hang of it.

Sally came back to their table at the Bitterroot. She took Jody's lunch order and Caroline's for coffee and pie, then left them to each other. Jody, never one to launch into talk, slipped his menu deliberately into place and sat back on his chair. He nodded slightly to Caroline, along with a smile to indicate that he was ready for her to encourage him into conversation. His cool blue eyes locked onto hers and held them. Caroline unconsciously fingered her right earring.

"So," she said, perhaps a little too forcefully, "I just heard from Ray Banes that he's got my first run of hardwood already sold to some place in Butte." She paused to adjust the left earring. "He looks like he's pretty pleased about going to the rodeo, don't you think?" Caroline noticed that Jody had some folded papers stuffed into the front pocket of his light blue work shirt.

"Boy, I sure like the rodeo in Great Falls. Me and Steve . . ." He missed half a beat in his narrative. "We used to get time off to go every year. You should go see it yourself sometime, Caroline. It really is something." He looked to her to pick up the conversation. He raked his hand through the hair that had fallen over one eye.

"Tell, me," Caroline continued valiantly, "what have you been doing on the ranch this week?"

"Well, it was fences last week and this week, too. They're all mended up now." He scooted his chair closer to the table and drummed his fingers a couple of times on the place mat. His fingers, long and straight, reminded Caroline of those of the guitar players she used to watch on MTV. Remember MTV? she mused to herself. She wondered what Jody would make of a channel like that should it ever come to Hawkeye. He was still smiling at her, waiting. Caroline felt like a second-grade teacher patiently drawing out the details of a timid child's show-and-tell recitation.

"What brought you to Hawkeye today, Jody?"

"Well . . ." He caught and held her eyes again. "I've got to get the spring schedule of vitamin supplements for both the calves and the heifers at Lowell's Feed and Grain." He patted the papers in his shirt pocket, where Caroline surmised the details of the vitamin list were written.

Caroline looked at the shirt pocket and found herself wondering what Jody looked like without the shirt. In this heat did he work at his ranch bare-chested? She started to imagine what he might look like like that.

Probably pretty good. She fingered the earring again and tried to twirl it around as her imagination led her on.

"We'll be having a busy time with these vitamins," Jody continued, oblivious of her thoughtful interest. "You should see the cycle of doses we've got to follow. Looks like a regular train schedule."

Caroline quickly changed her attention to Jody's face. Tugging at her earring, she smiled at him in silence.

"Nice earrings," said Jody, his eyes full of admiration.

"Thanks." She made herself rest her hands in her lap. She knew it was her turn again to run a few yards with the conversation, but she didn't.

After a moment Jody ventured, "This is some dry spell we're having."

"It sure is. Is it always like this in the summer?"

"Last summer and this one have been real scorchers. Been real bad for grazing. I've had to buy nearly twice the feed than usual."

"Oh," said Caroline, wondering what to answer to that. Nothing came to mind. She watched Jody's eyes. They had little white crow's-feet at the corners—not the kind you get from wrinkles, but the kind you get from squinting a lot in the sun. Caroline followed the line of his neck down and across to his wide shoulders.

Thinking about her shower this morning, Caroline asked, "Has the drought brought the water pressure down at your place, too?"

"No, nothing wrong with it. Are you sure it's not your well?"

"I have a well?"

Jody's eyes smiled, and the white crow's-feet dis-appeared. "Well, sure." He was clearly amused by her ignorance. "Did you think you were hooked up to Hawkeye's water system so far out?"

"Well, yes," she answered a little defensively. There was a lower button missing from his shirt. "I guess I never thought about it before."

A surge of combined voices interrupted from the direction of the cash register. Both Caroline and Jody glanced toward the commotion. It was a group of peo-ple laughing and looking for an empty table. Caroline turned back to Jody for the answer.

"You have well water out there." Jody beamed at her. His expression told her that he was pleased to be her guide in the ways of country living. "Probably not an artesian well if it's drying up midsummer like this." He waited for his revelation to sink in. It didn't.

"So what does that mean? Do I need to call a plumber or a well digger?"

"I'll come out and have a look at it."

"No, Jody. Thanks. Thanks a lot, but it's a busy time on your ranch—like you said. I'll get a name of someone to fix it at Fairbanks."

Jody looked perplexed at her, his jaw suddenly set tight.

"Look, Jody, you've really done a lot for me lately—too much, in fact—and I really do appreciate it. But you've got a place of your own to see to. Really, you don't have to take care of my problems all the time."

"But I would like to," he said in a surprisingly earnest tone. Then, in an even more serious voice, "All the time."

Their eyes held. Caroline had never seen Jody

quite so solemn before, his white crow's-feet even more noticeable. It was Jody this time who abruptly broke their mutual gaze, and Caroline, herself feeling suddenly shy, too, directed her eyes to the shirt pocket full of papers.

"Geez, you two," said Sally as she began to arrange dishes in front of Jody. "You ought to see yourselves—straight out of high school." She poured Caroline's coffee. "Don't forget to eat, okay?" Sally left, shaking her head in mock concern.

Caroline watched Jody as he ate. His appetite even surpassed Ray's as he wholeheartedly attacked his food. At least now they didn't have to talk. Caroline relaxed on her chair and toyed with the point of her pie. Again, she listened in on the buzz of conversation around her.

The group of people—three businessmen and one matronly looking woman—whose commotion at the cash register had caught Caroline's and Jody's attention before were seated at a table behind Jody. All four of them were in a loud, lively discussion. Caroline couldn't hear them very well and only caught, from time to time, the accented words: trash, energy, money, pollution. She wondered idly what it was all about. They certainly were at boisterous odds with each other, whatever it was. She waited for Jody to pause in his eating.

"Jody?" she asked quietly. "Those people behind you—what are they arguing about?"

He sat up straight and tilted his head to listen. All but one of his shirt buttons strained tight.

"It's that trash-to-energy thing they're talking about. Some company wants to start up a project around here to make electricity or something out of garbage."

"Garbage?" Caroline's mind flashed to a smoldering mountain of rubbish she'd seen in Gary, Indiana, like a scene from hell.

"I think so," said Jody. "I'm not so sure on the details, but it's supposed to be ecologically okay."

Caroline wondered what it meant. "Is that all you've heard about it?"

Jody slurped his coffee. "Bob Sanderson—he's got a good-size spread just north of Hawkeye—he just sold it to them. Made a fortune on it, too. Probably double the going rate for clear land. He and his wife are going to move up to Missoula."

"What do you think this project is?" asked Caroline, remembering the word *pollution* associated directly with the word *money* in the overheard argument.

"Don't know." Jody grinned at her. For some reason he seemed entertained by her interest in it. "We'll have to wait and see."

Wait and see, huh? Caroline mused. She would always distrust that phrase. The last time someone spoke those particular words to her, her life had looked pretty grim. She looked at Jody. His amused expression over her interest in local industry remained unchanged.

CHAPTER

6

CAROLINE AND JODY parted on the sidewalk in front of the Bitterroot. Jody headed left toward the feed-and-grain depot. Caroline crossed the street to the fabric store. She paused under the awning of the fabric shop long enough to watch Jody as he walked away. His jeans fit him nicely, Caroline observed with appreciation as he strode confidently down the sidewalk, his arms slightly akimbo. Her eyes lingered just a moment longer on Jody's retreat before she pushed open the door of the store.

A small bell tinkled her arrival as the smell of fabric sizing greeted her senses. Caroline really liked fabric stores. She likened this to the way her father used to relish a trip to the hardware store just to see what there was to see in it. Caroline had already sewn all the curtains that hung in her farmhouse from what she'd bought in this store. She'd taken a sewing class in high school once and found she had a talent for making her own clothes. It came in handy, especially in college when she was strapped for wardrobe money. After she got her job in Chicago, though, she'd parked her Singer at her mother's house in favor of department store clothes. She had her sewing machine back now.

Caroline fingered a bolt of fabric here and there as she serpentined her way through the store, then found the back table that held the pattern books. Forty-five minutes later she still hand't found a pattern she was keen on making. Really, she had all the clothes she needed. Besides, she was in no mood to gamble: her theory on sewing patterns was that one out of every three you made both looked good and fit well upon completion.

Caroline looked around for inspiration. Her gaze alighted on a quilt pattern book. After looking through it, she decided that she would make a living room lap quilt for wintertime. There was plenty of lead time. Then, she figured, if the lap-size model turned out well, she'd have a full-size quilt project to keep her busy during the dead of winter. The pattern she chose was called Log Cabin. Caroline's enthusiasm built as the saleslady cut the lengths of her chosen fabrics: yards of both solids and tiny-flowered reds and pine greens. Nice, warm, cozy colors. Caroline left the store, enjoying the weighty heft of the fabric in its bag and happy that she had a new project to tackle once she got home.

She headed toward Fairbanks Hardware and Army/Navy. She needed that new spring for the kitchen door, and it wouldn't hurt just to meander through the wooden-floored store beneath the old, squeaky ceiling fans. Inside, the Fairbanks family sup-

plied Hawkeye with the basics: work and cowboy
boots, guns and targets, video rentals, chain saws, blue
jeans, axes; stovepipes, and all the no-nonsense hardware items not sold at the coffeepot-and-housepaint-
oriented True Value.

When Caroline had finally left with the door
spring, she passed a beefy, teenage Indian boy sullenly
loitering out front. He was draped listlessly over the
kid's mechanical pony ride, sucking deeply on a cigarette. Looking into his eyes, Caroline suspected that he
was just on the functional side of being either drunk or
stoned. He wore the nationally recognized punk-teen-
age uniform: black T-shirt with rolled-up sleeves and
black jeans. His dark, heavy-lidded eyes were half-cov-
ered by a shock of long, greasy, straight black hair. Even
though it was pretty obvious that he was probably
Hawkeye's own town hood, Caroline inexplicably
found herself liking him. It seemed to her that here was
just a vulnerable kid with the odds against him, hiding,
as best he could, behind a tough facade.

"Hi," she greeted him, smiling.

Mildly startled at her addressing him, the kid nodded at her subtly, then broke into a fleeting yet winsome
grin.

Caroline sensed that he might be embarrassed to be
caught with his armor down, so she too nodded, making brief eye contact before continuing on her way. She
walked back in the direction of the fabric store, past
Paquette's Insurance, which was just across from the
IGA supermarket. Paquette's was the last building on
Main Street. If people needed goods or services beyond
what Hawkeye had to offer, they could travel ninety
minutes to either Missoula or Butte. Both of those cities

had a hospital-clinic, a K mart, and a McDonald's. The neighboring town of Novi, just forty-five minutes away, had a little less than what Hawkeye had for the consumer, but it was important in that it was the area's entertainment hub, offering a movie house, a honky tonk, and a bowling alley.

Caroline crossed over to the IGA parking lot, dumped her purchases in her car, and entered the supermarket, pushing a cart she found at the electric-eye door.

In the social fabric of Hawkeye, the IGA was cousin to the Bitterroot Cafe in that it was an informal meeting place, but on a more practical level. People came here to shop and to talk about the weather. And Leon, the butcher, a man who had never been in a hurry in his life, even when it wouldn't have hurt, was the welcoming host of it all. When he wasn't behind his meat counter, he cruised the aisles, joining in on customers' conversations in progress and initiating new ones.

The IGA was where Caroline had learned her first lessons on the slower pace of life in Hawkeye. People actually seemed to enjoy grocery shopping here. This was mostly because shopping was regarded as a social event rather than, as Caroline had always viewed it, one of life's essential chores to be speedily completed, the faster the better.

Caroline now pushed her cart toward the meat counter and surveyed the homemade sausages. Suddenly Leon was talking to her from behind the clear-plastic partition of the meat room.

"Hey, little lady. . . ." His deep and jolly voice rang out like Santa Claus's. "Now, don't miss out on the fresh corn today. It's good and sweet. I picked it myself early this morning, before the sun started drying things out."

"Okay"—she smiled at Leon—"thanks for telling me."

Caroline wheeled her cart around the store, gathering what she needed. She stopped at the meager frozen-food case: not a Lean Cuisine in sight for the ranks of the cooking-impaired like herself. She supposed she was actually going to have to learn how to cook this winter. She picked up her recent standby, fish sticks, and headed for the checkout line. It was an unwritten rule of etiquette, Caroline had recently perceived, that old people and people with only a few items were automatically given room in line in front of those whose carts were full. She hesitated to let a young mother carrying a baby and a box of Pampers go ahead of her. Caroline could have easily swerved to the other checkout line, but she preferred to wait. The checkout lady in this particular line had been helpful in telling her about the ins and outs of Hawkeye. It was she who'd told Caroline where the library was and explained about getting the sticker that gave permission to dump garbage at the landfill.

Today, while a teenage boy bagged the groceries, Caroline and the checkout lady chatted about the dry weather and the price of bottled water. She also gave Caroline the name of her brother-in-law's brother, who dug wells. Caroline left the supermarket and loaded her car. She returned her shopping cart to the store entrance, another unwritten rule of IGA etiquette.

✻ ✻ ✻

It wasn't long before Caroline was out of Hawkeye.
By the time she was driving past the high school, her
mind was busy replaying the events of her day, notably
her conversation of sorts with Jody. What exactly had
he meant when he'd said he wanted to take care of her
problems all the time? He'd seemed, Caroline recalled
now, so very serious when he'd said it. And why would
he say something so unabashedly obvious like that
when he was usually so ill at ease to say anything to
her? Well, as her mother used to say, still waters run
deep. Still, she had to admire his finally coming to the
point about his intentions, even if she didn't know how
she felt about them.

Things would have to blossom slowly with Jody,
Caroline reckoned. Truly they were very different people, and while opposites attract, a possible romance
between them would need some time to evolve. Just as
well, she mused. Jody was the patient type, and aside
from the ever-present fact of his unnervingly good
looks, she was in no real hurry anyway.

Caroline thought about the steady patience she
saw in Jody's character. He seemed to possess a self-
taught confidence that applied, probably, to everything
within his sphere of living except her. And he had the
honesty not to disguise his feelings about her, she realized, which most men would have taken at least some
precautions to camouflage. But, again, that was what
was so charming about Jody. His whole personality was
open and unpretentious. In fact, Jody seemed, in his
simplicity, the personification of Montana itself. In time
Caroline would adjust to him, just as she was getting to
feel comfortable in her new surroundings.

Caroline recalled Jody's tight-set jaw, today, when

she'd refused his offer to see about her well. He was
hurt, and she probably should have accepted the offer,
but she was thrown off balance by the seriousness of his
words. She pondered over what it all meant. Maybe she
simply wasn't ready to embark on a love affair. Maybe
she still needed to find her bearings in this new home
of hers alone and on her own before relinquishing some
of herself to a relationship. Maybe it was just a desire for
Jody's body that was making her attentive. Really, she
had to admit, they were not an ideally matched pair.
The country mouse and the city mouse described them
a little too well.

On the other hand, Caroline reprimanded herself,
wasn't that exactly why she'd left the urban world?
Hadn't she come to Montana with the intention of embracing all those qualities that Jody represented? The
fact that Jody was as lovely to the eye as Montana itself
was simply a pleasing bonus. Caroline's face clouded.
Might she be rationalizing? Jim had been extremely
attractive, too. Now *there* was a sobering thought—
perhaps a testament to her own bad judgment when it
came to men.

Lightly pumping the brakes, Caroline drove carefully down the steep mountainside. "Take it easy down
this stretch of road," she warned herself. She realized
the deeper implication of her advice and scolded herself, "And don't ever forget what happened with Jim."
Her knuckles were white from gripping the steering
wheel. She willed them to relax. No, she wouldn't forget. She would never forget what happened with Jim.

She had met Jim a little over two years ago. They'd
immediately fallen crazy in love with each other, al-

ways looking forward to the nonworking moments they could spend in each other's arms.

He was a corporate options trader: charming, successful, and aristocratically handsome with alabaster skin and fine-boned features. His shock of black hair gave him a rakish quality in spite of the oxford shirts and gold collar pin he always wore. But beyond his exceptional looks, the most striking thing about Jim was his affable nature. He would often joke mischievously with Caroline, and only Jim, with his humor-filled talk, could pull her instantly away from her preoccupations with work. Caroline had genuinely enjoyed his company. She saw in Jim a blend of sophisticated businessman and impish schoolboy.

To Caroline, Jim was exciting in both mind and body, and for two happy years they'd enjoyed a perfect romance. They were enthusiastic lovers and intellectual peers. Caroline had heard that a kind of electricity could exist between certain people, and she was sure this was so of them. She and Jim were also a good match in that both of them understood that job demands might often have to supersede their time spent with each other. Neither minded. Caroline felt especially lucky that she was loved by a man who understood her needs, both at home and in the office. So when they found the time to spend evenings, weekends, and vacations together, their love continued to be exciting and to thrive. In fact, Caroline came to depend on it. She felt that Jim was a man whom she could trust her love to. It came as a complete shock to her to realize she was wrong.

It happened just one month before her even bigger troubles started. With Jim's cheerful understanding, Caroline had worked through the weekend before. But this weekend she had kept clear for him. It was unusual that he didn't call and the answering machine on his end didn't explain. Well, she had told herself, it was her turn to be cheerful and understanding.

Back at the office on Monday, she heard it, thunderstruck, from Mort Zinder. Poor Mort—he didn't want to be the one to tell her but felt he should. He'd closed her office door and explained in the most diplomatic way he could: he and his wife had attended a party held by an influential business associate up in Evanston last weekend. They were introduced to the host's daughter, who in turn introduced her fiancé. The fiancé didn't seem at all discomfited to greet Mort in a warm and affable manner. Mort wondered if the fiancé recognized him but was pretending that he didn't or if the fiancé didn't connect Mort's face with the office where he'd so often picked up a friend after work. But Mort recognized him. It was Jim.

Caroline confronted Jim, hoping that it was a terrible misunderstanding. It wasn't. He'd been engaged for the past year but just couldn't bring himself to break it off with Caroline. And so they'd parted, Caroline hurt and uncomprehending, Jim merely wearing the wry expression of a guilty child.

During the weeks that followed, Caroline wondered if she was to blame for Jim's infidelity, that perhaps her compulsion to work long hours at her job had pushed him away. Perhaps she had placed far more importance on the depth of their relationship than he ever had. Maybe it was her own fault for romanticizing the affair—now she could see that it had been no more than that—into something it wasn't. It shamed Caroline to think that she had fantasized Jim's feelings for her way out of proportion. He had always been ambiguous about declaring his heart to her. Why had she been such a blind fool? she had asked herself. But she already knew the uncomfortable answer: When a man leaves the areas of love and devotion blank in a relationship, the woman will always fill them with what she wants to believe. And Caroline had done just that.

Her self-blame lasted for a long time. Eventually, however, just before the hospital, Caroline's view evolved into the more healthy belief that she had been a trusting, if romantic, dope and that Jim was just an unfeeling, two-timing son of a bitch.

Driving down the last stretch of the mountain pass, Caroline wondered if, underneath, all men were like that.

CHAPTER

7

*T*HE DASHBOARD CLOCK read a little past six when Caroline's home came into view. The wooden-frame, many-gabled house had a steeply pitched roof that continued well over and past the long front porch. Considering the vastness of the land surrounding her house, there was only a modest amount of bare front yard between the road and the front door. When homesteaders built this place, their only connection with the human world was the road Caroline now traveled, and they didn't want to be out of earshot of a single thing that might pass by. As Caroline neared, she could see that Humphrey was upholding that tradition as he sat perched atop the white spindle railings that surrounded the expanse of both front and side porches. Looking up at the gray-blue house, Caroline spotted Tinky's black silhouette waiting for her in the white-trimmed gable of her bedroom window. "Home at last," Caroline sighed as she drove the car back around to the barn.

Hot, her energy sapped from the exertion of the day and the long drive back, she began to unload the car. Groceries came first. This time she'd been clever: she'd bought a white Styrofoam cooler at the IGA and packed all her frozen foods in it for the scorching drive home. Hauling the cooler onto the antique kitchen table, she reached in for her favorite ice cream: heavenly hash. Even as she grabbed for it, she knew: the sloshing sound told all. When, she asked herself, would she be able to enjoy just one lousy little dish of ice cream like normal people? In January, came her own answer, but who the hell wanted ice cream when it was forty below?

Suddenly she was overcome by an irrational, yet very real irritability. Slamming the rest of the dripping groceries onto the refrigerator and freezer shelves, Caroline returned to the car to unload the rest. One of the eight plastic jugs of bottled water had sprung a significant leak. She left the car doors open to let the carpet dry out.

"Maybe I need to eat," she grumbled to herself.

It was seven-thirty by the time she had unpacked the purchases of the day and finally sat down to dinner. Her mail lay in front of her on the kitchen table. Feeling calmer, she opened the package from Celeste. It was a tape by an Irish folk-rock band called the O'Reillys. Caroline would listen to it later. Now she opened up Celeste's accompanying letter. Summer term was easy, her younger sister reported. Her grades were up, her boyfriend had just passed his bar exams, and Celeste was confident that when her turn came, she would, too.

Also, Celeste wrote in her barely legible scrawl, she'd gotten a perm that made her look just like their old cocker spaniel, Honey; she'd been spending many of her Saturdays at Fenway Park; and she hoped Caroline liked—no, loved—the O'Reillys' music as much as she did. Caroline smiled in fondness for her sister, then opened the letter from her mother.

Her mom was full of chatty news of people and places they had in common in St. Louis: Roselynn across the yard was expecting; she'd run into Dr. McAllister last week and he'd sent his regards; Aunt Libby had decided that they should make a rock garden around the side walkway. Caroline smiled wistfully throughout her mother's letter, at least until the part about Aunt Libby.

Having finished her food, she sat at the kitchen table, sipping from a sweating glass of iced tea. Sturdily lathed oak legs and thickly hewn side frames upheld the sprawling marble tabletop. The marble was predominantly gray, of more practical quality than asthetic and of an enormous weight, which was why, Caroline surmised, it had come with the house when she'd bought it. She ran her palm along its surface. It was the coolest thing in the house. Caroline wondered who the woman was who'd lived here so long before her: a woman who must have felt so strongly about making perfect pastry that she'd insisted on having this tabletop travel all the way to this hinterland. Caroline slid the dishes and letters away and laid her cheek on the marble. It felt wonderfully cool and good to her. She closed her eyes, trying to relax, but she found that she couldn't.

Getting up, she cleared the table, found the quilt

pattern book she had bought, and headed out the
kitchen door. The back porch flanked both sides of the
door, hugging the house. A series of white painted posts
supported the roof overhang, but still, with the angle of
the evening sun, there was no shade back here. Caroline
walked around the side porch to the front porch. It ran
the length of the house and was shady and cool under
its overhang.

She settled onto one of the wooden chairs and
looked down both ends of the road. She didn't expect
to see a soul in either direction, but she couldn't help
herself from automatically checking the terrain anyway.
Finding things just as she expected, she opened her
quilting book.

Evening dusk crept up without her notice until,
finally, she realized she had the book practically up to
her nose in order to read it. It was nearly dark. She
gathered up Humphrey for the night, speaking to him.

"Time to go in, my friend. I don't want you tan-
gling with the nighttime wildlife." She scooped the
unwilling animal into her arms, then paused to calm
the cat by petting it. As she looked out across the distance, Caroline's attention was caught. It was that ne-
thertime of evening when daylight hadn't completely
surrendered itself to darkness. Caroline saw, or thought
she saw, a faint twinkle of light coming from the direction of her mystery neighbor's house. It was like the
feeble flickering of a distant star. Now you see it, now
you don't. And, now, Caroline didn't. Stare as she
might, the brief twinkle didn't repeat itself, and she
wondered if she'd really seen it. A mosquito buzzed her
ear, Humphrey began to wriggle, and Caroline headed
for the front door.

It was a lot hotter once she was inside the house. Caroline turned on the lights and took her quilting book upstairs to one of the spare bedrooms. Sparsely furnished, it contained her kitchen table from Chicago, piled with the stacks of fabric she'd bought earlier that day. All manner of fabrics and spools were neatly housed within the white wooden shelves that covered the white planked walls. In the daytime this room was filled with sunshine from a bank of windows, so Caroline had made it her sewing studio and already had used it to make all the curtains that hung in the house.

Caroline stood in front of the table and thumbed through the new folds of fabric. She opened the quilt book to her chosen pattern, double-checked the colors, fingered the acetate templates, then paused to imagine the end result. This was the best part of making something, she mused—the gathering of the components, the beautiful expectations your mind envisioned as to the outcome of the project, even the pleasant debate you had with yourself as to exactly where you would use or display the finished work. Never mind that you hadn't made the quilt yet. These were all so much more fun to dwell upon than the actual chore of making the quilt. Caroline thought about starting the project then and there but talked herself out of it. It was late. She was tired. She felt fidgety, antsy, and concentrating on a quilt pattern wasn't the solution to this kind of restlessness. Instead, she headed for her bedroom where she got into a ruffled nightgown. Then she went back downstairs.

She turned on the television in the living room, plopped down onto the cranberry red sofa, and put her feet up on the wooden steamer trunk that served as the coffee table. Sinking deeply into a comfortable position, she was ready to surrender to whatever the television wanted to hypnotize her with. It was a car commercial.

"Aw, damn!" She hauled herself out of her sloth-like posture and padded toward the kitchen door. She had left the car doors open.

Outside, it had turned completely dark except for the dim glow from her car's map lights. Caroline felt strange walking toward the barn in her nightgown, even though she knew that she could be walking around stark naked and no one would see her. She banged the car doors shut, and total darkness enveloped her. That was when she noticed the lights. So she hadn't imagined it. Across the side meadow at a pretty far distance, there were lights inside the house that belonged to whoever her neighbors were. Caroline saw that they shone from the downstairs windows, dim and flickering as if produced from a candle or lantern. They don't have their electricity turned on yet, Caroline guessed. She squinted to see into their windows, but the flickering prevented her from focusing on anything. Caroline wondered what they would be like when she met them. Whatever they turned out to be like, it was nice to finally have some neighbors nearby.

Caroline stretched out her arms into the total darkness. She couldn't see them. Smiling to herself and recalling a movie called *The Miracle Worker,* she groped her way back through the pitch darkness until the halo of light from the back porch ended the game. Once inside, she went to the kitchen, found the box of herbal tea called Mellow Evening, and made herself some in her favorite red mug. She returned to the sofa, parked her mug easily within reach, and watched the television show that was in progress. She reached for her tea, only to realize that her hand trembled visibly as she brought the mug to her lips.

Quickly Caroline ran through a mental check-up: she didn't have a fever; her appetite was good; no panting, no pains anywhere. She held both her hands parallel, out in front of her. Yes, they were shaking, but that was no reason to panic. It could just be the heat or simply this restlessness she'd been feeling today, she assured herself. She thought about that for a while. Maybe her future in Montana *was* on her mind a lot lately, whether she realized it or not. Maybe she felt more pressure about how well she was adapting than she cared to admit. Well, she *had* to adapt, and that was all there was to it.

Caroline reached for the mug, willing her hands to be steady. They tried, but some tea spilled on the sofa. She sipped carefully from the mug and remembered the precise day that had begun the chain of events that placed her here. Her hands had betrayed her then, just as they did now.

It was the day of her big presentation, and Caroline's hand had trembled as she set the hot mug of coffee atop her rosewood office desk. She had been deliberately careful, but some coffee spilled anyway. Sinking onto her upholstered desk chair, she felt dazed and light-headed.

This is just some kind of flu, she told herself, you'll simply have to work through it. She tried to remember which desk drawer contained the aspirin. Instead she found herself dreamily gazing out the huge office window. Out there, at eight-thirty A.M. on a mid-December morning, Chicago's North Michigan Avenue shone brillianuy under a recent dusting of snow. Beyond, the sun sparkled clear and bright over Lake Michigan, but Caroline only winced at the light.

What lousy timing, she thought to herself. She had the Garner-Rolke combined advertising and public relations campaign presentation scheduled for ten o'clock that morning—the one she had been working on for nearly half a year. She knew that if her presentation today won that account, Mort would make good on his promise to promote her from account executive to vice president.

She felt strangely giddy as she proceeded to pull open each successive drawer in search of the aspirins that would mask this miserable flu. But even as she reached for the big plastic aspirin bottle, some nagging intuition bothered her. Maybe this was not the flu at all.

Caroline leaned her head back into the comfortable, high-backed chair. She rested there, staring vacantly at the coffee mug with the puddle around it, then at the silver-framed photos nearby. Several times she tried to rouse herself, but she only continued to stare. Ninety minutes later, three sticky circles of aspirin still lay in her sweaty, upturned palm.

Mort stormed into her office. "Caroline," he snapped quietly, obviously irritated. "Have you lost track of the time? They're all waiting. Where are the—" He stopped short. "Jesus H. Christ! You look horrible."

Caroline focused on his face, smiled wanly, and said, "Thanks, Mort. Thanks a lot."

Mort was too surprised by what he saw sitting at Caroline's desk to notice the listless sarcasm. Usually Caroline's oval face was both sweet and attractive, always animated by warm hazel-brown eyes that spar-

kled with intelligence and humor. Today, Mort plainly
saw that her eyes were heavy-lidded, glazed over, and
dull. More disturbing still, he saw that Caroline's normally flawless complexion had turned ash gray. This
wasn't just a paleness that so contrasted with her short
copper hair: her face held an unnatural pallor that triggered an alarm in his mind.

"How do you feel, Caroline?"

"Not so good. Some kind of bug."

Mort watched her shallow breathing. "How long
have you been feeling like this?" he pressed.

She shrugged. She had a childish, almost silly grin
on her face.

"Okay," he said. "Then where does it hurt?"

"It's just a stomachache that I've had for a few
days. It's only the flu, Mort. I'll be okay." She didn't
sound all that convincing, and she kept grinning stupidly at him.

Mort took her hand. "You're like ice." He immediately pressed his hand on her forehead. "Oh, hell, Caroline." He reached for her telephone and barked at the
switchboard operator, "Quick! Get 911. Tell them we
need an ambulance up here. Fast!"

Caroline watched all this from very far away. Her
ears, she realized with an inner giggle, were buzzing.
Mort's voice echoed and was muffled at the same time
so that she couldn't understand what he was saying.
She didn't care, really. Caroline sat back in her chair,
her ears buzzing even louder. She saw that Mort was
pacing in her office and that there was a fuzzy frame
around him. It was buzzing, too, and closing in. Caroline closed her eyes to a deep, enveloping darkness.

CHAPTER

8

CAROLINE OPENED HER eyes and took in the details of a pale blue hospital room. Calmly she tried to piece together the reason for her being there when a stout, redheaded nurse appeared at her bedside. Caroline tried to lift her head, but the nurse cheerfully stopped her.

"Don't even try it, dear. You want to stay flat for now." Reading the confused expression on Caroline's face, the nurse explained: "You've just had an emergency appendectomy, and it was a real close call, honey. Your appendix had burst some days before the surgery, and gangrene set in. You got here just in the nick of time. I'll tell you, it was real close. The doctors weren't so sure you were going to make it."

Caroline tried to absorb this as the rosy-cheeked nurse bubbled on.

"So now, sweetheart, even though your appendix

is gone, you've got yourself a nasty case of peritonitis."
The nurse's smile faltered for only the briefest moment
before she continued, "And, dear, there may be some
possible complications. The surgeon will be up to explain it to you." She smiled encouragingly. "But don't
worry. My name is Betty, and I'll be taking real good
care of you." As she left, Nurse Betty smiled so forcefully that Caroline felt compelled to smile, too. It faded
quickly, however, as she began to think about what
Nurse Betty had really said. Fortunately she didn't get
to think long before a heavy, fevered sleep overcame
her.

Caroline spent the next three weeks barely conscious, barely aware of anything as her body battled
with peritonitis and the subsequent pneumonia. Sometimes she dreamed she saw, even felt, her mother
nearby. She was never sure about this, but it was a
comfort to her anyway. At one point she pulled out of
the fog briefly enough to realize that, indeed, her
mother was there at her bedside. But there was no
longer any comfort in it. Even through her drowsiness,
Caroline could see the dark circles of sleeplessness
under Virginia Atkinson's eyes and a puffiness around
them that indicated she'd been crying. Caroline re-
lievedly drifted back into the fog.

At last the fog lifted and Caroline slowly won back
some strength. She also came to realize what her
mother, Nurse Betty, and the doctors already knew: she
could no longer move her left arm or leg. She couldn't
even sit up independently. Her mother was standing
next to her bed when the doctor came in to tell her the
official diagnosis. He didn't know why yet, but the left
side of her body was paralyzed.

Caroline received the message with remarkable calmness, but once the doctor had gone, she called out in terror.

"Mom?!" A wave of hollow panic rushed over her. "Paralyze `.!"

Virginia's anguished eyes answered as she held Caroline's one good hand.

Caroline was carefully tested for every ailment under the sun. Still, they could find no physiological explanation for her problem. The final diagnosis was that in conjunction with the trauma of the burst appendix, she had sustained a kind of stress-related trauma. It was the latter that somehow affected control over the left side of her body. They offered her no answers, no hope or encouragement beyond that. There were no prescriptions past "You'll have to wait and see."

So her health, if not her body, finally restored, Caroline left the hospital. She left just as she had entered—flat on her back. Her mother, crushed with the knowledge of what was to come and grieving over the unfair tragedy that had ruined her daughter's young life, sadly made arrangements to take her home to St. Louis to begin her next ordeal.

Virginia Atkinson shared many of her daughter's features. She, too, once had the same warm, copper-brown hair, only now it had turned nearly all gray. Virginia's eyes were a darker brown than her daughter's, and although until recently, they, too, sparkled with humor, Virginia's held a shy, retreating quality that Caroline's had never had. Virginia had been widowed two years after Caroline graduated from college. Caroline was then living and working in Chicago, and her kid sister, Celeste, was a freshman at Urbana. Both girls had offered to return home to Springfield that year, but even though it was a tempting comfort, Virginia decided instead to move in with her older sister, Libby. Libby lived alone in a large, slightly crumbling Victorian house in one of St. Louis's older neighborhoods. Since Libby was more "set in my ways," as she had phrased it, and because Virginia's personality was such that she always avoided arguments, Virginia agreed to sell her Springfield home and join Libby.

It was to this house that Virginia now brought Caroline. Caroline had never been overly fond of Aunt Libby, who she felt was a fusspot who bullied her mother, no matter how sweetly it was done. But Caroline realized that she was in no position to choose where she went, and she was thankful that Aunt Libby had miraculously agreed to allow Caroline's two cats to come along with her. Caroline wondered why Aunt Libby, who was allergic to fifty-one percent of what the world contained, would allow the cats. She could only conclude that, for once, her mother had insisted on something.

So Caroline came to live with her mother, two cats, and Aunt Libby in St. Louis. Now that all the excitement of leaving the hospital and the trip was over, now that she no longer had a parade of relentlessly cheerful nurses and office friends coming by her bedside to bolster her spirits, now that she was suddenly all alone, flat on her back in a strange bed, she had time to think about what had changed.

Staring out her window at a gray and snowy backyard somewhere in St. Louis, Caroline began to persuade herself that surely those doctors in Chicago were a bunch of idiots and could be entirely mistaken about the diagnosis. She would be okay, she told herself. All she needed was some more time to recuperate. Lurking just beneath these thoughts, though, was the recognition of the grim facts for what they were.

Soon she passed into a phase of fiery outrage. "Why me?" she would argue to herself. "I've been a good person. I don't deserve this." But Caroline also knew that "deserve" had nothing to do with it.

Once she'd passed through both denial and anger, the enormity finally hit her. She was worse than crippled. Her job and her home back in Chicago were gone forever. Her once vibrant young life had spiraled down to lying in an upstairs bedroom in her aunt Libby's house. And all she could do about it was wait and see.

It was the first week of February, and Caroline had lots of time to herself. Her mother came and sat with her every day, trying to interest her in books and idle talk. But her mother's generally timid nature had become even more so lately. It was a relief to them both when she would leave Caroline's room.

Clearly her mother didn't know how to handle what had befallen her daughter. Throughout Caroline's childhood even up until now, Virginia had been able to mend any problem Caroline had come to her with. Both of them had shared a rock-solid security in the knowledge that Mom somehow always knew how to make things all better again. But, unlike chicken pox, bad permanents, or bouts of lack-of-self-confidence, this time Virginia had no cure, no answer. This time she felt powerless. And worse yet, Caroline readily sensed her mother's feelings and was convinced that, indeed, things must truly be hopeless if her mother believed them so. Virginia tried to mask her emotions, but as any mother and daughter know, acting is both useless and unnerving in front of those who know you well. Virginia's pretense only underscored the despair in both women. So there evolved an unspoken agreement between them that at least until each had come to terms with what happened, Virginia's daily visits would be short.

Caroline wished that were the case with her aunt, but Libby showed no such sensitivity. Daily the stout, buxom woman barged into Caroline's privacy, smelling of face powder. Her white-to-blue hair was always poofed and sprayed into stiff curls, and she wore a different pastel-colored polyester pants-with-matching-jacket outfit for every day of the week. Aunt Libby chattered purposefully to her prisoner with less-than-flattering news about neighbors and relatives, the alarming murder rate in St. Louis, the latest plane crashes in the world, and how new findings showed that cat dander caused lung cancer.

It was more froth and gossip than Caroline could stomach. She told herself that Aunt Libby meant well, but her tolerance waned when her overbearing aunt concluded the daily tirade with her usual speech, a heavy-handed blend of sympathy and recrimination.

"Well, I must be leaving you now, Caroline, dear." Aunt Libby jabbed a finger behind her ear, reaching deep beneath the helmet of her hairdo, and scratched a spot on her scalp. "Oh, it just breaks my heart to see you lying here like this. You're much too young for something like this to happen to you." She shook her head soberly. "I can't understand what the good Lord had in mind when He sent this. But you must understand, dear, that sometimes He works in mysterious ways." Aunt Libby's baby-doll face stared into Caroline's intently.

Here it comes, thought Caroline.

"You know, dear, your mother was extremely foolish in letting you run off to Chicago like that. I've told her that over and over again."

I bet you have, thought Caroline.

"Really," continued Aunt Libby, "it's a wonder you're here with us at all. Chicago, of all places, is no place for a single young lady. You know, you broke your mother's heart when you took off like that. And your poor father's even more, God rest his soul."

Aunt Libby nodded for emphasis, then became encouraging. "But things will look up, dear. You'll be up and around in no time. It's much healthier here, so just be patient."

Aunt Libby smiled benevolently while Caroline wondered which loony theory her aunt would explain today.

"Perhaps I've mentioned this before, Caroline, but I am just so sure it was radon poisoning that did this to you." Aunt Libby's finger made another quick jab at her scalp, this time behind the other ear. "The entire city of Chicago, I was reading, rests squarely on the biggest radon deposit in America. It's no wonder that this has happened. I told your mother all about it when you moved there."

Caroline wished she could turn her head away from Aunt Libby. She tried to move it but couldn't. Aunt Libby saw her grimace, and fearing that her niece was about to cry, she poked her finger deep into her hair, found the itch, and quickly concluded.

"So cheer up, Caroline, dear. There's absolutely no radon here. I've had the house tested every year. Soon all the poison will leave your system and you'll be as good as new. You'll see." And with that, mercifully, Aunt Libby left the room.

Caroline knew that Aunt Libby would return tomorrow with more absurd theories as to the cause of her paralysis. Besides radon, she had also already covered air pollution, deadly fumes from office carpeting, and stress damage from fluorescent lighting. And even though these theories were silly, Caroline shared one not-so-silly thing in common with her aunt and her theories: she, too, needed a reason, a tangible explanation, for what had happened to her.

Now, with plenty of time at her disposal, Caroline began to think about what her life in Chicago had been, to look back and identify exactly what had led up to her present condition. Perhaps she had been pushing herself too hard at work. But she'd had a goal to meet, and she was just one step away from getting it. There had been no choice but to push herself. It meant beginning her workday at six A.M., attending scores of tedious conferences. It meant writing press releases while waiting in airports, missed lunches, working dinners, Saturdays spent in the office, and knowing more about computers than she cared to. Still, for all her constant flow of productivity, she'd never held that sense of satisfaction that you were supposed to get from working. Every night, Caroline recalled, she would lie awake in her bedroom with the classic agency phrase nagging over and over in her mind: "But what have you done for me lately?" Maybe that, more than the job overload, was what really caused the stress.

The way her relationship with Jim ended had caused plenty of stress, too. Now as she lay there thinking about it, the whole affair rankled her even more. It still bothered her that Jim had never inquired about her at the hospital, that he had never really loved her, that he'd been committed to another woman all along. It still bothered her that he had lied so charmingly when she had trusted him so completely. But most of all, now that the first waves of betrayal had passed, what continued to gnaw at her was that she had been such a willing fool.

By the end of March, Caroline was even more gaunt and listless than when she'd come home from the hospital. She had spiraled down a bottomless hole, deep into a sullen depression. She stopped speaking to her mother in anything but vapid monosyllables. She stared blankly when Aunt Libby appeared at her doorway and, in a whispered monotone, told Libby to go away, until she did. Caroline had lost her interest in life.

When Celeste, dressed in her usual shapeless corduroy jumper, arrived home for Easter break, Caroline was forced to regard the situation through Celeste's horrified eyes: Caroline was paralyzed physically and well on her way to mentally; their mother was not much better, parked in front of the TV set all day, mesmerized by loud, gonging game shows.

Celeste asked a lot of questions of Aunt Libby, who seemed to be the only person left in the house willing to carry on a conversation. From this she pieced together the whole story. Celeste had been at law school in Boston when her mother had called to say that Caroline was in the hospital. She'd wanted to fly out to visit her sister immediately, but her mother had told her it would be pointless: Caroline was too sick and drugged to recognize anyone. Celeste had questioned the wisdom of this. After all, she and Caroline were pretty close, but she sensed a firmness to her mother's orders, so she'd obeyed.

Celeste was in her second year of law school, and her grades were only borderline passing. She had been given a warning last term that she must either improve or drop out. The final exams she was to take just before Easter break would be what decided her future. Now it became obvious to Celeste: her mother must have felt that the knowledge of Caroline's paralysis would disturb her so deeply that she would never be able to concentrate enough on her studies to stay in school. Celeste said a silent thank-you to the woman in front of the television and decided to have another shot at talking to her sister.

Celeste arrived at Caroline's bedroom, grinning and cradling a six-pack of Diet Dr. Pepper in the crook of her arm, a bag of Fritos in her hand. She pulled the bedroom chair closer to Caroline's bed, sat down, and set the goodies on the nightstand.

"Hi, 'line!" said Celeste, tucking her long, baby-fine blond hair behind her ears.

Caroline, sensing the exaggerated cheerfulness in her younger sister's tone, offered a wan smile.

"I think I did okay," Celeste continued, "on my finals. At least enough to keep me in the running for another term, thanks to you and Mom." She shook her head slowly. Her grin subsided. "I wish you had told me, though. You and Mom, you're two of a kind that way, you know. It makes me crazy sometimes, the way you're always keeping things to yourselves, never letting your feelings show, never burdening others—even if they are your own family." Celeste tugged a can off the six-pack. Quickly she sneaked a glance to Caroline's limp left hand.

"But," she continued, "I shouldn't be so surprised. You always were stubborn—extremely stubborn, even when we were kids. Remember when we used to play hopscotch after dinner? And it'd start to get dark outside? You'd make me stay out there with you, hopping around in the pitch black until one of us finished the whole game right up to sky blue. That's stubborn." Celeste opened the can with a loud pop. "You know, there wasn't a person left in the neighborhood who'd play Monopoly with you." She pointed to the can. "You want one?"

Caroline listened to the soda fizzing. She didn't answer.

"In fact," Celeste went on, "you were so stubborn when you were a kid, you were downright weird. When everyone else was playing hide-and-seek, you were the kid who would purposely try to get lost in the woods or see if you could walk down the street with your eyes closed."

Celeste ripped open the bag of Fritos and waved it under Caroline's nose. Fritos were Caroline's all-time favorite, and Celeste knew it. Caroline recalled the sensation of just one corn chip laid with its curve over the tip of the tongue, how the salty-sharp sting would melt away into the gritty corn crunch.

"Want some?" Celeste asked politely.

Caroline hadn't had any Fritos since before the hospital. The familiar, pleasantly greasy aroma made her salivate. She didn't answer.

"Haven't changed, either." Celeste grinned, retracted the proffered bag, and began to munch. "Do you remember that time we went, umm, you had a name for it"—Celeste paused to think—"exploring, that's what you called it. You were in the sixth grade and I was in third. You had read all kinds of books about camping and living in the woods like Indians. Remember? Then one night, after Mom and Dad were asleep, we climbed out our bedroom window, shinnied down the drainpipe, and headed for the woods. We spent the night under some sagging lean-to you'd built. Me, whining and terrified the whole time, and you, cramped and cold and loving every minute of it."

Celeste popped open another can of Dr. Pepper. She tilted her head back and guzzled down half the contents. Caroline thought again about the Fritos.

"Geez, did we get in trouble for that one!" She took another gulp. "I always wondered what possessed you to do it. I was too stupid not to follow you, but, I mean, you knew we'd get caught trying to get back into the house. I never figured it, 'line. What made you do it?"

Caroline thought back to what Celeste had described, remembering clearly. She'd never been a foolhardy or danger-seeking child. She had done it simply to see if she could do it. The independence, the adventure of it, the getting by on one's own wits—that's what had been so appealing, even if the consequences later imposed by her parents were not. She'd never once regretted that night in the woods because it had taught her that she was capable of adapting to whatever was placed in front of her.

Celeste wondered if her sister was thinking about anything. She didn't really expect an answer, so she continued her monologue.

"Well, I guess we were pretty different from each other. You were always going off to see those grisly horror movies, and you had a thing for amusement park rides, didn't you? It was like you were always testing yourself with that stuff. I was just the opposite, even though I tried to be like you, 'line. But I found I could always handle things by arguing, sometimes even filibustering myself out of them." Celeste smiled. "Not as direct as your approach, but it worked. Usually."

All day and every day for a week, Celeste talked to Caroline. She spoke of her hopes for better grades and for a certain young man, of all the shared childhood memories of people and events that she could remember. At times Celeste talked till she was hoarse, always trying to draw Caroline out of the gloom she had sunk into. And even though Celeste often felt it, never once did she let her sister see any sympathy or sorrow.

By the time a week was gone, Celeste's throat felt raw, but she had Caroline sitting propped up in bed—even if she was listing heavily to one side, and she had gotten her to talk—even if it was just a protest at being made to sit up. Then, with eye contact that Caroline couldn't avoid, Celeste pulled out the heavy artillery and went in for the kill.

It was Mom's canned "Lecture #23" from their childhood, and Celeste hammered it in long and eloquently: "Stop being so sorry for yourself" and "You're not as helpless as you think." She topped it off with the God-helps-those-who-help-themselves speech and the seek-and-ye-shall-find speech for good measure. It was a shamelessly dirty trick she had stooped to, spewing out these well-worn childhood sermons to a captive audience, but they were not lost on Caroline.

Celeste stayed on an extra week because she could see the glimmer of resolve taking hold in her sister's eyes. She had one more task to accomplish before she returned to school. And she did it. Rather, they did it. By week's end, an exhausted but smiling Caroline had lifted her head and propped herself up on an elbow, completely unassisted. Celeste left the next day. She knew her sister's drive well enough to be sure that this was a good start.

CHAPTER

9

*C*AROLINE SPENT THE months of May and June working the hardest she had ever worked in her life. The methods she had learned at Cahill, Flynn and Zinder she now applied to herself. Set yourself a goal, she told herself. Meet that goal, then reach for the next one in line. Don't stop and don't look back.

So she set her next goal. She intended to grab her bed railing with her useless left hand and try to sit up by herself. It was a lot to aim for, and even though her determination was strong, she failed every day for two months. She was constantly frustrated from the strain that her mind demanded of her body and exhausted from the physical effort it required. She became angry and then furious that she couldn't do it.

But sometimes anger has its place, and for Caroline, it served to fuel her intent. Stubbornly and constantly, she repeated the elusive motion of reaching for that railing, so that by the end of May she began to inch just a tiny bit closer. It wasn't much and it was a grindingly slow process, but finally she knew the railing would eventually be within her grasp. And when it was, she locked her grip on it, her right hand clamping down heavily over her left-hand fingers to hold them there, and, grinning, she pulled herself up.

She began a long program of physical therapy in July. Every one of her physical therapists, Caroline became convinced, was a closet sadist bent on unrelenting goals of pain. Each of them was possessed by a drive to conquer Caroline's "physical challenge," as they called it, that made her own past career drive pale by comparison. The process was exhausting, painful, and frustrating, but she pursued it with determination.

After five months, Caroline's mother held a small celebration at their house. Caroline could raise her left arm over her head. At this point Virginia turned off the television and reentered the world of the living, as if on a parallel line with Caroline's recovery. Caroline now looked forward to Virginia's daily visits. They spent hours talking with each other, sometimes as mother and daughter, sometimes as peers. Caroline was surprised to realize that her mother, as if by some natural intuition, could understand and put into words Caroline's own thoughts and feelings. So there evolved a new phase of closeness in their relationship.

By mid-December Caroline could walk. It was a slow, deliberate walk, and her leg dragged a bit, but to Caroline, it was an achievement. To Virginia it was a bittersweet blend of happiness, answered prayers, and the certainty that Caroline would someday leave.

Celeste came home that week for Christmas break and suggested that she and Caroline do a little shopping. Aunt Libby protested vigorously when she learned that Caroline intended to walk on her own at the mall. Libby delivered her usual double-edged message about how well Caroline had improved while simultaneously undermining her confidence with worries about possible disaster if she tried to do too much too soon. Caroline glowered at her. Lately she had been squelching a hearty and steadily growing dislike for Aunt Libby.

The sisters went to the mall, where Caroline walked slowly, stopping to pause and rest at all the store windows. It tired her out, but with frequent stops she realized that no one in the mall crowd had looked at her as if she were a limping cripple. At last Caroline felt she was a member of the ordinary world again. They stopped for ice cream at a Friendly's, where Caroline told Celeste of her plans for returning to Chicago someday. As Celeste spoke of her own hopes and plans after law school, Caroline noticed that they had returned to two-way conversation. Not only that, their relationship as big sister and little sister had equalized. Caroline became aware of the incredible debt she owed to her sister, who no longer stood in Caroline's shadow. Celeste was going to be a fine lawyer someday.

After Celeste returned to law school, Caroline took to going out by herself, as much to escape the sweet-and-sour Aunt Libby as anything else. Caroline was confounded and saddened that her mother had chosen to share her remaining years with this perfectly awful woman. It seemed to her that the more stridently critical Aunt Libby was, the more self-effacing her mother became.

Caroline was required to have bimonthly medical checkups in conjunction with her physical therapy. Today she drove her own car to see the white-haired Dr. McAllister, who had become her friend and confidant.

Dr. McAllister was sitting behind his desk as she entered his office, his gaze fixed on her ankles and pink flats. "Well, you've lost the limp, young lady. Pretty dress."

Caroline was wearing a flowered springtime frock with a dainty collar. Now that she was mobile, she had replaced her severely tailored business suits for more feminine and comfortable apparel. She found that wearing long, swirly dresses and full skirts made her feel graceful and lent her an aura of confidence. Even though her determination to overcome her handicap had been iron-willed, it was as if, equally, a softening process had evolved subtly alongside it.

Dr. McAllister took her blood pressure, checked her reflexes, and began with what had lately been on his mind.

"I think this is your last checkup, Caroline. I'm writing you down for a clean bill of health."

Caroline wasn't really surprised at this news. She had suspected that soon she wouldn't be needing to see Dr. McAllister anymore. The only thing that kept her coming was the talks they had.

The doctor continued, "Have you thought about what you're going to do now?"

"Do you think I could go back to my job in Chicago?"

"Nope." Dr. McAllister's kind face looked hard at her. "Absolutely not. You're okay now, but from what you've told me, your career back in Chicago was demanding and stressful. It's my feeling that any kind of strain or tension might trigger what happened to you all over again. It was a burst appendix last time, but next time it could be something else—pneumonia, a car accident, even a bad case of the flu. Any physical distress combined with the constant pressure of your old job could land you flat where you were. It might even be stress alone that could do it next time."

Dr. McAllister read the crestfallen look on Caroline's face and softened his own. "Look at it this way, sweetheart. You've got yourself a second chance to learn how to live. You're extremely lucky in that respect, and you also know that if you want to live a normal life, you must not return to Chicago. It's very simple: something connected with stress triggered your paralysis. You must, therefore, protect yourself from it ever happening again."

Dr. McAllister let Caroline think about that for a while. From past conversations he knew the irritating situation Caroline faced at home with her Aunt Libby and the apparent sway the woman held over Caroline's mother. This situation might someday lead to more aggravated tensions, and he told her as much, concluding with the advice that she should remove herself from both the Chicago and St. Louis fronts.

"The wisest thing you can do, Caroline, is start all over. Find yourself a new place to live—a place that puts no demands on you. Where that may be I'm sure you will figure out for yourself. The important thing," he emphasized, "is that where you live has to be peaceful so that *you* can be peaceful." He looked at her sternly and made her promise to give the idea plenty of thought.

That evening Caroline eyed a pile of magazines Celeste had left behind last Christmas. She leafed quickly through *Tattoo News* and *World of Doll Collecting*, but she read *Montana Highways* from cover to cover. As it lay in her lap, she thought about her mother's reaction to Dr. McAllister's advice. As was her way, Virginia seemed already to have known.

"Caroline, honey, we both know that you have to go. Neither of us wants to say good-bye, but we've got to face the facts, and that's all there is to it. You'll do just fine on your own. I've seen you overcome what we all thought was impossible. So if you can overcome what you already have, then you mustn't have any doubts that you can overcome whatever comes next." Virginia smiled bravely.

"You know, sweetheart, I'm thankful for this past year. It's been hard—no, it's been absolutely horrible— but it's given me the chance to find my daughter again, and I'm thankful for that." She squeezed Caroline's shoulders and, smiling, said, "So, go sweetheart. It's time for you to go." Virginia abruptly hurried away, Caroline knew, because she didn't want Caroline to see her crying.

Caroline fingered the pages of *Montana Highways*, suddenly recalling Celeste's first monologue from a year ago. There was something very intriguing here, Caroline thought, something that hearkened her back to those childhood cravings to explore an unknown place. The beauty within the magazine appealed to her, the uncertainty even more. Here was a place where she would have to adapt to a whole new set of rules and surroundings; where she could explore a different life-style, conquer it, make it her own. Dr. McAllister's face floated into her mind's eye, just as she'd seen it when she'd left his office for the last time. He had certainly wanted to impress upon her the seriousness of his mes-sage: "If you want to live a normal life, Caroline, you've got to go to a peaceful place." Caroline recalled how pointedly he had looked at her, repeating with empha-sis so that he nearly barked it out, "Peaceful!"

The recollection was interrupted by Tinky half jumping, half clawing her way onto Caroline's lap. An-noyed, she leaned down to pick the talons out of her nightgown, then sat back so that the cat could settle into her lap. Her reverie broken, Caroline directed her atten-tion to the television's evening news. A toothy young man spoke with manic cheeriness about warm-weather fronts and the jet stream. Caroline turned off the TV and headed for the kitchen with her mug of cold tea. Her hands were steady now.

She fed the cats and climbed the stairs. As was her nightly ritual, she paused to listen to the utter si-lence when she got to the top of the stairs—no sirens, no gunshots cracking, no sidewalk voices, no motors. Upstairs, the evening breeze had cooled things down a bit. Pausing at her bedroom window, Caroline looked out over the black velvet landscape. Any hint of the lights she had seen earlier that evening had disappeared. Lying in bed, just before drifting into sleep, Caroline wondered if, perhaps, she had only imagined them.

CHAPTER

10

*C*AROLINE SPENT ALL morning upstairs in the sewing room, cutting out the quilt pattern. The solitude and silence of the day weighed particularly heavy on her this morning, to the point that sometimes she half imagined the peripheral noises of office phones, muffled talk, computer bongs. She looked out the bank of windows often enough, but she remained less than relaxed despite her preoccupation with the quilt.

By eleven o'clock it was getting uncomfortably hot in the sewing studio. Caroline really hated having to drop a task midstream, though. Something about not completing what she'd set out to do rankled her. She ought, at least, to get all the red pieces of fabric cut. That was foolish, she knew, especially in light of the increasing heat, but she gave in to her compulsion and changed into her two-piece swimsuit. Thus clad, she better endured another hour in the ovenlike room until she was satisfied that she'd cut out every one of the red pieces. Laying the red rectangles in stacks where the cats couldn't nest in them, she headed for cooler territory.

It was quiet as a tomb downstairs. Caroline found the tape she'd received from Celeste yesterday and placed it in the living room stereo. The O'Reillys wailed in wistful, folksy tradition about love that was pure and true. Dulcimers and mandolins twiddled along with marching drums and a painfully whiny fiddle.

"Oh, Celeste," Caroline spoke out loud, wincing. "Where do you find this stuff?" She reached for the tape deck but stopped herself. Even the O'Reillys were better than the dead silence surrounding her today.

Caroline sat down on the living room couch and propped her feet across the length of it. She thought about the kitchen screen door and decided that it was time to fix it, but still she didn't move. An hour later, after she had read *Time* magazine from cover to cover, she stretched and rose. It was time to get those tools and fix the door.

On the way to the basement, Caroline heard the doorbell ring. She wondered who it might be, then guessed that it was Jody when she saw the tall, cowboy-hatted silhouette behind the front door's curtain. Preparing herself to tell him that she'd already called a well digger, she tucked her hair behind her ears and clasped the doorknob. Suddenly she remembered that she was wearing only a bikini. Aah, what the hell. She smirked, imagining what Jody's reaction might be. She opened the door wide.

A dark, mustached man in a black cowboy hat

stood on Caroline's porch. He looked to be close to her age, although it was hard to judge since dark, aviator-style sunglasses shielded his eyes and expression. He wore a red cotton plaid shirt, blue jeans, and a grin like the Cheshire cat's. He removed his hat to reveal a shock of dark wavy hair cut slightly longer than the usual Montana length.

"Hi," he said in a deep-toned, warm voice, "I'm Matt—Matt Van Zandt." He twitched his head in the direction of the road. "Your neighbor." He took off his sunglasses and surveyed Caroline with what appeared to be genuine appreciation.

It took a while for Caroline to absorb both the information and the appraisal. There was something about this man—or maybe it was just the surprise of the situation—that prevented her from immediately assembling a coherent response. This was decidedly not what she'd expected her retired mystery neighbor to look like. The man's widening smile clearly told Caroline that he was enjoying her flummoxed reaction to him. His chestnut-brown eyes sparked a brief, sly twinkle before he remembered his manners.

"I was just on my way home from Hawkeye, so I thought I'd stop by and introduce myself." It must have been an effort, but his eyes focused only on her face. "When did you move in?"

"Last April," said Caroline, having found her composure. His eyes, soft yet mesmerizing, held steady. There was a thin scar along his cheekbone and deep dimple creases to his grin. "I've been busy settling in and renovating since then, but I'm pretty well done now. What did you say your name was?"

"Matt."

"Mine's Caroline Atkinson."

Matt nodded.

"You already knew my name?" Caroline asked.

"It's a small town."

Caroline regarded Matt's vibrant eyes once again. She liked him.

"How about joining me for some lemonade or some iced tea?" she asked.

"Well, thanks. Some iced tea would be nice. I can't stay too long, though, some lady from the power company is supposed to be calling me later."

"Have a seat." Caroline indicated a chair on the porch. "I'll be right back."

Caroline raced upstairs, slipped on a tank top, and zipped a skirt over her swimsuit. She hurried down to the kitchen, poured the tea, dumped a pile of Oreo cookies onto a dish, set everything on a tray, and skidded to a stop. Sedately, she walked to the porch. She noticed, now, that a red, wide-bodied pickup truck was parked in the front driveway and that Humphrey was in Matt's lap, purring loudly at the petting he was receiving.

"He likes you." Caroline smiled as she found a place for the tray. She handed Matt a glass and said, "And he's usually pretty picky about who he'll allow to touch him."

Matt smiled under his mustache and regarded Caroline as she sat there before him. He raised his glass to her. "Welcome, neighbor," he said by way of a toast, then he drank the tea in a long, unhurried swallow even as Humphrey climbed his chest and nosed at the bottom of his glass.

"Thanks," said Caroline, much pleased by the

warmth of this man. "Welcome, neighbor, to you, too." She drank so deeply that an ice cube touched her nose. Around the glass she could see Matt watching her. She put the glass down. He was still watching her.

Suddenly serious, he said, "Tell me about yourself, Caroline."

"Didn't they already tell you back in Hawkeye?" she asked.

"I try not to listen to town stories."

Now that the initial strangeness was wearing off, Caroline recognized a rugged handsomeness in Matt's face. What captured her attention, though, was the expression in his eyes. There was a sophistication, even a world-weariness, just under the surface of his good nature that didn't immediately blend with the country surroundings. She shot a fleeting glance to the unadorned fingers of his left hand.

"Well," Caroline began, "I guess I've got a long story for being here." She looked to Matt to see if he was really interested or if he was simply making polite conversation. His expression seemed sincere—intent, even—so she continued.

"Well, briefly, I used to work for a PR agency in"— she was just about to explain what the letters *PR* stood for but could see that Matt, nodding at her, knew—"in Chicago. I was driving myself hard—so hard that I messed up my health. . . ."

Matt's eyebrows shot up at these words, then smoothed.

"And landed in bed for a good year—well, hardly a *good* year," she corrected herself sarcastically. Caroline felt unexpectedly relieved to be telling Matt about this. "Anyway, I lived with my mom and her sister in

St. Louis until I got better. And, now, I'm here." She shrugged and smiled.

Matt absorbed her words, nodding at her understandingly. "Can't go back, huh?"

"Nope."

"It's a no-win rat race, anyway."

"I know. But I still miss it."

"What spot did you have your eye on in the agency?"

"How did you know?" Caroline marveled at this man who in the middle of rubedom actually knew about what was so foreign to everyone else. She leveled her gaze at him. "VP."

Matt smiled with sympathy at her, then his lips, partly hidden beneath the mustache, returned to their straight line. He appeared to be deliberating over what he might say next. "Your health is all right now?" he asked.

"Yes, as long as I don't go back."

Matt looked as if he wanted to question her on her last answer, but he checked himself. His friendly concern retreated a few steps and settled into a mood that seemed to Caroline purposely distant, as if he were holding something back.

Caroline reached for an Oreo, bit into both layers, and gestured with the remaining cookie. "You know you're a grownup when you eat them like this." She looked pointedly at Matt. "So, now, you tell me about yourself."

Matt's dark eyes narrowed at Caroline for a moment, then he smiled slowly as he absentmindedly stroked the purring cat behind its ears.

"I've got a business in San Francisco that keeps me

busy from time to time. In theory, it's supposed to run itself—but not always. In any case, I try to spend as much time as I can here in Montana. This is home, really. I spent way too long in San Francisco this last visit, but I think I've ironed out all the glitches that would make me have to go running back."

Caroline studied Matt's expression. It looked as if he were thinking something through to a conclusion. Their eyes held as he continued.

"On this last trip, I got an old college buddy of mine—I can trust him—to take charge in my absence." Matt's friendly eyes bored straight into hers, then abruptly focused on the horizon. "So," he went on without looking at her, "I plan to be here for some time."

"What line of business?"

"Computers."

"Specifically?"

"Lots of areas." He held the glass of iced tea poised at his mouth.

"Have you had the business long?"

"Twelve years." He slurped the tea through ice cubes and winked at her. "Good tea. You have any more?"

When Caroline returned with refills for them both, she found Matt tilted on two legs of his chair, his long legs outstretched and his pointed boots resting on the porch railing. He sat up and looked at her.

"Thanks," he said, taking the glass. He pulled his chair closer to Caroline's. When she'd settled onto it, he asked, "Have any of those trash people approached you yet?"

"Trash people?"

Taking a careful tone, Matt explained, "There's a corporation, Sanborne Inc., which in the past three years has established a string of what they call 'waste-to-energy plants' around the country. Most of them are in Maine, Minnesota, and Georgia—all places where population density and, hence, resistance is low and where wide tracts of timberland can be had for a good price.

"The idea is that Sanborne Inc. builds a trash incineration plant in these remote areas, then cashes in in two ways: first, it accepts, for a fee, all the rubbish, garbage, and trash that cities and towns within a one-hundred-fifty-mile radius can cart in. In our case, that means Butte and Helena, which are running out of landfill or at least clean landfill sites to dump their trash.

"Second, Sanborne takes the collected trash—I think the figures I read were three hundred tons of rubbish per day—and puts it on a series of grates under a high-combustion mass-burn incinerator. Then, as the trash burns, it heats up troughs of water set beneath it, and steam from the water is used to generate electricity, which . . ." Matt gave Caroline a sly smile. "Which Sanborne sells to people in the same one-hundred-fifty-area radius.

"It's a great deal—especially if you're Sanborne Inc. Sanborne gets paid for accepting the garbage that Butte and Helena have no more room to dump, legally, anyway. And . . ." Matt's eyebrow arched in pure cynicism. "Sanborne claims its plant can handle everything that isn't governmentally graded as either sludge or toxic waste. Then, Sanborne gets paid for selling us the electricity that they made out of the trash that they already made a profit on."

Matt sat back on his chair to await Caroline's reaction. She was dumbfounded.

"Oh, in all fairness," he interjected, "Sanborne will sell their electricity to Hawkeye at a discount because we are, after all, the host town." He smirked and shook his head. "Kind of makes you wish you thought of a scheme like this before they did, doesn't it?"

"No," said an angry Caroline. "What you've just told me is obscene. What about the pollution we'd get from burning three hundred tons of garbage per day? Per day? Nah, that's got to be impossible. Are you sure you heard correctly?" She stared at him and suddenly remembered the conversation she'd heard yesterday at the Bitterroot Cafe.

"They claim," Matt answered, "that they've devised a way to reduce the air pollution so that it infringes on from one to three percent of the atmosphere. And, who knows, maybe they have."

"I find that hard to believe, don't you? Besides, that's still one to three percent more crap in the air than we didn't have before."

"Sanborne claims it's well under the federal standards."

"Hah!" Caroline snorted in disgust. "I can't believe that people around here would swallow something like this."

"It means jobs for a lot of folks around here who are just barely getting by, Caroline. It means money."

"Oh," she said, her anger deflated. She thought about the punk Indian boy in front of Fairbanks. "I suppose it does." She faced Matt with a troubled look. "Still, it's a high price to pay, don't you think?"

"Yes, it is," he said soberly. Brightening, he added, "There's a town meeting coming up about it. Maybe we ought to go."

Caroline nodded in agreement, thinking it certainly was nice to be with someone who shared her opinion.

Matt stayed to a dinner of fish sticks and corn. The fact that both of them came from a cosmopolitan background before changing life-styles in Montana gave them much in common to talk about.

When he left that evening, Caroline waved goodbye from her front porch as he backed his truck out of the driveway. She watched him drive off, clouds of road dust trailing behind him, and kept him fixed in her sight until the red truck disappeared behind the last rolling hill.

Only when the last of the road dust had settled did she notice the spectacular sunset playing out before her. The long, feather streaks of clouds began with a blush of rosy lavender illuminated from behind by the yellow sun. Soon, with imperceptible changes in gradation, oranges and shadowy mauves gained precedence until the feather streaks elongated and broke to reveal a fiery, golden glow beyond the horizon.

Fine as the sunset was, what really absorbed Caroline's thinking was that, today with Matt, she'd had the first serious conversation since coming to Montana. Here was a man, Caroline realized happily, who was her peer in both age and background and in whose company she actually lost track of time.

The more she thought about it, the more pleased she became. She had a friend. Finally. The kind of friend whom she had immediately hit it off with—and those were hard to come by anywhere, much less in the middle of nowhere. Matt was a kindred spirit. He understood exactly what it was like to have to adapt to a foreign life-style. And with Matt, she felt completely comfortable.

It was both relief and an excitement. Maybe things in Montana weren't going to be so bad after all.

CHAPTER

11

*T*HE QUILT GOT WELL under way during the week that followed. Mornings, Caroline machine-sewed the rectangular strips of scarlet and pine fabrics that would make the concentric squares. Later she would join them all in sets of four to form the center cross of the Log Cabin design. For now, however, sewing the hundreds of strips into identical squares occupied Caroline's hands if not her mind. Her mind was left free to dwell upon her new friendship with Matt, and it did so, replaying various snatches of what they'd talked about.

Caroline stacked another completed quilt square atop the others and winced at the pounding of the well digger's drill outside her sewing room windows. She wondered idly if yet another week would pass before she'd get to see Matt again, when her curiosity evaporated instantly.

"Damn it!" she grumbled aloud. There wasn't enough of one of the fabric strips—the tiny red-and-green strawberry vines on the ivory background: the very fabric that gave contrast to the whole design. Now she'd have to drive all the way to Hawkeye and hope that the matching bolt of fabric was still there.

Caroline switched off the sewing machine, brushed the fabric bits off her shorts, and went downstairs. After telling the well digger that she was leaving, she headed for her car. If everything went smoothly and if she didn't have to find a substitute fabric, she might be able to accomplish the whole task in less than ninety minutes. Just in case, though, she decided to bring Humphrey inside to keep him from wandering near the well hole.

Caroline found the little gray cat napping at his usual spot on the front porch railing. She gathered him gently and laid him, still sleeping, just inside the front door and quietly closed it. Looking up, she caught sight of Matt's bright red pickup speeding toward Hawkeye, accompanied by a distorted surge of blaring music. The high-wheeled truck screeched to a halt, ground its gears into reverse, and whizzed backward to a spot in the road directly in front of Caroline's porch. Several horn honks and Matt's beckoning brought Caroline to the open passenger window. It was chin level to her as she peered in. Inside, Matt grinned from behind the aviator sunglasses as he snapped off the music.

"Hey, neighbor. I'm going into Hawkeye. You need anything while I'm there?"

"Well." Caroline paused. "Do you know where the fabric store is?"

"Yeah." His grin faded. "I guess so."

"If I gave you a swatch of fabric, do you think you could find the matching bolt?" Caroline began to look doubtful. Men were no good at this. They always returned with something completely out of left field. Still, she didn't want to insult him. "You could ask the saleslady to match it?" she suggested by way of question.

"Uh . . ." Matt's eyes were hidden behind the sunglasses, but his voice conveyed the doubt. "Listen." His deep voice brightened. "You better just come on along." He reached across and swung open the door.

Relieved, Caroline climbed up. Inside, the cab was roomy and red-carpeted. For a pickup truck, Caroline thought, this was rather comfortable. She sat on the long front seat across from Matt, a large sliding window behind her.

"This is nice." Caroline smiled, bouncing once on the seat and looking down and around. "I like how high up it is."

"Yep," Matt replied more to the windshield than to Caroline. He propelled the gears of the vehicle forward.

Today Matt made no attempt at conversation. Caroline followed the mood, staring forward as they picked up speed. The grasses on either side of the ribbon of blacktop were even more parched now that late August approached. Caroline could see from her elevated perch in the cab that knapweed was creeping, irreversibly and unchallenged, into the plains area. Even as a newcomer she knew this was a sure sign that serious drought had grabbed hold of the land.

Looking upward, she regarded clumps of fat, flat-bottomed clouds. They floated by, casting moving shadows over the rolling land, but Caroline knew they held only a slim promise of rain: the air was bone dry, and the clouds were traveling way too fast. She was about to break the silence with this observation, but she stopped herself. Surely she could think of something more intelligent to talk about than the weather.

"So," she chirped, perhaps a little too brightly, "what have you been doing with yourself?" She leveled her gaze on him.

Matt's black cowboy hat cast a shadow over the dark-tinted sunglasses and the rest of his features. The only clue to whatever expression he might be wearing was his mouth, and that was hidden beneath his dark mustache. It was like talking to a mask.

"Well," he drawled to the windshield, his baritone voice both serious and resonant, "been settling in. Taking care of details." He seemed to be concentrating on the roller-coaster road that lay ahead.

"No time to yourself yet?" Caroline continued gamely.

"Soon," was his terse reply.

Caroline settled back onto the seat and watched the road, too. She wondered if maybe she was imposing by joining Matt on his trip to Hawkeye. After all, he hadn't initially asked her to join him. Well, too late, now, she thought to herself as they entered the uphill tunnel of road surrounded by pines and ferns. She tilted her head back and smiled at the sweet and shadowy coolness now blowing through her open window. She gulped once as her ears popped.

At first she sensed it. Then, she sneaked a sideways glance to confirm that Matt's face was turned slightly toward her as he drove. Was he watching her? It was hard to tell just what he was looking at from behind the hat and glasses, but Caroline's intuition told her that she and the road were receiving equal attention. It made her uncomfortable. Still, she told herself, she couldn't be sure. That made her uncomfortable, too, so she turned her head and looked at him. He appeared to be concentrating intently on driving when he spoke.

"Did you get your well dug?"

"The guy is still drilling. I guess he has to go pretty deep to reach the water level, but I hope he finds it soon—you wouldn't believe how noisy it is." She grimaced, remembering. "Is yours an artesian well?"

"Uh-huh. I hit it lucky and got a hot spring bubbling up, too." It seemed as if he were about to add something, but he didn't. Instead he steered the conversation so that Caroline found herself explaining the whole process of making a Log Cabin quilt. Their talk then turned to Matt explaining the pros and cons of the various makes of four-by-fours Caroline would someday exchange her Camaro for. This carried them through the roadway's uphill climb and halfway into the mountain descent, but when they reached the place where maneuvering the steep grades and curves became tricky, they fell mutually silent so that Matt could concentrate on driving.

When Caroline was sure that Matt's attention was riveted to the road, she took the opportunity to study him. Today he wore a navy blue shirt. It billowed with the air that rushed in as they gathered speed down the first mountain descent. Rolled-up sleeves revealed a deep, rosy sunburn on sinewy arms, telling Caroline that many of Matt's settling-in details were done outdoors. Even seated, it was obvious that he was tall. A lanky, blue-jeaned leg hovered over the brake pedal, and although the truck cab was roomy, his black hat approached the ceiling.

Caroline's ears popped as Matt competently steered their rush down the mountain road. Now she watched him outright. She sensed something altered in his demeanor today. He looked the same except that, unlike at their first meeting, he kept on all the face camouflage. But, Caroline reminded herself, it was very sunny and he was driving. She regarded him with mild puzzlement. She thought about what they'd talked about—or, rather, what Matt wanted to talk about— quilts and trucks. Nothing revealing there. And that was it: what she sensed in Matt was more of a feeling of purposeful distance than there had been before— nothing rude or impersonal, Caroline felt, just an aura of privacy that he cloaked around himself today.

Caroline wondered about it for a while, then shrugged it off. She didn't know him well enough to figure out why, so she turned her attention to their progress down the mountain. Not long after, they were coasting over the flatlands near the high school. Caroline swallowed to relieve her ears.

"What do you need to do in Hawkeye?" she ventured.

"I'm expecting some business papers to arrive at the post office today," Matt answered gravely. "That's all. You want me to get your mail while I'm there?"

"Thanks." Caroline wanted to ask him exactly what kind of computer business he had in San Francisco but remembered how vague he'd been when questioned about it before. Considering his mood, she didn't think she'd get any better explanation today. Asking him again would feel akin to prying. She regarded the passing outskirts of Hawkeye and wondered less about what Matt's business actually was in San Francisco than why he didn't want to tell her.

"I'll meet you back here," Matt announced. He turned off the engine in front of the fabric store, and they each went where their chores led them. Matt was already lounging in the truck, hat sloped over his eyes and the tip of his nose, head tilted back as if in deep repose, when Caroline returned.

"I was so lucky," Caroline marveled enthusiastically as she heaved herself onto the truck's bench seat. She laid a flat paper bag on her lap, patted it noisily a few times, then spoke directly to the hat. "Someone bought nearly the whole bolt of material, but there was just enough left for what I needed."

The hat was guided back to its regular spot on Matt's head as he straightened up. "Good," he said, then added with a bit more sincerity, "Glad you found it."

"D'you get your papers?"

"Yep," Matt answered, and paused. "But something else has come up."

Caroline waited for him to explain. By habit, she looked straight into the speaker's eye but found only her own reflection in the sunglasses. A sudden surge of irritation welled up in her from the disguise and the advantage Matt held. She spoke to her own mirrored image, her voice teetering at the edge of annoyance. "What?"

"Irwin at the post office said I've got to see Ray Banes as soon as possible." If Matt sensed any of Caroline's irritation, his voice didn't show it.

"Uh-huh?" Caroline half stated, half asked. Figuring that it would be pointless to ask for an explanation, she was startled when Matt offered one.

"I signed up to be on the volunteer forest fire squad this year," he said, turning fully to Caroline as he spoke. There was a small scar on his neck she hadn't noticed before. "Ray Banes—you know him—he's in charge of it. Now, though, the postmaster tells me that I'm not allowed to do anything for the squad until I sign some insurance papers. And with this dry spell, I guess good ole Ray's getting a little itchy for me to sign them." Matt put one hand to his sunglasses and lowered them halfway down his nose. Tilting his head downward, he peered across into Caroline's eyes. "Would you mind if we took a detour to Ray's house before heading home?"

"Sure. No problem," Caroline replied, smiling directly to the revealed dark eyes. It was an instant relief to be talking to a person instead of a mask.

"Good." Matt flashed a quick grin and pushed the dark glasses back into place. Turning his back to her abruptly, he pulled something out of the storage pocket in the side door: a stack of mail.

"Here," he said, handing Caroline a few pieces off the bundle. "These are yours." He laid his portion of the bundle on the seat between them.

"Thanks," Caroline answered quietly. It was apparent that Matt had returned to his original distance.

He started the truck and steered it toward the north fork out of Hawkeye while Caroline busied herself by looking through her mail. Silence filled the cab, interrupted only by the sound of Caroline slipping her mail into the bag of fabric. Her gaze rested on the bundle between them. Curious as she was, she couldn't tell what Matt's mail was or where it was from without demonstrating blatant nosiness. Instead she looked straight out the windshield and recognized the stretch of road that she'd taken from Butte the very first day she'd arrived in Hawkeye. She hadn't been down this road since then—and, in fact, had avoided it. Coming ahead was the spot where that poor doe had been: a bad omen to start out with if ever there was one, she had thought at the time. Looking back on it, she realized that there was a certain amount of good fortune attached to it, also. After all, it had enabled her to meet Ray Banes—but, still, it had been a lousy way to meet him. Caroline's head turned to the spot as they passed it. Purposely she focused straight ahead as Matt drove on silently.

CHAPTER

12

"WE'LL BE THERE
soon," Matt announced, drumming his fingers on the
steering wheel. "I'm glad it's Ray who's tending to your
timberland," he continued, abruptly talkative. "He's the
best there is."

"Have you known him long?" Caroline asked.

"Well, I guess I have. Ray and I go back to when I
first settled here. He's not much of a talker, except if he
gets going about the rodeo." Matt flashed a toothy grin.
"But he's a good man and a good friend. Ray's wife,
Winona," he added, nodding, "you'll like her."

He turned up a narrow, uphill, dirt driveway
arched over by fluttering aspens. The truck bounced
over bumps and ruts for some distance until it reached
a flat clearing where the sun shone uninterrupted. Several rust-colored Herefords grazed behind a rail fence.
This was the Banes's front yard. A lone white pine

stood magnificently in the distance, its massive branches reaching out in horizontal planes. The tree shaded and hovered over a sprawling, rust-colored ranch house, as if it knew it was protecting it.

Caroline knew immediately, as they walked up the concrete ramp to the dark green front door, that someone inside was in a wheelchair.

Ray answered, opening the door wide. "Good you showed up. Come on in."

Matt entered, but Caroline stood motionless. She wasn't prepared to see a wheelchair again. A sudden rush of memory overcame her: all those trips to and from physical therapy when she was strapped in like some drooping rag doll completely under the control of whoever held the chair handles, always looking up to the rest of the walking world. She felt weak-kneed at the thought of confronting another person imprisoned like that.

"Caroline?" Matt turned to her from inside the doorway.

Biting her bottom lip, she walked inside. The tantalizing aroma of a cake, almost done baking, grabbed her attention. She concentrated on the smell and took a deep, relaxing breath. Possibly an almond cake, she told herself as she gazed across the parquet floor of a spacious yet cozy-feeling living room. A dark green, flowered couch and a wing chair nested in front of a white brick fireplace that contained a jet black woodstove. At the opposite wall, an oaken upright piano predominated. It was cluttered with sheet music, all askew, and open music books. There was no bench.

Caroline turned to Ray and tried to smile. "Hi, Mr. Banes. How are you?"

"Ray," he answered.

Caroline smiled more easily this time.

"Winona'll be out." Ray twitched his head in the direction of a wide, arched doorway from which the cake smell was emanating. "Papers are over here, Matt." Ray turned abruptly and walked toward a wooden desk in the corner of the room. Matt slipped his sunglasses into his shirt pocket and followed.

Caroline heard pots and pans clattering in the kitchen but made no attempt to enter. Instead she fingered an earring and looked around the living room. Several pieces of framed crewelwork graced the ivory walls. The coffee table in front of the couch held a stack of magazines, a historical romance paperback, and a television remote box. Built-in wall shelves contained a disarray of hardcover books and a jumble of yarns and knitting needles.

From the direction of the kitchen, an oven door slammed and the enticing smell of just-baked cake wafted over to Caroline even more strongly. Now she wasn't sure if it was almond or cherry. Consciously letting go of her earring, she walked over to the white mantelpiece. Two framed photographs were displayed there. One was an old-looking, black-and-white wedding picture—probably of someone's parents. A stocky man in a three-piece suit stood soberly, ramrod straight, his straw-colored hair nearly as bright as the watch chain hanging from his vest. Beside him, perhaps a tiny bit taller, stood an equally sober-looking woman in the straight, chemise-type wedding dress of the 1920s. Her long black hair, high and wide cheekbones, and almond-shaped eyes bespoke her Indian ancestry. The photograph that was set next to this was also a wedding picture, the color-tinted kind where people's cheeks seem unnaturally rosy. A young Ray Banes stood stiffly in a khaki, World War II uniform, his tie tucked into his shirt. One hand grasped a folded air force cap, the other rested on the handle of a wheelchair. On it sat a strikingly beautiful, almond-eyed young woman in an ivory satin bridal gown. Her raven hair was done in the shoulder-length, pageboy roll of the 1940s. While Ray's eyes stared stoic and solemn, his bride's practically twinkled.

Caroline's attention turned to the kitchen doorway. A woman, somewhere in her early sixties, wheeled herself through the arch. A big black dog followed her. The woman had aged since her wedding photo, but the eyes had remained the same. She spoke to Caroline as she approached.

"Sorry to keep you waiting, dear." She looked around and directed her next words with deliberately increased volume at Ray. "What? Did they leave you just standing here?"

Ray paid her no mind, but Matt's smile answered to Winona's mock scowl and stern head shaking.

"Well, I'm Winona." She returned to Caroline, offering her hand. "And you must be the girl with the deer. Caroline, right?"

"Yes," Caroline answered. As they shook hands, her attention was caught more by Winona's warm grasp and friendly face than the chrome wheelchair she sat on. Winona's hair was short now, curled in the style of Caroline's mother's generation and mostly gray with a peppering of black. Her wide, ample smile and high cheekbones told whose parents were in the other wedding photo. Winona's expressive, almond-shaped eyes seemed to be, at the same time, both serious and vibrant. She was slightly plump, dressed in a tan skirt and a white knit top over which she wore a loose, emerald-green shirt. A small silver locket, the size and shape of a watermelon seed, hung around her neck. Black canvas mary janes covered limp, bony-thin feet. Caroline figured it had to be polio.

The dog sniffed at Caroline, so she scratched it on the head the same way she petted her cats. The animal looked to be more black lab than not—sloppy and a little goofy.

"This is Tyrone," said Winona. "If he gets to bothering you, just tell him to sit." The dog sat. Its tail noisily *thwap*ped the wooden floor. "He follows me everywhere." With that, Tyrone forgot the sitting order and shambled eagerly, nails clicking on the floor, back to Winona's side. As Winona petted him, Caroline realized that her fear of seeing the wheelchair victim had all but vanished. It was obvious that Winona was anything but a victim.

"Come along with me, Caroline," said Winona. She adroitly maneuvered the wheelchair around Tyrone. "I need to get those cupcakes out of their pans before they stick."

Caroline followed through the arch into one of the most cluttered kitchens she'd ever seen. The countertops under the wooden cabinets practically spewed forth a riot of kitchen equipment. Sets of crocks holding bouquets of spoons, a microwave, a minitelevision, stacks of mixing bowls, and stacks of cookbooks all lent to the general hodgepodge. It wasn't really a mess, Caroline noted, looking briefly at a table topped with several big bowls of tomatoes and a cluster of canning jars. And under the scrutiny of sunshine from many windows, everything was certainly clean. Caroline looked around again and decided that although Winona's kitchen seemed a jumble at first glance, there was an underlying practical order to it.

"How about if you heat up that pot of coffee?" Winona suggested as she tumbled the cupcakes out of their pans.

"Sure." Caroline went over to a stove surrounded by hanging pots and pans. By the time she'd found the coffeepot and turned around, Winona had arranged a setting for two at one end of the long wooden table in the center of the kitchen.

"Come and sit down," Winona said, wheeling herself to the table. Tyrone settled comfortably on the floor beside her. "Ray and Matt have gone outside, so we'll have to start without them. Besides"—Winona's eyes twinkled now as they had in the photograph—"I've been hoping to get you all to myself." She tapped the table and motioned for Caroline to come over. "Now sit down and tell me all about yourself."

Caroline sat obediently and wondered what to say. Her hand automatically traveled to her earring.

"Just a second, dear," Winona said, "I think the coffee's boiling." She backed the wheelchair, bumped it into the counter, and began to turn the tight corner to get the the oven. Tyrone got up slowly.

"Let me get it." Caroline jumped up, fetched the pot, and poured the coffee into their cups. After she'd sat down again, she realized her mistake.

"I can't believe I did that." Caroline turned to Winona apologetically. "I'm really sorry."

"For what?"

"For what I did just now. For treating you like you couldn't get the coffee in your own kitchen."

"I'm sure you only meant to be helpful."

"No, I was treating you like you were useless. I was treating you exactly how I hated being treated once myself." She looked contritely into Winona's eyes and repeated, "I'm sorry. This isn't a very nice way to start being friends with someone."

"It's for the best, because now we will become good friends for sure." Winona smiled warmly at Caroline's puzzlement. "It's a Nez Percé belief that says 'A bad beginning will mean a good end.'"

Winona was silent for a moment, as if lost in a thought. "You know, when Ray told me how he found you with that deer, I knew there would be something special about you." Winona placed a cupcake on each of their dishes. "Now, why don't you tell me all about yourself?"

And Caroline did.

"Looks like you and Winona really hit it off," Matt commented as they drove back home. He seemed in a more open mood now that he'd lost the state trooper look.

"Well, as it turns out . . ." Caroline paused. She thought about the empathy she and Winona had so quickly discovered for each other that afternoon. "We've had a lot in common."

Matt stared at her with an intrigued expression for as long as he could before driving took precedence.

"Why'd she call you 'the girl with the deer'?" he finally asked.

"Oh, that." Caroline sighed, looking out the window. They'd already driven past the spot. "That's how I met Ray."

Matt waited for her to continue. When she didn't, he stared at her with dark, demanding eyes that made Caroline wish he'd put the sunglasses back on again.

"The very first day I got here," she began, "I was driving down the road we're on now. It was dusk and I was following a car pulling a trailer-camper."

Caroline thought to herself how it had all happened so quickly, yet in recollection it seemed to replay in slow motion.

"This deer came leaping from out of nowhere, and the car with the trailer-camper hit it."

Caroline flinched, remembering the awful sound of the car thudding into the deer's back legs. "And that damn car didn't stop. It must have been going at least sixty-five and it didn't even slow down. It just hit the gas and sped away. I couldn't believe it."

"Believe it. It gets lots worse when Yellowstone reaches its peak season," Matt said wearily. "Did you get the plates?"

"No. I was looking at the deer. After it got hit, it kind of hobbled into the field next to the road and then it collapsed."

In her mind, Caroline recalled the heart-wrenching way the animal crumbled onto its side.

"So I stopped the car and walked over. I knew it wasn't going to be good because the car had really hit it hard. And by the time I reached it, I don't know who was more scared, me or the deer."

Caroline's memory drifted back to the fallen deer. It had been a doe. She was a beautiful, light ash brown and of formidable size, but her hind legs were splayed out at her side at an uncomfortable-looking angle. She panted rapidly, and her huge brown, thickly lashed eyes bulged with terror. Instinctively Caroline knelt at the doe's head and stroked it tenderly. She didn't know what else to do.

Caroline now summarized for Matt. "It was a doe, and her legs looked—I don't know—wrong. Luckily, Ray was driving by and he stopped."

Again, Caroline's mind traveled back to the scene where Ray examined the fallen doe. It had seemed that the animal's fear relaxed visibly under his confident hands.

"Here's the story," Ray had finally announced. "She's young and there are no broken bones. But she may have a bigger problem."

Caroline didn't understand. She watched the gruff man soothe the animal under its jaws. He stared straight into the doe's round eyes when he next spoke, as if more for the doe's comprehension than Caroline's.

"We need to get her to stand up. Then she'll be okay and she'll run off on her own. But if she can't get up right away, then . . ." Ray broke his eye contact with the doe. "She's gonna die."

Caroline understood. She was no stranger to the doe's predicament.

Ray began to coax the deer in a gentle but urgent drone, and after a time her legs twitched nervously. Ray continued his level coaxing, and the doe's back legs stirred convulsively, then became still. She struggled and halted several more times, while each time Caroline remembered the frustration of reaching for that bedrail.

Ray persisted. The doe rallied, then quit, her struggles becoming weaker with each attempt. Finally she stopped entirely.

"Nope," Ray announced, shaking his head. He stood up and looked down at the animal. "I got a rifle in the truck."

"No!" Caroline knelt closer to the doe's head and held it in her hands so that their eyes were forced to meet. She quietly cajoled the deer as Ray had done only with a remembered intensity that sprang from deep within her.

The doe's warm eyes locked directly onto Caroline's as if startled. Her legs twitched in a brief and violent spasm, but whatever shred of spirit Caroline had summoned from the animal now receded beyond reach. The big eyes blinked, glazed and dull.

"It's useless, young lady," Ray said from somewhere behind her.

Caroline wept quietly over the hopeless creature. Tenderly she stroked its head while Ray walked to his truck.

"So what happened?" Matt's deep voice interrupted Caroline's recollection.

Caroline ignored him. Intuitively she knew she didn't want to share this part of the story—or the reasons why—with the man sitting beside her. She knew that there was no logic attached to her thinking this way, just an instinctive need for privacy—or caution, she wasn't sure which. In any case, it was Caroline, now, whose mood edged as purposely distant as Matt's had been on their trip into Hawkeye earlier in the day. She would tell Matt the facts, but she wouldn't tell him the feelings.

"We tried to coax her up," Caroline informed the windshield. "But we couldn't, so Ray had to shoot her."

The rifle crack echoed in her ears as it had so many times during her first weeks in Montana. Ray had asked her to wait at her car while he dispatched the doe and got it into his light blue pickup. Wiping his hands on a bandanna, he approached Caroline at her car.

"I'll take her to the police," he said. "You can follow me there to fill out the report." He looked at the sporty Camaro packed with boxes and cats. "How bad did it damage your car?"

"It didn't. It wasn't me who hit her."

Ray regarded her with an astonished expression that softened toward respect. "Did you get their plates?"

Remembering Matt's identical words, Caroline concluded her summary. "And that's how I met Ray. We got to talking about my timberland and Ray offered to take care of it."

"Well," said Matt, "you were lucky to get such a good start."

Caroline puzzled over Matt's words. That poor, sweet-eyed doe. Her pathetic struggle and her pitiful death. She had always interpreted it as a terrible start. During her beginning days in her farmhouse, Caroline's insecurity and superstitious nature would surface, and she would wonder if the omen would ever come to mean anything. Now she smiled as Winona's words came to mind. "A bad beginning will mean a good end."

"Maybe you're right," she said more to herself than to Matt as they drove down their side of the mountain.

It was getting close to dusk when they neared

Caroline's house. They'd been silent for some time, Caroline lost in her own thoughts, but as they crunched over her gravel driveway, she snapped back to reality. She studied Matt. In one fluid motion he downshifted the truck to an idle and relaxed back against his seat. He draped one arm over the open window with a casual, masculine grace.

"Thanks for the ride," Caroline said. "And thanks for introducing me to Winona."

"My pleasure." He grinned the Cheshire cat's grin at her as he surveyed her next movements.

Caroline gathered up her belongings. She looked at the sack of tomatoes Winona had given her, hesitated a moment, then said, "You want to join me for dinner?"

"What're you having?"

"Fish sticks?" Caroline answered dubiously, taking a quick mental inventory of her ill-stocked pantry. "And tomatoes," she added.

Matt made the same exact face that Celeste used to make when it came to lima beans. The comic expression dissolved into a wide smile. "No thanks."

As Matt drove away, Caroline wasn't sure if she was insulted or amused.

CHAPTER

13

"WHAT'S THE MAT-
ter, Tinky?"

The little black cat had abruptly stopped eating
from her bowl on the kitchen floor and had spun
around. Instantly alert, she faced the wood-frame
screen door that separated the kitchen's well-lit brightness from the night outside. The cat's body fixed tense.
Her ears fidgeted, searching.

Caroline stood behind the kitchen table and
peered at the door, but she couldn't see through the
screen. She took a bite of the homemade lemon bread
and huckleberry jam that came from her second, and
solo, visit to Winona's that afternoon. She savored the
moist and tangy bread against the sticky-sweet jam as
she watched the cat.

Tinky's radar ears were still. She jutted her nose
up in the air and sniffed delicately. As she craned her

neck to sniff higher and higher, her front paws left the floor.

"Well? What is it?" Caroline puzzled. Still seeing nothing, she concentrated on listening. Outside, the cicadas' steady siren wail attested to the evening's heat, but Caroline heard nothing more. Inside, the kitchen was heavy with the gathered heat and smells of the day. Munching on the bread and jam, Caroline regarded the silent door. If there was a breeze, perhaps just outside, she might cool herself off. The actions of her other cat, however, riveted her with caution.

Humphrey came tearing into the kitchen at break-neck speed, his mackerel stripes a blur of gray. He rushed directly to the base of the screen door, skittered furiously from side to side, then stopped so short that Caroline jumped, startled, too. His ears did a brief rendition of what Tinky's had done, and then, with a jolting suddenness, he flew out of the kitchen, leaving an overturned kitchen chair in his wake.

"Humphrey?" Caroline's alarm was reflexive, and now it mushroomed because she didn't know exactly what she should be so alarmed about. Up until this moment she'd been nothing but tired and droopy from a very long day. By the time she'd sunk deep into the pillows of her couch that evening, she was too hot to move. But now that was all changed. Even if she didn't know why, she was as agitated as her two cats. She sensed it, too: something was out there.

Oh, God, she thought, looking at the still unfixed screen door. The old wooden frame anchored the hanging hook, unconnected with its eye. Staring apprehensively at the bowed-out screen, she wondered what wild thing lurked beyond it.

Mimicking Tinky's rather than Humphrey's instinctive behavior, Caroline stood perfectly still. She heard it now: a slow shuffling and scratching against the back porch floorboards. All of a sudden the top section of screen bowed inward and a blackness filled the entire door frame.

Quickly Caroline tried to remember whether the screen door opened inward or out. The distended screen filled in blacker, and her question was answered as the screen made a ripping sound. A pair of rectangular paws—huge, black, and leathery—pressed into the mesh. A face loomed into view that reminded Caroline of a German shepherd's, except that it was much, much larger.

A bear! her mind screamed. A six-foot bear on its hind legs—and only a quickly ripping screen between it and her.

Tinky, instantly unfrozen, bolted a hundred miles an hour in no particular direction. Her little cat's paws scurried on the linoleum without actually touching, so that she looked like a cartoon animal, legs whirling wildly but getting nowhere. Caroline wanted to laugh—or cry, she wasn't sure which. Once Tinky finally found some traction and tore out of the kitchen, Caroline's giddiness passed. She wished that she could muster at least as much motor control as her cat just had, but she couldn't. She remained transfixed, clutching a crumbling piece of lemon bread.

The massive black paws pushed hard into the top screen section. Caroline watched in horror as a row of straight ivory claws sliced effortlessly into the mesh. The screen ripped more ominously as a wet black nose pressed what was left of the screen inward. Beady gray eyes set deep in brown-black fur looked stupidly into the kitchen. The nose sniffed visibly.

Caroline dropped her bread and jam onto the table and covered it hastily with a nearby towel. "Shoo!" she said meekly. "Go home!"

To her surprise, the bear returned to all fours and backed into the shadows of the kitchen porch. Caroline heard the claws scraping slowly down the wooden porch. Tiptoeing as if in pantomine, Caroline took long strides to the solid kitchen door, closed and bolted it. Looking out the door's top window, she could see the bear swinging its heavy head from one side to the other as it ambled toward the side porch. Caroline tried to remember if the front door was open. No, she was almost sure it wasn't, but the front and side windows of the dining room and living room—every one of them a floor-to-ceiling window—were all open wide.

Caroline stood fear-stricken in the kitchen, trying to think what to do. Could she manage to run in and close all those windows before the bear noticed her activity? She remembered how easily the knifelike claws sliced through the screen, and she shuddered. Which way would she run if the bear got in? Upstairs where it might corner her? In the basement? She shivered, remembering both the claws and the flimsy basement door. Maybe she could make a dash for the car?

A crash on the front porch interrupted her escalating panic. The bear had found the porch chairs, and they were not to its liking. Caroline rushed to the telephone on her kitchen wall.

"Please! Oh, puh-leeese be in the book!" She fumbled through the phone directory, willing her hands to work through their jittery shaking. She found and dialed a number.

"Hello, Matt?" she squeaked into the receiver.

"Can't hear you. Who is this?"

"Matt!" she stage-whispered while listening to her porch furniture overturn. "Matt! This is Caroline. There's a bear on my porch!"

There was no immediate answer. Even the porch furniture was silent. Caroline gripped the receiver twice as tightly, as if to squeeze a response from it.

"Okay, I'll be right there. Don't go outside."

Caroline hung up on the dial tone, giddily asking herself, Now why on earth would I go outside—unless, of course, the bear had already got inside. She peeked into the empty living room and tugged on earrings that weren't there, wondering how fast she could cram herself into the broom closet if she needed to.

Caroline's sense of rational time was suspended as she waited frantically in the kitchen. She folded her arms in front of her and hugged them tight into her ribs while she listened hard for bear sounds around her house. All was frighteningly silent. How long does it take to get here? her edginess nagged. Maybe he's not coming. Maybe I misunderstood him. Maybe I'm supposed to not go outside and that's all!" She was pacing the kitchen floor, wondering what to do next, when she heard the sound of an engine approaching. Tires crunched over gravel; the door of a pickup slammed. In a flash Caroline ran through the living room and threw open the front door. She peered out into empty darkness.

"Get inside!" Matt's voice snapped from around the side of the house.

She closed the door and backed into the living room, listening. The sound of Matt's cautious footsteps traveled toward the back, then faded. He was circling the house.

A quiet rap on her front door, and Caroline let Matt inside. Wordlessly he took the rifle he'd been cradling and laid it on the floor just inside the door. He stood before her in blue jeans and a faded black T-shirt.

"I think it's gone," he said, scratching at the dark stubble on his cheek.

"You sure?"

"No. It could come back. Depends on how hungry it is." Matt plopped onto the couch. "How big was it?"

Caroline felt safe now, even if it was still out there. She described the bear and her fear of it to him. She was both thankful and relieved that Matt was there with her and that he was taking her seriously—perhaps even more seriously than she was.

"It sounds like it was a black bear looking for food," Matt said. "This dry spell lately is making them have to look for food in places besides the woods. Sometimes they'll stick around if they smell something good to eat, so your instincts were good when you covered up that jam. From now on, keep the kitchen windows closed when you're cooking, even if it's those fish sticks of yours." He shot Caroline a fleeting, suddenly boyish grin that vanished when he added, "The important thing is, you've got to be careful not to startle them. Bears are real unpredictable. They're just as apt to go after you as not. You never know with them." He lowered his dark gaze away from Caroline and added quietly, "I'm glad nothing happened to you."

Caroline looked at him queerly. It seemed to her—

for a moment, at least—that another, more vulnerable man existed beneath Matt's confident exterior. She stared at the black-lashed eyes. Aware, they flashed and stared back into hers with a suspended intensity that held her mesmerized.

"On my trips," Matt said softly, breaking eye contact, "I've met up with a few bears, both black and grizzlies." He regarded Caroline with renewed intensity just briefly before he continued. "Lots of bears are persistent, but mostly they're pretty stupid. The best thing you can do is be passive. Either stand your ground or play dead and let the bear make all the moves. Let him do all the sniffing he wants. Usually, sooner or later— that is, if there's nothing for him to get interested in— he'll forget you and what it was he was looking for and leave on his own accord. As long as you don't spook him, that is." Matt regarded her outright and added mock seriously, "Screaming only sets them on edge."

"I didn't scream," Caroline said defending herself from the tease.

Matt chuckled, then turned serious. "Your cat—is it in or out?"

"They're both inside." Caroline noted that whatever softness she might have glimpsed in Matt had receded beneath the armor again.

"Good. Do you have a gun yet?"

Taken aback, Caroline replied, "No," in a tone that said "Are you crazy?"

"Matt ignored her tone but not her answer. "Okay, just in case our big black friend is the persistent type and decides to try it again, I'll camp out on your porch tonight."

It was a statement more than a request, but Caroline was grateful.

"And tomorrow we'll go to Hawkeye," Matt continued, "and buy you a gun."

"I don't want a gun."

"Maybe. But you need one to protect yourself."

"No, I don't."

Matt arched an eyebrow at her but said nothing.

"I don't like guns," Caroline countered. "They're for killing, and I could never use one."

"Don't worry. I'd be glad to teach you. We'll start with targets."

"That's not what I meant. What I meant was that I don't need a gun."

"Just what are you going to do," Matt persisted, vexed, "if another bear shows up in your kitchen? What if I'm not around? What if it's hungrier next time?"

"Then I'll do as you said and be passive until it leaves," Caroline answered smartly, realizing all the while that she was bluffing.

"Malarkey." Matt's eyes narrowed on hers. "You'll probably scream."

"No, I won't—" She didn't much care for the way he grinned at her. "Wouldn't," she corrected herself angrily, making her next retort perhaps a little more haughty than she intended. "And I neither need nor want a gun."

Matt glowered. Caroline got the feeling that he was about to growl something at her but that willpower stayed his tongue.

"So"—Caroline switched tracks determinedly—"do you want to sleep upstairs in the guest room or down here?" In her mind she added, *Where you can* shoot at things, although she dared not voice the thought. But her tone had implied her mood, and Matt responded in an overly composed manner.

"Down here is just fine," he answered, smiling wanly.

Silently Caroline watched Matt gather some couch pillows and stack them at one end. He pulled off his boots and slid back, catlike, into the couch. Just before he switched off the lamp, Caroline noted how strikingly his black shirt contrasted against the cranberry.

" 'Night," he said much too pleasantly as Caroline climbed the stairs.

"Good night," she answered, confused, the wind out of her sails.

Caroline hesitated on the staircase. She wanted to thank Matt for coming when she needed him. She wanted to tell him that she felt safe because he was there. She wanted him to know that she was grateful for his staying the night. But now, somehow, she didn't know how to say it. Anger, pride, stubbornness—or maybe something else—paralyzed her words, if not her feelings. Sadly she clicked off the upstairs light and went to her room.

CHAPTER

14

$``T$HERE SHE IS," MATT told Ray Banes as they entered the blessed coolness of the Bitterroot Cafe. Looking across the mostly empty tables, Matt had spotted Caroline sitting at a booth with Jody Landis. Matt was surprised. For some reason he had always assumed that he and the two Baneses were Caroline's only friends in Hawkeye. Matt pocketed his sunglasses. From the casual way they were talking, it appeared that Caroline knew Jody pretty well.

Matt and Ray wended their way toward the booth and said their hellos.

"Been here long?" Matt asked Caroline. She had accepted his invitation for a ride into Hawkeye today to tend to some chores, and they had arranged to meet at the Bitterroot when they were done. It had been nearly a week since the bear scare, and he had been careful not to mention bears or guns even once while driving in today. Maybe that might make it easier, later.

"No, just got here, really." Caroline slid over to make room for him to sit. Across from them, Jody did the same for Ray.

"Here's your mail," Matt said. He handed Caroline the bundle while noting the look of confusion on Jody's face.

Matt looked around the eerily quiet Bitterroot. It was the midafternoon lull, when the mealtime crowds and conversations were replaced by the silent loners of Hawkeye. Earl Bullchild, that sullen Blackfeet kid, slouched at the corner table. He was nursing a Coke while adding another cigarette butt to the pile in his ashtray. At the lunch counter, old Ed, the town drunk, huddled catatonic over an untouched cup of coffee. Matt winced involuntarily to look at him. A sunburned-faced man sat at a center table with two desserts. He wore what Matt recognized as an expensively tailored business suit that proclaimed him a stranger to Hawkeye. Sally stood at a table near the window, completely engrossed in filling up the sugar dispensers. Yellowing philodendrons drooped above her head, considerably worse off from the sun's unrelenting glare.

Caroline hurriedly leafed through her mail just as Matt's gaze returned to their booth. He wondered who wrote her personal letters from Boston in such scrawly penmanship. Caroline's copper, silky straight hair kept falling into her eyes, and she would periodically blow upward to clear her vision. Matt thought it made her look alternately girlish and exasperated. When she was done, she laid her mail to the side and lifted up her eyes to Jody and Ray.

"Heard you had a time with Winona's huckleberry

jam," Ray stated levelly, although Matt recognized this as lighthearted talk by Ray's standards.

"I sure did." Caroline smiled, immediately picking up on Ray's mood. "I didn't much care for the bear at my door, but the jam was really great."

"Winona always makes fine jam," Ray replied. A crease flickered at the corner of his eyes.

Jody looked questioningly from Ray to Caroline. "You had a bear at your house? When?"

Clearly, Matt thought, Ray's brand of humor was lost on Jody.

"Were you all right?" Jody's concern rose. "Did it try to get inside?"

"Well, it was thinking about it," Caroline replied. "But it went away when Matt came over."

Ray, his moment of whimsy behind him, directed his interest across the table to Matt. "Did the bear come back that night?"

"I'm not sure," Matt answered. "I thought I heard something out there, maybe one or two in the morning, but it didn't come in close this time." Briefly Matt regarded the look of concern on Jody's face, which seemed to deepen rather than ease at this information.

"But, Matt," Caroline interrupted, "why didn't you wake me up if the bear was out there again?"

"There was no need to," Matt answered abstractedly. His attention was drawn to the tight expression on Jody's normally placid face. Why the look of disapproval? he puzzled. He turned his attention to Caroline and made a point of adding, "You were safer upstairs. And I had it all under control from my post on your living room couch."

Jody visibly relaxed, but Matt wasn't sure if this

was due to romantic reasons or a prim sense of propriety on Jody's part. He had no time to come to a conclusion before Sally whisked up to their booth in a rustle of pink-and-black nylon.

"Sor , 'bout the wait, folks. I didn't even hear you all come in. What can I get you?" She was back in no time, pouring coffees all around, and when that was accomplished she took a square of paper out of a pocket of her pink smock and laid it on the table in front of Ray. "Paul Grandmaison," she said, "asked me to give one of these mimeos to everyone who comes in. Enjoy your coffee, folks."

As Sally returned to her station, a chair squeaked at one of the center tables. Matt saw the red-faced stranger make a show of forking into one of his as-yet-untouched slices of pie. When Ray pulled the mimeo closer, however, Matt saw that the lowered gaze of the well-suited man studied Ray intently.

Silently Ray read the lavender-lettered paper. He nodded slowly in sober comprehension, then slid the paper to the center of the table.

Jody took it up and read aloud: "Open Town Meeting regarding Trash to Energy Project in Hawkeye, Montana. Sanborne Inc. to present proposal. Question and Answer period to follow. Everyone invited. Tuesday, November tenth. Seven P.M. Medallion Regional High School Auditorium." Jody put the message down. "Well, that's a long time from now," he said as if to dismiss the matter as unimportant.

Suddenly it seemed unimportant to Matt, too, as he witnessed the look on Caroline's face. She'd been watching Jody, utterly absorbed in him, as he read. Matt had seen that look on a woman's face before. It had been on Sheila's face a lifetime ago. And here it was on Caroline's. It didn't make sense that someone like Caroline could possibly be interested in a hayseed like Jody. And yet, Matt knew from the look on her face, making sense had nothing to do with it.

Ray's gruff voice brought Matt away from his thoughts. "Checked with the cooperative extension about those maples," Ray told Caroline. "Gave them samples." Never in a hurry, Ray sipped at his coffee before continuing. "And damned if they know what's defoliating them like that. Their advice was an all-purpose spray next spring until they can pinpoint the specific pest. They said Jack Mackenzie's timberland's got it even worse than yours."

Caroline let this information settle in before speaking. Matt saw neither girlishness nor worry on her face, just the concentration of a businesswoman weighing her options. "What sort of loss does that mean?" she asked Ray.

"Nothing in numbers yet." Ray was equally businesslike. "It could kill off a portion of your maple hardwoods outright, or it could temporarily damage them enough for us to have to postpone the harvest till next season. Depends on the name of the pest, and we can't find that until the eggs hatch next spring."

"I see," Caroline said quietly.

"It's a hardwood pest. It won't affect the pines," Ray added as if presuming her next question. Ray was aware of the economic importance Caroline's timberland held for her.

Caroline nodded. "Good," she said finally. "What about the oaks and the cherries?"

"They're in the lower tract, away from the maples. So far, they look clean," Ray said.

Matt's attention was interrupted for a moment by the sound of a chair's legs scraping the floor. The sun-burned man appeared to be searching his inner suit jacket pockets for something. It struck Matt as foolish for anyone, no matter what his profession, to be wearing a coat in ninety-two-degree weather.

"You say Mackenzie's timberland has got the same problem as mine?" Caroline asked.

Ray sipped coffee and then nodded.

"Where's his tract in relation to mine?"

"Right next to yours." You're Medallion County lot number 037, Mackenzie's number 036—only yours goes a lot deeper north to south."

Matt glimpsed at the stranger again. He was scribbling in a small Day-Timer's notebook.

"Would it help any," Caroline asked Ray, "if we cleared a swath between us?"

Matt looked at Caroline with increased respect. Besides being so feminine-looking, she had a remarkably quick mind. The only reason he comprehended the solution she proposed was because of his fire-fighting training.

Ray said, "Nope. Too late for that."

"Okay," Caroline murmured. "Please tell me if you find out anything more."

"Yup," said Ray before plowing into his next piece of business with Caroline. He was ahead of his own logging schedule and was outlining a slightly amended schedule for her next harvest.

Uninterested, Matt watched the stranger shriek his chair out and leave. He'd left his two desserts uneaten.

While Ray and Caroline went over the dates, Matt took the opportunity to try to catch Jody's attention. He hadn't really spoken with Jody since last year. Maybe there was more to him than met the eye. Looking directly at him, Matt found him to be oblivious of everything except Caroline. He identified in Jody the vulnerable look of one hopelessly smitten.

Regarding him further, Matt was impressed by his good looks and saw a man who was animated and vital. Matt also saw a man whose hopes were fully resting on Caroline.

He had always liked Jody, but now Matt felt a vague sense of annoyance with him for wearing his heart so prominently on his sleeve.

"Oh, come on!" was Matt's irritated answer to Caroline's last statement. She certainly had an abrasive way of rearranging his words. "That's not what I said at all."

"Of course it was," Caroline replied a bit too coolly, her chin a bit too high. "You just don't like hearing it stripped of its euphemisms."

Matt accelerated into fourth gear as they approached the last major incline on the road home from Hawkeye.

"What euphemisms?!" Matt burst out heatedly. He exhaled long and hard to regain his composure. "Look, I'm not saying it should be used all the time . . ."

"It should never be used!" Caroline exploded, her coolness evaporating.

"But if some sicko who's seen one too many slasher movies goes around hacking up innocent people just for jollies, then don't you think we'd be doing everybody a big favor by getting rid of him?"

"Just off with his head," she retorted airily. "Is that what you mean?"

"Yes, exactly. Some people deserve it."

Caroline narrowed her eyes and frowned at him. In a mock-cowboy twang, she growled menacingly, "He needed killin'."

"Yes!" he shouted, ignoring the sarcasm. Jesus, she was infuriating. "Some people do need killin'!"

"Why not just put them in jail? I mean, who are we to play God with someone else's life?"

"Because it costs a lot of money—*your* money—to keep all those nut cases in jail for all their lives. And someone who's dismembered an eight-year-old girl on a railroad track doesn't deserve to go on living even in jail."

"But what if it was a mistake? What if they convicted the wrong person? It's happened," she argued. "Then doesn't it make more sense just in case the jury goofed?"

"Oh, come on. How many times does that actually happen?"

"Even if it happens only once—isn't that one life enough?"

"No, Caroline. What happens is that we get a bunch of murderers walking the streets on parole after a few years."

"Well, what if a convicted killer changes? What if he's really and truly penitent, and he struggles and works hard to turn his life around?" Caroline shifted under her seat belt to face Matt when she said, "Then why not give him parole?"

Matt concentrated on driving, exasperated that he had no immediate answer.

"What if," Caroline continued, "the killer did some terrible things because he was mentally unstable at the time, or drunk or on drugs, or even crazed by anger or something—stuff that he'd never, ever do if he was his regular self and thinking clearly?"

"Why does the killer have to be a man?"

"It's usually a man," she continued matter-of-factly. "And what if the person—okay?" She glared at him. "What if he or she got a grip and straightened out into a regular person—like you or me? Then?" She was impassioned now. "Then don't you think they deserve another chance?"

Matt thought about this. She'd struck a chord that reverberated just a tad too close to home, and damn it, he knew she was right. Still, he didn't like the idea of ex-murderers walking the streets any more than he liked the idea of conceding to Caroline. Downshifting, he slowed the truck for the road's last descent.

"Well?" Caroline persisted.

"Well, what?"

"Another chance. Don't you think that everyone deserves another chance?"

"Maybe. It depends on the person," he answered, vexed. He pretended to concentrate on driving so they wouldn't have to talk about this anymore. While he drove, he began to ponder the day in Hawkeye. Caroline had handled the problem with her trees with remarkable stoicism, Matt realized, yet here she was, the perfect example of the bleeding-heart liberal—well, maybe not entirely: she had a few sensible opinions from time to time. And, truth be told, he enjoyed debating with someone of Caroline's quick intelligence. During all his years in Montana, he'd never known anybody, not even Ray, with whom he could match wits. Being with Caroline intrigued him, even though sometimes she infuriated him with her excessive contrariness. Being with Caroline, he also had to admit, sometimes made him extremely edgy, and as to that, he didn't know why.

"Did you get everything you needed in Hawkeye today?" he found himself asking her.

"All except for the vitamins. I can't believe that a drugstore wouldn't carry something as basic as B-complex vitamins."

"What do you need B-complex vitamins for?"

"That's pretty much what they said at Rexall's, too. But," she added, piqued, "if I didn't mind waiting six to eight weeks, they could order them for me. Do you believe that?"

"Well, yes." Matt smiled. "Did you order them?"

"I didn't have much choice. It's the only drugstore around."

"This isn't Chicago, you know."

"I know," she admitted. "Sometimes the rural-ness of it all just gets to me."

"You'll get used to it."

"I know I'll get used to it—people can get used to most anything. What troubles me is if I'll ever feel like I really belong here." She looked at him and asked, "What about you? Do you feel like you belong here?"

Matt's answer was immediate. "I belong here." He saw Caroline trying to compare her own situation with his and felt sorry for her. The adjustment would be harder for her. For him, the transition had been easy:

his wealth had always allowed him to vacation regularly in Montana even before the accident. And, by the time he came to actually live here, it represented a safe haven—a place of security that protected him from what he needed to forget. Looking now at Caroline, he saw that it was not the same for her. "Give it time," he said gently. "Hawkeye's a good place."

"I know it is. It's just that sometimes I'm both pleased with the smallness of it and resentful toward it at the same time. Hawkeye is like this walk-in closet I had when I was a kid. I used to hide in it with a flashlight and a book and lose myself in there. Wonderful stories about princesses and ogres would transport me so thoroughly that when I heard some noise outside, it was like waking up. And then I'd be reminded that there was a bigger world out there where interesting things were happening and I had missed them because I was in the closet."

"What you're missing isn't as good as Hawkeye."

"Well, that's what I've been telling myself. Besides, Hawkeye's my only chance, so I've got to make it work."

When Caroline turned her face away, Matt realized that she'd probably said more than she'd meant to. Not wishing to intrude on her pensive silence, he drove on and let his thoughts wander over what he'd learned about her today. Here was a woman who'd been through some major difficulties—whatever they were—which had made her strong but not hard: the determination hadn't overshadowed the femininity. Here was a woman who possessed an understanding of what made people tick. The way she'd picked up on Ray's sort of humor today was pretty sharp. Matt got the feeling that nothing escaped her notice when it came to people. Whether it was an innate talent or a practiced canniness, he didn't know, but he did know that it made him uneasy. Still, there was a fragile kind of sweetness to the apple-cheeked Caroline. And she had that empathy of feeling that only certain women possessed—the kind of warm concern that Margaret had. And Winona. Matt recalled how instantaneously Winona had befriended Caroline, or was it the other way around? Winona, he knew, was never wrong about people.

Matt snatched a curious glance at Caroline and wondered why such a beautiful, intelligent woman would choose to live so far away from the world that attracted her so. He dared not ask. Do unto others, he told himself.

He pushed a cassette into the truck's tape player. A thin, twangy voice warbled, "Oh, I'm a-hurtin' for certain . . ."

"You like country music?" Matt asked.

Caroline chuckled good-humoredly. At least he'd cheered her up. "Umm, some of it. But not this."

"You'll get used to it."

Not long after, they drove up Caroline's driveway. Matt let her walk halfway down the gravel drive before calling her back to the truck's open window. She returned and looked up at him.

"I'll be over tomorrow morning," Matt called down to her over the rumble of the engine. "Is ten o'clock okay with you?"

"Well, sure. Why?"

"I have a present for you."

"You do?"

She was playing right into it.

"What is it?"

Her look of appreciation dissolved in stages as Matt described the gift he'd bought for her and as Caroline recognized the description to be that of a gun.

"I'll be over to show you how to use it," he said. Before she could utter a word, Matt shoved the gearshift into reverse and floored the gas pedal. Even though he couldn't hear it, he recognized the emphatic *"No!"* on Caroline's lips as he zipped to the end of the driveway in a cloud of gravel dust. He waved and grinned at her just before he switched gears and drove down the road toward home. She certainly seemed angry, he thought. But, sometimes, there was only one way to deal with overly stubborn people.

CHAPTER

15

"*L*ISTEN, MATT, I DON'T want to do this."

He grinned, ignoring her as he hopped out of the pickup and squinted into the midmorning sun.

"I'd rather shave my head with the coarse side of a cheese grater, Matt, while chewing on a wad of tinfoil, than have a gun."

"How 'bout if you try shooting it just once," he said sweetly. He reached into the cab and proffered a jet black handgun.

"No! I hate guns."

"Well, okay, if that's how you really feel." He shrugged with an air of innocent indifference.

Caroline scowled at him suspiciously.

"Just do me a favor and hold on to it for me."

"No. How about if you just return it?"

"Can't. I pulled a whole lot of strings for you down

at Fairbanks so they'd sell it to me and then register it under your name. Bob Fairbanks, Jr., arranged it as a favor. I'd get him in big trouble if he had to undo all the paperwork."

"Okay. So I'll return it."

"That'd be better." He handed her the gun. It was plain, black, and blunt, like what a television hit man or detective would have, and a great deal heavier than what she'd expected. She stared at it as it lay in her palm, resisting the temptation to grasp it by its handle.

"Look, here's the safety catch," Matt said. "Make sure it's always in place like this." He advanced very near to her, took the gun, and showed her the catch.

Caroline was less aware of the gun than she was of Matt's presence. She felt small next to him, and he smelled pleasantly of spicy soap. "Is it loaded?" she asked.

"Yup. If you need to use it, just switch back this lever and it's ready." He demonstrated.

"Set it back. I'm not going to use it. I'm just going to return it."

"Suit yourself," he said easily. He recaught the latch, returned it to Caroline, and assumed his original distance. "Just one thing, though," he said. "Let's just say if—just if—between now and when you return it . . ." He paused to regard her with a look of absolute sincerity. "If you should need to use it—say, for example, maybe that bear comes in a little closer, a little more persistent, or if a pack of coyotes get your cat cornered—it's dry times for coyotes, too, you know. . . ." He trailed off to lift his hat, rake a hand through his hair, and return the hat. "Anyway, let's just say *if*, mind you, you should come across a situation where it would be safer to use a gun than not? Even, let's say, just as a warning shot that could save, if not your own life, then your little cat's life . . ."

Caroline scowled at him heartily. She hadn't thought about coyotes eating her cats. She hadn't considered a gun as something that could scare wild animals away without having to kill them.

"If between now and when you return the gun," Matt continued, "if you might want to shoot the gun as a signal to me that you were in trouble—say, just in case you couldn't get to a telephone . . ."

Damn it, Caroline thought. She hadn't considered that, either.

"Anyway," Matt went on in an easygoing, almost flippant way. "If—and this is purely hypothetical, don't you know—just *if* you needed to use the gun between now and when you returned it, well, I'd feel a lot better if you knew how to shoot it."

"I won't need to shoot it," Caroline grumbled, but her resolve had been seriously undermined. She glowered at the gun, then looked at Matt. What was it about him that made it so difficult to acquiesce? "Oh, okay," she finally blurted. "I'll keep it to use for a warning shot. How much do I owe you for it?"

"Consider it a housewarming present. Now, let me show you how to shoot it."

"I'm sure I'll be able to shoot it." She regarded the gun with open disgust. "I'm not going to be aiming to hit anything, anyway."

"Humor me," Matt said patiently. "Just so you get the feel of it. See that tree? Shoot at that."

Caroline aimed just as she'd seen it done in the movies, while Matt edged well behind her. The sharp crack pierced her hearing even as her arm was flung violently up and out. Her whole body walloped backward, throwing her off balance. She knew the bullet hadn't even gone in the same general direction as the tree.

"How about if I set up a few of those targets I brought?" Matt asked gently.

Awed by the power of the gun and by the strength that was necessary to control it, Caroline nodded in silent affirmation.

As they drove up the hidden driveway, Caroline saw that Matt's house was even bigger than she'd expected. Huge craggy boulders surrounded, but by no means dwarfed, the place on two sides, protecting it with a gray-white wall of natural privacy. The other two sides opened up to the same vast, rolling plain as Caroline's. A barn to one side connected with a large corral where two chestnut horses grazed.

Coming in closer, Caroline saw that even though the house was built entirely of dark amber logs, it was dramatically modern in design: a successful combination of the architecture of two different centuries. Traditional and contemporary blended into one, Caroline decided, very much like Matt himself. Heavy log walls of varying geometric shapes supported several rock-colored roofs that angled at steep planes. The two multifaceted stories blended gracefully into the slope of the land around it, and a sublevel opened out from under the railed deck hugging the house.

Even as Matt opened the wide, rough-hewn door, they heard the phone ringing from somewhere inside.

" 'Scuse me," he said as he dashed away.

Caroline found herself standing in a huge, cathedrallike room. The walls were logs inside, too, a little lighter amber in color, which offset the room's enormity with a warm, secure glow. The log-beamed ceiling traveled high and peaked, chalet style, while a massive fireplace made entirely from fist-size rocks formed the wall at one end of the expansive room. Everywhere, lots of curtainless windows sent in shafts of brightness. The whole effect surrounded Caroline with a sense of openness on all dimensions, and she liked the place immediately. The warmth of the wood, the solidness of the rocks, and the volume of unfilled space: it was almost like being outside, Caroline thought to herself. It was also a lot like Matt's personality: open yet controlled; rugged yet warm.

She could hear Matt chuckling on the phone. After shooting at targets that morning, they had spent a lazy afternoon talking on Caroline's porch, then Matt had driven her to his house to have dinner. In spite of, or perhaps because of, the frequently argumentative nature of their relationship, combined with their common backgrounds, their friendship had deepened that day. And now, after Caroline had entered Matt's house, she felt immediately comfortable, as if the wood and rock were an extension of Matt himself. Appearing from the doorway, he regarded her pleasantly before he spoke.

"Sorry I took so long." He smiled as if his spirits had been elevated. "It was the Fosters back in San Francisco. We keep in touch a lot."

"Oh." Caroline remembered a past conversation. "Is that who takes care of your business for you?"

"No." Matt paused a moment. "Well, once,

but . . ." He trailed off, then picked up the thread again. "The Fosters are kind of like my godparents. My mom and dad both died when I was seven, so my grandparents took me in and raised me. The Fosters, Wayne and Doc—everyone calls her that 'cause she's a pediatrician—had been my parents' best friends, and they recognized that my grandparents were pretty well on in years and rather Victorian in their attitudes toward child rearing. So, it was the Fosters who took me for summers and weekends and holidays—and who made sure I had a crack at a normal childhood."

"They sound like neat people," was all Caroline could think to say to Matt's story, but Matt wasn't paying attention anyway. A huge, hairy brown moth was buzzing in distress, slamming into one of the window screens.

"Ick!" Caroline retreated a few steps and imagined the awful crunching sound it would make when Matt squished it. She hoped that maybe he had a can of bug spray.

Matt, however, cupped both hands over the repulsive creature and carefully contained it within. It whirred and flapped horribly. He walked to the door, jiggled it open, stepped outside, and opened his hands. The moth flew away with a noisy flutter. Caroline regarded Matt, standing in the doorway, with heightened respect.

He grinned at her happily and said, "Come on to the kitchen and tell me how you like your steak done."

During dinner they debated the issues of country versus rock music, and then the welfare system. By the time they reached a heated standoff regarding flag burning, Caroline had come to the assessment that although a few of Matt's opinions were open-minded, mostly he was very old-fashioned for someone in his thirties. Still, she enjoyed both Matt's talk and Matt's company, enough so that when Matt asked her exactly why she couldn't return to the city, she freely told him everything about her history—everything except the part about Jim. Caroline asked a similar question of Matt, but he remained evasive. She was a little hurt by this at first, feeling that their friendship could now support a better trust. But when she saw how delicately and earnestly he tried to switch the conversation to another track, she accepted his wishes.

It was dark when Matt drove her home. His pickup crunched over her driveway, and he turned off the engine. Leaning forward and folding his arms over the steering wheel, he looked skyward through the windshield.

"Holy cow! Look at those stars." Suddenly he was out of the truck and pointing upward at the blue-black velvet dome of sky highlighted by stars that Caroline felt she might simply reach up and touch. As he pointed out this constellation and that to her, Matt's close presence and the smell of his spicy soap grabbed Caroline's senses. She thought briefly to herself that if Matt were interested in her as more than just a friend, it would be so easy at this particular moment for him to slip his arms around her and . . . The thought broke. Matt walked a few steps ahead of her, pointing out Cassiopeia and Pegasus. He wasn't interested, Caroline surmised, and just as well, because neither was she.

Caroline watched as the taillights of Matt's truck receded down the road into a pair of small red dots.

Only when they flickered out of sight under a hilltop did she turn and walk into her house.

Autumn arrived as abruptly as if it had been clicked on by a switch. With it came a strange feeling of emptiness that Caroline pondered as she turned her car up the long dirt driveway that led to Winona's house. Perhaps she was feeling this way because Matt had apparently disappeared without a word, or maybe it was the change in the weather.

As she looked around at the tunnel of aspens surrounding Winona's drive, she saw that the teardrop leaves now fluttered pale yellow. And during the drive over she had noticed that the deep green mountainsides were becoming dappled with splotches of paler hues. Even the solidly lapis-blue sky of summer was replaced today by feathery wisps of cirrus clouds: a sure sign of change.

Caroline had already sensed the change last night when she went outside to get some logs for the woodstove. A new smell filled the air: crisp from both pines and peppery sage. She had been standing there breathing in the tangy aroma when the reclusive Tinky sensed it, too, and trotted out to Caroline's side without any hesitation.

"Hey, Tinks! Welcome to the world." She smiled in happy surprise at the little black cat. She automatically turned toward Matt's house, and the smile faded. No lights on again. Eight days—not since she'd had dinner there—and still he wasn't home. He hadn't mentioned anything to her about leaving. Could something have happened to him? Caroline recalled how Ray's baby blue pickup had traveled toward Matt's house earlier that day and returned almost immediately. Surely if Matt was home or even if something had happened to him, Ray would have discovered it. No, Caroline surmised, shrugging away the edgy feeling, Matt had simply gone somewhere.

Caroline didn't even get spooked when she found a sizable, molted snakeskin in the woodpile, and eventually, after using half a box of wooden matches, she got the woodstove lit. She was as proud of these self-sufficient accomplishments as she was of Tinky, but still she remained puzzled over Matt. And not only Matt. That whole business this morning with that awful man, Norris Nims, puzzled her, too. There was nothing specific that she could put her finger on that made her not like Nims—aside from his incomprehensible offer, that is— but instinctively she knew she didn't like him at all.

All this morning Caroline's thoughts had flitted from Matt's absence to the red-faced Nims until she had finally decided that a visit to Winona was in order. She was pleased that only Winona was home today, and soon they were talking in the cluttered kitchen over thick blocks of steamy-warm gingerbread topped with heavy dollops of sweet whipped cream. Hoping for a handout, Tyrone paced from side to side around the two women.

"Do you bake something every day, Winona?" Caroline asked, inhaling the cake's spicy aroma.

"Ray's got a quite a sweet tooth, dear, but I made the gingerbread because I had a hunch you might drop by soon."

Caroline smiled. If Winona had announced that

she was telepathic, it wouldn't have surprised Caroline one bit.

"Now, Caroline, dear, tell me if there's anything new with you."

"Well, there is," Caroline told her. "This weird guy came to my house this morning—well, not weird, really, just . . ." She stopped a moment to think about the man's brightly sunburned face and white-blond crew-cut. Then she knew. "Well, it seemed to me that he was trying to look like John Denver or something. He was wearing the standard flannel shirt, blue jeans, and cowboy boots, but they were all stiff and brand new. You could still see the crease lines from where the clothes had just been unfolded from their packages. And he was so meticulously tidy for around here that it struck me as kind of strange, as if he were wearing a costume.

"Anyway," Caroline continued, "this guy was all sweetness and smiles and introduced himself as Norris Nims."

"Did he say who he worked for?" Winona asked.

"Uh-uh." Caroline shook her head. "But right off the bat, he started asking me all sorts of questions about my timberland. Did I do most of the cutting in winter or fall, where was the central location for cut timber; did I own or lease the logging trucks."

"What a nerve."

"You said it. But he did it so smoothly, so laid-back, and mild-mannered, that, truly, it didn't occur to me to get angry about it till later."

"Did you answer his questions?"

"No. That's what was so weird, too. He asked, but I got the feeling he didn't really need to know, either."

Caroline looked perplexed. "And he already knew that Ray was in charge of it."

Winona responded with a cynical nod.

"The upshot of all of this," Caroline concluded, "was that he wanted to buy my timberland. He offered me a figure that was two and a half times what I paid for it, and—are you ready for this, Winona?"

"Oh, yes." Her eyes narrowed knowingly.

"In cash. Do you believe that?"

"What did you tell him?"

"No, of course. I told him it was my livelihood and it wasn't for sale. He didn't look happy, but he was polite about it. And then he said he'd be back in a couple of weeks to give me time to change my mind. I told him that I absolutely wasn't going to change my mind, but just as politely, he said he'd be back anyway. What a jerk, huh?" Caroline thought over Nim's parting words. They seemed to be simply phony then, as he'd stooped down to try to pet Humphrey, but now they took on an oilier quality. "Meeting you, Miss Atkinson, has been the pleasure of my day."

"The man's a bit of a sleeze, dear. What he neglected to mention was that he's a representative for the Sanborne Trash to Energy Project. They've been buying up a great deal of local land—supposedly for their incineration site, but also as a way of monopolizing Hawkeye so that challenge to their proposal will be minimal. Your neighbor Mackenzie sold his tract a couple of days ago. Mr. Nims is bound to pay you another visit."

"Well, I'm not selling and that's all there is to it," Caroline announced. She had no doubts about it, and it was only her concern about her and Mackenzie's unidentified defoliation that made her voice sound less than confident.

"Don't worry," Winona said. "No one can make you do what you don't want to do."

Caroline nodded silently in agreement.

"Enough of that," Winona burst out cheerfully. "What else is new?"

Caroline hadn't planned on voicing her puzzlement over Matt's absence, but she should have known that Winona would see straight into her clouded thoughts. "I can't figure it," she began. "Matt seems to have disappeared for the last eight days. I was just wondering, I guess, if he was okay." She finally put into words her more selfish fears. "And I guess I was worried that I was out there all by myself again."

The wheelchair rolled in closer so that Winona could touch Caroline softly on the shoulder. "I'm sure Matt can take care of himself wherever he is. And so can you."

Winona's quiet assurances lifted all the clouds. Caroline smiled comfortably into Winona's twinkling eyes, then she dunked the last moist chunk of the gingerbread into a big blob of cream.

CHAPTER

16

"*H*IGH SIERRA, CO-manche, Honcho, Ram Charger." All the names in the brochures sounded like either Indians or heavy-metal bands. Caroline sat at her kitchen table and arranged the pamphlets over the marble surface. The Explorer appealed to her, but maybe it was because of the name. The Bronco four-by-four seemed more sensible for the winter ahead.

And, indeed, winter was zooming in at a swift and steady pace. Just this morning Caroline had rushed outside when she heard the honking clamor of what sounded like a major traffic tie-up. There must have been hundreds of Canada geese in the flock. They shadowed the sky and filled the air with their trumpeting din. Looking up at the handsomely marked birds, Caroline remembered Winona's Indian name for the recent full moon of Halloween: the Geese-Go-South Moon.

Winona had said it was the moon when the rabbit and the weasel began to turn white and when the coyotes had to swallow their solitary pride and form into winter packs.

Caroline was readying herself, too. She'd had the woodstove chimneys swept; she'd restacked the woodpile so that it was closer to the kitchen door; and she'd split a bunch of kindling. She'd also purchased a gas-powered electric generator. It was entirely possible a winter storm could wipe out her power and snow her in for who knew how long. She thought about how spooky it would be to be stranded. And Matt probably wouldn't be around, either—like now, two weeks and still no sign of him. Being self-sufficient, Caroline realized, went a lot deeper than the pleasant feeling of independence she felt out here: it was a matter of survival.

An insistent pounding sent Caroline to her front door. Opening it, she surveyed a darkly tanned, dirt-dusted Matt. His face was hidden by hat and sunglasses, but the wide, toothy grin was exuberant.

"Come with me. There's something you've got to see."

"What?" She was happier to finally see him than she had expected to be.

"Back at my place. Come on, get in the truck."

As soon as they were on their way, Caroline regarded the scruffy-looking, rumpled Matt and made a sour face. "Gaaack! You smell like a skunk."

"Sorry. It doesn't wash off too easily." He took off the hat and sunglasses and laid them on the seat between them. He had owl eyes from where the glasses had prevented a suntan.

"You got sprayed?"

"No. Caroline, wait till you see what I got! It's really great."

"Where did you go?"

"The woods. I spent the last few weeks living in the woods. It's something I like to do from time to time, just to be completely on my own out in the wilderness."

"Yeah?" Caroline was intrigued.

"Yeah. It's—I don't know—satisfying, I guess."

"What do you do out there?"

"Nothing you'd call exciting: fish, hunt, hike around, live only on what nature has to offer."

"That'd be a lot of fun."

"Well, it is. But it's tricky, too. You've got to know what you're doing."

Caroline nodded thoughtfully. This sounded a lot like what she used to call exploring, only grown-up style. "Where'd you go?"

Matt's enthusiasm rose as a result of Caroline's. "Well, I started out on one of Ray's played-out logging roads with both the horses. Rode one and packed the gear on the other. I got started at eight in the morning and followed a stream up into the mountains till about four in the afternoon. By then there was barely enough path for the horses, so I turned the horse I was riding back. She's a real homing pigeon, so I knew she'd find her way. I unpacked the other horse and set up camp.

"That night I was lucky right off and killed a couple of jackrabbits. You should have seen it, there were tons of them leaping all over the place. I dressed them, hung one on a tree to keep for breakfast the next morning, and spitted the other for dinner."

"Wait a minute," Caroline interrupted. "Are you telling me that you didn't take any food with you?"

"No. No food, except for coffee and salt."

"What about water?"

"I always follow a stream. And this one was so chock full of trout that all I needed was a grasshopper on a line to haul them in.

"Next day, I hiked farther up. Saw this incredible golden eagle. Found a crystal-clear hidden lake. Got a couple of squirrels and a sage chicken, so I salted them for later. Then, I went into thicker forest. That's where it's really beautiful but much slower going. Lots of fallen trees and brush. I climbed for a while, then all of a sudden there was this grassy clearing where I could see the tops of rocky peaks, bigger than life. Astounding. You know, when you get close to something like that, it reminds you how very small you really are.

"The forest got sparser after that, so I stayed on a lateral path so as not to go too high up. Saw lots of moose, some elk, a wolverine, some black bears, a couple of foxes, and a lynx. Spent one night in a cave and another next to a waterfall. And one night I woke up to find it snowing—just a dusting—outside the tent."

They were nearing the end of Matt's driveway. Both chestnut horses grazed in their corral, looking none the worse for the wear. A pile of camping gear lay in a heap in front of the open barn door, telling Caroline that, upon returning, Matt had called on her before tending to anything else.

"Come on!" Matt called excitedly. He sprang out of the truck. "You've *got* to see this!"

Caroline followed him to the side of the barn, where, atop a big, salted square of burlap, lay a huge and smelly fish. Its dead eyes protruded so round and googly that it gave the fish a loony look. Seeing that Matt was near to being thrilled about it, Caroline tried to share his exuberance. Actually, it wasn't difficult. She was happy to be included in his joys; happy to see Matt back again; happy, even, to see this ridiculously ugly, dead and stinking fish.

"What do you think?" he asked.

"It's really big, Matt. What kind of fish is it?"

"Striped bass. I haven't measured it yet, but I think it could be trophy size. And—this is the best part—I got him with a grasshopper!"

Caroline's returning smile was heartfelt. This was uncharacteristic of Matt to be so open, and it honored her to be privy to it.

"I got him in the hidden lake I told you about. There were all these otters there, too. You should have seen them, Caroline. What a bunch of goofy animals— all sliding and slinking around. They seemed to be just as happy with other otters as they were playing alone. If I couldn't be human, I sure wouldn't mind being an otter."

Matt continued in a more serious tone, "You know, I really enjoy these wilderness trips. They're always a good physical and mental challenge, but mostly I take them so I can be alone. There was a time, before I came to live here in Montana, when I couldn't stand to be by myself. Not even for a few hours. I used to have to be around other people because—I hate to admit this—because I needed to be around their emotions. I had none of my own. When I look back at that, I can't see—or don't like to see—how I could have been that person. So now, every so often, I like to go off on one of these solo trips—like a refresher course, you might say, to keep things in perspective."

It was more than Matt had ever revealed of himself, and Caroline saw that as a result, a stronger trust had been forged between them. She recalled her own deep-seated yet nearly forgotten need to lose herself in order to find herself. "I think I know what you mean," she told him.

"I thought you might." Suddenly animated again, Matt said, "There's one more thing. You've gotta see what's in the barn!"

The barn was dark inside. Its only light came from several skylights, but it smelled agreeably of fresh hay. Caroline's eyes gradually adjusted to the dimness. She walked beside Matt while he explained more about his trip.

"You should see it, Caroline. The higher you go up the mountains, the closer to winter you get. When I finally went lateral, it was like it was a whole month ahead of the season we're having down here. The ground was already covered with leaves, and the trees were all bare and that kind of gray color they get when all the sap is down."

They passed a series of open horse stalls and stopped at an open, hay-strewn spot at the center of the barn.

"Well, what do you think?" He looked to Caroline in anticipation.

Caroline stared down at the boxy, light brown body and the black eyes encircled by lighter fur. It had those same long eyelashes. Bending down, she gently touched the antlers, the pointed muzzle. She tried to close the eyelids, but they had already stiffened. Somewhere above her, Matt was talking about using a Sturm, Ruger with a Simmons scope, but Caroline wasn't listening. She stood up and regarded him, wide-eyed.

"Beautiful, isn't it?" Matt suggested.

"It's disgusting."

"No." He was surprised, but his enthusiasm remained unabated. "That's one beautiful buck!"

"Are you *proud* of that?" Her tone was flat and much too calm. It held the same kind of tight-reined reserve her mother's voice used to have when she or Celeste had done something seriously wrong.

"Yes, of course I'm proud of it. I stalked that wily old buck for three days straight. I set up the stand last year. I played cat and mouse with him one night till dawn. You bet I'm proud of him."

"You've got plenty of money." Caroline's voice remained level. "Why couldn't you buy your meat at the IGA?"

"I didn't kill it to eat it."

"Then that's even more disgusting. What'd you do, kill it just to see it die?"

"No, goddamn it!" He grabbed each set of antlers with both hands and lifted the buck's head.

Caroline saw that the fur was creamy white around the neck, making it seem as if the buck wore a wide collar. His black nose flared wide and his crown of antlers were gray and full. Even though the animal was dead, Caroline cringed to see Matt pulling at it like that.

"Look at the span of those antlers," Matt continued. "It's a trophy buck. And look at *him*. The weight is right, the legs are perfect." His mind suddenly pictured the buck's particular grace, the spectacular leaps that suspended him as if airborne until the effortless dive back to earth. "This is a magnificent animal."

"It's a *dead* magnificent animal."

"You don't get it, do you? I tracked this deer for three days. I got to know him. Besides being in the trophy class, he was sly, too. His movements were always deliberate. He never lingered and he could stand utterly motionless for hours. He knew the places I couldn't or wouldn't penetrate. He was cagey enough to glide noiselessly through the brush when I took a cat-nap, and he even shifted his daytime routine to a night-time routine and then back again, to throw me off. I know that, really, he was simply programmed by nature to be the master of his habitat, that his choice of action was nothing more than a repetition of whatever defenses worked for him before, but . . ." Matt shook his head. "This one—I could have sworn that this one was actually smart."

"You admired this deer?" Caroline remained overly calm.

"Of course I did. I respected him." Matt remembered how he'd finally surprised the tired buck. Hiding behind a log, he had him square in his sights before the buck even realized it. The buck stood there facing Matt, staring, sensing that it was too late to flee. After the shot, Matt knelt by the animal's head and touched the eyeballs to make sure it was dead. Remembering the Indian custom, he apologized to the buck and then thanked him.

"Okay," Caroline said. "Let me get this straight. You respected its size and its cunning. You respected it so much that you killed it. In fact, you went out purposely to find not just any old ordinary buck, but one of nature's finest bucks just for the purpose of blowing it away."

"It's a trophy buck."

"Okay. You killed it because it had nice antlers." Her voice was cool. She gave him a penetrating look that clearly implied that she thought of him on the same level as a writhing mass of maggots.

"Caroline, you don't understand." Matt shook his head in disappointment. He was sorry he'd asked her over and angry, too. He looked down at the buck and then back to Caroline, who was doing her best to look politely distant.

"No." She shook her head and frowned sadly at the buck's sunken eyes. Her voice turned civil and businesslike—a stranger's voice. "That is something I'll never understand." Her eyes flashed at Matt, and again they were filled with ill-concealed revulsion. Looking one more time with overt dismay at the buck, she whispered, "Matt, I think I've seen enough." She turned on her heel and walked out of the barn.

Cursing to himself, he, too, regarded the buck once more. Well, damn it all, this was the best hunting achievement of his whole life, and here she was throwing a wet blanket over it. Why the hell couldn't she see beyond that childish Bambi stuff? Surely she knew that life wasn't like that. Why couldn't she look beyond all those silly, sentimental opinions of hers and at least make an open-minded attempt to look at it from someone else's point of view? Hell, even the buck was capable of that. Matt looked out the barn door, but she was nowhere in sight. He glanced back at the buck and thought about having to dress him pretty soon.

Meanwhile Caroline, having marched to the end of

Matt's driveway, turned down the road toward home. It would be a long walk, but she was so busy grumbling to herself that she hadn't noticed yet. She couldn't, for the life of her, understand it. How could someone she considered a friend—a good friend—someone who shared her own basic sensibilities—how could he *do* something like that? Had she judged him all wrong? After all, her talent for judging people—men in particular—had never been any too good. No. She remembered the moth. "I don't get it," she mumbled to herself as she tramped down the center line of the blacktop. Here was a man who went out of his way to free an ugly moth, only to turn around and cold-bloodedly gun down a beautiful deer. It was absurd. He was absurd. No, he was worse than absurd. Only a heartless person could kill like that. She found a rock and kicked it as she trudged forward. Her house looked so small from this distance.

She was wearying fast when she heard the engine behind her. Scowling, she stomped ahead.

Matt paced the truck's speed so he could talk as she went on. "It's a long walk. Let me drive you home."

"No thanks." Her legs were fatigued, but she pushed them on at a brisker rate.

"Caroline, don't be so bullheaded. It'll take you thirty minutes to walk it."

"I don't mind," she said without looking at him. "And I am not bullheaded."

"Hah! You bet you are."

"Well, at least . . ." She walked faster to get away from the truck. When he caught up, she stopped short and turned to him. "At least I'm not a murderer." She returned her steps and attention to the blacktop.

"I am not a murderer, Caroline. I'm a hunter. There's a big difference."

"Until that buck has a rifle to aim at you, Matt, you're a murderer." Secretly she was pleased to see him punch his fist against the steering wheel, but she didn't show it.

"Do you want a ride or not?"

"Thank you, no."

"Fine."

She heard the truck's tires squeal and then barrel away, but she refused to look. By the time she got home she was thoroughly worn out and had a throbbing headache.

That night there was a terrific windstorm. It began as a long, drawn-out wail that sighed, melancholy, all around the house. Caroline felt that it sounded as if ghosts were moaning and scolding. Soon the winds howled and gusted at an alarming velocity. At their apex, the roaring sounded like an airplane taking off and all the windows in the house whined like an orchestra of high-pitched kazoos.

It stopped as suddenly as it had come. Caroline walked outside into the stillness. She was greeted by a new, winter cold, along with the most startlingly fresh, pine-spiced air she had ever breathed. A group of coyotes howled in a distant, mournful chorus as if in echo of the windstorm. Caroline wondered what made them cry so sorrowfully. Even when they joined in with other coyotes, they still sounded so utterly lonesome.

CHAPTER

17

*C*AROLINE STOOD INSIDE the doorway of the high school auditorium. The season's first blizzard certainly hadn't hindered a heavy turnout for the town meeting. She pulled off her mittens and looked around.

"Howdy," said a voice that approached from somewhere beside her. "You need a place to sit?"

She looked up to see Jody removing his cowboy hat and grinning eagerly.

"Yeah." She returned the grin and let him escort her down the aisle. When they found two seats, he helped her off with her coat and they settled in.

"I've never been to a town meeting before," Caroline said. "What are they like?"

"They're okay." Jody chewed energetically on some gum. "Mostly it turns into a big long argument and no one ends up agreeing about anything."

"Do you get to vote?"

"I don't think so. Or else they do it later. I'm not sure." He tossed his head to sweep the golden hair from his eyes. "You want some gum?"

Caroline accepted a piece of Hawaiian Punch–flavored bubble gum and looked around. There were more people here than she'd seen in quite a while. Mostly men in plaid flannel shirts and sleeveless down-quilted vests sat on the auditorium's theater seats. The baseball caps had been changed for woolen hats with earflaps. The expressions under the hats had changed, too. Wintertime had altered many of the relaxed and sociable faces of Hawkeye into faces, not unfriendly, but faces braced to meet whatever the weather held in store.

Caroline looked toward the stage and then behind her. Slouched deep on the corner seat of the last row was Earl Bullchild, surveying the crowd while twirling a toothpick in his mouth. In the rows behind her, Caroline spotted Matt, who was joking with a cluster of townsfolk much older than he. Matt's easy rapport with the next generation didn't surprise Caroline at all. If he saw Caroline, he didn't acknowledge it.

When she faced forward again, Jody took her hand, twined his warm, callused fingers with hers, and smiled, saying nothing. Caroline smiled silently, too, content to listen in on nearby conversations. There was talk of cordwood: who of the local timbermen slipped too much birch into their loads; who sold wood so green an ax bounced off rather than split it; who was charging too much. And, of course, there was talk about the blizzard: eight inches at six P.M. and still snowing strong.

On the stage, the members of the town council

filed in, followed by Mayor Gaynor, a short, retired postmaster dressed in two-tone gray checkered pants, a profoundly green sport jacket, and black galoshes. They sat facing the auditorium alongside three representatives, already seated, from Sanborne, Inc. Caroline recognized Norris Nims, who had traded his John Denver costume for a conservative business suit, a near match to the other two Sanborne reps. As Caroline studied Nims and his colleagues busy themselves with papers and a display easel, she recalled that Nims never did follow up on his land offer.

Mayor Gaynor spoke into the microphone to welcome everyone, then turned the meeting over to the Sanborne representatives.

They began by showing color slides of Sanborne projects already established in Canada and Minnesota, then distributed colorful brochures describing the incineration system that would turn trash into electricity. Most of the proposal was what Matt had already explained to Caroline last summer. She listened to the slick sales pitch completely aware, from her own past profession, of every well-plotted persuasion technique Sanborne was plying to sway the people of Hawkeye into acceptance. The news of a towering smokestack belching soot was couched cleverly between tax relief statistics and suggestions that Hawkeye be grateful for the myriad jobs the fifty-million-dollar investment would create. The three reps from Sanborne cited new jobs for plant workers, truckers, construction crews, service industries, and businesses. They invited the town council to talk to other Sanborne towns, where the incinerator was the savior of languishing economies.

Caroline had to hand it to them, they had a top-notch public relations department on their side. She sneaked a peek behind her to see what Matt's reaction was to all this, but his face told nothing. The rest of the faces in the crowd told plenty, though. My God, she thought in surprise, they're buying it! Facing the San-borne reps once more, she sincerely tried to listen more objectively, not from a newcomer's point of view, but from a native Hawkeyean's point of view.

As the proposal reached its conclusion, Nims took the forefront, his face much paler than last summer, and drove his message home. "Ladies and gentlemen, today we are offering you the rare opportunity to improve the very quality of your lives and of the lives of future generations. We at Sanborne are pleased to be able to present Hawkeye with the chance to save our precious environment and to do something positive about the ever-growing dilemma of Montana's shrinking land-fills." Nims paused in what could have been inter-preted as deep humility before his final statement. "There is no one around Hawkeye whose life would not be enriched from this worthy project."

With Sanborne Inc. at the head of that list, thought Caroline cynically. She wished for a moment that she was on speaking terms with Matt, if only to share her opinion of the bill of goods she just heard. Instead, though, she watched as Mayor Gaynor began the ques-tion and answer period. Bob Fairbanks, Jr., stood up with the first question.

"What about air pollution?"

"There would be no air pollution." Nims smiled.

"Aw, come on," Fairbanks replied. "Your brochure, here, talks about burning three hundred tons of rubbish a day."

"There would be a negligible amount of soot introduced into the atmosphere, and it would dissipate with the wind."

"Exactly what do you mean by soot?" It was Leon, the butcher from the IGA.

"Ash, sir."

"What's *in* the ash?"

"It's just an acid ash, completely nontoxic, that escapes up the smokestack. The bulk of it stays in the incinerator and is cleaned out daily."

"What do you do with the bulk of the ash?" Leon's normally jovial voice boomed in seriousness.

"We bury it."

"Where?"

"On several local Sanborne properties."

Oh, shit, thought Caroline, remembering Mackenzie's deal.

"What's to prevent it from draining underground into the water supply?" continued Leon.

"No, sir, it will not affect either land or water," answered Nims.

The next voice was Irwin Corwell's. "I have a question," said the postmaster with the Pepperidge Farm accent. "And that is, shouldn't Hawkeye get free electricity for bein' the host town tah all this trouble?"

"It's possible that Hawkeye might want to exchange free electricity for a commensurate break on Sanborne property taxes. . . ."

"How tall is the smokestack?" was the next question from somewhere on the left.

"Sixty feet," answered Nims.

"What happens when there's no wind to blow this ash away?" asked the voice from the left. "Aren't we trading our health for money?"

"No," Nims stated firmly. "It's completely safe."

"How does three hundred tons of garbage a day get here?" Caroline recognized Matt's deep voice.

"Trucks will haul it in from Butte, Helena, and Missoula," Nims answered cheerfully.

"Have you designated which road they'll use?" Matt asked.

"We have a few in mind."

"How much traffic does that mean?"

"That"—Nims took a deep, and serious-sounding breath—"will ultimately depend on the implementation ratio of truck tonnage to the amount of usable roads within the designated radius."

"How many trucks a day does it take to bring in three hundred tons of garbage?" Caroline, if no one else, heard the edge to Matt's tone.

"I would have to check on that for you, sir."

"Would it be more than one hundred trucks daily?" Matt pressed.

"I have no current figures to date."

"More than one hundred fifty daily?"

"Regrettably, sir, I have no data pertaining to your question."

"Say we had a ballpark figure of between one hundred to one hundred fifty trucks rumbling in and out of Hawkeye every day. Would you agree, roughly, to those numbers?"

"That could possibly be correct, sir," Nims replied less cheerfully than before.

"Then," Matt asked pointedly, "doesn't that mean

one hundred to one hundred fifty trucks' worth of diesel exhaust, noise, road repair, and traffic we will all have to look forward to?"

Up to this moment, the other two representatives had been silent. Now one of them rose and replied flatly, "Sanborne will do its best to route the haulage as far away from the population center as permits."

Caroline turned to see Matt arch a skeptical eyebrow to this reply. Turning back, she saw that Matt's silent response hadn't been lost.

"Sanborne would also be prepared," the representative added in a monotone, "to pay for certain selected roads to be widened. Next question?"

"Is the garbage they're gonna truck in," Sally from the Bitterroot wanted to know, "is it like everyday garbage from people's houses, or is it industrial garbage?"

"Both." Nims retook the helm. "The incinerator can handle anything that isn't governmentally graded sludge or toxic."

Up in front, a young man in a grimy jacket turned to the audience and spoke up next. "I don't think we should let them do to Hawkeye what they did to Butte!"

"Do you have a question, sir?" Nims asked.

"Look what happened to them," the young man continued. "The people in Butte are the worst off than anyone 'cause they depended on the mines and nothin' else. And then when the mines closed, so did all the jobs. There's nothin' left there."

Mayor Gaynor interrupted the young man. "If you don't have a question, Hank, I have to ask you to please refrain from speaking out."

Hank plopped onto his seat, and Earl Bullchild stood up. He spoke in a quiet, dignified voice that belied his looks. "I want to know if the jobs are going to be permanent." He slipped the toothpick back into his mouth and waited.

"Yes, young man." Nims smiled. "The in-plant jobs and the trucking jobs are all on a permanent basis with medical and dental benefits. The construction jobs will end with the completion of the plant, but you could always be rehired by then as a plant worker."

Earl nodded as if in approval, and the questions continued with Paul Grandmaison.

"What if some crooked trash company decided to slip some toxic waste in with the regular trash? How would you know?"

"We conduct spot checks from time to time." Nims nodded jovially at the crowd.

"But," Grandmaison continued, "that's only spot checks, and it's our children breathing this stuff and getting cancer. How can you guys guarantee that every truck coming into our town isn't carting toxic waste in along with the potato peels?"

Nims looked at his colleagues, then said, "Well, I suppose we could conduct an in-plant check."

"You mean you'd have people sifting through three hundred tons of garbage a day?" Grandmaison asked.

"It's something we would have to look into, sir," Nims answered pleasantly. "We will definitely get back to you with an answer, however, before the vote next July."

A nod from Nims to the mayor indicated that the question and answer period was over. The meeting concluded with the promise of another one in a few months and an auditorium full of people with split opinions. Caroline knew she was dead set against San-borne's project, but, still, as she looked around at the people filing out, she wondered how many of those who had remained silent during the meeting were just as silently hopeful along with Earl Bullchild. Turning to Jody, she asked what he thought about it all.

"It's a real tough one to call." Jody wasn't grinning. "And you just know that if Sanborne doesn't get the okay here, then they're bound to get it somewheres else." Broad shoulders shrugged fatalistically. He gave Caroline's hand a gentle squeeze. "As I see it, we can live eighty miles downwind from the one they build in the next town. We'd still be breathing the stuff, and it'd be us who'd be paying them to take our garbage away. Or else we can put up with one here and at least get some jobs and electricity out of the deal." He looked at Caroline with a Charlie Brown smile. "Sometimes, there's no winning."

CHAPTER

18

DURING THE WEEKS THAT followed the town meeting, Caroline saw a lot of Jody. He was with her as she drove her shiny, new, dark green Bronco out of the Ford dealers and with her as she first drove in the boxy four-by-four. After she'd steered down all the roads around Hawkeye, Jody asked for a turn at the wheel. On impulse, he drove them all the way up to Missoula. They walked around the Ag Hall displays at the university, where Jody talked about his plans for improving his herd, and then they ate at the McDonald's in town. Caroline hadn't had a Big Mac in what felt like decades, and she savored it as if it were a delicacy from a gourmet restaurant. Afterward Jody took her to a car race held on packed snow. High speed was out of the question, but the cars compensated by skidding, spinning around, and careening sideways off each other in a truly spectacular fashion. Caroline had

a great time and began to see that, as Jody's shyness
finally wore off, there was a certain recklessness to his
nature.

They spent Thanksgiving at Caroline's, and although Caroline's culinary skills were bumbling and
uncertain, Jody was complimentary enough to make her
feel comfortable. While the turkey cooked they went
sledding, with Jody steering them down the steep, tree-
encumbered slopes. Each time Caroline was both relieved and invigorated when they would finally crash at
the bottom of the hill. They returned to the house
breathless, red-cheeked, and encrusted with layers of
snow. Caroline's Thanksgiving dinner was of dubious
quality, but Jody regaled it as a sumptuous feast, right
down to the soupy pumpkin pie with the soggy crust.
Afterward they nestled together on the cranberry
couch, watched the Chicago Bears trounce the Detroit
Lions, and fell asleep, tired and full, in each other's
arms.

Jody was back on Saturday afternoon with a dozen
bottles of dry gas for the Bronco and a bemused expression at Humphrey sleeping on the floor in front of the
bottom refrigerator vent.

"What's so funny?" Caroline asked, seeing Jody's
broad grin.

"Oh, nothin'." Jody snapped his gum vigorously.
"It's just the idea of keeping cats inside the house." He
beamed at Caroline, carefully opened the refrigerator
door so as not to disturb the cat, and peered inside.
"You have any plans for this stuffing?"

They sat at the marble table and picked at the array
of leftovers while they talked—Jody, of winter ranching

chores; Caroline, of her plans to hire Earl Bullchild to split some wood and kindling for her.

"Steer clear of that kid," Jody cautioned, abruptly out of character.

"Why?" Caroline was taken aback. She'd never seen Jody scowl before.

"He's got a record. A couple of years ago he was arrested for arson, but they had to let him go."

"Did he do it?"

"They couldn't prove anything, but it sure looked like he did. As far as anyone could piece together, Earl was paid to start the fire by some guy who eventually collected a whole lot of insurance money."

"Is that what they said in court?"

"No, but that's what everyone in Hawkeye said." Jody wrestled a wing off the turkey.

"Well, then, that's nothing but gossip," Caroline replied indignantly.

"Maybe. Maybe not," Jody said while trying hard to swallow the overcooked meat. "But the guy is bad news, believe me. Don't let him over here. I'll be glad to chop the wood for you."

Caroline didn't answer. Her gut feeling about the Indian kid remained unchanged, except that now she felt even more sorry for him than before. She almost launched into an argument in favor of Earl, but something told her not to. Changing the subject, she clunked a compacted heap of stuffing onto her plate and regarded Jody thoughtfully.

"Jody, do you hunt?"

"Uh-huh. Rabbits and pheasant. I only take down one deer a year, though, 'cause I'm not too crazy about venison."

"Do you hunt for trophy bucks?"

"Yeah, sometimes, if I can get enough time to devote to it." He smiled at her quizzically. "Why?"

"Oh, I don't know. I guess it's kind of like you seeing cats in the house." She looked at the watery puddles on top of the pumpkin pie and wrinkled her nose. "Do you want a slice of this pie?"

"Sure," he said, gulping.

When Jody drove off that evening, Caroline watched briefly as his beat-up black farm truck retreated down the snowy blacktop. Her thoughts had already turned inward by the time she started clearing off the kitchen table. Why didn't she mind very much that Jody was a hunter? Could she be getting used to the idea of people gunning down animals? She pondered this, but the answer was no. Probably the reason she wasn't annoyed with Jody was that he had common sense enough not to show her the eyes of his killing.

"When I was a kid, we called December the Moon of Winter Cold," Winona said.

"No doubt about that," Caroline replied, remembering the snow she'd driven through to get to the Banes' house today.

"On the other hand," Winona continued, "it's also the Moon That Parts Her Hair Right Square in the Middle. That's because December marks the end of the shortest days of the year and the beginning of the longer ones. So, look at it this way," Winona said cheerfully. "Winter is halfway over."

Caroline looked out Winona's kitchen window at

the Baneses' small herd of Herefords huddled together against the cold, up to their knees in snow.

Winona followed Caroline's gaze, then added, "Well, nearly halfway over."

Caroline and Winona were spending a comfortable day together, talking about knitting, quilting, recipes, and local news. Caroline was glad that Winona enjoyed this kind of feminine exchange as much as she did. It was the one thing Caroline truly missed about her life in St. Louis.

Ray entered the kitchen, stomping snow off his boots and scratching the ebullient Tyrone under his ears. The three of them sat down to apple strudel and coffee. As Caroline bit into the flaky sugar-sprinkled pastry and the warm, just-the-right-side-of-firm apples, she confirmed something that she'd been noticing on each of her successive visits: Ray, when he wasn't completely taciturn, was at best gruff to those he spoke to; but around Winona there was something altered in his nature. The man whose favorite phrase for his loggers was "I don't give a rat's behind if . . ." was transformed to gentleness in the company of his wife. And today, as they sat in the warm, apple-scented kitchen, Ray entertained them with stories about his younger days when he did "cowboy work" for the cattle roundups.

Winona told stories, too, about growing up on a lamb ranch, about the haying season, and about each year's first frantic lamb drive when her sheepman father and the hands would work around the clock. Winona spoke of her mother, a woman named Pretty Robe, of her own middle, Nez Percé name, Keeps the Fire, which was given to her on her tenth birthday, and how, despite the polio that kept her alone at home throughout much of her childhood, she always had the company of everyone in Hawkeye because she was able to "listen in" on the telephone's all-county party line.

Late afternoon came quickly, and soon Caroline traded the warm security of Winona's kitchen for the snowy road back home. Driving, Caroline smiled at the bright red ribbon Winona had made her tie to the rearview mirror: good luck for a new vehicle, according to Winona. As she steered toward the ridge outside of Hawkeye, Caroline could tell where houses were scattered on the wooded mountainside by the solitary strings of rising chimney smoke. They reminded her of her own recent trial-and-error attempts at woodstove heating. Immediately her thoughts became wholly occupied with the hope that the huge logs she'd wedged into both woodstoves before she left today had been enough to keep her water pipes unfrozen. This attention to winter, Caroline was coming to realize, was serious business.

Besides the attention that the Montana cold was demanding, the solitude of winter was also something that Caroline was gradually coming—and sometimes not coming—to terms with. It simply wasn't easy to go anyplace anymore, not when you knew you had only the time it took for your fattest log to burn down, or when snow, swirling like a maelstrom, could strand you up to your radiator before you made it home, or when random bursts of howling winds could speedily plummet the temperature into negative digits.

As a result, Caroline was now spending her time indoors. She was glad she had started the quilt. The concentric Log Cabin blocks were all done, and she began the task of sewing them together into one big quilt top. Looking out the windows of her sewing studio, she paused to view the once magnificent vista of sky and land, today reduced to a bleak swath of gray and white. The windows she looked through were iced up around the edges, and that, combined with the knowledge that her farmhouse was buried in a sea of drifting snow, added to her feeling of isolation. Remembering that this morning the kitchen door had to be defrosted open with a hair dryer only accentuated the feeling.

Lately Caroline had been waking up earlier and earlier in the mornings. Her ice-cold nose forced her out of bed to build fires in both the living room and kitchen woodstoves. Days, she spent quilting and talking to Winona every so often, although more via the telephone than in person. Evenings, she had the companionship of her cats and the television. It was the commercials from the Great Falls channel—the ones for Red Lobster, J. C. Penney, and Taco Bell: the stuff of the real world, the reminder that there was so much more out there, always so far beyond her reach—that gradually began to turn her sense of isolation into a full-blown case of cabin fever.

That night, wrapped in an afghan, anchored by two sleeping cats, knowing just how much cold would chill her when she got up from the couch to feed the woodstove, and possessed by an insane craving for a flame-broiled Whopper with Cheese—to the point of imagining precisely how the extra pickles would taste on it—Caroline vowed that no matter what the weather conditions were tomorrow, she absolutely *had* to get out of the house.

It turned out to be a no-win situation. The next afternoon Caroline walked, shin deep, through a thick white blanket of snow while her sense of isolation increased with every step. She was trying to follow a blacktop road that had all but disappeared. Her only guidelines were the ridges of once plowed snow that paralleled either side. Quite sure that she was the only traveler on the pure white path, she walked down its very center. She had, she realized, simply traded the solitary, hemmed-in feeling of isolation of cabin fever for an equally solitary, adrift sort of feeling of isolation in the vast outdoor void. She felt like a single ant on a beach—except for the temperature.

She wasn't uncomfortably cold. The long walk had warmed her, and she'd dressed for the outing in her pink quilted eiderdown parka. For all the snow she'd trekked through, Caroline had made it all the way to the foot of the first mountain. She stood there now, wondering if the road was any clearer under the tunnel of pine trees that arched over the ascent. She thought about the steepness of the climb and concluded that she'd had enough exercise for one day. She pivoted in her boots and began her return home. Realizing how far she had to go suddenly made her feel a little tired.

It was late afternoon, the time when dusk crept up steadily but imperceptibly on a cloudy gray day. As Caroline trudged on, it began to half drizzle, half snow in a dreary mist that further quieted the muffled hush already enveloping her. The bare trees on the horizon began to lose their distinctive skeletal lines, giving way to a cold, blue-gray haze that veiled them as if phan-

toms. Now she was tired. Now she was beginning to
prefer cabin fever over the great outdoors. Somewhere
within the muted silence, a coyote yowled loud, long,
and miserably. Caroline reached one hand into her coat
pocket and found the acorn Winona had given her. She
fingered it through the wool of her mitten, remembering
that no harm could come to a person harboring an
acorn. Quickening her wearying pace, she was glad she
was headed home.

The sky was turning the color of faded denim
when she heard the engine approaching. Turning
around, she saw in the distant gray blur a bright yellow
snowplow—the only discernible color in an otherwise
dulled landscape. It was coming down the mountain
road. As the plow approached, Caroline saw that it was
attached to an equally bright red pickup. She edged to
one side of the road as Matt's truck came nearer. When
the engine rumbled close by, she turned her head to see
Matt pull up, his open window directly across from her.
They both stopped.

"You need a ride?" He neither frowned nor smiled.

"Thanks," Caroline answered quietly without
looking at him. She scurried around the truck and
climbed into a cab that smelled pleasingly of Matt's
spicy soap scent. She concentrated on clicking the seat
belt before finally facing him. "Thanks," was still all she
could think to say.

"Yup," he replied, and set the truck in motion.

Regarding Matt for a moment, Caroline realized
that it had been a long time: the last time she'd been
with him, he was in shirtsleeves. Today he wore a black
sheep's-hide rancher's jacket and amber buckskin mit-

tens. His wavy dark hair had water droplets sprinkled on it where fallen snow had melted.

Caroline pulled off her mittens and then her pink stocking hat. She shook her copper hair loose and looked straight out the windshield. Softly she said, "So, how have you been?"

"I've been okay." Matt's deep voice was guarded and serious.

"Mmmm," mumbled Caroline, nodding to compensate for her lack of words. The cab was warm and her thawing nose was beginning to drip.

After a while he asked quietly, "You?"

"Okay."

They drove on in awkward silence, Matt steering carefully down the snowpacked road, Caroline searching her coat pockets for a Kleenex. Finally it was Caroline who surprised herself by breaking the uncomfortable hush with a torrent of words. She hadn't a clue as to where they came from. Truly, she hadn't even pondered these thoughts before this very moment, but obviously they had been waiting there all along.

"You know, if I didn't value your friendship so much, then it wouldn't make a hill of difference to me if you went around shooting innocent animals or not." She found a Kleenex and paused to use it while Matt drove on with no expression to his face whatever.

Annoyed with her own lack of tact, Caroline continued. "I guess it's this—" She abruptly blew her nose again. "I've never really understood why anyone would want to hunt, you know?"

Matt's dark-lashed eyes narrowed slightly.

"And I always figured that the people who hunted were so far removed from me that I could easily be blind to how ugly it was because it had nothing to do with my life anyway." She knew she wasn't saying this well, but her words gushed out anyway. "And then you came along, Matt, and I'd never once thought that someone I liked so much could stoop to that." She sniffled, blew her nose, and looked confused. Even without looking at him, she scowled, knowing that she hadn't smoothed things out at all.

Matt steered the truck slowly around a curved hill. If he had an opinion about her outburst, he kept it hidden.

"I guess," Caroline finally blurted, her hands gesturing in frustration, "that it's a case of 'To each his own.' You're not going to change your mind about hunting, and I'm not, either. So let's forget it because the bottom line here is that we're friends and we're neighbors and I like you. And it just doesn't make any sense for us to be mad at each other."

Matt seemed to be thinking while Caroline watched him intently. He concentrated on driving but said nothing, and his expression, as far as Caroline could read it, remained pensive. The truck rose and fell over the first of the roller-coaster hills.

Caroline turned her gaze back to the road and sat there, disgruntled. She blew her nose again even though she didn't need to, smoothed her mittens out on her lap, and continued to wait, vaguely aware that the truck was slowing down. Matt downshifted, eased it to a stop, and parked it in the middle of the road. In one swift movement he had unclicked his seat belt and slid across the seat, the front of his bulky sheep's-hide jacket pressing gently into the quilted padding of her coat. His soft mustache tickled as silky lips descended upon and covered hers, gently at first, the closeness of his face warm. His kiss lingered, becoming steadily stronger while Caroline's wide-eyed alarm ebbed away to be replaced by a fluttery feeling from deep within. Matt's moist lips played over hers carefully, sustaining and prolonging the kiss. When at last, in slow, purposeful increments, he withdrew, Caroline found herself wishing that he wouldn't. Instead Matt edged away from her, although all the while their eyes held.

"I like you, too." Matt's resonant voice was at the same time playful and sincere. Breaking the mood, he flashed his Cheshire cat's smile at her, slipped into his seat belt, and wordlessly resumed driving.

The roller-coaster stretch of road combined with Caroline's own tumult of inner emotions kept her as quiet as Matt for the rest of the ride. What had just happened confounded her, astonished her—and not solely because of Matt's actions, either. She was just as befuddled by her own response. No one, she kept thinking to herself as the road rose up and down, no one has ever made me feel like *that* before. She stole a glance at Matt. He was driving, as relaxed and casual as could be. He looked for all the world as if nothing unusual had happened between them except for the slight, nearly imperceptible smirk beneath his mustache.

CHAPTER

19

"*R*EADY?" MATT ASKED.

"I guess so," said Caroline. She was beginning to shiver.

They were standing behind the double set of sliding glass doors that led out to the side deck on Matt's house. Outside, it was a cold, clear, moonlit night. It was barely fifteen degrees out there, Caroline knew, and here she was, clad only in her swimsuit with a thick Turkish towel wrapped around her. Looking down at her toes, she saw that they were tinged with blue.

"Are you sure we won't turn to ice out there?" she asked.

"No, not at all. Once you're in it, it's warm."

Caroline's eyes narrowed in suspicion. "This isn't going to involve whacking ourselves with birch trees, is it?"

"Just follow me," Matt replied. "Okay?"

"Okay," she answered dubiously. The steaming hot tub at the end of the deck looked awfully far away.

Matt slid open the glass door. Instantly a wall of bone-chilling, glacial air engulfed them.

"Jeez, Matt! It's freezing out there!" Caroline's teeth began to chatter.

Suddenly Matt tightened his Turkish towel around him and sprinted across the wooden deck. He flung the towel across a nearby bench, revealing a flash of navy swim trunks on a sinewy physique. In one fluid movement he sat at the edge of the hot tub and slid in up to his chin. He moved around the tub to where he could face her. Just above the waterline, Matt's ear-to-ear grin was so energetic that, for a split second, Caroline suspected it. Maybe the water was cold and this was Matt's idea of a joke? Sometimes she still didn't know what to expect from him.

"Come on in." Matt beamed at her. "It's great."

Caroline took a deep, invigorating breath and then followed Matt's example. The water was hot—almost scalding in comparison with the piercingly frigid air she'd just run through—but she welcomed it. Caroline found and sat on a submerged bench that encircled the inside of the hot tub. She could have sat up straight, but instead she slouched down low, keeping all but her head within the water's soothing heat. Steam rose from the surface of the swirling water in a dancing mist. It tickled Caroline just under her nose. From somewhere inside the tub, jets of water shot into the tub, gently churning the water in a natural whirlpool The water, Caroline realized, was still very hot, even after her body temperature got used to it. It was the kind of heat that could loosen every muscle in your body and then go on to warm your very marrow. Caroline gladly relinquished herself to it. Looking across the water to Matt, she smiled in appreciation.

"Not bad, huh?" he said.

"Mmmm," Caroline murmured. "This is wonderful." Slouching farther down, she tilted her head and let the water eddy around the nape of her neck.

Across from her, Matt described how he had first discovered the natural, bubbling hot spring and built his house beside it. Resting her head on the tub's edge, Caroline closed her eyes and smiled more lazily. She liked the low-toned quality of Matt's voice as he spoke to her. The deep sounds of his words were comfortable and relaxed, like the calm feeling that the hot, swirling water gave her. After all the buzz that had surrounded Christmas last week, this was the perfect balm.

Actually, Caroline now reflected, it wasn't Christmas so much as it was the buildup before Christmas that was the hassle. Trying to find gifts that were even halfway appropriate in a town that was never a shopper's paradise posed a challenge to Caroline. But as for Christmas itself, it had been a good day spent with good friends. Caroline had greeted and ushered out the holiday in the company of Matt, Winona, and Ray in the homeyness of the Baneses' house. The four of them had enjoyed a sumptuous afternoon meal prepared by Winona and then exchanged gifts. Later, while Ray leafed through *Hoof and Horns* magazine and Matt dozed in front of a television football game, Caroline and Winona talked and played cards in the kitchen.

They all grazed on the leftovers at dinnertime, and after Caroline and Matt took care of the dishes, the two of them went outside to take Tyrone for a walk. They'd spent a lot of time together lately, but while their friendship had reblossomed, Matt had shown absolutely no further romantic interest. This, Caroline firmly believed, was for the best. A comfortable chumminess had developed between them, and Caroline knew that she didn't want to lose it. It was far better, she was certain, and far safer to have Matt securely as her friend than to mess things up with anything beyond that. When she considered his comradely behavior of late, she was relieved to see that Matt felt that way, too. Besides, there was Jody, visiting his mother in Helena for the holidays, to consider.

The water in the hot tub prickled at Caroline's nostrils like the carbonation from a glass of ginger ale, and, after a time, the temperature seemed to rise. Caroline sat up so that the water was shoulder high. Looking skyward, she saw a display of stars shining brightly despite the glow from a full moon.

"Over there," said Matt, pointing straight up, "there's Perseus. And over to the right is Orion's belt and then Aquarius."

Caroline nodded when she found them. "Do you see that darkish spot on the moon?" She said, "Winona told me an Indian story of how it's really a frog that's sticking to the moon's face." She squinted at the moon in doubtful scrutiny. "I don't know. It sort of looks like a frog."

Matt smiled at her. "This water's getting way too hot." Abruptly he lifted himself halfway out of the tub and sat on its edge.

"You'll turn to ice," Caroline said.

"Nah, I must be a hundred and twenty degrees inside by now. Try it."

Caroline, too, felt as if she were being boiled alive. She sat at the tub's edge and dangled her legs in the water. It was weird to be sitting outside, exposed like that and surrounded by a snow-covered landscape, but it was refreshing and not at all cold. Looking across to Matt, she was about to tell him as much, but what she saw on his torso suspended her words. Long, raised, and ragged scars, at least four or five of them, criss-crossed Matt's chest and shoulders. Obviously they had been serious wounds at one time. Their haphazard design told that they were not the work of any surgeon.

"How'd you get *those?*" Caroline blurted.

"They're from a long time ago," he replied casually. He seemed unconcerned by her reaction.

The scars didn't look like "a long time ago" to Caroline. More gently this time, she rephrased her question. "Matt, what happened to you?"

"I had an accident."

"I'll say," she agreed. "A car accident?"

"No."

Caroline waited for, perhaps, an addition to his answer, but none came. "Motorcycle?"

"No."

She waited again. Staring at the biggest foot-long scar that traveled from his sternum over one broad shoulder, she finally asked, "Then what?"

"Bungee jumping," he answered calmly. "I was bungee jumping and the cord broke."

Caroline thought about this for a moment before asking, "Where?"

"From the Golden Gate Bridge."

"No one jumps from the Golden Gate Bridge."

"Okay. It was Tibet."

"Hooey."

"You're right, Caroline. It was really aliens. Fiendish, evil aliens." Matt shuddered convincingly. "They had powerful laser swords."

"I see," she replied patiently. "Green, bug-eyed, fiendish, evil aliens or the mutant, two-headed kind?"

"No. Strangely, they all looked like Elvis, only they were shorter."

"Was this in Tibet, too?"

"Edison, New Jersey."

"Of course." Caroline nodded while, to herself, she wondered why Matt wouldn't be straight with her. Often, lately, he had been falling into this mildly teasing style of conversation when he was uncomfortable with certain subjects. It was always amusing, but it was beginning to bother her. Regarding him seriously, she asked quietly, "What really happened?"

"I made some really big mistakes," Matt answered solemnly. "The bad part was this." He pointed to the scars. "But the good part was that it taught me a lesson I will never forget." He slipped off the edge of the tub, back into the water.

Silently Caroline did the same. Hot, swirling water engulfed her. Looking up at the snow white moon, she could clearly identify the frog-shaped blotch marring its face.

CHAPTER

20

*J*ANUARY, THE MONTH
Winona called the Moon That Helps Eat, was living up
to its name. Helps eat, Winona explained, because the
temperatures outside get so bitterly cold that everyone
has to stay indoors; and when people are inside and not
far away from food, they are always tempted to eat. So,
January helps the food get eaten faster. It was certainly
the case with Caroline. An empty pantry, plus the news
of a winter storm watch, sent her to Hawkeye to stock
up.

Inside the IGA, she meandered with her shopping
cart. She hadn't come with a list, so she was browsing
each aisle for things that appealed to her. She thumped
four boxes of fudge-nut brownie mix into the cart, then
wheeled it on. The IGA was crowded today. People
who had been imprisoned indoors for too long were
talking more than shopping, and the talk was about the

Sanborne Trash to Energy Project. A heated discussion of "lost rural character" versus "necessary growth" flared in one aisle. One of "I'm still listening" versus "I've heard so much, I don't know what to think" simmered in another. One thing was clear as Caroline traversed the supermarket aisles: people's opinions were well divided over the project.

Caroline heard the scuttlebutt, too: Sanborne was in cahoots with the local construction company; Sanborne was suing a town that had withdrawn approval of the project; Sanborne was actively purchasing more land around Hawkeye. Caroline had reason to believe the last rumor. The oily Norris Nims had repeated his buy-out offer to her twice since the town meeting—once in person and shortly after, via a breezily worded note on a Christmas card. With her shopping cart full, Caroline left the Great IGA Debate.

The sky was a thick blanket of steel gray clouds when she got home that afternoon. The air was so heavy, it felt as if the snow would bear down any minute. Not long after she'd rekindled the woodstoves and put the groceries away, Caroline heard a knock on the front door. Opening it, she found gathered on her porch an elderly man in a down vest and a crowd of schoolchildren, nylon backpacks hanging off them at various angles. Everyone was grinning except the man.

"I'm sorry to bother you, miss," he began before interrupting himself. He turned around to address two boys who were bopping each other with their lunch boxes. "Now settle down, you two, or we'll all be sleeping in the bus tonight." Returning to Caroline, he smiled courteously and continued. "The school bus broke down a ways past here. . . ."

"Oh," Caroline said. "Do you want to use the phone to call for another one?"

"There isn't another one," the bus driver explained, "and on accounta this storm that's about to hit, even if all their parents drove out here to get 'em, they might not make it home safe through the snow. So I was hoping you could put them up for the night."

Caroline looked at the gathering. There must be about twenty of them, she counted in alarm.

"Just the girls," the bus driver interjected. "I'm gonna take the boys over to Matt Van Zandt's place. I'll call to get the plows out here first thing in the morning and get the kids picked up for school."

"Okay," Caroline answered cheerfully, "sure." She looked at the smiling young faces and thought that, in fact, this might be fun. "Please come in." She opened the door. Eight girls, most of them from seven to nine years old, rushed into the living room, dropped their backpacks midrun, and, as if propelled by one mind, made for the two startled cats on the cranberry couch. Tinky escaped behind the pile of kindling that Earl Bullchild had recently stacked in one corner. Humphrey, however, was snatched by the moiling swarm and was receiving more attention, giggles, and baby talk than he'd had in his life.

The next morning, after a station wagon had picked up the girls, someone knocked at the front door. Splayed out on the couch, Caroline considered not answering it, but the knock persisted. Feebly she called, "Door's open."

Matt entered. He looked even more dazed and exhausted than Caroline.

"Wow," he said, marveling at the devastation. "It

looks like someone came through here with a giant eggbeater."

"You want a cup of coffee?" Caroline asked, ignoring his statement.

"Yeah." He tiptoed his way through jumbled pillows and heaps of twisted blankets strewn over the floor. "Do you have anything to eat? They cleaned me out."

The kitchen wasn't in any better shape. Evidence of brownie preparation covered nearly every flat surface. Caroline shoved a heap of eggshells and dirty mixing bowls to one side of the marble tabletop and set up the coffee along with a plate piled with rock-hard brownies.

"I think," Matt said, dunking his brownie into his coffee, "that everyone who ever entertains the idea of having a baby should have to have a bunch of kids overnight—just to make sure they know what they're getting into."

Caroline shook her head. "People would stop having families."

"I don't think so," Matt said. "It wouldn't stop me." He seemed lost in some inner train of thought. He didn't even seem to notice when Humphrey leaped onto his lap, although he petted the cat absentmindedly. Finally, after attempting to bite his still unsoftened brownie, he looked at Caroline, his expression pinched into disgust. "Eeeeew, these brownies are bogus, gross, and toxic."

"No way, dude." Caroline applied her new vocabulary. "Those brownies are mega-awesome."

"You learned well," Matt said, putting down the brownie and attending to the gray cat.

"I also learned," Caroline went on, "that if you point at a grave, your finger will rot off and that if a cat jumps over a grave, it will turn into a bloodsucking vampire. Can you tell we told ghost stories last night? What did your kids do?"

"Mostly they just talked about themselves and about the people in their families. I had to stop one boy. He started telling us this remarkably detailed account of an argument between his mom and dad, complete with a cast of some very crazy relatives." Matt shook his head and smiled. "That's what's so neat about kids. They're so forthright."

Caroline recalled the barrage of forthright questions the girls had had for her last night: How rich are you? Why did you come to Hawkeye? Are you going to marry Mr. Landis? And then there was that one little girl whose words still troubled Caroline.

"Matt?" Caroline asked. "Do you think I'm too much of an outsider to really belong in Hawkeye?"

"No. You live here just like anyone else." He looked at her curiously. "Why?"

"Well, there was this one little girl last night—she was really a sweet kid, and I'm sure she was only repeating what she heard at home—but she told me I was a stranger who had no right taking jobs away from people who'd lived in Hawkeye all their lives."

Matt frowned. "She—or rather, her parents—probably heard that you won't sell your land to Nims and they wish you would."

"Well, I don't know. I don't want to be the reason why people won't get the jobs they need. Maybe I should sell a portion of it."

"You're tired, Caroline," Matt said in his deep,

soothing voice. "And it's not just *your* property that's the keystone in this land buy-up. There're plenty of landowners all over the place who aren't selling out either. Sanborne's targeting you because they think you'll crumble the easiest under pressure."

"But what if Sanborne isn't successful and all those people are blaming me for the jobs they lost?"

"That's malarkey and you know it. Besides, do you really want to see Sanborne succeed?"

"No, not at all."

"Then stick to your guns. Don't let them bully you into feeling guilty enough to change your decision."

"Well, that's just it, Matt. Maybe I don't have as much right to make a decision on everybody else's fate. I mean, here I am, I just waltzed into Hawkeye last April, and there they are, people who have invested their entire lifetimes here."

"Do you live here in Hawkeye and no place else?" Matt asked patiently.

"Yes,"

"Do you plan on moving away?"

"No."

"Do you own land and pay taxes on that land?"

"Yes."

Didn't you tell me once that this was the only place left where it was safe for you to live without stress ruining your health again?"

"Yes."

"Then as far as I can see it, Caroline, this is your one and only home and you have as much right as anyone else to decide what happens to it." Matt glanced down briefly to smile at the cat asleep on his lap.

Caroline nodded slowly. There were times when

Matt could be dead wrong about things, but this wasn't
one of them. She was glad of his patient assurances and
the way he could corral her worries back into perspective. "Thanks," she said softly.

Matt pushed the plate of petrified brownies toward
her. "Have another?" he asked.

"No thanks." She smiled wryly. "They really are
bogus, gross, and toxic."

CHAPTER

21

"SORRY TO DRAG YOU up here," Ray began as soon as they each emerged from their respective pickup trucks, "but Winona said to be a hundred percent sure before breaking it to her."

Matt nodded in understanding. He followed his friend up the snowpacked road that led to Caroline's timberland. The morning light was pale, and his breath hung in clouds as they approached the entrance to the main logging trail. Although Ray didn't say so, Matt knew that Ray wanted it down before his men came to work today. Both men stopped when they saw it.

"Think it's hers?" Ray asked gruffly.

Matt made himself look hard at the stiff and blood-ied little gray cat. Its front paws were bound helplessly together by a rubber band. Its mouth was wide open in a frozen scream. It had died long and horribly, nailed eye level to a tree. "Goddamn it," Matt snapped. Even the seasoned hunter in him was repulsed by the sight.

"Is it Caroline's then?" Ray wanted to know.

Matt moved toward it warily. The bedraggled fur was gray with mackerel stripes just like Humphrey's, but its body seemed scrawnier. Still, considering what it had been through, it was hard to say. Matt tried to picture exactly what Humphrey looked like—all those times he'd hopped so trustingly onto Matt's lap to be petted. But all Matt could remember clearly was the cat's rumbling, satisfied purr. Goddamn it! Looking at the lifeless creature cruelly impaled on the tree, Matt thought that maybe its head and ears were smaller and its nose a little too pointy. Maybe this was some hapless stray cat, sacrificed because it was a close enough match—for the purpose of providing Caroline with a meaningful threat. He couldn't be sure. He checked for the familiar white flea collar. There was none, but it could have slipped off or been removed during the capture. Perplexed, Matt said quietly, "It's hard to tell."

"Should I tell her about it?" Ray asked. "Winona seems to think it could be a little tricky."

"Let me take care of it," Matt answered.

Ray looked relieved, but not entirely so. "There's something else," he said.

"What?" Matt turned to face Ray fully. He was glad not to have to look at the cat anymore.

"She's got a more serious problem with this lousy defoliation thing than we knew about before." Ray frowned as he explained. "The guys at the extension service say that there have been reports of this kind of defoliation from all over the state. Turns out, some timberland to the east got it earlier than here, so they sprayed. Same all-purpose spray we were planning on using next year." Ray paused for effect. "Didn't work. Now they're thinking it might be a virus and not a pest." Ray concluded in his typical style, "Spray doesn't work. Extension bozos can't identify it. There's the possibility that it can't be stopped."

"Have you told her?"

"Yep. And she took it on the chin." Ray made a slight motion with his head to indicate the tree with the cat. "But that was before this."

Matt answered with a nod. Both men, in their own way, wished that they could shield Caroline from the troubles that seemed to be raining down, but neither of them knew exactly what to do. Matt broke their silence at last. "I'll go visit her," he told Ray, "and see if, maybe, the cat's around or if she mentions him being missing."

"Good," said Ray. He turned away from Matt and proceeded to remove the stiffened animal from the tree.

Carefully Matt steered down the mountain road. He'd be at Caroline's soon. The sun was shining at an angle, reflecting pinkish white on the snowy plain that rolled ahead, but he didn't notice its beauty. He was planning things out. If the cat wasn't there, he'd stick around as long as he could in case it showed up. If Caroline mentioned that it was missing, he'd have to convince her that it could have gotten lost in the snow—and possibly died. He didn't relish telling her that. A picture of the crucified animal flashed gruesomely in his mind. Still, he decided, it was the lesser of two evils. Caroline could deal with the uncertainty of Humphrey's fate far better than she could deal with the knowledge of what really happened. The imperative to avoid stress that she'd told him about was nothing to sneeze at, Matt reminded himself. Apparently Ray and Winona had thought so, too.

Matt wondered what her limits were. Caroline presented herself as a strong and competent young woman, but he was beginning to see her vulnerabilities. Just how much stress could she withstand before her paralyzed nightmare began again? Unaware that he'd cast his habitual caution aside, Matt raced his truck faster down the road.

Caroline answered the front door in a bubbly mood. "You're just in time," she told him excitedly. "I finished the quilt. Come take a look."

She was wearing a pink chenille bathrobe and the stupidest slippers Matt had ever seen. They appeared to be fuzzy gray lop-eared rabbits with big buck teeth and googly eyes. Briefly Matt wondered why a seemingly sensible person would own slippers like that.

Caroline tromped the rabbits across a living room floor scattered with spools and sewing tools. The television blared out the morning newscast. Caroline snapped it off and, with a flourish of her arms, presented the quilt, draped over the couch. "Whaddya think?" she chirped brightly.

Matt regarded the patterned blanket bordered in dark green, his favorite color. The red, green, and white fabrics crafted into geometric strips made an attractive design. "You did a real fine job," he commented. To himself he mused that although she was the world's worst cook, she had considerable talent as a seamstress. "Real fine." He nodded appreciatively as Caroline, standing in those ridiculous slippers, enthusiastically disclosed her plans for her next, even bigger quilt. Matt smiled, touched by her girlish effervescence. Funny that he hadn't noticed before this, how simple and naive she actually was. While Caroline bubbled on, Matt surreptitiously sneaked some quick glances around the living room. Tinky, the black, aloofish cat, slept in a corner next to a pile of kindling sticks, her front paws folded tidily under her. There was no sign of Humphrey anywhere. Again Matt worried: Would losing Humphrey be the straw that broke the camel's back? Or would the next nasty threat Sanborne delivered be the one?

"Matt," Caroline spoke enthusiastically, "I made one of Winona's recipes last night—cherry streusel cobbler. Would you like to try it?"

"Sure," he answered bravely. He snatched one more searching look around the room, then followed her into the kitchen. The cobbler was a lumpy collage of white cake, gooey cherries in syrup, and, probably, some kind of icing, but it tasted pretty good. Matt was pleased not to have to rehydrate it in his coffee. Sitting at the marble kitchen table, he complimented Caroline on the recipe while taking notice of the two cat-food bowls on the floor near the broom closet. A few stray morsels remained in one bowl. The lump of cat food in the other hadn't been touched.

Looking across the table into Caroline's merry eyes, Matt opened the conversation with the other thing that had been on his mind all morning. "Ray told me the latest about your hardwoods."

"Yeah. Doesn't look too good."

Matt arranged the words in his mind beforehand. He took a slow, deliberate sip of black coffee so as to seem casual before speaking. "Tell me, has that Nims character been around lately, wanting to buy your land?"

"No." The merriment faded from Caroline's hazel eyes. "But Jack Mackenzie, of all people, wanted to buy me out. Jeez—you'd think there was gold on that land instead of a bunch of dying trees," Caroline said. "Mackenzie handed me this line about having second thoughts and wanting to go back into business again, and I almost believed him. But when he offered me the same exact price that Nims offered, I knew what he was up to and exactly who put him up to it."

"Was the offer any good?"

"They offered two and a half times what I paid for the land, if that's what you mean."

"Maybe . . ." Matt paused in order to look as earnest as possible. "Maybe you ought to sell."

Caroline regarded him questioningly before delivering her flatly stated, "No."

Her answer had the ring of finality, but all the same Matt saw Caroline's hand travel to her ear and nervously finger a plain gold earring. If he had merely sensed it before, he now knew for certain: cautioning Caroline about her susceptibility to stress—even though it was the very heart of the problem—was the wrong tack to take. He watched Caroline tug at the earring while he considered the familiar question. Exactly where did strong-willed resolve cross the border into self-destructive stubbornness? Matt had been around the block and back on that one and still hadn't found the answer.

"Two and a half times the price is a terrific offer," he said, trying to sound positive without overdoing it. "You could probably up the price to three times the amount and make a killing, Caroline. Then all you need to do is buy a new tract of timberland somewhere else— with money to spare."

Caroline smiled sweetly at Matt as if to thank him for the role he'd assumed for her sake. "The new tract would have the same problems. And selling my land would only make things that much easier for Sanborne to succeed. I'd still be living in Hawkeye, and their smokestack would be spewing all that junk."

"Oh, I don't know," Matt replied. "They practically swore on their mothers' graves that the air would be safe. They're probably telling the truth."

"You were at the town meeting," she answered. "You know what a bill of goods Sanborne's trying to foist on us." Caroline smiled wistfully. "Industry and all that comes along with it . . . that's not why either of us came to Montana."

Matt couldn't argue. From the corner of his eye he saw a cat's nose poke into the kitchen doorway. It was only Tinky. Returning his attention to Caroline, he said, "You know that Sanborne is going to keep harping at you to get you to sell."

"Yes, I know."

"They're dirty players. They could get dirtier."

"I wouldn't doubt it. But that would only make me dig my heels in deeper."

"And you know that the spray Ray was planning to use on your hardwoods doesn't work."

"Yes, I know."

"You could lose your entire hardwood crop."

"Yes, I know that, too. But even if the worst happened and my hardwoods were wiped out completely—and they probably won't go completely, a percentage of them are bound to survive—I'd still have the pine trees to see me through."

"You'd lose an awful lot of money if you had to go with your softwoods alone. The whole state's got this defoliation problem. The market's going to be glutted with softwood. Maybe you ought to get out while you can." All of a sudden Matt thoroughly believed in what he was urging Caroline to do. "Caroline, you could go broke with this."

Caroline continued to twirl her earring, but a look of resolve had settled on her face. "It's really very simple. When I first came to Hawkeye, I was committed to staying because I promised myself I would stay. But now I'm realizing that living in Hawkeye is kind of like that quilt I just finished."

"Uh-huh," Matt replied, trying not to sound completely bewildered.

"I really worked hard on that quilt. And I cursed it an awful lot, too, because it was a brand-new skill and most of the time I didn't know what I was supposed to be doing. But I put so much time into it that now it feels as if that whole quilt is a part of my life—like Hawkeye. I've invested so much time and effort in it that I'm willing to stick around and take my chances." She smiled into Matt's eyes.

"Are you sure?"

"Hold on a minute." She got up from the table and opened the kitchen door to let Humphrey trot in, his tail straight up. She shuffled back toward Matt in her silly slippers. "Am I sure?" she repeated Matt's question. "I'm positive."

An unexpected wave of relief rushed over Matt as he looked across the table at the combination of Caroline's disheveled copper hair and resolute expression. Humphrey vaulted onto Matt's lap and began to purr.

CHAPTER

22

MATT SLIPPED A CAS-
sette tape into the truck's player as he started down the
road for Hawkeye. The recent dustings of snow had
finally abated, leaving the big sky cloudless in an infinite azure expanse. Matt's appreciative mood soured,
however, when he drove past Caroline's house. Jody
Landis's black heap of a truck was parked in her driveway again. Matt scowled. That made the third time that
he'd driven by and Jody had been there. Jody was wearing his welcome thin, Matt observed, unless of course
he was there at Caroline's invitation. Annoyed, Matt
turned the tape up louder and drove into Hawkeye with
the music blaring.

Toward evening, Matt drove home from Hawkeye
even more annoyed than before. The April weather was
still ice cold, but the sky was beginning to look as if
springtime might make an appearance. The sunset Matt

headed into was illuminated by a mass of low-lying, cotton-ball clouds reflecting rose to dusky blue as the warm front pushed its way toward Hawkeye. But Matt gave no more than cursory heed to the beauty before him. He was remembering that miserable old busybody at the post office.

"Come for your mail, then?" Irwin Corwell's clipped manner of speaking had greeted him as he stood at the postmaster's counter.

At the time, it had struck Matt as a superfluous question. Looking back on it, he realized that it was nosy old Corwell's way of wedging open the conversation he'd been just waiting to have as soon as Matt arrived.

Corwell continued in his curt way. "Your neighbor lady, Mizzz Atkinson, hasn't come fer her mail in close tah two weeks."

Matt nodded politely at the report.

"She must be pretty busy not tah come and fetch it," Corwell added abruptly.

"I suppose she must be."

"You ain't seen much of her, then, I take it?"

"No," Matt answered flatly, himself abruptly aware that Corwell was fishing for information.

"Well, I'm sorry tah hear that things didn't work out between you two."

Matt wondered at the blatant, meddling stupidity of the man. Did Corwell really think he could maneuver him into revealing his feelings? He addressed the man with firm formality. "Caroline Atkinson is my neighbor and my friend, nothing more than that and nothing less."

"Well, I'm glad tah hear that, sir," Corwell replied

assertively. He turned away to get Matt's mail from its slot and returned to stack it on the counter between them. Purposefully folding his hands atop the mail, Corwell regarded Matt outright while he continued. "Especially since it's Jody Landis, I hear, who's been keepin' your friend so busy of late. I suspect you've already heard they were the most romantic couple to attend the VFW dance last Saturday night?" Corwell's eyes bored into Matt's.

Matt was taken aback, but knowing that Corwell was searching his face for even the slightest flinch of a reaction, he took care to show him none. "Irwin, may I have my mail?"

"Uh course." The postmaster slid the mail across the counter but made no motion to remove his hand from it. "You mind takin' your neighbor's mail to her? Jeezum! She's got more of those department store catalogs than anyone I can think of around here. There's one heck of a pile in her slot." Corwell's inquisitive gaze bored into Matt once more. "And who knows how much busier she's gonna get before she comes intah town." Corwell concluded with a humorless wink. "Huh?"

Matt regarded him blandly and nodded in wordless acceptance of both stacks of mail. He knew that the snoopy old coot wanted nothing better than to see some kind of emotion written on his face—anything that he could pass on to the rest of town.

But even as Matt kept his face steadily impassive, he knew only too well that it belied his real feelings. The fact was that he loved Caroline. He loved her deeply, perhaps too deeply. And while he knew he had to be careful this time, he wondered how much of his own damned caution he'd have to fight through, how much more trust he would, somehow, have to find in himself before he could tell her.

He was thankful that there was no sign of Jody's truck when he reached Caroline's house. She answered the door wearing jeans, a sweater, and a big fireproof glove that reached to her elbow.

"Matt!" she greeted him excitedly. "Oh, boy, am I glad to see you." Quickly motioning him to follow her, she led him into the living room. "I've got this big log wedged halfway out of the woodstove and it's starting to burn like crazy and I can't get it to move. Could you help me?" She took off the fireproof glove and handed it to Matt along with its mate.

The log was stuck halfway out of the stove, wedged in firmly at an awkward angle, which wouldn't have been a problem, except that it was birch. The white, curly paper bark had caught the flames and was crackling and popping well outside the woodstove, spewing sparks past the hearthstone. Matt donned the gloves, pulled the burning log out, and righted it while Caroline stomped out the burning embers on the floor.

"It's okay now," Matt announced while he watched the birch log flare against the closed, glass-paned stove door.

"Thanks, Matt." Caroline sighed in relief. "I don't know what I would've done without you." She, too, was caught by the sight of the flying birch-bark sparks and fell silent.

For a while both of them watched the fire, now tamed behind the glass door. Neither spoke for some time as, side by side, each stared into the hypnotic flames. Matt suddenly spoke what was on his mind, surprising himself with a forthrightness he didn't know he had. "Jody Landis has been by a lot. Is he sweet on you?"

Caroline looked uncomfortable. Fingering her earring, she said pleasantly, "He's such a nice person."

"Is that all he is?" Matt pressed. All of a sudden it was important that he get an answer. He wanted to know from her, not from Irwin Corwell, how she felt about Jody Landis.

But Caroline wasn't going to give him an answer—or, at least, not the answer he wanted. She made an enigmatic little gesture with her hands and gave him a look that communicated only that she didn't wish to talk about it.

The drive back home from Caroline's served only to escalate the fears engendered by the postmaster. Why wouldn't she give him a straight answer? Matt asked himself. She'd never been evasive with him before. That in itself, he reasoned, ought to tell him something. Maybe she did love Jody, but she was too shy to talk about it with anyone. The feeling, familiar and frightening, seized Matt like a net thrown over a pursued animal. As always, it began with a jolt—a completely hollow sensation in the pit of his stomach clutching at him with a sudden iciness, bedeviling him with frozen, unutterable emptiness. Recognizing it, Matt recoiled reflexively. As always, there was nothing he could do but retreat from it. But it wasn't finished with him yet. A picture flashed into his mind: last summer at the Bitterroot Cafe—the smitten look on Jody's face and the one on Caroline's—the one that had been just like Sheila's. Again, the feeling slammed into his stomach.

This time Matt shoved it away from him just as forcefully as it had been delivered.

A week later Caroline was at Matt's front door. Smiling and friendly, she asked him why she hadn't seen him in so long. Matt's first instinct was to invite her inside, but he stopped himself. Instead he stood in the doorway and answered her question. "Been busy."

"Doing what?"

"Just stuff."

Caroline looked at him queerly for a moment, then continued. "I've got a favor to ask you. Ray's really busy lately with his last harvest, but he says that now is the week I have to check the leaf buds on my hardwoods for whatever this pest might be. So, I was wondering if maybe you would come with me."

"Yeah," Matt mumbled. "Sure." Slipping on his coat and sunglasses, he followed her to her Bronco.

Once they were on their way, Caroline spoke as she drove over roads wet with melting snow. "Ray says I'm supposed to bring him back some branches from the main tract, and also, I'm supposed to open up a whole lot of leaf buds and see if there's anything like larvae or bugs inside. The leaf buds are supposed to unfurl sometime in the next few weeks, and if we can find anything inside, then Ray might have some clue as to what kind of insecticide to buy. It's a long shot, but it's worth a try."

Matt waited for her to return her attention to her driving before saying what was on his mind. "Jody Landis knows lots more about this sort of thing than I do. Why didn't you ask him to come with you?"

"Well . . . I missed seeing you, Matt."

"Why?"

Caroline turned to him with a puzzled look on her face. " 'Cause I did. 'Cause you're my friend."

"Isn't Jody your friend?"

"Well, sure, but . . ."

Matt noted the way she hesitated.

"But," Caroline continued, "I haven't seen you or heard from you in so long . . . I was getting concerned."

"So, you were checking up on me."

"Well . . ." Caroline looked through the windshield. "Yeah, I guess," she answered vaguely. "I just wanted to see how you were."

"Thanks," Matt said, carefully keeping his voice in check. He hated being pitied.

They must have checked over forty random maple trees, but there was absolutely nothing to be found in them. The morning was cool and pleasant. In spite of his mood, Matt enjoyed the particularly nutty aroma of last year's leaves fallen into the ground and now thawing with the advent of warmer weather. But Caroline, he knew, found no comfort in this forest.

Driving back home, Caroline was subdued and uncommunicative. She was probably worried about her trees, Matt surmised. Actually, he was glad for the silence. It gave him the opportunity to sort things out logically. Laying the facts squarely in front of him, he concluded that, yes, there appeared to be a romance beginning between Caroline and Jody. The fact that when questioned about Jody, Caroline's reply was nervous and noncommittal implied as much as an admission. And there was no denying that Matt had witnessed an unmistakable attraction between the two of them, even though it was Jody who seemed farther along in infatuation. As far as Jody went, Matt admitted, he was a good man. He had enough to offer a woman in the way of security and surely had decent intentions. And, Matt had to concede, Jody was both likable and good-looking in a baby-faced sort of way. That Caroline hadn't noticed Jody's attractiveness was not in question. But how could she not notice that the handsome Jody had no more than a pea brain? She would have to become bored with his cowpoke mentality eventually. Or would she? Opposites attract, Matt recalled uneasily—all that stuff about Ying and yang. . . .

Matt began to think that maybe he'd better *do* something. Maybe it was way earlier than he'd planned it, but maybe it was time anyway. He would declare his feelings for Caroline and win her away from Jody. Thinking about it didn't offer much comfort, though. For one thing, he wasn't sure if he could do it yet. It was still way too scary. And even if he could, the timing was all wrong. Caroline seemed keenly interested in Jody right now. What if he tried to win her away but couldn't? That was an even scarier thought. Maybe, Matt decided, once begun, Caroline was destined to have her romance with Jody.

Matt's thoughts rushed through his mind faster and faster. Even if he succeeded in tearing Caroline away from Jody, it could all backfire. What if Caroline might someday look back and regret never having allowed Jody his chance? Would it haunt her? Would she always wonder if she'd made the decision of her own free will or if she'd allowed Matt to push her into it? No, Matt concluded, sweeping her away, fighting for her, could be a big mistake. Caroline had to be sure about how she felt or didn't feel about Jody. And Matt knew his own imperative only too well: he needed to be absolutely sure, too. Better to step aside, wait patiently, and let this thing with Jody reach whatever conclusion it was going to come to. If Caroline chose Jody, then so be it. But if she didn't and if her own love for Matt was ever to be, then the waiting would be worth it.

The tough part, of course, would be the waiting. Matt grimaced involuntarily as he began to mull over the excruciating details that would be part of the waiting. He wondered grimly if he was capable of being quite as cavalier about not interfering when it actually came down to seeing Caroline and Jody close together. He had never, ever, counted willpower as one of his talents. Staring out the window over the rolling hills nearing Caroline's house, he sank into deep and deeper brooding. From far away, Caroline's voice penetrated his dark thoughts.

"Would you like to stop inside for lunch?" she asked.

"No. I've got lots to do," he found himself saying. Suddenly, looking at her bright, apple-cheeked face, he knew what he had to do.

"You sure? I made some coffee cake."

"Nope. Nope. I've got some packing to take care of. I'm leaving on a business trip."

"Oh," Caroline said resignedly. "How long will you be gone?"

"I'm not sure," Matt answered. "A month, probably. Maybe more. Depends on how long it takes for some things to get resolved."

CHAPTER

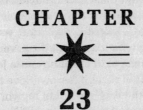

23

MAY IS THE MOON OF
Green Grass and Leaves, the month when the grass
comes out of the ground and the leaves appear on the
trees. But no leaves had appeared on Caroline's trees,
and none were going to. Ray drove out to her house one
rainy morning to tell her why.

"You got pear thrips," he began in his usual blunt
way. "Used to be a fruit tree problem, but the little
buggers shifted to maples, probably on account of such
heavy spraying programs in orchards. They're these
flea-size things. The eggs winter over in the soil around
the base of the maples. When the ground gets warm,
they hatch, fly up into the branches, get into the
swelled-up buds, and eat the leaf from the inside. Kills
it even before it has a chance to unfurl."

"But we checked. Matt and I opened up scores of
those buds last month and there weren't any bugs,"
Caroline argued.

"Ground was cold. Thrips hadn't hatched yet." Ray shrugged fatalistically. "Wouldn't of done any good, anyways. Orchard sprays don't work anymore."

Caroline let this sink in, putting her mind to work. "About what percent of the hardwoods, would you say, are affected?"

"Looks like all of 'em," Ray replied flatly.

Caroline hadn't expected that. "Oh," she said, trying to think calmly. "Will any of the trees survive to next year, or should I harvest them all right now?"

"Cooperative extension's talking fast and fancy about sap reduction percentages and root stress," Ray said, shaking his head in derision, "but looking at your maple stands, I'm seeing a wipeout. Most of those trees have no leaves and no buds. The rest have gnarled-up leaves that aren't gonna make it. You got ground suckers all over, but with no known insecticide, that'll only end up in major limb damage. Wood's getting brittle already. No leaves. No sap. It'd cost you more to cut it than you'd get selling it." Ray paused and looked disgruntled even for the stoic that he was. "Best to look to your softwoods for income from now on."

Ray waited to make sure that Caroline had absorbed his disheartening information. In a less businesslike tone he added, "Softwood prices are gonna drop all over on account of this. Can't say for how long, either. You think you'll be able to make it?"

"I'll get by for however long it takes."

"You could always sell it off to Sanborne, you know, before it turns into a bigger problem."

Caroline smiled at Ray. She knew exactly what he meant by this, but she felt sure about what she could tolerate. However difficult economic pressures might get, it was not the kind of thing that would lead her into a relapse. The corrosive stress of her old life was one thing. Caring about staying here enough to weather the struggle was quite another. Caroline answered with conviction, "I'm okay on this, Ray. It's not going to be a problem."

Ray nodded in acknowledgment. He paused just a bit longer than was his usual brusque manner before announcing that he had to go feed Matt's horses.

Caroline stood on her front porch and watched Ray leave. The combination of rain and melting snow caused a curtain of water to drip from the gutterless overhang as her gaze followed Ray's truck down the road. All over the countryside, she saw snow melting everywhere as springtime approached, however hesitantly. A blush of apple green peeked out of the snow patches over the valley's rolling plains, and the pines along the mountain ranges seemed a more vivid green. Snow still streaked the mountain, however, and while the melting snow formed new and gushing creeks down every hill, the frigid winter wind blustered so noisily as to crash.

Caroline knew that she ought to be thinking of Plan B as far as her luckless timberland was concerned and perhaps to start to refigure her budget for the next year. But, strangely, she wasn't all that troubled by these considerations. What preoccupied her thoughts had more to do with Matt: his terse and unexpected goodbye to her; the feeling of purposeful distance she'd sensed from him the last time she'd seen him. That was about three weeks ago, Caroline realized, and the fact was that she was becoming increasingly lonely—even restless—without his companionship. True, she'd had plenty of Jody's companionship recently, but it wasn't the same. Jody was a lot of things: sexy, exciting, attentive—Caroline's mental list faltered for a moment—but even after being with Jody time and again, it never got any easier to talk comfortably with him. To be perfectly honest, she told herself, it probably never would.

Caroline thought about her last date with Jody. They'd ended up on the cranberry couch, where Jody's advances became far more ardent than ever before. Not that Caroline didn't mind being so eagerly desired by a man, and not that she didn't have desires of her own, but even as Jody's hands traveled her body, luring it into compliancy, even as his kisses pressed and teased, Caroline's heart was unwilling. She'd retreated, feigning virtuous values, but that wasn't really it at all. Something was troubling her. Something was missing. What it was, she still didn't know.

Looking past the waterfall cascading from her porch roof, Caroline searched the dreary landscape for the word that would describe that missing ingredient. Instead, one of Winona's Napi stories began to run through her mind—the one about how Old Napi was responsible for bringing all the Indian men and women together.

In the old times, Winona had related, men and women lived separately in different camps. Men had bows and arrows to hunt with, but not much else going for them. They lived in shoddy lodges and wore crude animal skins for clothes because they didn't know how to tan or sew hides. Women, on the other hand, had figured out how to run buffalo over cliffs to get their food, plus they were skilled in tanning and knew how to make beautiful clothes and sturdy tipis.

Old Napi figured he'd be crafty and strike a deal, so he went to the women's camp and told Chief Woman how men lived and how they could hunt game. Chief Woman listened patiently and began to feel sorry for the primitive way the men had to live. Out of pity she asked Napi to bring the men over to the women's camp tomorrow and the women would choose mates.

The next day the women were busy butchering buffalo when the men arrived at their camp. Chief Woman announced that she would be first to choose a man, and she chose Napi. But Napi refused her because she had been cutting the buffalo meat and did not look appealing. Chief Woman got angry and instructed the men to leave and not come back until tomorrow.

The next day, Chief Woman was dressed in her most beautiful clothes when the men came. This time Napi liked what he saw and tried to get her to choose him, but she took another man. And when all the men were chosen except for Napi, Chief Woman turned Napi into a lone pine tree. So now, if you ever see a pine tree on the side of a hill, it should remind you of Old Napi and how foolish he was to judge by looks alone.

Caroline stared into the rain, knowing, now, what was missing between her and Jody. Jody was attractive to her, maybe even blindingly attractive. But as much as she wished it could be otherwise, she had to admit it: there was nothing deeper to her attraction than that. Suddenly it was crystal clear, as if the rain had instantly stopped and the sky had brightened. The only thing that edged into Caroline's sense of peace and relief was how she was going to tell him.

✳ ✳ ✳

Caroline stood just inside the door of the Bitterroot Cafe, waiting for Jody to meet her there. She had decided that today she would break it to him, even though she still didn't know exactly how to say it. Turning her back on the noisy din of the lunchtime crowd, she faced the community bulletin board and began to compose an opening sentence. "Jody, you are one of the sweetest men I have ever known but . . ." The Bitterroot Valley Plowing Association was going to hold its match just south of the Holton Farm. "Jody," her mind rephrased, "it wouldn't be right if I didn't tell you this . . ." The Hawkeye Congregational Church was having a ham and bean supper next Saturday. "Jody, you deserve better than—"

"Howdy." Jody's hand squeezed her shoulder. "It's real crowded," he said, motioning to the dining area. "You mind if we sit with Bob junior?"

"Sure," Caroline replied cheerfully, even though sharing a table was going to throw a monkey wrench into her plan.

Bob Fairbanks, Jr., beckoned them over to his table, obviously pleased to see Jody. Irwin Corwell was already seated with Bob junior, looking and sounding, as ever, like the Pepperidge Farm man. Once the usual greetings were exchanged, Bob junior spoke to Caroline.

"I heard about those pear thrips, Caroline, and I'm real sorry they hit your timberland so bad."

"Well, that's the breaks," Caroline answered with a shrug. "But, thanks."

"Are you planning to sell your land to the trash people now that your hardwood stands are gone?"

"No." Caroline remembered Jack MacKenzie's

offer and wondered what Bob junior was getting at. "In fact, they called me with another offer just last night— maybe you heard about it—and I turned it down."

"Well, I'm really glad you did that. Those trash guys are one pushy bunch of s.o.b.'s, pardon my French, and they're using this thrip disaster to their advantage. Matt's told me how much those creeps have been pestering you, so I'm happy to see you're still holding your ground."

"Thanks," Caroline replied, pleasantly surprised that she had found an ally in Bob Fairbanks, Jr.

"Speakin' of our friend Matt," Irwin Corwell interjected, "has anyone heard from him of late?" When no one rose to the postmaster's bait, he continued. "His mail's been rerouted tah California, I notice. I've been havin' tah pack up all his letters and such and send 'em tah that different address again—same one as usual— care of someone by the name of Margaret. Margaret somethin' or other, I ferget what her last name is. Do you happen to know of her, Mizzz Atkinson?" The postmaster bored into her eyes for an answer.

A stunned "No" was all Caroline could muster.

Corwell adroitly turned his query to Bob junior. "How 'bout you, Bob? Matt ever mention to you his livin' with this Margaret?"

"I'm not sure. Well, maybe. The name sounds like it might be familiar," Bob junior began. "Once in a while Matt will talk about some woman he stays with out in California. He always speaks real well of her. From what I gather, it sounds like he's been going there for a long time."

Corwell studied Caroline's face while concluding his inquisition with the relish of a true busybody. "Surprised your friend Matt never mentioned this tah you, Mizzz Atkinson." Seeing Caroline glower with a sharp expression that was barbed with both hurt and reproach, Corwell retreated, adding hastily, "But, after all, I didn't mean tah pry into anyone's business."

Caroline's tone was barely civil. "Of course you did," she told him.

Caroline remembered little of lunch. Her thoughts were commandeered by the revelation that Matt was living with a woman in California. Corwell's report jabbed relentlessly inside her head. Bob junior's testimony gripped icy cramps into the core of her heart and smashed down her spirit with the weight of a tombstone.

Whether lunch was over or not when Caroline got up and excused herself, she neither noticed nor cared. All she was aware of was the pain simmering to intolerance within her and that she had to get away from it. Once outside the Bitterroot, she ran faster to escape it, fleeing toward the refuge of her Bronco parked on Main Street. When she got safely inside, she let herself cry, at last giving in to what she had been denying for so very long. What she felt for Matt went well beyond friendship, and it went far deeper than simple companionship. She knew that now, but what hurt and jealousy had brought forth, they could not satisfy: Matt had a lover in California. Sobbing, Caroline abandoned herself to the grief of this unwelcome knowledge. The discovery of her love for Matt and the hopelessness of knowing that her love would never be returned were bound wretchedly together.

Jody had followed and stood witness on the sidewalk in front of the weeping Caroline. Telling him what she had meant to say before would be unnecessary. He could see for himself. Silently, grimly, Jody walked away.

CHAPTER

24

*C*AROLINE WAS FUZZY
with sleep when she got the four A.M. call about the fire.
It was her timberland, Winona told her, and Ray had
left specific instructions that she come to their house
and not the site of the fire to await the outcome. Once
she was sitting amid the clutter on Winona's kitchen
table with a mug of steaming coffee in front of her, her
worries began to dawn along with the sky outside. With
her hardwoods wiped out already, would the fire de-
stroy what was left, and with it, her livlihood?

"Not to worry," Winona said, sensing Caroline's
anxiety. "Ray's in charge of the fire fighters. He'll make
sure they do their extra best to put it out."

Tyrone, as if in support, shambled over to Caroline's side. He laid his head in her lap and panted
shallowly. Caroline stroked his black muzzle, wishing
she could know for sure.

"Here's some cinnamon toast." Winona placed an aromatic stack in front of Caroline and parked her wheelchair beside Tyrone. "Now, have some while it's warm and we will talk about something that has nothing to do with the fire."

"Like what?" Caroline asked, biting into a butter-soaked slice of sugared toast despite her apprehension.

"Like the town meeting yesterday. You did go, didn't you?"

"Oh, yes. I went." Caroline rolled her eyes.

"Well, then. What happened?"

"A lot of nothing. It was basically another question and answer forum—same stuff as before, only this time there was a lot more niggling over the details. It spiraled down to two sides pretty fast. There are a lot of ranchers now who are throwing their weight in with Sanborne because it looks like we're in for another dry summer. They're predicting that it might be even worse than last year and the ranchers are going to need any tax break or, for some, any land-parcel buyer they can get hold of. I guess you can't really blame them," Caroline said. "It beats getting wiped out entirely. And then there are the timberland owners who, all of a sudden, are ready to sell out to Sanborne because of those crummy thrips. I guess you can't blame them, either."

"But it's not up to the ranchers or the timber owners," Winona countered. "Ultimately the decision belongs to the town council. Right?"

"That's true. They've got to weigh what they heard at this last town meeting and vote to either approve the project or not by the July third deadline. They're supposed to vote with their constituents in mind, and that's what's going to be the problem. They didn't dare take an audience vote. All hell would have broken loose if it was by ayes and nays, and they wouldn't have been able to count it accurately if it was by hands. It looks like Hawkeye is pretty well split right down the middle."

"Oh, I'm not so convinced of that," Winona said. "I think that some people have been more demonstrative than others."

"Like who?"

"I get the impression that it's the Sanborne sympathizers who've been making the most noise."

"Well, it's probably true that the word you hear most at these meetings is 'money.' But, then again, last night Bob Fairbanks, Jr., was in the high school lobby, signing people up for an antitrash group."

"Did many people sign up?"

"There were a lot of people there. Enough, I guess."

"Did you sign up?"

"Yes. I did." Caroline lifted her hand from Tyrone, who was alerted to a noise outdoors. Caroline shrugged her shoulders and added dubiously, "For what it was worth."

Whatever Tyrone had heard, Caroline and Winona now heard, too. Soon Ray was in the kitchen, shedding his canary yellow fire fighter's jacket and backpack gear. He unstrapped his yellow safety helmet to reveal a face smeared with soot and water streaks. The part of his face that had been protected by goggles contrasted white against the black.

"Fire's out," he announced. "Only got some of your hardwoods anyway."

"The pines are all okay?" Caroline asked.

"Yup. We snuffed it pretty easy."

"Ray," Caroline said, "how can I thank you?"

"No need. Good practice for the boys for what's in store. Two months further into this dry spell, though, woulda been a different story."

"You were lucky, dear," Winona said to Caroline.

"Debatable," Ray replied to this. He wiped his sooty face on a paper towel before continuing. "You might as well know"—he repeated the motion with a fresh paper towel—"arson. Found the gas can. Folks are saying it was Earl Bullchild doing it for Sanborne."

"No," Caroline said firmly. "I can't believe that."

"Nor can I," added Winona, shaking her head.

"There's no proof to it," Ray replied, "but that's who folks are blaming anyway."

"Whoever it was," Winona addressed Caroline in a more serious tone than before, "they want you to heed their warning. Now you know what your signing up with the antitrash group was worth."

Caroline was absorbed with assimilating this while Ray started out of the kitchen. Only Winona was able to interpret the look on his face as worried.

A week after the fire, Caroline sat at her kitchen table. Paper, bills, and payment booklets fanned out everywhere over the marble tabletop while she worked a calculator and wrote the numbers on a yellow legal pad. So far it looked as if she'd be able to get by this year. The thrips and the fire had taken a chunk out of any profits she might have made, but she would probably break even. Not wonderful, Caroline told herself, but at least she owned all her land outright, so it wasn't terrible, either. She would simply have to write out a strict monthly budget and hold herself to it until next year's harvest. Ripping off a fresh sheet of paper, she began the task, but her mind roamed away from the legal pad while Tinky roamed over it.

"Tinky! You know you don't belong on the table," Caroline scolded, even though both her hands petted the length of Tinky's silky black body. "Now, come on," she said, giving the cat a final scratch on the head, "that's enough attention. What you need is to go outside and do whatever it is that cats do out there. Check out the barn, sleep in the grass, be on your own."

Tinky responded by pushing her head, much like a bulldozer, into Caroline's chin and purring louder than before. Even when deposited onto the kitchen linoleum, the little black cat persistently rubbed against Caroline's ankles. Caroline whisked the cat fur off her legal pad and tried to readdress herself to the budget, but with no success. She knew that she was just as restless as the cat nudging at her feet. In fact, she'd been feeling this way for some time, except that lately her agitation seemed to be mushrooming. She'd started taking long walks recently, as a balm for the restlessness, but even that had produced the opposite effect. Yesterday she had stopped to throw a stone into a creek at the foot of the mountain range behind her house when, looking back, she'd suddenly realized that she had absolutely no recollection of how she'd arrived there. Whatever it was that she was restless about was beginning to preoccupy her mind to the point of becoming unsettling.

Caroline surveyed the budget and scowled fiercely. There were too many things going wrong lately, too many annoyances, she thought with increasing irritation—fires and thrips, whatever it was that was wrong with the well pump, the sudden solitude of not having Jody come around anymore. She gathered the papers into a disheveled stack and angrily began to jam them into a manila envelope—the miserable way Matt had up and left, the miserable reason why. Caroline opened a kitchen cabinet and pitched in the envelope, legal pad, and calculator—and the miserable way his absence had created a gaping, lonely hole in her life. She slammed the cabinet shut with vehemence. Through the rattling of the dishes in the cabinets, Caroline heard the knock at the front door.

It was Earl Bullchild on the porch, his chunky physique slouched in black T-shirt and jeans, his raven hair cleaner and longer than when Caroline had last seen it, tied back behind his neck.

"Earl," Caroline said, surprised. "Won't you come in?"

He frowned and mumbled something monosyllabic and negative sounding. He flicked the lit stub of a cigarette off to the side in an arc and watched it land before he addressed Caroline. "It wasn't me who torched your trees."

"I never thought you did, Earl. What people are saying is nothing but gossip."

"Yeah, but since they're saying it, I wanted you to know." Earl's voice was sullen, but it also possessed a maturity that belied his looks and age. "It's 'cause I'm different. I don't fit in. I never have. And, okay, maybe people are scared of that, but that don't mean I'm bad. It only means I'm different." Earl stopped abruptly to light a fresh cigarette, and then, to Caroline's surprise, he continued. "It used to bum me out, people ragging on me like that. Used to make me real mad and lonesome. But now—hell, I don't know—maybe I got stronger from it or something, but what they say just won't cut anymore. I go to sleep every night with a clear conscience, and that's all that matters." Earl grinned fleetingly at Caroline before returning to his customary solemnity. "Gotta go." Motioning his thumb toward the driveway, he added, "Borrowed truck." And with that he turned and left.

Caroline watched Earl's borrowed truck disappear back toward Hawkeye and thought about his extraordinary speech. Extraordinary because such wisdom came from one so young and unlikely; extraordinary because Earl's words pared to the very heart of her restlessness. Whether he knew it or not, Earl was talking about having found a state of individual independence, an inner strength to live by. He no longer required other people or relied on their judgments. He was happy to be with himself, content in his own company. That, Caroline told herself, was the very thing she, too, must learn to be. Finding that inner strength was the next step. She had come to Montana in order to live peacefully. But peace wasn't going to come from a physical place. It wasn't going to come from Matt, no matter how lonely and hurt she felt with or without him. And it wasn't going to come from the town council's decision whether Sanborne triumphed or not. The only place it was going to come from, she now knew with absolute certainty, was from within herself.

Caroline surveyed the plains that rolled toward Hawkeye. Clouds were lying in low wisps in the foothills of the greening mountains. Wildflowers—pink and white columbine, orange Indian paintbrushes, and purple-pink fireweed—graced the fields in bright profusion. Smiling, she recalled the Nez Percé name Winona had for this month: the Moon of Hatching, when birds' eggs hatch open with life. To this, Caroline tacked on her own addition. June meant springtime: the time of hope and renewal.

CHAPTER

25

*C*AROLINE WAS AWAK-
ened by a pebble hitting the side of her face. Opening
her eyes to the ceiling of dawning sky above, she kept
still and listened. There was something creeping
around on the bluff just above her, probably the animal
that had dislodged the pebble, but it didn't sound as if
it were big. Propping herself up on an elbow, she listened more carefully to hear the creature loping away.
Probably just a jackrabbit, she told herself. She sat up
and right away noticed the thick layer of yellow dust
over her dark green sleeping bag. Touching her face, she
felt the gritty pine-tree pollen sprinkled there, too.
Maybe sleeping inside the tent was the better idea after
all.

Wriggling out of the sleeping bag, Caroline headed
sleepily for the backpack she'd set near last night's fire.
In the cool, early morning light, food took precedence

over cleanliness. She could wash off the pollen later because today's breakfast was something she'd been looking forward to since yesterday. There was, Caroline had realized after three days, just so much trail mix a person could stomach.

Soon a tin cup of hot coffee from the revived campfire was in one hand and a pot filled with sweet, ripe mountain raspberries in her lap. She'd picked them last night after dinner, all the while thinking of Winona and her Indian calendar, glad that July was the Moon of Ripe Berries. Caroline put a handful of the juicy-sweet berries into her mouth and regarded the cloudless morning sky surrounding her, a breathtaking vision of heavenly vastness. Content, she rolled just a single raspberry inside her mouth and toyed with its fragility while she thought about her wilderness journey so far. She'd started out one morning in her Bronco, following the old dirt road that forked off a few miles past Matt's house. It was a road she hadn't yet traveled, and as she'd had no definite route in mind, she'd taken it. After an hour, when open fields turned into woods, the road narrowed, eventually becoming two dirt tire ruts marking a dim path surrounded by thick side growth. When even the ruts faded away into solid overgrowth, Caroline parked the Bronco where it stood, fetched her backpack, and set out on foot to whatever might lie beyond.

She kept close to a creek, following it even when straying from it would have meant traveling over easier ground. But it was worth it. She'd pitched her green dome tent each of the first three nights amid clusters of lush green grasses near clear running water. It meant easy cooking and cleaning plus access to the water she needed after all that trail mix.

Yesterday she hadn't set up camp until nearly sunset, much later than she'd done so far. But the day had gone slowly and she'd barely covered any ground at all. She'd seen the signs of drought that day. The creek she was following thinned down to a narrow line while fields of wildflowers were replaced entirely by purple, cornflowerlike knapweed. Caroline followed the knapweed fields that morning but soon found herself trudging uphill on rocky ground. Once in a while she would lift her eyes to see the distant spires of a glacial mountain range. It stretched across the entire horizon, its rugged gray peaks soaring to connect with heaven itself. Leveling her gaze, Caroline saw jackrabbits jumping about, oblivious of her presence, and several antelope. A young bull moose emerged from a thicket and stood in her view. His gaze was so riveting that Caroline stared back too hard and nearly tipped forward with the weight of her backpack.

Lovely as her surroundings were, Caroline began to ignore them entirely as the uphill climb took its toll on her tired legs. She stared only at her feet and at where she placed them. Just fifty more steps, she would tell herself each time she'd counted out the last goal of fifty. By late afternoon she'd had enough. She had camped early and considered the big accomplishment of the day, the raspberries she was this morning twirling around in her mouth.

When she'd eaten the last of the berries, she washed the pine pollen off her face in a spring-fed creek. The water was ice cold and invigorating. Looking to the sky, she saw an eagle dive from a cliff in a slow, graceful glide. As suddenly as it had appeared, it vanished. It was time for Caroline to decamp and take off, too.

Her progress was even slower and more difficult than the previous day as she walked through thicker woods. Tree branches were low and had to be pushed to get by, while others grabbed into her T-shirt and snagged her hair. Fallen trees lay crisscrossed everywhere, but still Caroline kept to her creek. It was dark, akin to the dusk before sunset, from the forest's impenetrable leaf cover, when she came to a rubble of rocks. Strange, Caroline thought, to find so many rocks all heaped in one pile out here in the wilderness. Walking on, she discovered another set of stones and understood. The first rubble pile of rocks had once been a fireplace and chimney, now all that remained of a homesteader's house. The other stones, a few still standing upright, were all that remained of the family that had lived here.

Caroline pushed through tangled underbrush, land that had once been cleared by the very people whose names she was about to read. The gravestones belonged to the McDermott family. The father and six children had died between 1909 and 1913, except for the mother and two babies, who'd died between 1905 and 1907. They'd all died young by Caroline's figuring, and except for the parents, they'd all died without bringing anyone else into the family through marriage. Staring at the headstones, Caroline wondered what it would have been like to be the last one left in this failed attempt at family and homesteading. Did the last McDermott stick around or leave? If he did stay, then who buried him?

Caroline continued following her creek, now widened into a steady-running stream. The incline and the tangy balsam-and-sage-spiced air told her she was climbing higher into the mountains. Finally she reached the clearing that took her out of the forest. It was perfect, Caroline decided: a pond to one side, a sheer wall of rocky-cragged, balsam-scattered mountain to the other. Well, it wasn't quite perfect: the quivering wail of coyotes echoed from the mountain ridge, and it wasn't even dark yet. Still, Caroline reminded herself, coyotes never attacked people. She would set up camp here.

Something that wasn't a coyote yowled. She'd heard of catamounts and of wolverines, but she didn't know what they sounded like. The spooky noise repeated, setting Caroline's teeth in a clench, but at the same time she was too tired to hike even another fifty baby steps that day. She looked around, hoping to find a more secure place to spend the night than in her flimsy nylon tent. A hiding place was what she wanted, and the huge Douglas fir nestled at the edge of the mountain looked about right. Its lowermost branches came clear to the ground, and they were dense enough to form a giant green tipi. Going to it and peeking inside, Caroline felt her spirits rise. She unpacked for the night.

Since the raspberries this morning, Caroline's mealtime standby of trail mix was looking less appealing than ever. Remembering the fishhook she'd packed, she cut a cottonwood pole, caught a few baby grasshoppers, and headed for the pond in hope of snaring something. She caught three fat trout speckled and pinkish silver and was swelled with the pride of self-sufficiency as she lit the campfire that would cook them.

Picking the meat off the very last fishbone, Caroline sat in the evening's long shadows while her thoughts traveled back to the homesteaders' graveyard. Obviously the McDermotts had come to their place by the lure of free land for the working of it. And, obviously, they had believed in themselves enough to think they could succeed. They must have been aware that they'd be completely on their own out there and that the very remoteness of their situation could endanger their lives. And yet they took the chance and stuck it out. Why? Caroline asked herself. For a parcel of land? To risk so much, there had to be more at stake than that. Maybe it was their chance to be independent—to be free to steer their own course on their own land instead of working their lives away for a mining company in Butte. That would be, Caroline decided, the only reason for their staying after so many successive gravestones. But if the price of freedom is uncertainty and solitude, the McDermotts paid dearly. Then again, Caroline concluded, maybe that's the price everyone must pay if they want something as precious as that.

Caroline thought about the risks that she herself was taking by going on this wilderness trip alone. Today, walking between the fallen logs of the dense forest, she'd very nearly twisted her ankle but saved herself from an immobilizing sprain by using a tree for support. What if she hadn't been so lucky? Who would ever find her up here? Only Winona and Ray knew of her plans, but they didn't know where she was headed. In fact, they both had tried to talk her out of the trip, but Caroline had insisted that this was something she needed to do. Besides, she wasn't taking any foolhardy risks. Other people did this sort of thing all the time— Matt, for one, and lots of those Yellowstone types as well. If they could take care of themselves, she could, too.

Bringing Matt to mind sobered Caroline's bravado. She had almost reached a point where she was resigned to it. "Matt loves someone named Margaret," she had repeated to herself lately, just so that it would become perfectly real to her. And although this information was, indeed, perfectly real, it still bothered her.

Sunset came, but the mountainside blocked most of it. Caroline heard a cricket begin chirping close by and suddenly remembered one of life's great tidbits of outdoor information. She'd memorized it for the time when, as a kid, she'd dragged Celeste down the drain-pipe with her and out into the night woods to go explor-ing: to tell the temperature without a thermometer, count the number of times a cricket chirps in fifteen seconds, add the number thirty-seven, and that's the Fahrenheit temperature. Caroline counted and cal-culated. It was sixty degrees. Much pleased about fi-nally putting this knowledge to use after so many years, Caroline stirred the campfire embers and added enough wood for the night. Through the slim shafts of many cottonwood trees, the sky loomed an inky, evening blue. Caroline crawled into her evergreen tipi. With its soft carpet of fragrant pine needles, it was as cozy as any bedroom. Snuggling into the sleeping bag, she stretched out and listened while a chorus of coyotes sang her to sleep.

The next morning, Caroline emerged from her sleeping shelter to a thick, chilly fog that hid even the mountain that rose behind her. Blundering around, she found a creek and washed her face in water that tasted of snowmelt. That meant she'd traveled higher up. Maybe some lateral traveling today was a good idea.

Within an hour a brilliant sun had burned off the fog and Caroline was on her way. The route she chose took her through a sun-shafted pine forest. So many layers of fallen pine needles blanketed her path that she got the sensation of bounding across a bed.

Eventually she reached a clearing with a crater-size cobalt blue lake. It was early afternoon, time for lunch. Once she'd assembled her primitive fishing tackle, Caroline sat in the soft, lakeside grass and waited, basking in the sun's warmth. Soon she hauled in a fat trout and re-baited her line. Not long after it sank into the crystalline water she was fast asleep on the warm shore grasses.

She awoke to a magnificent sunset painted brilliantly against the horizon in cloud-trails of bright oranges and burnished yellows. The same colors shone their reflection on the calm lake in front of Caroline giving the whole world a fiery glow. Renewed by her nap, she set up her tent as close as was safely possible to the mirror lake. She was famished, and the trout was going to taste wonderful.

Velvet darkness crept in as the fish sizzled in its pan over the campfire. Caroline sipped some coffee and waited for it to cook, listening to the wood pop, watching it spew sparks into the night. Looking up, she saw the first evening stars and recalled the names Winona had for them: the Star That Stands Still, the Dusty Trail, the Seven Persons.

The trout was even more delicious than she had anticipated. The thin outer skin had crisped to a crunch, while the pink flesh within remained juicy and delicate, falling away in successive layers. Sated, Caroline lay on her back, arms folded behind her neck, and watched the sky above. This time, though, the stars paled next to what glittered in the distant sky over Hawkeye. "Ah, of course!" Caroline said. "It's the Fourth of July. Independence Day." In honor of the occasion, she ransacked her backpack for the treat she'd been saving: a box of Milk Duds. Sinking her teeth into the chocolaty wads of caramel, Caroline delighted in one dazzling fireworks display after another: giant pom-poms, the traditional sparkler burst, triplets that thud-ded in succession.

Briefly Caroline wondered if the fireworks was a celebration for whatever happened with the Sanborne Trash to Energy Project. The decision had come yester-day. But somehow that didn't matter out here, nor would it when she got home. She would adapt to what-ever had to be adapted to. This trip had helped her with that. Caroline was suddenly and immensely happy that she'd made this journey to the wilderness. She had derived such a great satisfaction from it, although a description of that satisfaction was difficult to express in exact words. You had to actually go on one of these trips to really understand, she reflected. Matt would understand. He would know what kept the McDermott family out here and why counting out another fifty more steps was an all-or-nothing achievement. Matt would be able to agree with her on how a trout and a handful of raspberries could taste of ambrosia, and how the sky and the stars could humble a person so. He'd see the reason for a human staring down a moose.

Caroline stopped herself from going on when the

bittersweet realization hit her. Yes, it was true that there was no one in the world but Matt who could really understand these personal discoveries with her. But Matt loves someone named Margaret, she reminded herself. Sharing her innermost feelings with Matt about this trip or anything else, for that matter, just wasn't going to happen.

CHAPTER

26

MATT STOOD ON THE
flat, tarred rooftop of the Fosters' brick, two-story house
and looked up at the darkening sky. No stars shone
through the cloud cover, but soon, he knew, the Palo
Alto sky would be sparkling with a riot of Fourth of July
fireworks. He inhaled the old, familiar fragrance of the
neighborhood's huge eucalyptus trees, then peered into
the shadows of the low-walled rooftop. Matt smiled to
himself. He'd spent many a happy childhood Fourth of
July evening here. He walked to the roof edge, then
looked down and retreated in one swift motion. This
was his first time on the roof as a grownup.

Something thudded from behind the rooftop door
before it creaked open. Doc, wearing her usual sporty
shirtdress, backed herself through. She had a folding
lawn chair wedged under each arm and a pop-top can
in each hand. As soon as Matt slipped the chairs out

from her arms, Doc immediately set down the cans. "Holy Hannah!" she exclaimed. "Those cans are freezing cold." She rubbed her hands together while Matt set up the lawn chairs.

"That's very nice," Doc's silky voice told Matt after he was done, "but the fireworks always go off over there." She pointed to the next side of the roof. "Maybe if you took off those silly sunglasses, Matty dear, you could see where you are," she scolded him gently. "I've only been saying it for—how many months have you been staying here with us now? Take them off. I want to see you."

"I'm right here. You can see me."

"Besides, I hate to tell you this, but they make you look . . ." She stopped to make sure she'd hooked him.

"What?" he asked impatiently, recognizing, yet still not immune to her age-old strategy. "They make me look what?"

Doc raised her eyebrows in exaggerated haughtiness. "Snooty, Mr. Mathew Michael Van Zandt. They make you look snooty."

"Well, all right, then," Matt replied, matching Doc's mock loftiness. "I will remove them just so that you may see me, Dr. Margaret Mary Foster."

As Matt and Doc repositioned their chairs, Doc's mood turned thoughtful. "It's too bad Wayne's going to miss the fireworks tonight. We've been married, what?—forty years, and I don't think we've ever missed an Independence Day display together. I don't suppose he'll be seeing one in London, either."

"Do you miss him?" Matt wondered at this. After all, Wayne's private practice as a lawyer had sent him away on business trips all their married lives, and Doc, a pediatrician, had led a hectic and independent schedule of her own. Before this moment, it had never occurred to Matt that either of them had ever wished things otherwise.

"Yes, I miss him," Doc answered, pushing her page-boy hair behind her ears. "The best part of my day is the part when I get to share what happened in it with Wayne."

"Can't you share it with me?"

"Not all of it." Doc smiled sweetly. "There's a whole background of things I can talk to Wayne about that no one else could understand. I mean, sure, someone else would grasp the surface of it, but only Wayne knows me well enough to see into things and know what I'm really feeling. Sometimes I don't even know myself what I really feel until I tell it to Wayne. And whatever that happens to be—insecure, happy, worried, or frightened—I know that he will never criticize or judge me by it or use it to his advantage. I can trust him with anything."

She handed Matt a can of Seven-Up and then apologized. "I'm sorry, Matty. It completely slipped my mind inside and I grabbed myself a can of beer. I'll be right back." Doc headed for the doorway.

"No," Matt said quietly. "You don't have to. Go ahead and drink it."

"Uh-uh," Doc protested. "Not a good idea."

"Honestly, it doesn't bother me."

She deliberately pushed aside her wariness and said, "Okay."

They sat on their chairs and popped open their respective drink containers. Surveying the rooftops of Palo Alto, Matt saw that soon, but not quite yet, the sky would be dark enough for the fireworks to begin. He caught a whiff of the yeasty beer smell and was pleased. It wasn't a matter of willpower anymore. It didn't even appeal to him. But the beer had been only a bit player at the tail end of the problem, when his money was running out. Cocaine was what began it. Six years, Matt remembered, not really that long ago, was when it had started. And it had been so easy to get started. He'd had a lucrative computer business whose coffers easily supported the regular purchase of cocaine in a variety of designer forms; a wife who with her own brand of self-serving greed supported it, too; and, of course, his own unquenchable obsession. But a year later the supports were crumbling. His business was failing. Sheila, incapable of accepting money shortages, used her position as his wife to create and dip into new lines of credit, using Matt's business as collateral. And Matt, oblivious of anything beyond his need to remain perpetually stoned, added vodka as an adjunct to his daily habit.

Once, in a lucid moment, he'd begged Sheila to send him to a facility where he could get straight and sober. He never forgot her answer, even through his farthest journeys from reality. It was the word *impractical* that stuck in his mind. It was impractical, she'd reasoned with him in her sweet-and-helpless style. The facility would cost three times as much as the coke habit itself. After that, his addiction worsened.

He snorted his Cessna, and then his Porsche. He grieved over Sheila, realizing painfully that she had always loved his wealth but she'd never loved him. Thoughts of suicide, some drug-induced, some not, plagued him, and he decided that a trip to his mountain cottage in Montana would help him forget his problems. And in a harrowing kind of a way, it did. He went mountain climbing alone; got very high in both senses of the word; and fell. His body was critically ripped and crushed, and his spirit offered no encouragement to fight for life.

The Fosters stepped in after that and somehow convinced him that he did, after all, have reason to continue. The physical healing of his injuries began in a Montana hospital as he struggled to get off the critical list and then continued under Doc's constant care back in California as he fought to get the mended bones and stitched muscles to work again. And all of that was the easy part—in fact, ridiculously easy in comparison to the process of beating the cocaine and alcohol addiction. If it hadn't been for Wayne's strong support, Matt knew, he never would have been able to do it. Eventually Wayne sent him off to a rehab facility in northern California to complete the job.

When Matt returned he found his business smaller but salvaged, thanks to Wayne, and his divorce papers finalized. Recovered, Matt resolved never to relive the experience. Keenly aware of his vulnerability to dependency and never forgetting the pain that came from his commitment to Sheila, he moved to Montana with a vow he would live by, an oath that he would carry like a protective talisman: he would be cautious in all things, Matt had sworn to himself, forevermore.

The first fireworks starburst exploded in the horizon. Matt and Doc watched the display to its conclusion, each absorbed in thought. Doc twirled her empty beer can between her palms and broke the silence.

"Matty," she began in her husky voice, "now,

please don't misunderstand me because I absolutely adore having you stay here with us, but . . ." She turned on her chair to face him. "You've been here for three months and seem kind of at odds with yourself lately. Is there anything that's preventing you from returning to Montana? I mean, anything that you're afraid of back there?"

"No," he said, all the while marveling at Doc's ability to see more than he wished to show.

"Aren't you getting a tad tired of business lunches and working out in the gym every day?"

"Well, sort of," Matt conceded with a smile.

"How is your neighbor-friend, then?" Doc said, deliberately jumping tracks. "Caroline," Doc added.

"I don't know." Matt realized that Doc's sixth sense had him cornered. There was no way he could escape telling her the truth of his self-imposed exile.

"Did you quarrel?"

Matt explained about stepping aside for Jody as his reason for leaving Montana and waited for Doc to say something. When she finally did, it was more than he was prepared to deal with.

"Matty, did you leave because you don't really want her?"

"No. I left because I want her too much."

"So you decided to leave her to someone else." Doc's face showed puzzlement.

"I thought that it'd give her the chance to be surer about me."

"Do you mean to tell me—" Doc stopped herself. She had been going to ask if he had so little confidence in himself. But the answer was best left unspoken. She knew of Matt's fears. Instead she asked, "Well, did she run off with this cowboy or not?"

"I dunno. I'll find out when I get back there."

"Have you called or written her?"

"No."

"But you and this woman spent a lot of time together, as friends, as I understand it. And then, Matty, you go and vanish for three months without a trace, not even a phone call? And you expect to sashay back there and see if she loves you or this cowboy? Holy Hannah, Matty! What were you thinking?"

"Okay. Maybe I was taking cover, but I was only trying to protect myself until things got clearer."

"Clearer." Doc shook her head. "So you would prefer to wait until things got clearer, is that it?" She shook her head again. "You would prefer to hand her over to another man than take the chance on telling her how you feel? You know, Matty dear, there's nothing wrong with wanting someone too much, but sometimes you have to work for it."

"I was going to. This time around, though, I needed to know for sure—for absolutely sure. I needed to know if she was going to care as much as I did."

"You can't know for sure unless you lay your cards on the table, Matty. And that's hard to do if you're a thousand miles away."

"You make it sound like gambling."

"Well, of course. That's exactly what it is. It's what life is all about. Believe me, Matty, the one thing I've learned being a doctor is that for all our efforts to the contrary, there are no guarantees in life. It's all a whopping gamble. There are no guarantees in love, either,

Matty dear. Sometimes you lose and sometimes you win."

"I don't like playing at gambling."

"If you don't mind living with the alternatives, then you don't have to play." Doc's tone became serious. "That's what you're doing now—not playing."

Matt said good night earlier than usual that night. He needed time alone to think—the very thing he'd been actively avoiding up until now. Pacing the length of his childhood bedroom, he remembered what Doc had said when she spoke of Wayne as her confidant. Wayne and Doc's marriage was built upon more than their being just confidants to each other, Matt realized. Indeed, they were well matched in intellect and temperament, and they seemed romantically inclined toward each other. But there was a deeper strength to their relationship that Doc had described tonight. Carefully Matt reconstructed her words: "I can trust him with anything."

Still pacing, Matt recalled the last time he'd seen Caroline. Her wispy copper hair had been flying from the wind. Her cheeks dimpled with a smile. In another moment, he was in Wayne's home office. He found the black desk phone and smiled as he dialed. He let it ring ten times just in case she was outside, while in his own neighborhood, firecrackers popped in series of bursts. Two hours later there was still no answer, and none at three A.M., either. Still picturing Caroline's face, Matt was gripped by an icy fear that he was too late.

CHAPTER

27

*T*HE CABDRIVER HAD THE radio turned up full blast all the way to the airport. The traffic report blared of an accident on a northbound access lane plus heavy delays on incoming arteries. Even in the day's dawning hours, San Francisco was keying itself up into a state of agitation. Matt, sleepless from the night before, had already achieved it. Looking out the taxi window, he spied Sirius, the Dog Star. It rose, Matt remembered, with the sun, adding its heat to make July's days the hottest of the year. During that time, he also recalled, rain seldom fell, flies increased, and, supposedly, snakes went blind and dogs went mad.

The part about the rain seemed true enough as Matt's airplane made its landing approach over Great Falls later that morning. The terrain he observed from his aerial view was parched and straw-colored—much worse than last summer. Still, he rejoiced to see it.

It was around lunchtime when he drove into Hawkeye. Everything was comfortably unchanged, except that it was a whole season further along than when he'd left it. Sobered by this realization, Matt decided to stop at the Bitterroot instead of heading directly for home. He couldn't stand to wait even another hour. He had to find out right now no matter what the answer was. Maybe, if he was lucky, Ray would be having lunch. Ray would know, and Ray would tell it to him straight.

Luck was with him. He sat down to join Ray, who was eating his lunch alone at a table. Ray looked up from his brussels sprouts with no more surprise than if he'd seen Matt just yesterday.

"Glad you're here," Ray announced, preoccupied with chasing the last brussels sprout around his dish with a fork. Once he'd stabbed it, he regarded Matt and added gruffly, "Got some new fire equipment you need to learn how to use. It's looking like we got no time to lose, either."

"Okay." Matt hoped he hadn't shirked his duties as a volunteer on the fire squad. "Have there been any fires?"

"Just Caroline's."

"Her house or her timberland!?"

"Timber. Hardwoods. We put it out pretty easy." Ray pulled his side dish of hash browns in closer and motioned to the menu with his fork. "You want lunch?"

"No. I ate on the plane." Matt was about to ask more concerning Caroline, but Ray launched right into a new subject.

"Your horses are all okay, but they seemed kinda spooked last time I was out there. Only thing I can think of is coyotes. Folks have spotted them coming in closer these nights. Hungry on account of this drought, no doubt. Bob junior says he lost near to a dozen chickens to them." Ray stopped to eat some hash browns. "Pass the salt, would you?"

Matt slid the salt and the pepper shakers together across the table. He toppled the pepper shaker in the motion.

"Spilled pepper," Ray stated, using the salt, then righting the pepper, "means an argument between friends. Hope it's not us."

"You sound like Winona." Matt smiled. "Tell me something, Ray," he said quietly. He was unable to postpone it any longer. "Is Caroline still seeing Jody Landis?"

"Nope."

"You're sure?"

"Yup."

Matt waited while Ray finished all his hash browns.

"Didn't last more than a few weeks after you'd gone." Ray started on the dish of applesauce, then continued. "Just for the record, town gossip had you living with a girlfriend in California."

Matt frowned in puzzlement.

"The name Margaret . . ." Ray paused to spoon up more applesauce. "Mean anything to you? I'm not asking for an answer. It's nobody's business but your own. It's just to let you know what everyone else knows—or thinks they know."

"Aw, Jeez." Matt shook his head and looked disgusted. "That jerk Corwell started it. Right?"

"Don't know. Just heard it around town."

"Do you think Caroline heard it, too?"

"You know how stories can fly around here." As was his way, Ray answered his friend levelly, without a hint of visible curiosity. As to whether the girlfriend story was true or not, he figured that Matt would tell him if he wanted to.

But right now, Matt's fatigued mind was swirling with an overload. His relief at Jody's fade-out had just transformed into galloping alarm over the gossip. He had to tell Caroline the truth. Abruptly he squealed back his chair and stood up. "I've gotta go, Ray. Catch you later."

Ray watched Matt hurry out of the Bitterroot. Thoughtfully he swept the spilled pepper off the Formica tabletop and onto the floor.

When Matt finally located Caroline she was way across the field behind her house. Unaware of his approach, she was gathering wild blackberries into a basket. Every once in a while she knelt down to pet Humphrey. As Matt walked toward her, he was struck by how gracefully her lithe figure moved in her lavender-print sundress. Her copper hair, tied loosely with a ribbon of lace, seemed much lighter and longer than before. While her willowy arms reached for the berries, she appeared to be talking earnestly to Humphrey, just the sort of sweet-silly thing Caroline was apt to do, Matt reflected tenderly. He hastened his approach. As she walked to the next blackberry bush, a breeze blew the flimsy sundress close against her, silhoueting the curves of her body and filling Matt with yearning.

He was nearly at her side before she noticed him.

And although Caroline's immediate reaction appeared to be genuine happiness combined with a quick movement that made Matt think she was just about to embrace him, she hastily checked herself. Visibly subduing any further outward expression, she spoke to Matt in an uneasy and unaccustomed tone.

"Welcome back," she said in a stranger's voice.

"It's good to be back." Matt fought back the desire to simply clasp her close to him and thereby get to the heart of the matter. Instead he pocketed his sunglasses and asked, "What's been happening around here?"

"Not much." She shrugged, then held on to an earring while she continued. "Lots of dry weather. I had a forest fire, but nothing bad happened. And when I got back this morning, Winona told me that the trash to energy thing got defeated."

"Wonderful!" Matt said, adding, "About Sanborne, I mean."

The stranger possessing Caroline retreated slightly while she mustered a smile.

"Where'd you go, anyway?" Matt asked her. "I called you last night, but you weren't home."

"Oh," Caroline answered vaguely. For a moment it seemed that she was about to say something more, but again she stopped herself. "Just out," she replied, regarding him as if for the first time that afternoon. "You look thinner," she observed wanly.

"I've been working out every day," Matt replied distractedly. He was wondering about Caroline's last answer. "What have you been doing?"

"Not so much." She frowned at Humphrey, who was affectionately rubbing against Matt's ankles.

She seemed annoyed with something, Matt

thought. Was it him or the cat? Out loud he asked, "What's the story on your timberland?"

Still using a stranger's tone, Caroline explained about the pear thrips.

"Wow, Caroline," Matt said with concern. "I'm really sorry."

"That's the breaks," she replied, shrugging.

Matt stared across the empty plain and wondered what to say next. There was so much he wanted to tell Caroline now that he was finally with her, but the words dried up inside him.

"How was your business trip?" she asked coolly.

"It was okay." Matt knew from her stiff manner that she had indeed heard the town's gossip. He needed to straighten it out. It would be easy enough to explain how Doc and Margaret were really the same person. The tricky part would be explaining his absence without baring his entire soul to her. He had hoped to tell Caroline that he loved her in a more gradual way.

"That's nice." Caroline's voice filtered through his thoughts. She had a tense expression that reminded him of someone trapped, and she seemed as if she were about to edge away from something. Positioning her basket handle onto the crook of her arm, she started to leave.

"Wait!" Matt said, following her in the direction of her house. He wanted to explain, but not while trotting after her through a field. "Wait, a minute, okay?" He jogged to keep up with her.

"What?" Caroline stopped short.

Maybe it was her annoyed impatience that threw his tired mind off track or maybe it was his own incapacitating fear, but suddenly Matt knew that this wasn't the right time, the right place, or the right mood to tell her. He needed more time. He needed to prepare. He had to do this right, say it carefully. "How about dinner?" he asked.

Caroline looked at him, perplexed.

"Dinner," Matt said. "How about if you come and have dinner at my place?"

"No," she snapped. Realizing her rudeness, she tried to soften it by adding, "You've just gotten back. . . ."

"Okay. How about if we have dinner at your place, then?"

"No, Matt. Not tonight."

"Okay. How about if . . ." Matt paused to watch her. She seemed as perched on the edge of anxiety as he was. "How about if I come by to see you tomorrow?"

"No, Matt," she replied immediately. Whether she was aware of it or not, her steps were slowly backing her away from him. "I've got plans made already. I'm going to be busy."

"Fine!" he practically shouted, angry with her, frustrated with himself. "Fine," he repeated, regaining his composure. "I'll see you around, then."

Caroline bit her lower lip and nodded wordlessly. She stood motionless now, no longer in a hurry to flee.

Matt strode away through the long field, wanting to but willing himself not to run.

Nightfall found Caroline eating blackberries outside on her side porch, catching what slight breeze the night air could offer. This was her first day back from her wilderness trip and she still hadn't spent more than an hour inside her house. Each time she stepped indoors, the oppressive heat trapped within the walls made her feel stifled. Reflecting on it, she wondered if it was really the heat or the walls themselves. She ate another blackberry and leaned forward on her chair to watch Humphrey cautiously stalk something in the field at the back corner of the house. When he hadn't advanced for a while, Caroline eased all the way back onto her new wicker porch chair.

Thoughtfully she raised a plump blackberry between her fingers, then squeezed it until it bled. She hadn't handled it well today with Matt, she told herself. When she first saw him, all kinds of things rushed into her mind that she wanted to talk to him about, and the only way she could find to stop herself was to be rude. She pressed the blackberry harder and put it in her mouth. Licking the juice off her fingertips, she wondered if perhaps she'd been too harsh and pushed away his friendship entirely. She picked at the berries in the basket and thought about it. If she had any brains at all, maybe that would be the best approach. That way she wouldn't come to depend on Matt's companionship, only to have him snatch it away and leave for three-month business trips. Business, hah! Why couldn't he at least admit that it was to see his girlfriend?

Caroline squeezed another blackberry. The dark juice was down to her knuckles before she could get it into her mouth. That, of course, was no good, either, she realized, tending to her fingers. Today, in the field, Matt's troubled expression had warned her that he was going to explain something about this Margaret of his; Caroline just knew it, sensed it with a certainty. And with equal certainty she knew that she didn't want to, couldn't bear to, hear it. Her reaction had been instinctive, and without even thinking she had tried to flee from him. Maybe, she reflected, she needed more time. Maybe this newfound independence of hers needed to grow deeper roots before she could allow herself to be friends with Matt. Or maybe she was just fooling herself, she thought just as Humphrey rushed and pounced upon something in the tall grasses.

Caroline told herself to look squarely into her heart. Do you really think you can listen to him talk about his life in San Francisco with someone else? She asked herself. Can you turn your true feelings off like that just for the sake of companionship? The answer, illustrated this afternoon, was clear and immediate. It filled her with anger, not only at the impossible situation, but at Matt for taking from her that which she was not prepared to give and for returning no more than friendship—a friendship she was happy neither with nor without.

Caroline looked bitterly across the field where Humphrey had been rustling in the grasses. The slow-motion stealth not far from her cat drew her attention, but the glint from the deep, close-set eyes were the giveaway. Caroline's reaction was just as instinctive as it had been with Matt this afternoon, but this time it was not to flee. Soundlessly she slipped into the house and swiftly returned to perceive that there was another one crouched just behind it. The first coyote poised itself, motionless, but Caroline spotted it by the faint outline of bent field grasses. Now, it was less than four yards away from where Humphrey was. No sooner had Caroline spotted it than the coyote leaped into the air toward Humphrey, jackknifing midflight. The crack of the gunshot obliterated Caroline's hearing while she watched Humphrey shoot away at rocket speed toward the barn. The second coyote sped through the dry grasses toward the far mountains.

More angry then afraid, Caroline clutched the black handgun and walked toward the field. Her only thought through the high-pitched ringing in her ears was that she hoped the animal was completely dead. In the near darkness its coat looked reddish tan, and it seemed more like a dog than a wild creature. It lay on its side, its beady eyes vacant. A spreading blotch of blood stained its neck fur, and its mouth was frozen open in a silent howl. Caroline scrutinized the coyote intently, satisfied that it was dead, perhaps too satisfied. She stared at the lifeless animal and tried to feel some remorse over her deed. She had none.

CHAPTER

28

"I'VE HEARD THAT PEO-
ple get more stubborn as they grow older, but you,
Caroline, you have no place to go!" Matt stood on her
front porch, his fingers tapping out his frustration on
the cardboard crate that stood between them.

The "older" accusation stung Caroline, although
he was completely correct about her being stubborn.
That was her plan of defense, and she intended to stand
fast. He'd been knocking at her door every day for the
past two weeks—stopping by "just to say hello," even
bringing her mail from Hawkeye, anything to wear her
down and get close to her again, but she'd done her best
to repel him. Now here he was with the wicker porch
table she'd ordered from the Sears catalog, along with
his cheery explanation that he thought he'd save her
the trouble of having to fetch it from the post office.
Well, at least he'd been cheery up until now. His pa-

tience seemed to be rapidly unraveling on a par with her own.

"Why?" Why won't you come to the movies with me?"

"Oh, Matt, I just don't want to, that's all." Caroline was becoming confused by his pushy insistence, while at the same time she held herself in check even more carefully than usual. The impossible situation was of her own doing, she reminded herself, not Matt's. And although it would be easy to put him off by blurting out something nasty, he didn't deserve to have his feelings hurt like that.

"Caroline," Matt half stated, half pleaded, "you haven't let me talk to you since I've been back. . . ."

"You're talking."

"You know what I mean." He said it levelly, but there was an edge to his voice.

"Matt," she interrupted quickly, assuming a firm and combative attitude, "I don't see what—"

"Look," he interrupted just as swiftly without concealing his temper, "have I done something wrong? Have I insulted you or something?"

"No," she said, even though her private answer was yes.

"Then why won't you listen to me?"

How could she tell him her reason—that his very presence was like a torture to her, that her fear of him speaking of his Margaret only increased the torture? How could she announce that she loved him in spite of the knowledge that he didn't love her? No, she couldn't. She wouldn't. She'd been a fool once, but she wouldn't be again.

"Why?" he demanded persistently, maddeningly.

"Oh, okay," she burst out in exasperation, thinking to herself that, yes, it would be torture, but she would endure it. It was, after all, still the path of least resistance. She glared at him as she answered his original if not his most recent question. "Okay, I'll go to the movies with you."

"Fine," Matt said, purposely ignoring both her evasiveness and her annoyance. "How about if I come round for you tonight at . . ." He paused a moment, wondering if adding dinner out to the proposition would be pushing it. He looked at Caroline's irked face and saw that it would. "Eight?"

"Eight is fine," Caroline said politely as she clicked the front door closed on him. Back in the privacy of her own living room, she grimaced and slapped her hand over her mouth, but it was too late. She'd already accepted.

Walking down the front porch steps, Matt fought back the disturbing feeling that he wanted—no, needed—a drink.

The only movie theater in Medallion County was in the neighboring town of Novi. At eight o'clock Matt's red pickup carried its two uneasy passengers there, one intent on delivering a message that he still didn't know quite how to reveal, the other just as intent not to hear what she thought he might say.

"How far is it to Novi?" Caroline asked, glancing across the seat at Matt.

Even though the sun was setting, eye level to his left, Matt remembered to take off his sunglasses. He wondered briefly at what she had chosen to wear tonight: a dull and shapeless dress, uncharacteristically long for Caroline and uncharacteristically unattractive, too. He thought it best not to mention it. "It's about a forty-five-minute drive," he replied.

Caroline averted her eyes, miserable in the knowledge that Matt's nearness was stirring her more basic responses. The way he rolled up the sleeves of his dark navy shirt; the relaxed, masculine grace with which he draped his arm to the steering wheel; the teasing slyness barely concealed in his lively dark eyes. Even without looking at him, she was both unnerved by and drawn to the familiar smell of his closeness. Caroline's helpless misery turned back on her. How could she ever have allowed herself to be talked into this? Why, when at this very moment her common sense was blaring the alarm that this was a very bad idea?

Matt flashed a mischievous sort of grin at her. "Don't worry. Going to the movies with me won't be so bad."

Not trusting herself with words, Caroline shot him a quick but pointedly sarcastic look.

"Besides," he continued blithely, "how long has it been since you've been to the movies?"

"A long time, I guess," she confided to the windshield.

"Doesn't Jody Landis ever take you?" Matt teased, fully aware of the unfairness of his remark but unable to stop himself.

"No," Caroline replied, an unmistakable chilliness to her tone, "he never did." Scowling, she focused her attention on what passed outside her side window.

Silence prevailed as the mountain road into Novi turned into a flatland road over empty prairies. Matt squinted into the western sun. Finally, more subdued, he reopened the conversation.

"Novi got its name because it was a stagecoach water stop back in the 1800s, did you know that?"

"Nope."

"Uh-huh," he continued, trying hard. "It was just a water tank at first with its station number written on it. And that's what they ended up calling the town that sprang up later. The abbreviation for 'number' was 'no.' and 'six' in Roman numerals was 'vi.' So, they called it Novi."

"That's nice," Caroline answered, polite yet aloof. She was wishing that she were out of this mess.

Matt drove on, wondering what to say. Nothing sprang to mind. The straight prairie road stretched on, and the sun set in an orange blaze. After a time he broke the silence with a question for Caroline. He had intended it to be heartfelt and thoughtful sounding, but even as he spoke the words, his voice betrayed him with a slight hint of teasing.

"Did you miss me?" he asked her.

"Oh, I don't know," she said lightly, "I kept pretty busy."

"Doing what?"

"Stuff."

"Well, I missed you." This time he said it as honestly as he really felt, but even though he wanted to elaborate, he found he couldn't.

Caroline shot him a quick, and fretful glance before returning her attention to the road ahead. She once again wished she were anywhere but where she was. This whole going-out thing was truly a mistake.

Matt was suddenly thinking much along the same lines. Things were not going as planned. He should have told her who Margaret was by now. Maybe he should just forget about paving the way to explanation and say it outright, right now. Watching Caroline in her troubled silence and her ugly dress, he tried to speak, but the words wouldn't come. Was it his own lack of confidence or Caroline's strange behavior that was stymieing him? he wondered. She used to be so sympathetic to his moods, but now she seemed to have a chip on her shoulder. If she'd only meet him halfway instead of being so standoffish, he could tell her.

They were nearing a place where they would soon drive through a railroad underpass when Matt saw that a freight train was rumbling across its overhead tracks. Remembering something from his childhood, he floored the gas pedal so they'd be under the tracks while the train was above their heads. "Quick!" he told Caroline. "Put your hand on the ceiling and make a wish." They both did so while the last of the boxcars thundered above them.

"I didn't know you were superstitious," Caroline said, momentarily letting down her barriers. She smiled briefly before adding, "What'd you wish for?"

"I wished that you'd stop being mad at me."

"I'm not mad at you."

Matt was about to argue the point but stopped himself. "What'd you wish for?"

"It's private." She rubbed her itchy nose. When pressed to wish quickly under the bridge, she had wished without thinking, and now she was sorry she had because she'd wished for the impossible. She rubbed at her nose again and scowled out the window.

"Aw, come on," Matt chided. "What'd you wish for?"

"No. It won't come true if you say it."

Now Matt scowled, too, as he drove, close-mouthed, toward Novi.

Novi was smaller than Hawkeye but more interesting. Instead of hardware and fabric stores on its main street, it hosted a veritable wealth of entertainment options—a bowling alley, a honky-tonk, and a movie theater. Matt parked the truck in the fenced-in graveled lot behind the movie house, and they walked to the theater. The crunching of the stones beneath their feet was the only sound they made. The movie was a clone in the Mafia-saga category and not worthy of much discussion as they left the theater.

"You want to get something to eat at the diner?" Matt asked once they were outside. "Or a drink?" He motioned to Perk's Place and hoped she'd choose the diner.

"Thanks, but I'd rather not."

Their footsteps crunched slowly over the gravel in the empty parking lot, where the night had deepened since they'd entered the theater a few hours before. Walking toward Matt's truck under the glow of one dim, bug-swarmed lamppost, they heard a snap and a small, high-pitched squeal from the open field beyond the gravel lot. Both Caroline and Matt, as if by some unspoken mutual curiosity, walked straight to the farthest fence rail and peered out to see what animal it might be. Although they saw no other signs of wildlife, Caroline's mind sprang into thoughts about catamounts and wolverines, although she suspected there was nothing more out there than a weasel. Matt's thoughts seemed to be running on a parallel course.

"You know," he began quietly in the hush that now engulfed them, "you got me in deep trouble with

Ray and Winona. They think it was me who suggested you go off on your wilderness hike. Why didn't you tell me you went, Caroline? Where'd you go? What'd you see?"

His interest was so sincere that Caroline was gripped by the need to share with him the experiences only he would understand. In spite of herself, she found she was softening, wanting to open up to him. She steeled herself and reined back the temptation, but her inner turmoil was getting the best of her.

"You should see yourself," Matt chuckled gently, referring to the play of emotions taking turns on her face.

Quickly she rubbed her itchy nose as if to rub away her countenance as well.

"Nose itches." Matt smiled, raising an eyebrow at her. "Means you're gonna kiss a fool." He moved toward her and delicately held her face between his thumbs.

His chestnut eyes had never looked so intently serious to Caroline as they captured her own helplessly mesmerized eyes. Gently stroking his thumbs down her cheeks, he lifted her chin with a deliberate tenderness and kissed her with an intensity that suspended all rational thought. The overwhelming rush of yearning that besieged Caroline left her at a loss to protest. It angered her to realize that she didn't want to protest. Not while his hands pressed the small of her back, urging her into a stronger embrace that she herself was much too willing to answer. Not while his moist lips played teasingly over her own tingling mouth. Flushed with a breathless mix of helplessness and desire, Caroline pressed her hands against his shoulders to push him away. She was incapable of carrying out her intent. But when Matt's embrace tightened stronger around her, it brought her to a point that required every shred of her being to rebuff. Pushing away and trying to catch her breath, if not her composure, she was suddenly furious with herself for her weakness. Stepping backward, she said shakily but with angry conviction, "Can we go home now?"

Matt fought down his own swirl of feelings and answered with a gleam in his eye, "Sure." He arched an eyebrow at her. He knew teasing was unwise, but he said it anyway. "Your place or mine?" Silently he followed in her wake toward the red pickup, wondering if it was just him or if all men were such gluttons for punishment.

They drove back to Hawkeye in complete and utter silence in a pickup truck cab where the tension hung so heavily it could practically be touched. Matt's concentration seemed aimed on the road he steered down, but his real focus was on the words he wished to speak but couldn't. In fact, he was realizing that the longer he stalled, the harder it became to speak at all.

Caroline, on the other hand, was boiling over with things to speak of and was working hard on keeping her mouth shut. Why was he toying with her like that? Damn it, he already had a girlfriend in California—and that made him nothing but a lousy two-timer, not one iota better than the last son of a bitch she'd let herself get entangled with. Who did he think he was? she snarled to herself. A sailor with a woman in every port? Did he actually have the gall to think that she would be the country girlfriend when he was in Montana? Well, hell no! This was the absolute end between them, Caroline decreed. No friendship was worth this kind of grief. Why couldn't he have just respected their friendship and simply left it at that? And why, she continued, her fury stoked and turning inward, why had she let him kiss her like that?

The pickup turned into Caroline's driveway, and Matt spoke in a serious tone, quietly pacing his words. "I want you to know, Caroline, that it's been a long time since I've gone out like this. I enjoyed our evening."

Caroline couldn't tell if she detected sarcasm in his voice or not. How could he have possibly enjoyed the evening? They'd had a terrible time, for goodness' sake.

"I hope we can do this again sometime," he said, turning off the engine.

He had to be kidding, Caroline decided. But why, she asked herself, did he seem so damn sincere?

He was toying with her again, she concluded angrily, that's why. Well, damn it, she could toy with him, too. "Didn't you go out in California?" She glared at him meanly. Without waiting for a reply, she opened the truck door, added a crisp, "Good night," and jumped down.

"No."

She turned around and was about to slam the door, but first she shot him a disgusted sneer that implied he was lying.

"Just in case you were wondering," Matt added quickly, the last-minute pressure of the situation finally summoning some of the words he sought, "you're the only woman in my life, Caroline."

Caroline stood speechless on her driveway. She looked eye level into the truck's front seat while her face registered a confusion that quickly jelled into annoyance. "Who, then," she asked, "is Margaret?"

"How did you hear about Margaret?" one part of Matt asked aloud, while another warned him simply to seize the moment and explain.

"I heard it around town."

"And you believed what you heard around town?"

"What I heard seemed to be based on fact—that your address in California was not your own, but that of someone named Margaret. But, okay, you tell me. Was that true or not?"

"True. And I suppose," he said, suddenly buoyed by the consternation written on Caroline's face, "you want to know who Margaret is." He grinned at her, delighted by the suspicion that she was, perhaps, jealous, and waited for her to reply.

"Not really." Caroline feigned indifference. "If you never mentioned it before, it's none of my business now."

"Margaret is a friend," Matt said pointedly. "A very dear friend who, at one time, used to be a big part of my life." He shrugged as if to say there was no more to it than that.

Caroline regarded him skeptically. He seemed so flip with his answer. Just a friend, huh? Wasn't that how he always labeled her, too?

Really," Matt continued, "there isn't the slightest need for you to feel jealous over Margaret." His eyes gleamed at her with the implication.

Caroline scowled at him darkly.

A voice in Matt's head screamed at him. *Dummy!* it nagged. *Tell her it's Doc, for Chrissake!* But it was as if he were paralyzed. The words that would explain would have to say more than he was able to say, so no words came at all.

"I'm not jealous," Caroline muttered, but it was barely audible because of her embarrassment.

"You could fool me." Matt taunted, retreating to his last line of defense. Again, he reprimanded himself. If only he could somehow be more forthright, she'd be in his arms instead of glowering at him from outside the truck door. But, again, no words would come. Instead he grinned at her heartily. "Just look at your face, Caroline," he said with ill-timed amusement. Jealous of someone you shouldn't even be jealous of at all."

"I am not jealous of anyone," she hissed through clenched teeth. Caroline slammed the truck door shut with a jolt that underscored the extent of her rage, and then she stomped away from the source of it.

CHAPTER

✦

29

"*I* DON'T KNOW, RAY,"
Matt said, shaking his head. He raked a hand through
his hair. "She's making me crazy with all of this."

The two men walked unhurriedly down the caked-
dry dirt ruts of one of Ray's logging trails. It was so hot,
even under the shady canopy of maple trees, that none
of the usual August insects had the energy to swarm
around them.

"Mmm," Ray answered, stopping to examine a
maple sapling for possible signs of thrips.

"It's like she's some kind of yo-yo or something.
Last night I could have sworn she was interested in me.
Today, I drive by her in her yard, I honk, wave, say 'hi,'
and she ignores me, turns her back on me entirely."

"Damn," Ray announced after finding what he
feared under a new leaf.

"You said it. You know, ever since I got back, I've

been groveling around her door like some homeless dog just so I could clear up this town gossip. And finally, *finally* she agrees to go out with me. Even though she shows up wearing a flour sack, for Chrissake, and even though she won't say more than two words to me all the way to Novi, later on she warms up a little. So, I explain to her how Margaret is someone who used to be a big part of my life but not anymore, and do you know what?"

"Mmm."

"She ends up being even more angry at me than before." The two men walked on in silence for a distance. Matt was accustomed to waiting for Ray, who checked two more maples before speaking.

"Maybe," Ray drawled, "she's thinking that you just broke up with this Margaret lady and that she's catching you on the rebound. Caroline's got a good amount of pride, you know."

"Aw, Jeez. That's not it."

"Then you need to explain it better."

"Hell, I tried hard enough last night and look where it got me. Maybe what I really need to do is take things slower, steadier. Maybe I'm rushing into this too fast, Ray. Maybe I should be learning from one mistake instead of leaping headfirst into the next one."

"To be fair," Ray said, slowing his pace, "sounds like she's got more to watch out for than you do."

Matt nodded in thought. That Caroline needed to be cautious had never occurred to him before this. "Maybe I'm not ready to give up my independence just yet."

"She's got that problem, too. Her and that idiot

camping thing of hers. Could'a independenced herself to death out there."

"Well, then, it's just possible that neither one of us is ready for each other, that's all."

"Who do you think you're fooling here?" Ray stopped in front of a maple and got as close to smirking as Matt had ever seen.

"I'm not trying to fool anyone."

"Right. And I am the king of England." Ray checked another maple leaf and threw it down, scowling. "Admit it. Now that you've got her where she wants you, you're scared."

"Scared of what?"

"Commitment, of course."

Matt didn't care for what he heard and even less so coming from his trusted friend. He regarded Ray with suspicion. "Whose side are you on, anyway?"

"Yours." Ray's eyes met his directly. "You know that."

Later that day, Matt clicked on the tape player as he drove home. Usually loud music had a way of capturing his attention and diminishing his concerns, but today it irritated more than it soothed. So, okay, maybe he was a little nervous about this commitment thing. Ray was right to point it out, but still, it didn't make things any easier. Disgruntled, he clicked off the music. And, okay, he probably should have told her right up front who Margaret really was instead of being so coy about it. But on the other hand, why couldn't she have just taken his "good friend" explanation at face value? Why did she have to be told everything? His privacy and furthermore his past—those were his own business, no one else's. Where does it say that he should be required to account for every single detail of his life?

Either he was way too wrapped up in thinking about this mess or else he was speeding, he realized. He was nearly home. Unconsciously he slowed down as he passed Caroline's house. She wasn't anywhere outside, and the front door was, unaccustomedly, shut. Slowing down further, he surveyed the barn area, but her Bronco wasn't in sight. He wondered where she might be then, with an effort, he made himself stop wondering.

Accelerating, Matt looked over amber plains and an idea occurred to him. That it might be just a little too dry to chance it now also occurred to him. He considered the sun-dried land in the distance. It would certainly be more of a challenge than usual.

"That means company is coming," Winona announced from across her kitchen table. She handed Caroline the slice of bread they had both just reached for. In the course of their assembly-line sandwich making that afternoon, Caroline had also learned that it was bad luck to cut bread from both ends or leave a knife stuck in a loaf or turn a loaf of bread upside down. The sandwiches were part of the twenty-two dinner boxes they were preparing for the volunteer fire fighters. The squad, Ray and Matt among them, was out battling a brushfire, and it looked as if they'd be at it well into the night. Although this blaze, a wildfire that had sprung up in the valley east of Hawkeye, was the biggest brushfire of the summer so far, it wasn't the first. The squad had been called to duty on three other occasions during the past two weeks.

"You don't suppose the fire's going to spread to the woods this time?" Caroline asked as she sliced generously thick slabs of smoked Virginia ham on a cutting board.

"It depends on which way the wind is blowing," Winona answered. She interrupted her sandwich making to take two large pans of brownies out of the oven. Stuffy as it made the kitchen, the rush of chocolate-scented heat was enticing. "But sooner or later, you know it is going to be a forest fire. I don't see that we can avoid it," Winona added, returning to the sandwiches. "I suppose it's one way of getting rid of those nasty little thrips."

"I heard that you and Ray have them, too. I'm sorry." Caroline smiled at Tyrone, who was trotting faster than usual away from Winona's side.

"There's always next year."

"Mmmm. That's what I'm counting on, too." Caroline slipped Tyrone the chunk of ham he had come for.

When forty-four jumbo sandwiches were made, wrapped, and stacked in their boxes, Caroline brought in the Granny Smiths she'd bought at the IGA. Winona took the first one and rubbed it briskly over her heart before placing it in a box. "To eat an apple without rubbing it first is to challenge the Devil," she told Caroline. "They'll be too busy, so we'll do it for them."

"Do you worry about Ray when he's at these fires?" Caroline reached for an apple and followed Winona's example.

"Of course I do. But not nearly as much as you appear to be worried about Matt."

Caroline unconsciously rubbed her apple more vigorously. "I suppose I am worried about him. Even though I told myself I wouldn't rely on his companionship so much anymore, we seem to have fallen into our old routine of doing stuff together these past few weeks. I guess that even in spite of my trying to be more independent, I can't deny that I enjoy his company."

"Is that all you can't deny?"

"Yeah. That's all." Caroline knew immediately what Winona was hinting at. "I've thought about it a lot, Winona. I really have. His friendship is all I can handle right now." She held her apple poised as she thought again about how she'd arrived at this decision. For the past few weeks, Matt's words—that she was the only woman in his life—had rung with equal clarity with his words explaining Margaret as once being a big part of his life. Caroline had concluded that even if he had just ended an affair with this Margaret, more dust needed to settle on it. What if he changed his mind and returned to her for another three months? Caroline wondered if she'd ever be able to recover her independence all over again. Or, instead, would she have to leave Montana in search of a safer, more peaceful place to live?

"Does Matt feel this way, too?" Winona asked.

Caroline finished rubbing her apple, remembering how he hadn't touched her or, for that matter, even come close to her since their evening in Novi. "Yes, I believe he does."

Winona nodded silently in that wise-and-patient, nonjudgmental way Caroline had seen her use on Ray so many times, and it said, however wordlessly, more than Caroline wished to hear.

"Are the brownies cool enough to cut?" Caroline asked.

Again, Winona nodded in eloquent silence.

CHAPTER

30

*C*AROLINE CAREFULLY transferred the leather reins to one hand and swatted at the horsefly near her face. She watched it buzz to Matt's horse, directly in front of hers. Their chestnut mares followed a thin trail that only Matt was able to discern while Caroline, finally accustomed to the rhythmic bounce and sway of riding, observed their surroundings. The afternoon's ride had brought them to a series of rolling hills speckled with yellow wildflowers and outlined by scattered lines of pines. The hills, stretching on for miles, and the limitless sky above filled Caroline with a swelling sense of freedom. Her gaze returned to Matt, riding confidently ahead of her, keeping a cautious pace to accommodate her amateur equestrian skills. Candidly regarding the easy way his broad shoulders moved in harmony with the horse's gait, Caroline reflected that lately, at a similarly cautious pace, something was changing between them. Before, she used to know exactly where the boundaries were. The areas that defined simple friendship with Matt were always just as clear as her awareness of what edged beyond friendship. But now, as if imperceptibly, the distinctions were beginning to blur.

The horses plodded through a ridge of pine trees. When they were through to the other side, Matt turned to Caroline. "It's down this hill," he said. "We'll tether the horses here." He dismounted with the grace of an acrobat while Caroline sat puzzling as to how she might accomplish that, too. It was a long way down to the ground.

"Just sit sidesaddle," Matt said from down at her side. Gripping her securely, he allowed her to slide off the horse. He lingered a moment longer while they stood face to face on the ground then released her when she tensed. He led both horses to the shade of the pine trees. Caroline stood watching, feeling bowlegged and wobbly from riding for so long.

"It's over there," Matt said, pointing. "Down by that bunch of aspen." He was referring to his favorite fishing spot.

Together they unpacked the fishing gear and headed down the hillside until it leveled at the banks of a wide, running stream. Matt's fishing spot was cool from the dancing shade of aspen leaves and covered with lush green grasses fed by the water nearby. Caroline plopped down on the oasis. Discovering how close-cropped the grass was all around her, she unstrapped her sandals and squeezed her bare feet pleasurably into the soft, verdant carpet. Matt assembled the two fishing rods, then opened a dirt-packed container of night crawlers. Joining him, Caroline took up the hook of her fishing line and began to bait it.

From the corner of his eye, Matt studied her. There she sat in a frilly, feminine, pink-blushed cotton blouse. Eyelet lace ruffled demurely around her shawl collar while, without the slightest trace of squeamishness, she impaled a fat, fighting worm, weaving it repeatedly, oozing, onto a barbed hook. Nothing had changed, Matt observed. She still confused the hell out of him.

They cast their lines into the stream and reeled out enough so that they could sit on the bank and wait for fish to bite. Matt's line pulled right away. He was kept busy with a series of catches while Caroline waited, content to break into the bag of Fritos she had brought. She watched Matt standing beyond her. His lanky-legged blue jeans and dark navy shirt contrasted sharply with the cloudless azure sky as, in one fluid movement, he cast off another line. He stood there for nearly half the bag of Fritos before he reeled in his next catch. Sitting beside Caroline, he unhooked it and added it to the fish basket.

"I wonder how many I've got in there," he said, squinting into the basket. "A whole lot more than you," he added, grinning.

"If you count the number of fish you catch," Caroline replied, ignoring the taunt, "you won't catch any more."

"One, two, three rainbows," Matt said, lifting the basket lid, "and one . . ." He stopped when he saw what Caroline was suddenly reeling in. "That's a nice one," he said of the hefty steelhead trout thumping before them.

"Worth at least three little rainbows, wouldn't you

say?" Caroline returned the taunt while she unhooked the fish. She handed it to Matt to put in the basket. "May I have another worm?"

"Sure." Turning to her, he dangled the biggest of the night crawlers in front of her face and grinned the grin of a fifth-grade boy. The gray-and-red night crawler writhed angrily, fat and dirt-blackened in some places, thin and slimy in others.

Caroline regarded both Matt and the worm with equally cool disdain. He held the wiggling creature closer, nearly touching her nose with it. Making a show of how unruffled she was, Caroline looked upon Matt with the forbearance of a tolerant parent as she calmly snatched the sticky night crawler from him. In one swift motion she had pulled the neck of Matt's dark shirt and dropped the worm within. Much pleased, she smirked at him, waiting for results.

Matt gave the appearance of complete composure. Overdone composure, Caroline commented to herself, still waiting. He arched an eyebrow at her in superior reproach but remained silent, seemingly untroubled by the slithery intruder crawling inside his shirt. To Caroline's annoyance, he maintained this stance for a remarkable amount of time. All of a sudden, however, he was on his knees, vigorously yanking his shirt out of his blue jeans, a queasy sort of alarmed expression overtaking his face. Despite some initial hasty fumbling, he got his shirt buttons undone with lightning speed. He peered into each open shirt flap and then, with an amazing amount of energy, into his waistband. Retrieving the invader, Matt reassumed his composure and advanced toward Caroline, the night crawler drooping off his fingers.

"Oh, come on, Matt. That's enough," she said nervously. "It was only just a little worm."

Smiling, he came closer. Caroline crossed her arms, King Tut-style, tightly over the front and neck of her blouse and glared at him defiantly. But her glare dissolved into consternation when she perceived that Matt's mischievous gaze focused not on her blouse, but somewhere above it. He raised the worm higher, his dark eyes even more intent.

"What are you doing with that?" she demanded.

"Your hair. I think it'd look especially nice"—he smiled slyly as he advanced—"in your hair."

She crab-walked backward a few paces, but Matt matched her retreat, proffering the writhing worm aloft. When it came too close to her ear, she abruptly covered her head with both arms. She missed seeing Matt's triumphant grin, but the slimy clamminess of the night crawler wiggling down the inside of her blouse was unmistakable.

"Eeeeew!!" Caroline furiously unbuttoned her blouse.

"Aw, come on," Matt teased. "It was only just a little worm."

"Uugh!" Caroline yowled in reply as she extracted the gooey fish bait from the center of her bra. She stared, disgusted and enraged, at the curled-up worm, then confronted Matt with the same black expression. He responded with a leer that conveyed how pleased he was with the results of what he'd done. His face fell, however, as Caroline, glowering evilly, raised the hapless worm menacingly toward him. Seeing that she meant to put it, now, in his hair, Matt reflexively clasped his hand around Caroline's wrist, swiftly raising her arm high and away from their faces. It brought them unexpectedly close, a closeness that startled and seized them immediately. Instantly the struggle halted, leaving both Caroline and Matt struck motionless. They stared, as if suspended, into each other's eyes. Caroline, softening to what she beheld in Matt's intense regard, unconsciously let the night crawler fall to the ground. Carefully Matt scooped her into his arms and laid her tenderly on the soft grass carpet. He lowered himself onto one elbow beside her, facing her as aspen leaves fluttered above his head. Spellbound, Caroline stared into his eyes, recognizing in them the same pent-up yearning as in her own. And she witnessed something that she'd wanted to see since the day she'd met him. Looking long into his dark-lashed eyes, she saw Matt as she'd only glimpsed him fleetingly before: guileless, unguarded, and without pretense. Seeing that, Caroline knew, then and there, and she knew it with a certainty. She loved him, utterly and completely. And for the first time ever, she rejoiced in that knowledge.

The stream murmured peacefully in the distance, and aspen leaves rustled serenely overhead, flitting their shade all about them as Matt drew nearer to Caroline. He met her lips with his own, kissing her full and long with a depth of tender passion she had never even imagined before this. It released from somewhere once lost within her an equal reserve of passion that surprised them both. Deliberately, in slow motion, Matt turned his body halfway onto Caroline's, their lips still touching, wordlessly speaking of love and desire long denied. Caroline felt the bare skin beneath their unbuttoned shirts meet, touch, cleave together. She felt their hearts, close-pressed, pounding, thundering, hers or his, she couldn't tell.

Breaking slowly away from their kiss, Matt looked into Caroline's face, seeking what was most important, the thing that Doc had spoken of, the thing that he needed even more than the surrender of Caroline's body. Holding himself in check, he regarded the woman he loved, searching for and finding the assurance he sought. It was there, unmistakably there, in Caroline's trusting hazel eyes. Smiling gratefully into those eyes, he continued without hesitation. Slowly he completed the job half-begun on her blouse, unfastening the buttons, lingering on them one by one, then untrussing her breasts and gathering their ample softness in his sinewy hands. He felt the buds harden while Caroline's tentative fingertips slipped lightly over his chest. He covered her with soft kisses until Caroline involuntarily hummed a small moan and her blue-jeaned legs allowed his body to press fully upon hers. Soft kisses became stronger and deeper, and their embrace tightened.

Again, beneath the quiet of the aspens' dancing shade, Matt pulled away to regard Caroline's face. Once more seeing the sweet, wide-eyed trust written there, he unfastened and slipped his hand into her blue jeans, his palm gently circling the soft satin of her belly. He felt her back arch as he reached the smooth line of a raised scar, but then he jolted to a stop.

Confused by his suddenness and, further, by the mix of alarm and concentration on his face, Caroline began to ask why. But Matt's salty fingers rested lightly upon her lips as he shook his head in silent warning. He swiftly fastened her blue jeans and reclasped the front of her bra, all the while listening, on full alert, to something she couldn't hear. He motioned her to, ever so slowly, get up onto her knees. And now Caroline heard it, too, along with the terrified whinnying of the horses. Matt didn't have to tell her. She'd heard the heavy thump of those lumbering footsteps before.

CHAPTER

31

*W*HAT CAROLINE DIDN'T
expect was for the bear to be a grizzly. She saw it appear,
hulking on the hilltop above them, more enormous than
any black or brown bear she'd ever seen. It stared with
what seemed a mixture of annoyance and curiosity,
poking its mammoth triangle of a head out at them to
better catch their scent. Beady black eyes stared from
beneath a thick-furred brow. The huge, black-nostriled
nose twitched irritably. Sitting on its hind legs, the
grizzly rested to watch them, the massive bulk of its
shoulder muscles forming a furry mane around a face
that remained fixed on the two humans. Caroline, mesmerized, could not help but return the same unblinking
stare, although all the while she was struck giddy by the
incongruity of the monster's cute little ears.

Matt, however, viewed the grizzly for what it was:
the symbol of all that was truly wild in the wilderness

at its best, a walking nightmare at its worst. In either case he didn't like what he was facing: a 1,300-pound carnivore that could sprint fifty yards in three seconds, run at a speed of thirty-five miles an hour and bring down prey with a single swipe of a razor-clawed paw. Its hearing was sharp and its sense of smell so keen, it could detect food from a mile's distance. Matt had long ago memorized the options he would have upon a grizzly encounter, and now he reviewed them along with the added complications of insuring Caroline's safety and without knowing if the horses stood anymore. They could run: knowing that the grizzly could run twice as fast as they could and, like a dog, its instinct was to chase and kill things that ran away from it. They could climb a tree: the spindly aspens wouldn't hold them, and even if they both somehow made it to the pines, the bear could climb, too. They could stand their ground in hopes that the bear was bluffing: standing together probably wouldn't work; and if they stood separately and the grizzly wasn't bluffing, it would attack the smaller human first. The last option was playing dead: with one person it held a fifty-fifty chance of working; with two, the odds worsened.

Matt looked at Caroline beside him and struggled with the choices. Which course of action would keep her safe? His thoughts froze instantly. The grizzly rose from its spot. Its taupe-brown fur rippled with sunlit silver as it ambled, pigeon-toed, along the ridge of the hilltop. Matt held his breath. The grizzly sat down again, having achieved a better view of them. Pushing down panic, Matt told himself that he must act quickly. If only he knew whether the horses were still there. He reticked off their options and added one more variable.

He stared at the grizzly's mouth, looking for the telltale white flecks that signaled a bear made edgy under stress. With a suddenness, the face of Leon's brother, Jimmie, passed before Matt's mind's eye: Jimmie's ruined half of a face because he was mauled by a grizzly—the huge eye patch; the stretched skin where his cheekbone and jaw ought to have been; the deformed mouth.

Matt flung off the awful image and assessed the grizzly's size. Great, elephantine forearms supported bulky, hunched shoulders like some exaggerated gorilla. He and Caroline were as mice to it. All it would take was one strike. Collecting himself, he listened, hoping the horses might announce their presence, but all he heard was the gushing of the fishing stream. Regarding it, he wondered. Was the bear drawn here because of the good fishing or by the smell of the Fritos? The red-and-ocher-colored bag nearby had given him an idea—if only he could be sure about the horses. Realizing there was no time to spare, Matt knew that he had to gamble on it anyway. He looked into Caroline's wide eyes. They were frightened, but their trust in him had remained constant. This in itself restored in Matt the calmness and confidence he needed.

"Okay," he whispered. "We're going to make a run for the horses." Caroline nodded solemnly in acceptance as Matt noted that her being barefoot would slow her down. "You have to get beyond the bear," Matt continued softly. "But the thing is, you can't let the bear see you running."

Caroline shot him the look of a person with a migraine. "I thought you said," she whispered, remembering the bear on her porch last year, "that they were stupid and always went away."

"Not this one."

At this, the grizzly rose threateningly on its hind legs, revealing its frightening enormity and the reason Indians named it the Bear That Walks Like a Man.

"Yikes!" Caroline squeaked.

"Listen . . ." Matt spoke quickly now. "First you have to get to the edge of those aspens over there. Slowly. So it doesn't notice you. Once you get there, just stand there and don't move at all. Okay?"

"Okay. But what about you?"

"Okay. Then I'm going to divert the bear's attention towards me just long enough so that you can run like hell to the horses and get them untethered." Matt prayed silently that at least one of the horses would be there. "Okay?"

"Okay," she answered unsteadily.

"And now, listen: If it gets near you, you've got to roll up on the ground like a ball with your face and your stomach down and your hands clasped behind your neck." He pushed away the vision of Jimmie's face. "You got that?"

"Yeah," she answered, now even more unsteadily.

"And no matter what, you have to keep that way and keep perfectly still. Okay?" He looked into her frightened eyes and wanted to hold her and tell her that everything was going to be all right, but that wouldn't do them any good right now. He shot a glance at the grizzly on the hilltop. It was on its haunches, scrutinizing them.

"But," Caroline whispered fretfully, "what if it comes after you? How will you get to the horses?"

"Don't worry. I've got a plan."

"Why don't we just run for it together?" she persisted.

"Trust me. Okay?" He stared solemnly into her hazel eyes.

"Okay."

She nodded, and he knew that she did.

"Now?"

"Now."

Caroline began her interminable, slow-motion journey to the cluster of aspens as both she and Matt fixed their wary eyes on the grizzly. Remembering the sneaky baby steps of her childhood game of Mother May I, Caroline edged surreptitiously toward her target. She got a little over halfway there before the grizzly began his pigeon-toed lumbering down the hillside. Instantly Matt leaped to his feet. He scooped up the Fritos from the grass and began to noisily shake the bag and crinkle its cellophane to capture the bear's attention. Shouting, he knew, would only enrage it. At the bottom of the hill, the grizzly kept Caroline fixed in his sights. Matt ran erratically with the noisy bag until he lured the beast's attention out of Caroline's range.

"Now, Caroline!" he half shouted as the grizzly pounded dangerously close behind him.

Seeing this, Caroline froze with horror.

"Run!!" he yelled, and she did. Just as swiftly, Matt sprinted toward the stream, the grizzly in hot pursuit. In the blink of an eye, Matt veered away from the stream and darted inside the protective spindle trunks of the aspen trees. Marveling at how fleet the huge grizzly was, he had only a few seconds to wait before the right moment arrived. He dumped the contents of the Fritos bag in a heap outside the maze of aspens and fervently prayed that the bear's attention would be snared more by the scent of the corn chips than by his own crazy actions.

The grizzly shambled to the aspen cage, completely oblivious of the aromatic treat lying so close by. With one angry swipe of a gargantuan forearm, it felled the first four aspens, cracked down as if no more than brittle twigs. Matt's heart skipped a beat in pure terror as he crept slowly backward, trying to keep within the dubious protection of the trees. The grizzly gave a horrible, blood-chilling roar, showing a set of even more horrible, yellowed canine teeth. Matt stood trapped, motionless, fighting off a quaking in his knees as he understood the intent in the nightmare's beady eyes. Abruptly, the grizzly's rage broke as if shattered. It turned its huge head toward the smell of the Fritos.

Matt rocketed out of the aspens and up the hillside with the velocity that only a torrent of adrenaline can fuel. Caroline was with both horses, holding on with all her might to keep them from bolting. Feverishly, wordlessly, Matt snatched the reins and boosted her onto a jittery horse that was prancing high in nervousness. With demon speed, he scrambled onto his own chestnut mare. They beat a hasty retreat, flying like the wind on horses that were only too eager to race headlong away. Three miles later the horses finally slackened to a gallop, as did Caroline's and Matt's thundering hearts. Only then did they button up their wind-whipped shirts and smile at each other in relief.

CHAPTER

32

*C*AROLINE PICKED UP THE menus and handed one across the small round table to Matt. "Perk's Place," the laminated menu cover announced, "Dancing, Beer, Wine, Liquor, and the Home of the Best Hamburgers in Western Montana." She leaned back onto a wooden cafe chair to read what else Perk's had for dinner. Deciding quickly enough, she looked around, accustoming herself to the dusky, beer-smelling atmosphere of a honky-tonk on a Saturday night. Her second visit to Novi, she knew, would be much better than the last.

A waitress in a carpenter's apron took their order, then they waited amid the steadily increasing racket of people talking and beer bottles clanking and the jangle and thud of the nearby cigarette machine. Oblivious to, at least, most of this, Matt and Caroline smiled at each other as a jukebox bellowed syrupy twang in accompaniment to country-western music's perennial message about being a fool for love. Matt's smile widened at the lyrics as he moved his chair next to Caroline's.

"You know," Matt began, locking Caroline's eyes with his own. He placed his hands on top of her knees. "I've never been here before." He indicated he meant their surroundings with a quick motion of his head while his dark eyes became merry. Caroline felt his hands slide leisurely up the outsides of her thighs, confidently creeping well under her short denim skirt.

"Nylons," he commented, much pleased with their silkiness. "Nice," he added appreciatively, and she had to agree. His hands advanced beneath the denim, hovered, then rested heavily on the tops of her legs. Caroline quickly broke from his merry gaze to give a visual check.

"And high heels." Matt nodded approvingly. He slipped his hands disconcertingly to the insides of both her thighs.

"Mmm," Caroline answered abstractedly as, once more, Matt's eyes magnetized her own in a compelling gaze. Smiling from both the pleasure of where his hands rested along with the anticipation of their next logical advance, Caroline heard the jangle-thud of the cigarette machine. "The nylons and heels," she said, returning a merry look of her own, "are because someone I know led me to a place where I had to leave my regular sandals behind."

"If you want, we can always go back"—he paused while, deliberately, he glided his hands down to her knees and then, with equal deliberateness, slid them back up to where they had been resting just a short moment ago—"and find them."

Even the situation at hand couldn't erase Caroline's vivid memory of their hell-bent horseback escape. "You'd really go back there?"

"Not a chance." His voice was still merry, but his eyes were not. "Once a grizzly bear gets your scent, he remembers it." His hands played thoughtfully over the weave of her nylons. "At least that's what some people say, and I'm not up to the finding out." His hands resumed their animation but stopped when the food arrived.

They ate prodigious portions of thick, crusty steak fries and the most colossal hamburgers in western Montana. Balancing the nearly pie-size burgers before them, Caroline and Matt looked about as they ate, watching Perk's Place fill up with people—men in jeans of a deeper indigo than ordinary work pants and well-polished cowboy boots, and women in blue jeans and a variety of fringed and ruffled tops. A four-man band straggled through the tables and set up on a low stage. By the time Matt and Caroline had finished all they could of their food, Bashful Bob Owens and the Showmen, as their drums proclaimed them, were tuned and playing a swaying country-western waltz. Bashful Bob sang from the heart, and to Caroline's surprise, he wasn't bad. Caroline and Matt sipped their lemonade as they watched the first few couples take to the dance floor. The following song was slow and steamy, doubling the amount of people dancing.

"You want to dance?" Matt asked. They walked across the slick brown floor. Caroline lifted one hand to Matt's shoulder as he took her other hand in his, stroking her fingers, plying her palm as if, she reflected, it were more than just her hand, as if it were an extension of her whole self. In one motion Matt sensuously turned his hand in upon hers, enveloping it entirely. Caroline watched as he guided her hand against his chest. She rested it there, her hand both embracing and being embraced as if, again, it were something more. Slowly, in deliberate time to the bluesy dance music, Matt pulled her closer until their embrace pressed complete. Relaxing, Caroline rested her head on the dark cotton of his shirt, languidly snaking her arm from his shoulder to his neck. Matt held her tighter, temporarily oblivious of the music, not even moving while he breathed in the sweet, intoxicating fragrance of her coppery hair. When Caroline's other hand also entwined around Matt's neck, he began ever so slowly to sway in halftime to the music. Shifting his weight to the underbeat of Bashful Bob's song, he danced to some inner, personal music. And Caroline, hearing it, too, followed, their hips touching, their legs close upon each other's. Their surroundings, the dance floor, in fact, Perk's Place, entirely vanished for both of them as they lost themselves in their sinuous partnership. As if of a united mind, both Caroline and Matt could think of nothing except the warmth of each other's bodies pressed so close together. Suddenly nothing else existed. They had no other thoughts, no doubts, no tensions. There was for them only the pure embrace they shared at this moment.

Bashful Bob had long since launched into the next dance before Matt and Caroline realized it. Caroline untangled her arms from Matt's neck and rested them lightly over his heart. Solemnly she looked up into Matt's eyes as he held her silky head tenderly between his hands. He caressed her cheekbones, her temples, repeating the action in lieu of doing anything beyond that. He knew the strength of his willpower, and he knew its limits, too, and he knew that if he kissed her right now, he wouldn't know how to stop. Again Caroline's hazel eyes looked into his, spirited intensity taking turns with shy self-consciousness. When he caressed her again, her hands fluttered as birds upon his shirt. He held her hands steady, surrounding them in his own, tenderly enveloping them against his own drumming heart. Matt buried his face into the sweet perfume of her hair and spoke only to her. "Let's go home."

Hazel eyes locked on to his. They were no longer shy as Caroline answered, "Yes."

CHAPTER

33

NO DOUBT ABOUT IT, Caroline thought to herself, it was going to be a long ride home. The flatlands surrounding Novi were pitch dark as Matt drove headlong into the starless night and Caroline gave in to some speculation. You know, she told herself, you're not a dumb twenty-year-old anymore. You can't just rush into this like it was some kind of a lark. There's stuff like commitment and consequences to think about. She frowned, wondering if Matt might be having these thoughts, too. Turning to see if anything of the sort was written on his face, she regarded him, seeing an openness to his nature that evaporated any doubts she may have had. She already knew that she'd rushed into love with him, and she knew, equally, that it was not just a lark.

"Caroline." Matt spoke from the darkness, his gaze briefly alighting on her before returning to the road.

"Before things go any further . . . I mean, before any- thing happens, uh, between us . . ." He said all this calmly, but both of them were aware of the unaccus- tomed strain in his voice. "There's something you have to know. . . ." He trailed off, gripping the steering wheel, groping for the right words—words that were honest because there was nothing to be gained by sugarcoating it, but at the same time words that wouldn't drive her away from him in loathsome contempt. He pushed down the dread pummeling his stomach. In all fairness, he had to tell her and it had to be right now.

"There's something I want you to know, Caroline," he said, somehow plucking his composure out of the churning swirl of apprehension, "about the person I was before I came to live here."

He told her everything, and he didn't camouflage it. He told her of all the greedy excesses and of all the losses, too, including willpower and self-respect. He told her about Sheila. He described how he'd get up in the morning and have to do a couple of lines and a couple of beers just to get himself out of bed, just to get himself functioning enough to go out and cop some more. He told her how he'd lived for it, and it only, and of how many times he'd thought his mind had snapped. He told her of the shameful helplessness of it and the resolve of a recovery that can never be completely guar- anteed. And when he was done, he waited. He waited for the hazel eyes to lose their trust about who he was, about what he'd so carefully kept hidden from her before this. He stared into the dark road ahead and waited to hear what she'd say.

Caroline also stared into the black night as she digested what she'd just heard. They reached the rolling prairies beyond the flatlands before she finally spoke. "You could have told me," she said, much subdued.

Matt nodded. He concentrated on driving, still waiting.

Caroline was suddenly saddened by the lonesome secret Matt had locked inside him for so long, unable to share it, unable to shed it. "Matt," she said quietly, "you could have trusted me."

"I'm trusting you now."

Caroline accepted this as certainly as she accepted that the Matt who sat beside her at this moment was much changed from the one he described six years past. She sat in silence for some moments, then touched Matt's arm tentatively before her heart found the words to say. "Matt, the past is past and it no longer matters. Nothing can change how I feel about you." Her eyes turned solemnly to his. Even through the darkness, he could see and rejoice that this was so.

At last, the familiar gravel crunch of Caroline's driveway delighted Matt's ears. Humphrey was at the front steps, greeting Matt in his usual way, but tonight the little gray cat didn't receive his accustomed attention. Once they were inside Caroline's living room, Matt closed the front door and surveyed her.

"Would you like a cup of coffee?" Caroline asked, smiling playfully at the expression on Matt's face.

"No," he replied, advancing.

"A glass of lemonade?" Her smile widened as she slowly backed toward the nearest wall.

"Uh-uh." Matt replied, smiling slyly as he hemmed her against it. He took her face tenderly between his hands and, as before, carefully caressed her cheekbones, gently stroked her temples. Sensuously he kissed her with a yearning intensity that snatched the breath from her. Unabated, his mouth played over and into hers with an unrestrained hunger that Caroline, still pleasurably breathless, easily surrendered to. Charged with an urgently mounting passion of her own, she broke from the kiss. She took Matt's hands off her waist and sandwiched them between her own smaller hands. There she held them, between their hearts. Caroline smiled into his eyes. "Come with me," she said quietly. Gently she tugged at Matt's hands and led him upstairs.

He chuckled as he entered the pink-blushed, dust-ruffled world of Caroline's bedroom. It was, Matt mused briefly, as feminine and uncluttered as Caroline was herself. A little black cat scooted off a cluster of dainty pink throw pillows on the white four-poster the minute Matt sat on the edge of the bed. Caroline stood just beyond him, her hazel eyes regarding him outright. Suddenly Doc's words echoed in his mind: "I can trust him with anything." Remembering what he'd told Caroline tonight, he knew that it was true of her. He wondered if she could say the same of him.

She stepped in closer. Standing before him, he undressed her slowly, reverently. When he was done, he laid her down gently onto the sea green cotton coverlet and watched her smile as the coverlet's coolness greeted her naked skin. Looking upon her heart-stopping, willowy form, he turned to her. "Caroline . . ." he said, stroking her silky breasts, sensuously following the contours of her satin-smooth body, touching her hips, her abdomen. Caroline's fingers began delicately to unbutton his shirt, while his own found and played thoughtfully over a raised and recent scar. "Caroline . . ." he said again, still searching for the words that would complete what he wanted to say. Not finding them, he instead fixed his eyes on hers.

Silently Caroline watched him take off his shirt. When he turned to tug off his boots, she sat up and touched him lightly on the shoulder. "I'll be right back," she whispered, and slipped off the other side of the bed. Scurrying down the upstairs hall, she was vaguely aware of the phone ringing from the sewing room.

"You look like a giant rosebud," Matt said when she returned to the bedroom. He was referring to the long pink kimono she had wrapped around herself.

Caroline smiled wistfully at Matt as he sat amid her pillows, grinning at her from under the sea green coverlet. "That was Ray on the phone," she told him. "He says there's a real big fire up near the north Medallion line and he needs you on the squad."

Matt set his jaw tight and regarded Caroline, already inaccessible, tightly enfolded in the pink fabric of her robe, her expression meditative. She knew it, too. He couldn't ignore a duty like this one. Not when Ray and, possibly, people's lives were depending on him. She sat on the white wicker chair in the corner of the room and watched him get dressed, becoming even more wistful as she eyed his lanky, unclad form. Silently they walked downstairs.

"I'll wait," Caroline told him at the door, knowing just as well as Matt that it wasn't likely he'd return before dawn.

"It could be a while."

"You never can tell." She smiled at him. "Maybe we'll get a break this time." Her smile faded as she spoke her concern. "Be careful out there. Okay?"

"Okay," he said. Then he was gone.

The possibility of the break that Caroline had hoped for diminished as the evening wore on. Television channels signed off the air, and from time to time Caroline went out back to her barn. She looked for lights at Matt's house that might announce his return, but there was nothing but blackness out there. Back inside, she sat on the cranberry couch, waiting, mulling over the events of the evening. She thought about the story of Matt's past, and one thing kept bobbing to the surface until it began to prick at her mind like a burr. She remembered how Matt had mentioned that the Fosters, specifically Wayne Foster, had helped him out of his troubles. And on one halting occasion Matt had spoken the name "Margaret" with similar gratitude. Caroline scowled, gripped by a sudden black jealousy. That Matt had already described Margaret as no longer a part of his life did nothing to assure her. All the doubts she'd had earlier that evening about commitment and consequences suddenly exploded back into her mind. More of her own words returned to her, too. "The past is past and it no longer matters," she had told him. Could she put her own past far enough behind her to stand by those words? She smiled at the simplicity of it. She had dismissed everything else in Matt's strange past. It was time, Caroline concluded, to dismiss Margaret, too.

CHAPTER

34

"*H*ERE," MATT SAID as he reentered his kitchen, carrying two thick, white Turkish towels. He waited for Caroline to latch the dishwasher before handing her one of them, then placed the other on the countertop. "I better quick go douse the fire," he told her. "You can go and put your things in there." He pointed beyond the kitchen to a doorway off the living room before he left via the kitchen's sliding glass doors.

Caroline headed in that direction, happily knowing that the only fire he was going to douse was in the side-deck barbecue grill. She also knew that this would be the night—the night she'd been anticipating since Matt had returned at six o'clock that morning, soot-covered and exhausted from the wildfires on the Medallion line. He'd slept the day away, but tonight, Caroline knew, would be different. Tonight they'd already en-

joyed a romantic dinner together and were now about
to relax a bit in Matt's hot-springs pool outside. Caroline walked through the doorway Matt had pointed to
and smiled immediately. It was Matt's bedroom. Slope-
ceilinged by beams of whole, bare logs and wide pine
planks that matched those forming the floor, it was as
wholly wooden and amber as the rest of the house, only
much cozier. A plain, white-painted fireplace fit solidly
into the irregular, floor-to-beam space of one wall, a
wooden bowl perched on its simple mantel. A sky blue
woven rug graced the cool pine floor next to an oversize
hewn-log bed. An old cotton blanket of a navy, tan, and
red geometric Indian design lay tousled over a
plumped, down-filled mattress. Caroline pictured herself slipping into the soft clouds of Matt's feather bed
and of Matt there with her, both of them sinking together, deep into the cozy billows. As she thoughtfully
unfastened her clothes and looked about the snug, low-
ceilinged, amber bedroom, she was pleased. It made her
feel as if she were standing, as if transported in time, to
a small room of a pioneer's log cabin. This was, she
decided, the perfect little haven to make and be made
love to.

She hung her clothes over a low, log bedpost and
wrapped herself several times around in the thick
towel. Walking past the bedroom door and toward the
kitchen, she heard Matt talking to someone.

"Uh, hi, Ray." She positioned herself behind a
kitchen counter and wrapped the towel tighter.

Nonplussed, Ray nodded a silent greeting to her
and continued his words to Matt. "So that leaves four
men out, eighteen left. Mackenzie and Reaves are still
claiming they got smoke inhalation problems. That's a

big, steaming pile of gorilla shit and everybody knows it, including them. Their wives are sisters, you know. Both just now figured it out that firefighting puts 'em in harm's way." Ray looked disgusted as he slowly shook his head. "Don't give a rat's behind who they leave in the lurch, that's what stews me."

"Forget them," Matt advised. "We'll manage without them."

Ray nodded, regaining his stoic composure as he continued the roster of casualties. "Bill Goodnight is still under observation for a concussion, but that's only for another twenty-four hours. And Connery is definitely out. Broken leg."

"But he was hopping around all over the place last night even after that tree hit him," Matt replied in surprise.

"Yup," Ray nodded sagely. "Ether. Damned stupid thing to be carrying in his pack, but . . ." He nodded again. "Old rodeo trick. Connery knew it, too. You pour a little from a can of ether on a break, and it'll freeze up a leg so you can just about gallop on a broken bone without feeling it. 'Course when that freeze wears off, you got a lot more feeling than you bargained for, but the point is, it'll get you through. I remember when I was rodeoing at Bozeman, right before the war, and there was this . . ." Ray halted when he saw the distressed expressions, identical on both Matt's and Caroline's faces. Usually they liked to hear his rodeo stories for hours on end, but that didn't appear to be the case just now. Ray shot an exaggerated look at his wristwatch. "Whoa," he said, tapping it. "Gettin' dark. Gotta go." Done with this particular brand of hilarity, he resumed his usual tone as he walked toward the door.

"Just wanted you to know about this regional fire alert," he told Matt. "It's serious. With so few men left on the squad, you know I'm really counting on you."

"I'll be there when you need me," Matt promised his friend as he walked him back to the baby blue pickup.

Caroline walked out to the deck to wait for Matt in the hot spring. Outside, it was the end of another parched-dry, drought-stricken day. Looking all around her at the straw-colored landscape, she understood Ray's concerns and prayed from both selfish and un-selfish reasons that no fires would start anywhere. The last of the sunset's long rays were twinkling their re-flection over the hot spring's quivery surface when Caroline got there, and gray dusk was closing in rap-idly. Tossing her towel to the side, she eased herself into the swirling water. It was hot, but not as hot as she remembered it from last winter. Caroline waded to the center of the pool and surveyed the waist-high water that churned all around her. Hovering her hands just above the water's surface, she smiled to feel the dancing spray prickle at her palms. She looked beneath the water's bubbling surface, where a submerged bench encircled all but one side of the pool. Caroline walked to face the plain-walled side.

Propping her elbows over the side, she rested her chin in her hands, and relinquishing herself to the mus-cle-loosening water, she lazily viewed the dusky pano-rama that lay before her. Darkening plains rolled in varying, shadowy hues until, many miles beyond, the charcoal-gray mountain range rose jaggedly against a vast navy sky. The night was so still that Caroline could hear sounds from the open kitchen windows and doors—Matt shutting the refrigerator, the rattle of ice cubes clunking into glasses. From somewhere very far off, a mourning dove played its haunting, drawn-out hoot and was answered softly, oboelike, by another. Looking up to the endless sky, Caroline listened to the gentle drone of water eddying at her waist and was filled with tranquillity.

She heard Matt walking barefoot down the side deck and listened more carefully as he slipped into the water from somewhere behind her. Then, the sounds of ice cubes jiggling. She sensed his approach, waiting, until, hovering close at her back, he leaned into her, silently placing a tall glass of lemonade at either side of her elbows. Slowly Caroline straightened, holding on to the wall as cold, wet hands traced down her ribs, reached beneath the misted blanket of water, and rested on her hips. Adeptly he guided her willing body against his own, easing her closer into him while water swirled hot around them as if to further melt them together. She tilted her head back and rested it serenely against his shoulder. Together they stood in silence, each content to savor this moment of peace and promise, each content to gaze into the darkness of the evening without needing to know what lay beyond. Stars were peeking through the curtain of sky as wordlessly the lovers watched them grow brighter.

By slow degrees Matt gradually crept his hands up the satin skin of her torso, leaving a cascade of warmth from the hot spring. Cupping her breasts in water, he chuckled softly at her body's immediate response. "Caroline," he said in a deep, low tone. He groped for the words, hoping he could find them this time. "Caroline . . ." Under the water, he was now keenly aware of the path her own hands were taking behind him. "Caroline . . . I . . ." He tried again but did not know how to continue.

"What are you trying to say?" she chided him gently.

"I'm trying to say . .," As if of their own accord, his hands took over, pressing heavily down her front and into the water. Leaning into her, he pressed past the scar but willed himself to go no farther until he spoke the words. "I'm trying to say that I love you."

Her body spoke before she did. Gracefully, gently, she broke away and turned to face him. Hazel eyes searched his solemnly, finding their focus even through the darkness. "Well," she spoke, hushed, barely above the burble of the water. "Do you?"

Wordlessly he snatched her willowy form and lifted it up so that she sat on the edge of the wall. Hazel eyes continued to bore into his as he advanced, gently parting the legs that dangled in the water. She lost focus of his face, however, when it reached level with her shoulders. Passionately he kissed her throat, her shoulders, her breasts, gradually drawing one nipple into his mouth until she moaned. Her wet fingers dug deep into his dark hair as he gently pulled and then released her. She felt the night air blow cool against the heat of where he had just been, while from somewhere in the starry night, she heard the dim echo of a coyote. Cicadas buzzed a vibrato as Matt thoroughly, sensuously, kissed, then enveloped the other nipple. Caroline's fingers tangled tightly into his hair, while of their own will, her hips arched to him. Sinewy hands caught her legs, then slid past to capture her knees. Lowering himself, he kissed her shimmering torso, followed a trail over and past the scar, and then traveled purposefully, unstoppably lower. Stunned and then overtaken by an unrestrained trembling for him, from him, she cried out, "Matt!"

Pulling her back into the churning hot spring, he stared into her eyes as he deftly backed her against the wall, holding her, supporting her. Pressing her tight against him under the slippery blanket of water, he rejoiced, and he began, watching her beautiful eyes widen as he first started to guide himself to her, watching her catch her breath as he began to enter.

It wasn't the cicadas buzzing. *Oh, for Chrissake, no!* Matt's mind screamed. It was the phone ringing from the kitchen. Arrested, suspended, neither Matt nor Caroline made a sound. It rang again with shattering volume, but Matt heard, louder, the pounding need within him as he stood at the very brink of consummation. He stared into Caroline's eyes, now round as saucers. "Let it ring," he managed to mumble. Instinctively he went in farther, but again the harpy phone shrieked piercingly from the open kitchen windows.

Looking at Caroline, he searched her saucer eyes for a clue as to what to do. He could feel her trembling as she bit her lip, her body as taut as a bow wire. The unrelenting ache within him demanded that he seize the moment with a hastiness, but his mind and heart knew that this woman before him, the woman he loved, deserved better.

When the phone rang again, Caroline knew it was over. If it was Ray calling about a fire, then no matter what her need for Matt was right now, it had to wait. Sadly she regarded her hands, already splayed across Matt's shoulders, already prepared to push him away, but as yet incapable. Watching Matt's rugged face, she marveled at a willpower far stronger than her own. The phone rang again. In a mighty resolve, Matt broke from her.

He retreated a few small steps from her. "Uh," he began, "would you answer it?" Achingly he watched Caroline's lithe figure step gracefully out of the hot spring to become enfolded, flowerlike, by so many layers of white. The phone persisted, and she trotted off, away from him.

Caroline teetered, dizzy and rubber-legged, before the kitchen wall phone. Fighting off the wobbliness, she answered it on the next ring, ready to remember and relay Ray's fire information.

"Matty dear?" inquired the husky, sexy-sounding voice of a woman.

"Uh," Caroline replied, much confused. "Umm, this isn't Matt. . . ." Another segment of her mind told her that this woman, whoever she was, probably already knew that. "Um, hold on a minute and I'll go out and get him." Caroline's mind flared. Who *was* this woman calling him those names?

"No, no. Don't bother if he's outside," the silky voice said. Whoever it was, she spoke slowly, patiently enunciating every word as if Caroline were, perhaps, the cleaning lady or a child.

Caroline didn't answer immediately. She stood there, her legs and feet dripping water onto the kitchen floor while she wondered what to make of this phone call.

"I just called Matty to have our usual Sunday night chat, that's all," the annoyingly affectionate voice told Caroline. "If you would, please ask him to call Margaret when he gets the chance, would you? He knows the number."

Stunned for the second time that evening, Caroline flashed back to Matt and herself just moments ago in the hot spring. Dully she returned her attention to Margaret—Margaret! "Sure," she replied in a flat, preoccupied monotone. She stretched out her arm with robotlike slowness. Pensively she hung up the phone.

CHAPTER

✸

35

*C*AROLINE WAS DRESSED
and looking around the dining room for the keys to her
Bronco when a towel-clad Matt walked in.

"What's taking so long?" he asked. Seeing that she
was dressed, he waited to hear where the fire was.

"That was Margaret on the phone," Caroline announced calmly, perhaps too calmly. "Your old friend
Margaret. Correct me if I'm wrong, the once-she-was-a-
big-part-of-my-life-but-she-isn't-anymore   Margaret."
Caroline found her keys and continued, her calm trans-
forming to anger. "The Margaret who, even though you
don't live with her anymore, still calls you up every
Sunday anyway, Matty dear."

Matt's expression crumbled. Damn! he cursed
himself. Caught by the one thing, the single, solitary,
one-and-only thing, he hadn't told her. And now, by the
look on her face, she hated him for it. The words echoed

through his mind, nagging at him. "Everything," Doc had said. "I can trust him with everything."

"Caroline," he began plaintively, "it's not what you think. Not at all. Margaret isn't a girlfriend or anything like that. It's just Doc Foster's real name, that's all." He smiled weakly.

Caroline's hazel eyes surveyed Matt, smoldering. "Why?" she demanded, squelching the anger, trading it for a certain amount of self-possession. "Why," she asked him quietly, "after telling me your whole terrible past—Jeez, Matt—drugs, alcohol, your wife—why, in all of that strange history, couldn't you have included that Margaret was really Mrs. Foster? I don't understand. That doesn't make any sense at all to me." She held back the storm of tears that began to thunder from deep within, and in a strangled voice she went on. "What kept you from telling me something as simple as that?"

"Hell, I don't know, Caroline. I just never found a place to fit it in."

"Liar!" she hissed. Her lip trembled, and her eyes, burning, filled with contempt as she remembered with vehemence how easily men are able to lie.

Matt set his jaw tight as he witnessed what this was doing to her. "Look," he implored, "I was being too cautious. I'm sorry. Caroline . . . I . . ." Irritably he raked his hand through his dark hair. "I should have told you way before. For Chrissake, Caroline, I've got no idea why I didn't tell you. I just couldn't, that's all."

"You lied! Why?" she yelled at him, the ancient pain resurfacing. "You said she wasn't part of your life anymore, but she *is!*"

"Caroline, she's part of my life because she's Doc Foster!"

Caroline replied nothing to this. Her stricken look said it all. Suddenly drained of all anger, she shook her head slowly at him, pursing her lips to hold it all at bay. "I'm sorry, Matt." She regarded the man standing before her and fought down all the love she felt for him. After all, he was no different.

"Caroline . . ." Matt stopped short. He saw it in her red-rimmed eyes. Not one shred of trust remained in them. "Caroline," he pleaded, "have a little faith in me."

Hazel eyes looked bitterly into his. "I don't believe you."

"Pick up a pin, pick up a sorrow," Caroline recited to herself. She held the stray pin, one of her quilting pins, before her and allowed that she'd certainly done just that even if she had gotten the order of it wrong. She sank onto the white wicker chair in her bedroom and recoiled, blinded from the dazzling morning sunlight. Getting things wrong was par for the course, she reflected grimly through the kind of wincing headache that comes from a fitful night's sleep. It was wrong that she'd wakened alone this morning when she should have been with Matt. It was wrong that that horrible Margaret had called—or Mrs. Foster, or Doc or Sneezy or whoever the hell she was. It was wrong, all wrong, the broken way that Matt had looked at her when she'd left him last night.

The throbbing in Caroline's head crescendoed in tempo with her anger or chagrin, she couldn't say which it was. After this last sleepless night, Caroline wasn't sure exactly what she knew anymore—only that everything was wrong and that maybe, possibly, *she* was wrong, too. For the forty-second time, questions from last night jostled around in her mind: If that woman really was Mrs. Foster, then why hadn't Matt told her instead of allowing her to believe something else? Why had he kept it a secret?

Caroline squinted into the sunlight and grimaced as Matt's last words echoed through her mind: "Have a little faith in me." She fingered a piece of loosening lace on her nightgown and considered guiltily that she hadn't. Maybe what had happened with Jim had a lot to do with how she'd reacted last night, why temper had superseded reason, why fear had overshadowed faith. She squinted into the sun's piercing rays and thought hard about what had happened with Jim, how she had once felt about him, what she'd felt about him afterward. Most of all, she thought about the person Jim really was. She thought about Matt and knew that he was a different man entirely. Her feelings for Matt went far deeper than they ever had for Jim.

Her own words from just a few nights ago came back to haunt her now. When she had told Matt that the past no longer mattered, she had also spoken her heart to him: "Nothing can change the way I feel about you." It was true back in Novi, and it was still true this brilliant, sunlit morning. She knew that it had been true even from the minute she'd first laid eyes on him so long ago on her front porch. Caroline suddenly recalled what she had once read in a Greek mythology book. To the Greeks, it was common knowledge that each of us was part of someone else but we had been divided at birth; that the search for love was really a search for the other half; and that, when the two natural halves met, they would recognize each other. Caroline knew that Matt was that man. And with that recognition, her troubled thoughts cleared.

Suddenly she knew. All that she had experienced in Montana—her timberland losses, Sanborne's attempts to buy her out and burn her out, even shooting the coyote—all those things had taught her an important lesson: You have to stand your ground for what you want and sometimes you have to fight to keep it. Whoever Margaret turned out to be, Caroline realized, whatever the risk she had to take, she was prepared to take it. She loved Matt too much not to do anything else. Dressing quickly, she hurried downstairs and started the Bronco. As she drove down the road toward Matt's house, the words rushed through her mind that would tell him what was in her heart.

There was no answer at the front door, so Caroline went around to the sliding glass doors of the kitchen. Finding them open, she called, then entered. All was the same as it had been when she'd been there last night as she walked through the log-beamed dining room, except the house was ghostly quiet. Caroline meandered through to the living room, hoping that Matt hadn't been called away again by the fire squad. "Matt?" she called, but there was no answer. Resting her hand on the fireplace's stone mantel, she looked around, wondering what to do next. She saw that Matt's rifle, usually propped in the corner where stones met the log wall, was gone. On the hallway wall there was an empty space where his fishing basket traditionally hung by its leather strap.

"Matt?" she called again, louder this time. She stopped at the doorway of the cozy pioneer's bedroom, but the log-post bed was empty. In the next room, Matt's yellow fire suit and gear lay waiting, atop an otherwise bare desk.

Quickening her steps, Caroline went back outside. The red pickup was still parked in the garage. Out back, neither of the chestnut horses grazed in the corral. She ran to the barn and opened the door with a mighty heave. "Matt?" she called into hay-scented, sun-shafted darkness. Waiting, she knew there would be no reply as assuredly as she knew that the horses were gone.

CHAPTER

=✷=

36

"*T*HAT   RANGER wasn't any help at all," Caroline flatly told Ray as soon as they got back into Ray's baby blue pickup.

"Nope." Ray started the truck and aimed it back toward home. "But it was worth mentioning it."

"What they had just mentioned was that Matt, after being gone, most likely on a solo wilderness hike for ten tinder-dry days, might possibly be lost. Neither Ray nor Caroline was especially surprised by what State Forest Ranger Putnam had just told them, but neither of them felt very good about it, either. What he had managed to do was put to voice every single one of their unspoken fears. He expressed surprise that Mr. Van Zandt, an experienced fire fighter, would attempt such a trip during the most widespread regional fire alert of the decade. Ranger Putnam's surprise verged into gentle disbelief that Mr. Van Zandt, also an experienced outdoorsman, would venture into the drought-stricken wilderness, disregarding the fact that food would be scarce while bears would not. Beyond the troublingly obvious, Ranger Putnam explained that with the Labor Day weekend starting the next day, every ranger who wasn't on fire duty would be on crowd duty at nearby Yellowstone, but that the next time a helicopter went up, he'd get them to have a look around. Ranger Putnam had concluded by taking Ray's phone number and a description of Matt and his horses. He suggested they get back in touch with him in another five days, if need be, but seemed to think that more than likely Mr. Van Zandt would turn up soon enough.

Caroline surveyed the scorched vegetation of the countryside from her perch in Ray's truck cab while she gave thought to Ranger Putnam's words.

"He'll be back," Ray said gruffly. "He knows I need him on the fire squad."

"I can't help thinking this is all my fault," Caroline answered, fretfulness getting the best of her. "If we hadn't argued like we did, he wouldn't have gone."

"You didn't saddle up those horses. He did." Ray shot a glance at Caroline and wondered to himself. The two of them, cut from the same cloth—what new turn of events had it been between them this time? Scanning the heat waves over the asphalt, Ray reflected that there were advantages, after all, to being old and settled.

"But what if he can't get back, Ray? What if he's been trapped or hurt by a bear?" Suddenly Matt's very words plagued her mind: "Once a grizzly bear gets your scent, he remembers it."

"He knows better than to come close to a bear." Ray assured her.

"What if he's slipped off a mountain somewhere or twisted his leg and he's just lying there waiting for us to rescue him?"

Ray scowled at her, but she continued. "Maybe we should try to find him ourselves?"

Ray frowned at the road. He'd already had these same thoughts when Matt had been gone for just five days. Maybe Matt wasn't thinking too straight when he took off like that, but he wasn't stupid, either. It didn't make sense that he'd stay gone so long. By day number five, Ray had indeed started tracking his friend, but the trail was as withered as the weather, and both he and Tyrone had lost it entirely. Ray looked at Caroline beset with worry and told her of his failed attempt at tracking. "There's not much we can do," he concluded, annoyed by his own ineffectiveness. "We've just got to wait for him to get back to us." He watched her absorb this information with a stoicism that rivaled his own. He also watched it disintegrate.

"Ray?" Caroline's quiet voice quavered. "What if there's a fire?"

"Matt will be all right," he said forcefully, as much for his own benefit as Caroline's. "He can take care of himself alone better than any man I know. It's his specialty. He doesn't need anyone."

Caroline nodded silently at straw-colored hills, thinking that perhaps Ray was right on both counts.

Ray brought Caroline back to his house. He felt tongue-tied and useless at soothing her fears, fears that in truth had only mushroomed with their visit to the ranger. Winona would know what to say to her, he reflected as he drove past their rust-colored Herefords all grazing, not on the land anymore, but from unbundled hay in front of the house.

Winona did indeed know what to say. After dinner she hustled Ray off to the living room with his dessert and a copy of *Hoof and Horns* magazine and took Caroline back with her to the kitchen. Caroline served them each a wedge of huckleberry-lemon pie while Winona made a fresh pot of coffee and opened a window to let a warm summer breeze flutter the curtains. By the time they sat down at one end of the cluttered kitchen table, Tyrone was already waiting for them, nosing curiously around the table edge.

"Caroline, dear," Winona began in her usual way. Not one to beat around the bush, she got right to the point. "You've done what you can. Now you must put all this worry aside before it begins to hurt you." She was referring to the strain pulling on Caroline's face.

"Winona, how can I?" Caroline replied bleakly.

"Because," Winona continued solidly, "it's time for you to wait patiently and to trust that Matt will come back." Winona's almond eyes stared straight into Caroline's as if to underscore what she was saying. "There's nothing else you can do."

"But—"

"No. There are no 'buts' when it comes to this. You must have the patience to wait."

"Oh, Winona . . ." Caroline began weakly, but Winona wasn't about to hear it.

"Patience," Winona countered firmly.

Two days later, more to keep herself from climbing the walls than anything else, Caroline went to Matt's house. Outside, near the corral, she found one of the chestnut horses returned. It was hungry and its saddle-bags were empty. She filled the water trough, led the panting horse to it, and watched it eagerly quench its thirst while she squelched down her anxiety. Hadn't Matt once said that when the trail got too thin, he'd send one of his horses home? After all, the saddlebags were empty. Maybe, Caroline reasoned, this might be a sign that Matt was okay, even nearby.

She started unstrapping the horse's saddle. Poor thing, she thought when she saw how long the saddle had been on the horse's back. All her worries surfaced again. Maybe the horse had escaped what Matt could not. Carefully she led it to the barn, put it in a stall, and fed it the best she knew how.

Later, when Caroline got home, she still didn't know how to interpret the lone horse's return. After dark that night, she walked out on her back porch and looked to see if any lights appeared at Matt's house. As usual, there was nothing. Humphrey rubbed against her legs, mewing affectionately but she paid him no mind. As she peered into the infinite blackness of the night, nothing could diminish her sense of foreboding. A prickly chill shivered through Caroline engulfing her with the feeling that she might lose the only man she ever really loved.

CHAPTER

37

"*A*NYTHING IN THE saddlebags?" Ray asked.

"Yes," Caroline replied uneasily. "Coffee, salt, a box of bullets, and some cooking things." She was referring not to the lone chestnut horse she'd been caring for during the past two weeks, but to the second riderless horse she'd found teetering listlessly in front of Matt's barn that afternoon, saddlebags, bedroll, tent, and Matt's rifle still strapped to it.

"What kind of bullets?"

"The big kind. The kind that go in rifles."

"No smaller bullets anywhere?"

"No." Caroline answered, understanding and crushing Ray's hope. "I kept that handgun. Matt only packed his rifle."

Ray thoughtfully closed his copy of *Hoof and Horns* and leaned forward to set it on the coffee table next to Winona's knitting. "What'd the horse look like?"

"Starved. Barely alive, really."

They both knew what that meant—in terms of time, in terms of Matt's being left without basic survival equipment. Ray watched the worry grow on Caroline's already haggard face. You look like you've been drawn through a knothole backwards, his mind silently said of her. This last month had been hard on her, on everyone, Ray reflected. He had to admit that his own hopes for his lost friend had shriveled. Matt knew his way around the woods, and his hunting skills were good, too. But time and the elements—and now, it looked as if luck itself were playing against him. It had been four weeks, and Matt's chances of survival were shrinking fast. In another week there'd be no use even in hoping anymore. Ray wondered about Caroline's resiliency in the face of losing someone she loved. He wondered about his own. The worst part was going to be having to accept it without actually ever finding the body. Disconcerted by these thoughts, he sought to rein them in. Abruptly he spoke to Caroline. "What else about the horse?"

"Well, she hadn't eaten for a very long time, so I gave her just a little bit of food to start her out. You should see her, Ray, you can count her ribs right through her skin, and her legs and sides have all these long, deep scratches."

"Across or up and down?"

"Mostly across, like she'd been running through bushes and trees."

"Fresh or healed?"

"They're mostly healed."

"Okay," Ray said. He'd heard all he wanted to hear. "I'll go there tomorrow morning and see how she's doing."

Caroline nodded as Tyrone nudged her knees. Looking up, she saw that Winona had wheeled silently into the room and, like Ray, was piecing together the chronology of the information.

"Caroline, dear," she said, breaking the troubled tension, "I could use some help with dinner."

"Sure, Winona." Caroline and Tyrone followed her into the kitchen. Lately Winona had been asking for Caroline's help in cooking, end-of-summer canning, and even running errands into Hawkeye for her. It wasn't at all like Winona to shrink from self-sufficiency like that, and Caroline, aware of her friend's ploy, was grateful for it. With Matt gone so frighteningly long, with the unabating, daily torment over him, with her hopes withering before her, it was all Caroline could do some days to get up in the morning. Winona, sensing all of that, had prevailed upon her, had relinquished some of her own independence, and had seen to it that Caroline was kept occupied and in contact with other people. This afternoon was no exception as Winona handed her a peeler and began to instruct her through a recipe for potato salad.

"The trick to good potato salad," Winona began, catching Caroline's attention, "is getting all the—"

The phone rang in the living room, and both women instantly forgot about potato salad. Stopped motionless, they listened as Ray answered the call that might end the waiting.

"Where?" they heard him say. "Holy shit." An

excruciatingly long silence followed, after which Ray answered only, "Yup," and then, "Okay. 'Bye."

He poked his head in the kitchen door and regarded Winona with a grave expression that was, Caroline noticed, tinged with something akin to apprehension. "Fire, a real big one," he began. "The whole west Medallion line." He shook his head as if in disbelief. "The whole damn length of it. The guys from Novi are covering the south half of it. We're taking the north, so you know," he said pointedly to Winona. Then, as if it would somehow lessen the alarm on her face, he added, "They're calling in backup squads."

Caroline watched Winona during the short time it took for Ray to go get his fire fighter's suit. As Winona's mind registered the fire's level of danger, the anxiety in her almond eyes evolved to sober acceptance. By the time Ray reappeared at the kitchen door, bearing a mound of canary yellow equipment topped with a yellow hard hat, Winona's expression was as stoic as her husband's.

"Can't say when we'll be done," Ray said, patting the pile of rubberized yellow canvas to check for the boots. "Suppose we could use some dinner later on."

"Okay," Winona answered. "Do you have your gloves this time?"

"Yup."

He left by the front door. Winona's alert eyes followed his movements as he went. After a moment she turned to Caroline, her eyes bright. "Now I *really* could use some help with dinner."

A little later Caroline was speeding her Bronco toward Hawkeye, thinking of the curious farewell Ray and Winona gave each other. She was heading for the

IGA with a shopping list that would feed an army of fire fighters once she and Winona had busily prepared all the food. More than anything right then, Caroline was looking forward to the unthinking mindlessness of being entirely busy. She wanted to be busy enough to blot out the constant worry that had stung her heart and tortured her mind every day for the last thirty days— the gnawing worry, no longer simply for Matt's safety, but for his very life. She wanted to be busy enough so that she wouldn't have to hear and rehear those words anymore—those last painful words she'd spoken to Matt, the words that he remembered her by. And most of all, she wanted to be busy enough not even to think of where Matt might be in relation to the fire.

Driving faster past sun-scorched hills, she hoped for a relief from the strange mood swings that had lately begun to seize her: a leaden depression when she awoke in the mornings, an unreasoning fury thrashing through her head when she lay in bed at night. And then there were the nightmares that hounded her, jolting her awake so that she found herself gasping, her heart thundering, the bedsheets soaked in sweat. It was always the same nightmare, and it was always Matt. In the dream she looked upon him from some very high and distant place while he stood in a forest clearing. Whenever he took a step, the dry grass beneath his feet would burst into shooting flames. He would try to run away, but everywhere he stepped, flames lapped up his legs while Caroline watched, helpless to save him. Finally Matt would come to a creek bed, and although Caroline-in-the-dream knew it to be as combustible as the ground, Matt-in-the-dream believed it to be safety and would jump in. Someone would scream, "No!" and

Caroline would awake. And now Caroline shuddered.
The horrible nightmare could actually come true.

She parked the Bronco in the IGA lot and stopped
short when she got out. Beyond the IGA, beyond Hawkeye, she saw a smoke cloud rising high, brown gray and
billowy against the western sky. Caroline hurried into
the supermarket, its aisles already abuzz with talk of the
fire. She would have to get enough food to feed more
than just the Hawkeye squad, she thought to herself.
There were Novi and the backups to feed, too. That was
good, she decided resolutely. It would keep her plenty
busy. Leon, the butcher, came out to help her with the
list. In his usual jovial way, he helped her pack her cart
while keeping up a steady flow of conversation on
every subject pertaining to Hawkeye except for the fire.
By the time Leon had wrapped up enough meat to feed
Cleveland and escorted her down several more aisles,
Caroline had everything and more of what she needed.
She got into her favorite checkout lady's line and put
the massive load of groceries on the belt.

"I see you and Winona Banes are packing dinner
boxes again," the checkout lady observed. "I get off in
half an hour at five. Do you need any help?"

"Thanks." Caroline smiled at her. "But I think we
can manage it between the two of us."

"Okay," she said as she rang up the last of the
items. "Have you heard any word on Matt Van Zandt?"

"No, nothing yet," Caroline answered.

"Well, here," she said as she scribbled something
on a piece of paper and handed it to Caroline. "My
phone number in case you and Winona get tired." She
motioned to the pile of grocery bags the packing boy
had set in Caroline's cart. "Leon says there's no

charge." She snapped the register receipt off the machine, folded it up, and returned it to the drawer.

Outside, a steady, hot breeze blew through Caroline's hair. She busily loaded the groceries into the back of the Bronco, purposely ignoring the smoke cloud in the west. As she latched the back of the truck, a familiar voice spoke.

"Howdy." Jody Landis stood tall before her, tossing his head to get the golden hair out of his eye. He looked at her only for a moment, then set his ocean blue eyes toward the western horizon as he spoke. "That must be some fire."

Caroline turned to it. The smoke cloud had tripled in size and density since she'd entered the IGA. Now it loomed in the distance like a giant wall—white, boiling, cauliflowerlike clouds spreading left to right, mile-high thunderheads jutting into an otherwise clear blue sky. Both awed and troubled by its sinister bulk, Caroline was speechless.

"How have you been?" Jody asked her with a directness that self-consciousness had never allowed him to express before.

Caroline shrugged while still staring at the smoke cloud.

"Have they found . . ." Jody stopped and quietly began again. "Has Matt come back yet?"

"No."

"How about the forest rangers? Have they come up with anything?"

"They've sent helicopters and search teams. They've really done their best, but the problem is that no one knows which direction he might have set out in."

"Where does he usually like to go?" Jody asked, staring into the smoke-filled west.

"Usually he goes north so he can stick to the woods. Other times, though, Ray says he remembers him going west. He wouldn't have gone south 'cause that's mostly prairie, and pretty much the same for due east. But southeast and northeast's full of forests. Who knows? He could be anywhere." Caroline's face turned pensive as she remembered Ranger Putnam's awful words. They'd keep sending up helicopters, he'd said, but the range where Matt might be was so vast that it wouldn't be easy to spot him dead or alive.

"Don't worry," Jody offered gently. "He'll show up."

Winona was also ready to be busy when Caroline returned with the groceries. In fact, she had started. She had set up an assembly line that spanned the kitchen table—cleared of everything for the first time in recent history—that traveled out to the dining room table and ended with a line of kitchen and dining room chairs all stacked with empty, open dinner boxes.

"Not a bad job of furniture moving for a lady in a wheelchair," Winona proudly announced. "Now come over here so I can tie some knots in your apron strings."

Smiling, Caroline obeyed without even asking why. She knew it had something to do with luck, and she was glad to be starting out with a bit of luck on the all-consuming, all-distracting chore. Together they set to sandwich making at a bustling pace in Winona's breeze-filled kitchen. They talked, they listened to the local radio for fire news updates, they kept busy so as to suspend all thoughts of either Matt or Ray being harmed by the fire that was advancing across western Medallion County with alarming speed.

An hour later the radio stopped dead. Caroline went to it, played with its knobs, but got no sound.

"Look at the clock," Winona said. "The power's out."

Caroline flipped the light switch and verified this. She lifted the telephone receiver to her ear. "Phone's out, too."

"Well, let's get moving," Winona said. "We've only got a couple hours of sunlight left."

It was gray-black dusk when Caroline closed the very last dinner box and Ray tramped wearily through the kitchen door. He flicked the light switch up and down a few times, not surprised by the lack of results, then unstrapped his hard hat and safety goggles. Everything he wore that had been a bright canary yellow a few hours before was now an ugly, soot-smudged, black-streaked ocher. He smelled heavily of acrid smoke, and his face was as dark as charcoal. He tugged tiredly at the navy blue bandanna tied loosely around his neck, freeing it from under the blackened yellow jacket.

"Got to evacuate," he told Winona.

CHAPTER

38

*D*ANTE HIMSELF COULDN'T
have imagined the scenes that Ray began to describe as
he sat, exhausted, in the darkened kitchen. Gulping
down tumblers of water, he tried to communicate to
Winona and Caroline the frightening enormity of an
unstoppable inferno.

"We're throwing everything we have at that fire,
everything we can think of," he began, shaking his head
in amazement, "and still, that hell-roaring blaze is kicking our ass from one end of the line to the other." As if
he couldn't get enough, he quaffed another glass of
water before continuing. "We took our first position in
front of the power station, figuring to save it. But we
weren't counting on winds—fire winds like I've never
seen happen before, like you wouldn't believe." Ray
paused, suspended by the memory of an orange, hellish
landscape lit blindingly bright by blast-furnace pillars

of flame. "Those winds flashed up so high, it was like staring into a solid wall of fire. And the trees, they weren't just catching fire, they were exploding in our faces like bombs. They were so goddamn dry, it was like they were soaked in gasoline. And the air—we could feel it and then hear it being sucked up along with the trees, mixing with the flames, shooting straight up into the sky. Shit, it was too damn scary for any of us. And then that whole wall of fire roared into our faces like a freight train, and I knew we had to get the hell out of there.

"We took a position behind the next ridge and did what we could as fast as we could, even though the fire was kicking up so much ash we were working blind. Then it slammed into us again. Red-hot cinders the size of a man's hand were flying into us. I've seen fires before, but nothing ever like this. There was no way we could hold it back, so we headed north to the timber tracts and just watched it take the forest. Didn't take long. Some trucks came and brought us back. We set to work as a strike-and-move team and got a good amount of fire lines dug, but we had to leave on account of a grizzly." Ray paused for another drink of water and decided not to upset the two women with mentioning how hideously the bear, barely recognizable as a bear anymore, had been burned. "Wouldn't have done any good there, anyway." He snapped back into his tale. "The north line is already half gone. All that timberland's like a big, old lumberyard that's standing on end—millions of twelve-by-twelves spaced just perfect, far enough apart to let the wind come through, close enough together for one tree to torch the next one. And if that wasn't bad enough, those pear thrips have left all the hardwoods brittle dry and just ready to burn." Ray looked wearily at Caroline, sitting dull and impassive before him. "And that's what they did. Your timberland, the hardwoods and the pines . . . they're all burned out."

Caroline stared blankly, expressionless. "No matter," she answered hollowly.

Ray nodded and concluded his story. "It's spreading like a horseshoe shape. The western line keeps pushing in and the north, curving in even faster on account of all that timberland. The south line's fanning out as a grassfire heading towards Novi. That's why they called for the evacuation."

When he was done, Ray shook his head as if to shake off the memory of what he'd related. Caroline sat numbly, not from the fear of evacuation nor from the loss of her timberland. The single harrowing thought in her mind was that if Matt had somehow survived to this night, there was no way he could have escaped the paths of the all-consuming fire Ray had just described. Gradually a sickeningly familiar sort of trembling began to take hold of Caroline. Her hands turned icy. The shivering traveled slowly up her arms, possessing her in the darkness of Winona's kitchen as if emptying her of her will. She was aware of the trembling that mushroomed within her, yet she sat vapidly in the face of it. A voice jabbed into the emptiness.

"I need you to take Winona," Ray's gruff voice demanded. "Out to your place. You have a battery radio?"

Catching herself as if from a fall, Caroline concentrated hard on the necessity of the words she was hearing. She grabbed the table edge to steady her hands.

"Battery radio," she repeated aloud, gripping mightily until she was in control again. "Yes, I've got one."

"Then listen to it," Ray barked. "If Hawkeye goes and they tell you to evacuate farther, I'm counting on you to get Winona out of there."

"Do you think . . .?" Caroline began. She was almost relieved to be experiencing worry again.

"I'll find you when it's over," Ray cut in. He was already up and taking stacks of dinner boxes out to his truck.

It was easier getting Winona into the Bronco than Caroline thought it would be. In fact, she remembered the Seven Steps of Wheelchair Transfer with such a flash of clarity that she interpreted it as a warning. Ray had long since gone back to the fire only somewhat revived, and now they were driving toward the relative safety of Caroline's east-of-Hawkeye home. Tyrone howled piteously in the backseat, and Winona sat in the front, a small box of assorted, irreplaceable possessions on her lap. It had been hard, Caroline reflected, evacuating the Baneses' home as they'd just done, wondering if it would still be there the next time they came back, but Winona had taken it well. The only thing that bothered her was leaving her Herefords. Caroline imagined the possible fate of those poor, trapped animals. Wishing them a small degree of mercy, she hoped that the smoke might take their lives before the fires did. As Caroline drove steadily into the darkness, she prayed the same for Matt.

It was hot and strangely still outside when they got to Caroline's house. There was no power there, either, so they sat on the front porch in the light of a three-quarter moon. The radio mumbled low at the foot of Winona's wheelchair, but both women ignored it. Their real diversion lay in Humphrey, who alternately skittered like a dervish from one end of the porch to the other, then hunkered down suddenly, his eyes dilated circles, his tail irregularly thwapping the floorboards.

"Good," Winona spoke, commending Humphrey's erratic antics. "A restless cat means a storm is brewing."

"A restless cat means Tyrone is somewhere around," Caroline countered. "There isn't a cloud in the sky."

"You never know," Winona said of the sign. "September is the Moon When the Long Rain Comes." She paused to watch Humphrey shoot straight up into the air, then violently lick his tail upon landing. Winona smiled approvingly.

And hour later the lightning began, but no hope could be taken from it. It was heat lightning, the dry lightning that comes from long, arid stretches of brutally hot weather but brings no rain with it. Caroline and Winona watched in dismay as twisted bolts of electric white illuminated the sky. Each time, the ragged lightning found a place to touch the ground and hung on with rootlike tendrils. Sometimes it lingered for so long that they could see, menacingly lit up, the dense curtain of smoke that spread over the entire western horizon. Each time a crooked trail of lightning struck, it struck silently, crackling only as static on the radio. Each time the heat lightning found its way to the earth's surface, Caroline and Winona knew that yet another fire had been ignited somewhere else.

At first Caroline was too absorbed in the sky's

ferocious light show to notice it. The hot breeze that came as if from nowhere, that existed only on the periphery of Caroline's awareness, suddenly took center stage, building steadily to a point where it whipped her hair up from her head. As if competing for attention with the lightning, the wind hummed increasingly stronger, rattling all the windows, knocking over the radio and wicker porch furniture. Quickly scooting Tyrone into the house, Caroline gathered Humphrey and threw him in after. "Windstorm!" she yelled to Winona, barely able to hear herself over the whirring din. She began to wheel the chair to the door.

Winona's hand gently halted Caroline's. "No," Winona mouthed as she shook her head slowly.

Trusting to Winona's instincts, Caroline held her flying hair with both hands as they remained on the front porch and watched. Gale-force winds bent the sapling tree out front into a horizontal line, its big leaves a mere blur within the wind's velocity. Bigger trees in the distance seemed as if swept straight up like inverted umbrellas. Mesmerized by the strength of its force, Caroline imagined in horror what this tempest must be doing to the fires just begun and, worse, to the fires in progress. But Winona had been correct in her assessment: this wasn't a windstorm. As suddenly as it had arisen, the wind abated, traveling elsewhere. A sudden rush of cold air assaulted Caroline, shivering up her spine as she let go of her hair. She heard the first huge, ripe drops splat heavily, and she breathed in the wonderful, heady aroma of water meeting dry dirt. She and Winona were sprayed by the ensuing rainstorm, their faces dripping as the rolling claps of thunder began. In the next five minutes the once parched earth was suddenly drenched, and there was hope again. Satisfied, the two women went inside to await tomorrow.

It rained the whole night through and was only just stopping at first light as Ray, utterly spent and filthy, trudged zombielike onto the front porch. "Fire's out," he croaked hoarsely. He read the silent question in Winona's eyes. "Our timberland's all gone," he told her, swallowing. "The house is okay."

As she left Caroline's house, Winona saw the iridescent rainbow in the delicate morning sky. The most brilliant and vaulting she'd ever seen, it arched up so high into the sky that the top curve was lost in the clouds. Immediately, Winona remembered what her mother had taught her. Just as immediately, she rejected it. All of a sudden she hated all the signs that had guided her before. It was because of this one that she wished herself ignorant of every one. This beautiful rainbow, Winona sadly knew, was made of tears and light. It was the bridge over which souls were taken from earth to heaven.

CHAPTER

39

"*L*OOK AT THAT," RAY
said. "Two weeks and it just won't give up." He spoke
of the black-charred landscape still smoking in some
places beyond the roadside. Thin strips of glowing orange clung alive and smoldering deep within bare and
blackened tree trunks. Although the flames had passed,
it was as though the fire, refusing to release its grip
upon the land, had dug in and taken root.

Caroline did not reply. She had no desire to see
what remained of her timberland tracts today or any
day, but Ray had stubbornly insisted. She stared off
skyward, bracing against the jostling of the baby blue
pickup.

Winona bounced next to Ray as he steered carefully over heat-cracked pavement. She, too, had no desire to see the burned-out devastation but knew, as her
husband did, that it was time. She looked out the wind-

shield, up at a mountainside of pines burned crisp
except for an island of green that the fires had leaped
over and spared. It was like that on the next slope, too:
curious, hopscotch patches of green within the blackened and browned. But as they drove slowly on,
Winona saw an entire mountain where the flames had
spared nothing. Lodgepole pines, stripped bare of needles, stood as giant, black fish skeletons. Aspen groves
remained only as charred, broken rods. Winona regarded the lifeless forests and reminded herself that fire
was nature's plan sometimes. Half of all lodgepole pine-
cones would pop open only if heated. They would grow
again, as would the aspens, whose deep communal
roots would send up new shoots in response to every
burned tree. In spite of the scorched destruction,
Winona knew that death never stood alone. Wherever
it visited, a plan for life's renewal always accompanied
it.

Ray steered the truck off the broken pavement onto
the dirt road that would take them to Caroline's timberland. A huge swath made by a fire-lining bulldozer
gouged across the road, but evidence showed that it had
been to no avail. Poles that were once trees smoldered
still. What had once been a solid boulder stood entirely
shattered by the heat of the vulcan inferno. In the distance, a boxy, gray hulk stood in the road. Ray approached to view the shell of a pickup truck, its paint
scorched down to bare metal, its tires completely
melted off their rims. He slowed to a stop. He wanted
Caroline and Winona to see for themselves the physical
reality of the fire. That was why he'd brought them out
here today. He wanted them to understand exactly
what Ranger Putnam meant when he suggested that

Matt could have perished in the intense fires without leaving a trace. Most of all, Ray wanted them to realize that the frail hope they both still clung to for Matt's survival must be let go.

Utter silence filled the cab as Ray drove on. He stopped at the cul-de-sac that was the entrance to the main logging trail and helped Winona onto her wheelchair. It would be bumpy for her, he knew, but he needed her to see. Besides what it meant to the two women, he, too, had feelings about the death of his friend, feelings he didn't know how to face without Winona's help.

The ground was black with a carpet of singed pine needles. When they trod upon it, the ash and soot crunched and clouded beneath them. The trees surrounding them were all branchless. Burned bare beyond recognition, they rose from the ground as a towering legion of ebony pillars. In the distance an even stronger blaze had turned the forest into an alien landscape. The ground was burned beyond black and into a chalky gray, flattened and stark. It was crisscrossed by tree trunks that fell to a fire so fierce that it left nothing upright in its path. The fallen trunks were also an eerie gray white, the color of pewter. They rested as long, mummified mounds upon the ground until, jarred by footsteps, they disintegrated into ghostly clouds of ash dust. The fire here must have been so hellishly hot that it didn't simply consume the trees as fuel but, rather, it baked them throughout.

Caroline stopped at the sight of this, arrested by a bewildering mixture of awe and fear for what had been at work in this forest. Her face contorted in anguish as she imagined the unspeakable horror of dying in a fire such as this one. The guilt that plagued her, those last angry words she'd spoken to Matt, returned to stab her soul. The fact that she'd never told him how much she loved him tightened like a vise around her heart. She surveyed the ghostland before her while despair unfolded into sorrow. She looked upon the total lifelessness that stretched in all directions, and the sorrow became hopelessness. She regarded the hopelessness, and suddenly she was able to remember Matt without the torment—the warm expression she saw in his chestnut eyes when they talked; the toothy, crooked grin he flashed at her from under those sunglasses; the tender way his lips brushed over hers when they kissed. She remembered with bittersweet clarity, now, how only Matt could ease away her cares and make her laugh. She remembered how, for the entire time she'd lived here, despite all the ups and downs, he'd been the best part of her life.

"Look," Winona said quietly. She pointed into the distance, where a lone, charred log rested coal black, shimmery on the ground. A clump of verdant green shoots nestled around the scorched wood, sprouting anew from the dead ashes. As if by some life-affirming announcement triggered by the heat of the fire, a cluster of columbine flowers unfolded their pink-and-white star petals.

Caroline stared steadfastly at the wildflowers that blushed in contrast with the surrounding blackness, but she found nothing hopeful in them or in anything. There was nothing to be found in this forest but the beginning of grieving.

CHAPTER

40

A PALE HALF-MOON glowed high in the midnight sky, suffusing the front yard with an ashen ghostliness. Caroline sat on a wicker porch chair, listening to the distant coyotes' mournful evening song while Humphrey slept, a curled-up ball in her nightgowned lap. Caroline leaned back her head and closed her eyes from fatigue, but she knew that blessed sleep would not visit her tonight. It hadn't for so many nights that instead of going upstairs to lie wide-eyed and awake in the dark confines of her bedroom, she now came directly outside to the solace of the outdoors. The thoughts still slammed around in her head, but as long as she was outside in the warmth of the Indian summer, staring into the inky vastness of the night, the torment dulled into grieving, the wondering if the pain would last forever lessened into the hope that eventually the sleeplessness itself would bring a dazed and welcome numbness.

She wondered, as she had nightly, how she would be able to continue without Matt, how she could face all the everyday things and places that would pierce her heart with the memory of him. Even though Ray predicted a relatively quick regrowth and profit for her timberland, especially since the fire had solved the thrip problem, Caroline didn't care about it anymore. There were too many memories here. Her only escape from them, as she saw it, was to sell her tracts, her home, and leave. But where would she go? Where would she ever find a place that was as right for her as Hawkeye? And how could she face the added anguish of having to break the bond between herself and Winona? Everything she cherished was here, paired with everything that pained her, too. In frustration, Caroline raked her hand through her tousled copper hair. Realizing that she was unconsciously mimicking one of Matt's characteristic gestures only added to her distress. She gave an angry moan, but that was all she could do. Much as she wished it, she could not cry. Not after the trip to the burned forest, not now. Her feelings, deep as they were, refused to come out. Instead they had chosen to eat at her from the inside.

Humphrey's front paws jittered in response to his dreams, rumpling the lap of Caroline's long white cotton nightgown. Even a jittery sleep would be nice, Caroline reflected. Even a fifteen-minute catnap, just fifteen minutes without having to think these thoughts anymore. She stared ahead into the eerily lit night and knew that this one would be no different from the others. She would witness yet another night come to dawn without the balm of sleep, without the release of tears. The sound of another quivering coyote wail reached the porch. Humphrey awakened and leaped off Caroline's lap, and Caroline, also restless, rose and stretched. The painted floorboards felt cool and smooth beneath her bare feet as she walked the length of the side porch to the back of the house.

There, Caroline's steps were arrested when she saw in the distance a light shining from a window at Matt's house. At first she thought she was imagining it, or perhaps the sleeplessness was getting the best of her. It's only wishful thinking, she told herself, peering harder at the distant bright window. She focused on it for a full minute. The light was real. She hadn't seen or heard any cars come down the road all night, so it couldn't be Ray checking on the horses. And as much as her heart jumped at the possibility, she knew it couldn't be Matt. Perhaps word of the uninhabited house had gotten around, and it was a thief. But even a thief would have had to drive past her front porch sentinel tonight. Then again, maybe not. Truly, she didn't know what to think as she stared at the beacon glowing from Matt's window, except that she needed to find out right away.

Caroline dashed into the house and scooped up the keys to the Bronco. Quickly she grabbed her pink kimono and wrapped herself within its folds. Violently tying the sash, she rushed back outside. The gravel on the driveway alerted her that her feet were still bare, but suddenly driven by a wild hope she dared not even put into thought she hurried for the truck anyway. The same unreasoning yet burgeoning power compelled her to speed full tilt down the road until she reached Matt's driveway. Telling herself that it could just as well be an intruder she would be facing as not, Caroline hastily turned off the headlights and crept the Bronco silently up the long and secluded driveway. Cutting the engine, still at a distance, she got out and viewed the house in utter dismay. She ran swiftly around the front, sides, and back. No lights shone from any window.

Caroline stood facing the lifeless house, wanting to call out but not daring. Quietly, glad now that her feet were bare, she slipped into the house and tiptoed from one darkened room to another. There was no one, no signs of anyone having been there at all. Again she fought down the urge to call out to whoever had turned out the light—or whoever had turned it on—or, per-haps, no light had ever been on at all. Caroline stood in the dark kitchen, hearing only the sound of her own rapid breathing. What was she doing here? Maybe the lack of sleep was deceiving her eyes. Or maybe she was losing her grip on sanity. Dr. McAllister's words echoed in her mind. "Peaceful!" he'd barked at her. Maybe, Caroline reflected nervously, the stress was sparing her body this time but claiming her mind instead. She could have *sworn* she'd seen a light on here. The recol-lection of it addled her. Maybe she *was* going crazy.

All of a sudden, Caroline felt weird about standing in the empty house—weird and frightened. She ran outside again, this time hoping to discover a burglar or a horse thief. An intruder of *any* kind would be better than her mind playing tricks on her. Caroline's bare feet padded faster down the wooden side deck toward the hot spring. She stopped to listen to a noise that was more than just the familiar burble of water, praying that, indeed, she had heard rather than imagined the sound. If she was correct, it had come from somewhere below the deck she stood on, somewhere toward the garage.

Maybe it was someone planning to steal Matt's truck. In view of her alternate fears, she hoped that it was.

Caroline sneaked stealthily down the side path encircling the log house. It sloped down toward the bottom level. Its flat slate slabs buried at ground level formed a stepping-stone trail that meandered down a gentle hillside embankment. The nighttime iciness of the stone slabs halted Caroline's bare feet for just a moment, but then she continued, keeping to the shadows extending from the side of the tall, moonlit house. Ahead of her, down the path, a darker shadow edged quietly toward the corner of the house. The sound of leather soles scraping against the slate pathway greeted Caroline's ears. This was no apparition, nor an imagined sound: there was a person out there. Caroline stood breathless in the shadows. She wrapped her pink kimono tighter around her and fidgeted with the sash, retying it as she peered into the eerie moonlight. She followed the murky figure as it advanced, glimpsing now through the darkness that it was the shadowy form of a very thin man. Caroline halted. She retreated deeper into the protective shadows, her every movement suspended while she wondered what to do next. Should she hide or flee? The question, however, was as suddenly lost as her missed heartbeat. With the silent swiftness of an animal in the wild, the shadow-man spun around to face her.

CHAPTER

※

41

THE FEATURELESS FORM of the intruder was silhouetted black against the pale moonlight. He stood silent, a shadow riveted upon the slate path, then turned a bearded face, listening alertly, as a forest animal might, for the slightest hint of sound. Caroline held herself immobile, hardly daring to breathe while the long-haired man peered into the darkness. There was a kind of leanness to him that reminded her of a vagrant. Alarmed at this, she stole a quick glance behind her to see where she might run.

"Caroline?" a deep voice called. And with that, Caroline ran, but not away.

Their embrace was joyful, tearful, surfeit with all the love that each had mourned as lost. "Matt!" Caroline sobbed once the first, strong clasp of their arms lessened around each other. She looked at his weathered face and wept in a rush of emotion. "Matt," she repeated. It was all her heart knew to say.

His hollow eyes looked down at her, a gleam replacing fatigue. Tenderly he stroked the tears from her face. Smiling at her, he slid his hands to her shoulders, grasping them toward him as he walked backward out of the shadows. "Caroline, I want to see you." He pulled her gently toward him to a spot suffused in the chalky moonlight. He regarded her there, as he had imagined her for so long, only tonight, Matt reminded himself, she was real.

"Matt! Are you okay?"

"Yes. Now I am." He grinned at her. "I just ate something and got cleaned up and was coming to find you." He studied the way Caroline smiled at him as she stood on the grassy slope. All wrapped up in her kimono, she seemed like some delicate pink rosebud. To him, she was the very vision, miraculously realized, of what had kept him alive this whole time. Satisfied, he held her close to him once more, enfolding her in his arms.

Caroline rested gently against him, breathing in the familiar smell of his shirt and returning the embrace as she spoke. "Oh, Matt," she said, "I'm sorry for not believing you."

"I didn't give you much cause to believe," he answered soberly. Holding her closer, he stroked her hair as she continued.

"I was so worried, Matt. So scared for you. I really thought you were dead."

"For a while, I thought I was. And I was scared, too. But what scared me the most was the thought of never seeing you again." Once more, Matt loosened his hold around her, held her at arm's length, and smiled into her eyes. "Come on over here," he said, walking farther down the pathside slope. He sat down on the cool grass and beckoned again.

Caroline sat beside him to view the miles of rolling hills laid out as black shadows before them, leading into the distant mountain range. Above, in the murky sky, clouds were beginning to dissipate, revealing a smattering of bright stars. Sitting, arms about each other, looking at the stars, Caroline and Matt began to realize that the despair was over, that the ordeal had an end to it. It began to sink in that the world was safe now that they were with each other again. Caroline leaned into Matt to hold and to be held more securely. The sleepless turmoil of the last month slowly seeped away from her, and for the first time since then, she felt at peace. She rested her head against his shoulder. Sensing that Matt was savoring the same sort of tranquillity, she knew it was all right to ask, so she spoke to him softly. "Tell me what happened."

"It seems like so long ago." Matt shook his head at the memory. "After we argued—you know, after the hot springs and the phone call . . ." His grip around her tightened. "I don't know what I was thinking or that I *was* thinking, really. All I knew was that I needed to cool down, to get away from everything so I could find my balance again. So, early the next morning I packed the two horses and set out on one of Ray's northwest trails. It was dry, but the going was easy and I was getting a lot of small game for food. Toward the end of the week I still hadn't gotten clear of what happened between us. So I let one horse go to find her way home and decided to stay on longer.

"It wasn't long, though, before I had problems. Big problems. Maybe, like I said, I just wasn't thinking straight to be out there in the woods. Or maybe I was too preoccupied. But the upshot of it all was that I got careless about paying attention to the danger signals and I ran smack into the path of a grizzly. It happened so quickly, I didn't even have time to think. All of a sudden, no warnings, no growls, the bear charged. Its ears were flattened down and it looked all stretched out and streamlined. It was coming fast. And, uh . . . ." Matt paused to rake his hand through his hair. "It's . . . it's one hell of a scary thing to see coming at you like that and knowing that it's really happening. The next thing I knew, I was flat on the ground and the bear was on top of my back. It was moving around and I could hear my flesh ripping under those claws."

"Oh, my God, Matt!" Caroline quickly released her arm from around his back.

"Don't worry." It was bad before, but it's all healed up now. And it was so weird while it was happening. The ripping? I could hear it and I knew it was happening, but I didn't feel a thing. There was no pain, really. But I knew that I was yelling. And almost as soon as I realized I was doing that, I also knew I had to stop. My only chance was to play dead, so I got real quiet and the bear left me. I peeked at it just for a moment, and it was even bigger than that monster we ran into on our fishing trip. Caroline, it was huge! It went up a nearby hill, but when it reached the top, it came running back again. And this time it hooked its claws under me and pulled me over on my back. But it did it with enough force that I could use the push to get curled up and face down again. I didn't open my eyes and I didn't let the bear see my face, but it rolled me onto my back again. And so I rolled with it, face down again. And, damn it, that beady-eyed nightmare did the same thing, playing with me like I was some kind of soccer ball or something.

"I woke up and it was nighttime. I could hardly see, but I knew I was wedged tight between rocks and underbrush. There was this awful pain going across my back and I think I might have blacked out a few more times before I finally got myself standing. It seemed as if there were walls around me, so I figured the grizzly must have rolled me to the bottom of a dry ravine. I couldn't see so well and I was real woozy feeling, but I knew I had to get out of there. I couldn't climb up, so I started running down the length of the ravine, stumbling around for I don't know how long. It was daylight and I was out of the ravine when I woke up.

"Luckily, I found a stream, and I cleaned up the mess the bear had made of my back. The horse had bolted off in who knows what direction with my rifle and gear and I had no idea where I was anymore. I followed the stream as long as I could. I still had a fishhook and buck knife in my pocket, so I ate okay for a while. But then the stream dried up and I started running into grizzlies again—irritable grizzlies on account of the drought. So I widened my direction and circled around them, deeper into the woods. I lost track of where I was and I lost track of time. My only clue was that my back was beginning to feel better, so it had to be a couple of weeks. I ate mostly berries and got pretty good at throwing a knife at small game. But the more ground I traveled, the more lost I got.

"Early one evening, though, things got worse. At first it was the silence. Not a bird, not a cricket. It was like every animal had stopped to an alert. I felt it, too, and then I smelled it before I saw it—first the thin wisps of smoke hazing in like a mist. All of a sudden, more smoke rolled in like a wall of fog that thickened till it looked almost solid. Then, it turned brown and then black. Jeez, you just wouldn't believe how fast it came. It was all I could do to keep from gagging on the fumes. I ran ahead of it and up a high hillside so I could look down, and what I saw from up there was incredible. There was this monstrous swath of smoke and fire that was eating into the timberland. Every so often, huge orange flames would hurtle over another ridge and pour down the other side. It was like watching paper burn, only it was the whole countryside that was being consumed.

"I ran like hell with a blast of heat chasing me. I've seen fires before, but I never knew how swift a really big one could be. Behind me, the fire winds roared like an airplane taking off, and I heard trees actually exploding like they were bombs. Live embers showered all around me and I ran faster, hoping that somehow I could get to the top of the next mountain range. The smoke was so dense that squirrels and birds were dropping dead out of trees, and I had to crawl on my hands and knees to keep breathing. Finally, I don't even know how, I climbed to the crest of a rocky-topped hill and collapsed. It was late, I had no idea how long I'd been running, and I couldn't go any farther. Besides, it was hopeless. Looking beyond the timberland below me, I saw heat lightning start new fires while an incredible wind whipped them higher. So I sat on my hilltop and watched the main fire as it advanced. I figured it had a quarter mile to go before the smoke and cinders reached me, maybe another quarter mile before the fires came. I was surrounded and there was nothing in the world I could do about it except watch it come."

CHAPTER

42

"SO I SAT ON THE hilltop and watched each gust of wind fan the flames in closer," Matt said. "And even though I knew I couldn't save myself, that wasn't what frightened me the most. All of a sudden, nothing was as frightening as the thought of never seeing you again, never getting the chance to tell you."

"Tell me what?" Caroline dared to whisper from within Matt's embrace on the pathside slope.

"That I needed you, Caroline."

"I need you, too."

"For me it was different. I needed you so much I got scared. Scared because I couldn't control it, scared because of the power it held—or I thought it held—over me, scared enough to make me mislead you about Margaret and to let her remain Margaret and not just Doc for all that time without explaining. I guess I figured that as long as I held control over a threat—even though it wasn't even a real threat—to what was happening between you and me, Caroline, then I also held the excuse to bail out before you did.

"But it backfired. What I thought was my having the upper hand was really just my lack of trust in myself, in you . . . in us. But don't you know, I didn't figure any of this out until I was stranded on that hilltop with smoke stinging my eyes to tears. All I could do was regret my caution and watch the fire edge in closer and closer. All I could do was promise that if, somehow, I was allowed to survive, I would return to you and tell you. And then, as if by some miracle, it was raining. God! It was wonderful! It doused and dampened everything. By dawn the next morning only small fires were smoldering. The sky was a cloud of ashes and I still didn't know which way was home, but at least the path was clear. I walked for days on end through places that were so bad, Caroline, it looked like even the rocks had burned. Still, I was surprised that most of the small game had survived, and by the time I got back down in familiar territory, there were flowers springing up through the ashes."

Matt tightened his embrace around Caroline in her pink kimono and smiled at the recollection of those flowers. "Anyway," he continued, "I knew I was close to getting back home. I don't know how long it took me, but tonight, once I saw that I was close, I just kept going till I got here."

Matt let go their embrace as if with a conscious intent and faced Caroline where she sat beside him. She had never seen his dark eyes so unwavering as he spoke quietly to her. "And now I can tell you," he said, gathering her hands into his. "You're all I think about, Caroline, all I've thought about for the last year. You're the last thing on my mind when I go to sleep every night. You're the first thing I think about as I wake up every morning." Matt held her hands tighter while his eyes kept steady on hers. "I have never been so sure of anything in my life as this, Caroline. You are all I've ever wanted."

"Matt," she said softly, "I was scared, too." She faltered for just a moment before adding even more softly, "And I have always loved you."

Matt's hands squeezed Caroline's in response to what was in his heart. Caroline's words elated him, filled him with an immense sense of relief. The very thing that had scared the hell out of him for so very long was suddenly the source of his greatest joy. Catching Caroline once more into his embrace, he kissed her with a passion that was born of euphoria, gratitude, and yearning.

"Caroline," he said, pulling his lips away from hers, "Caroline, I . . ." But the words, simple as they were, would not come forth.

"What?" Caroline whispered. She knew full well what but longed to hear it from the lips that had just kissed hers.

Matt's arms tightened around her. He rose to his knees, bringing her up along with him. He clasped her close and kissed her long and deep as if his actions might communicate what words would not. His kiss held her even stronger than his embrace and spoke eloquently, if silently, to a Caroline left breathless by it. Matt lingered with her lower lip before releasing it, while his hands loosened the sash of the pink kimono.

Gently he pushed aside one layer of the thin pink fabric, then two layers, to reveal the white nightgown beneath. The swell of her breasts showed through the filmy white fabric, and Matt caressed their softness through the pull of the cloth. His hands coursed down slowly, sensuously, stretching out the fabric over her ribs and torso, and rested on bones he could feel, also, through the thin, taut cotton. The gown rumpled as he traveled back up again. He undid the row of little white buttons at the low neckline, then watched, smiling, as Caroline unfastened the cuff buttons of his shirt. No words were spoken between them, but when she was done he slowly combed his hands through her hair, shining coppery in the moonlight. His dark-lashed eyes gleamed at big hazel eyes, and he spoke softly. "Come on, Caroline. Let's go to bed."

Matt's house was dark as they walked through it, but Caroline was no longer spooked to be there. Delicate moonlight from the clearing sky shone through the many windows and lit the way to Matt's bedroom. The bedroom, too, was suffused in the moon's pale glow, low-ceilinged, amber-logged, and snug as Caroline remembered it. A pile of tattered clothes lay heaped in the white-painted fireplace, Matt's wilderness clothes. They gave the room a slight acrid aroma, the smell of the smoke and the fire that Matt had journeyed through. Caroline looked around, easily accustoming herself to the room's coziness. Turning, she smiled to Matt as he stood in front of the hewn-log feather bed.

"Caroline," he said, and then stopped to watch her. Without waiting for him to continue, she stepped to face him. She reached up with a slow, feminine kind of delicacy and began to unfasten the buttons of his shirt. Quiet and still, he watched her, wondering what she was thinking as dainty fingers worked their way down. Smiling mysteriously, she slid the shirt off his shoulders, caressing them as she did so. When the shirt got halfway down his back, she tightened the fabric into her fists so as to hold his arms immovable. She held him captive for a time, while Matt, although much pleased by her attentions, got a fleeting feeling that she was searching for something in his eyes. In another moment Caroline stepped deliberately backward, slowly pulling her willing prisoner along in her path. When at last she backed into the straight log wall, she smiled at him slyly, tugged the shirt fabric suddenly tighter, and yanked him in close. Unable to use his arms, Matt responded, pressing hard upon her, squeezing her against the wall until her hips arched in answer to him. The shirt loosened around him as their dance intensified, then dropped, forgotten, to the floor.

Matt willed himself to take a step back to release them from the steadily escalating demand. He slipped the loose pink kimono off her and let it fall to join the shirt. He grasped Caroline's shoulders, his eyes sparkling provocatively. His hands guided her arms up and out against the wall, then traveled up the length of them, his fingers entwining with hers. Still holding Caroline's hands against the wall, Matt kissed her, opening her mouth and surrendering to everything he was feeling.

Caroline let the passion of the kiss possess her. Her fingers, once outstretched between Matt's, now tightened into his, uniting their clasp as she, too, surrendered herself to everything she felt. "Matt," she said softly when the kiss had ended. "Matt, I love you."

Matt's jaw set tight, although his eyes, it seemed to Caroline, held what she sought. Silent, he backed away a few steps and sat on a straight-backed chair. After a few pensive moments, he motioned for her to come to him. What's so hard about saying it? Caroline thought perplexedly. But she came to him nonetheless. Standing in front of where he sat, she slipped her legs alternately between his. With all the buttons of her nightgown unfastened, he slipped the thin spaghetti straps off her shoulders and let the white gown slip down to her hips. The delicate moonlight shone through the room's one window and onto Caroline's tanned skin as Matt held her waist and tenderly kissed one silken breast, then the other. Caroline moaned softly as she pleasurably dug her fingers into Matt's hair, her perplexity dissolved.

"Caroline," he said, releasing her and trying once more to speak his heart. He felt Caroline's fingers grip tightly into his hair. Compelled, he slid the nightgown down past her hips. When it dropped to the floor and she stood naked before him, his hands moved from her waist and deftly traveled down her hips. His thumbs heavily traced the tender crease that led down to each inner thigh. Parting them slightly, he stopped when he felt her trembling. Leaving her body for the moment, Matt finished undressing himself, keenly aware of the hazel eyes that watched his every move in the moonlight. He stood before her and pulled her close upon him. The feel of her satin skin upon his and the arch of her hips touching him skyrocketed his desire past all words, past all restraint. He pressed even closer to her, his need rapidly increasing and instinctively searching. Caroline, too, reacted swiftly. Her hands slipped down his waist and over hard buttocks. They rested on the taut muscles behind his thighs then pulled him to her in unendurable closeness.

Quickly he scooped her up and laid her down on the plump, oversize bed. The sensation of sinking into the feathery depths was even more delightful than Caroline had once imagined. Matt sank in at arm's length above her, his lean, sinewy body contrasting with the surrounding billowy softness as it began to merge to hers. Caroline looked up, seeing both pleasure and restraint within the warm chestnut eyes. Her hands explored his lanky form while he positioned himself and hovered, steadily driving Caroline wild with the anticipation of what would come next. Her hands moved more urgently down his body, but still, excruciatingly, he waited, only touching.

Looking deep into the ever-trusting hazel eyes, Matt at last abandoned the very last of it. "Caroline," he said quietly, "Caroline, I love you." He watched her hazel eyes widen as he went deep, then deeper, inside her. And at his words and touch in the smoke-fragranced room, she blossomed for him like a flower.

Daphne Hartwig graduated from Michigan State University. She is the author of four nonfiction books and is a former editor in the book division of *Better Homes and Gardens* magazine. She lives in New Hampshire.

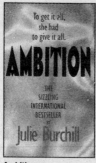